Everdene

MELANIE HOSKIN

Macde Publishing Ltd

Published by Macde Publishing Ltd
First published 2015

Print edition:
ISBN 978-0-9932004-3-4
Also available as an e-book:
(ISBN 978-0-9932004-0-3 Kindle)
(ISBN 978-0-9932004-1-0 ePub)

Cover art image credits:
Shutterstock/MaxyM,
Shutterstock/baoyan,
Shutterstock/Alekksall
Title, Heading & Decorative Symbol font:
NickyLaatz at CreativeMarket (Butterscotch font)

About the author

Melanie Hoskin lives in London, and Everdene is her debut novel, and the first in the Classic Cliterature Series.

She always loved writing stories as a child and finally set aside the time to write a novel. Inspired by classic literature, as well as raunchy romances, her bookshelves are filled with thousands of books.

When she isn't writing, working hard at the day job, or reading, she's probably travelling or watching International Rugby (or both).

You can find her on:
Twitter: @MelanieHoskin
Facebook: facebook.com/everdenenovel
Web: www.melaniehoskin.com

Coming soon:
The Thorn in Hale's side (Fall 2015)
Fine Eyes (Late 2015)

Dedicated to the Cheshire Cat,
and the willful hard-to-wipe grin that
always brings a smile to my face.
He appeared one day when I needed
direction, and encouraged me to be
imaginative alongside my everyday reality.
Without either of those things, this novel
would never have happened.
Sometimes you have to meet people
as mad as you are
before you find the courage
to reach for your dreams.

To the Kew Starbucks girls
Thanks for Coffee!
Melanie x

Acknowledgments

Many people helped make this novel a reality. Firstly, a big thanks to Thomas Hardy, for writing the original *Far From the Madding Crowd* story; one of my favorite novels.

Secondly, to those who read the earlier drafts and provided feedback—special mention to Natalie, Wendy and Caroline for your initial comments.

Thank you to the people who post information about the BDSM lifestyle—your blogs, forum posts and advice columns provided a wealth of research material beyond fictional novels.

Thanks also to Lucie for teaching me Twitter to the point where I think I know how to use the hashtag beyond only #Everdene.

Also thanks to my local Starbucks girls who woke me up each day with several caffeine shots, friendly smiles and enquiries about how the book was going, and to my personal trainer, Eddie, who kept up my energy levels (and motivation) each week.

Thanks to my family for your support in everything I do, and to Mum and Dad, for my education and all the books you bought me to read. My imagination wouldn't exist if it wasn't for reading extensively while growing up.

Thanks also to my close friends for your daily support—you know who you are—and to those friends further afield who have been a support network for many, many years; your continued encouragement means more to me than you know.

Finally, thank you to those authors who, in recent years, have brought the erotic romance genre to the masses (and to the inventors of e-readers), and last, but definitely not least, thank you to you—the reader. I hope you enjoy the story.

Prologue

A man can be attracted to a woman for many reasons. He may date her if she ticks boxes that fit with his short or long-term plans. His interest in her may be fleeting, it may last beyond a first date, or it may even stretch into years.

However, sometimes a man meets a game-changer—a woman who drives him to distraction with desire, makes him laugh until his face hurts, or cry when he's alone. His soul's on fire when he's with her, and his heart aches for her when he's not.

Without knowing it, she challenges everything he thought was a priority in his life, replacing it with a need to protect and support her, make her smile and give her pleasure. She will bring him to his knees, and he will gladly let her; surrendering to the magical power that she possesses. Unlike a man who says he will be with her through the ups, and downs, of life, he isn't just saying it—he's already proved it time, and time again without words.

He will want to be his best for her, identifying the flaws and fears that need overcoming within himself to be that man. He knows he would do anything for her, even if that meant putting aside his own ego and letting her go if he couldn't make her happy.

This is when a man knows he's truly found the *one;* the woman he will never forget if he loses her and the one he wholeheartedly would give anything to belong to for eternity—to love, honor and cherish.

He may perceive his love for her to be his greatest weakness, but if his love for her is a requited love, it has the capacity to be his greatest source of strength.

When a woman realizes she has such a man in her life, this is whom she should open her heart to, and this is the love that she deserves.

Chapter One

He saw her heels first; the unmistakable red sole of a Louboutin black stiletto was clearly visible on the glass step.

It was Dillon Oak's first day in his new job and he'd arrived early—far too early—and with every passing minute, he was dreading the moment they would meet. Everyone in the industry had talked about her—Catherine Everdene, and her no-nonsense approach, was legendary. While pleased about securing the role of Head of Commercial for the London office of the prestigious global media company, he'd been more than a little apprehensive when he'd found out the identity of his new boss.

Now, as he waited in the marble and glass lobby, watching the heels descend the almost invisible pristine glass stairs, he found himself hoping that this was her PA coming to greet him. More and more of the female's well-toned legs, enveloped in silk stockings, came into view. His hopes began to fade that it was a PA; very few personal assistants would be able to afford a designer outfit like the one this woman was wearing. A tight black pencil skirt, perfectly tailored and sitting just above her knees, had come into view and his heart began to pound. Two more steps descended and he could see her pink silk blouse, fitted to the curves of her breasts and waist, a loose V-shape neckline subtly enhancing her cleavage. It was a warm day; had it been cooler, he suspected the woman would have been wearing a black jacket to complete the suit.

Dillon could see all of her now; her glossy brown hair was in a classic up-do, her face adorned with classic blood-red lipstick. Having attended the London Olympics the previous month, he didn't doubt that if there had been an event for sophistication, she would've won gold; everything about this woman portrayed power, perfection and achievement.

"Mr. Oak?"

She'd crossed the lobby and was now holding out a hand to shake his. Her eyes were giving him the once over, and while his resume and references would have sung his praises, the frosty female seemed to be reviewing him in a completely different way.

"Yes, you can call me Dillon," he replied.

His heart was beating faster—no longer just a case of first-day nerves—and his hand shook as he reached to take hers.

"Catherine Everdene. It's a pleasure to meet you."

As their hands made impact, he felt a spark of electricity run through him, heading straight for his groin. His heart rate accelerated and he prayed she wouldn't notice; the tips of her blood-red polished manicured fingers tantalizingly close to the pulse points in his wrist. He swore he caught the hint of a naughty sparkle in her sky-blue eyes.

Does she know I'm on the verge of a cardiac arrest?

A shiver ran through him, not from fear or cold in response to her icy demeanor, but of something that was far more concerning to him—excitement and arousal. In those brief seconds, entirely inappropriate thoughts had come into his mind—fantasies that he shouldn't be having about his new superior.

"Follow me please," she said, before turning her back to him.

Keep breathing, I can do this.

Dillon obediently followed her across the lobby and up the glass stairs, desperately trying not to watch the provocative sway of her hips and toned bottom as she led him up the first of what would be far too many flights of stairs for his sanity. She didn't say a word; small talk didn't seem to be her style.

Reaching the fourth floor, Catherine led him across to an empty office. "This will be your office *Dillon*," she said, and another shiver ran through him as she emphasized his first name.

He walked into his new workspace, giving her as much of a wide berth as he could as he passed her in the doorway.

"As the Director of UK Operations, my office is on the fifth floor with the other directors." Her comment could have been one of arrogance, especially with the tone she used, but before he could respond, she added a twist, "I prefer to be on the *top* . . .," she paused for effect. "Floor."

He blushed and adjusted his suit trousers, his body language sure to give away his secret thoughts; her widening smile and raised eyebrows proof that she was aware her deliberate remark had had the desired result. Now he was sure there was a wickedly, naughty sparkle in her eyes. It wasn't like Dillon to be flustered to this degree—sure he was a hot-blooded male who thought about sex on a fairly regular basis—but he'd never felt an intensity like this; like someone had suddenly turned on a magnet inside not only his groin, but in his mind as well.

A romantic might have believed that this was love at first sight, but he wasn't a romantic—he was career-minded and practical. Dillon's life plan involved doing well in his job, finding a nice woman to marry and living a contented, settled life—just like his parents. He was determined to get that plan back on track after some wrong choices in his late teens and twenties; he didn't want to let his family, or himself, down again.

"I'll remember that," he finally replied, not knowing how else to respond to her comment; his palms and forehead still beaded with sweat from the physical assertion of four flights of stairs and the constant distraction in his eye line. Despite only knowing Catherine for a few minutes, he wouldn't have put it past her to have chosen the stairs deliberately; her heels didn't lend themselves to frequent stair climbing, and they'd passed four perfectly-working elevators in the hall.

The growing sexual tension in the room was disturbed as a man with greying-hair joined them. He introduced himself as the Finance Director and then launched into a speech about the company, apologetic that the CEO was unavailable to greet him personally. Dillon tried to pay attention, but he found himself unable to focus under the weight of Catherine Everdene's continued stare.

"If you'll both excuse me, I have a conference call. Good luck *Dillon*— you will find that I've itemized all of the tasks for you to focus on in an email. Your PA will have booked all the relevant meetings into your diary," she interrupted, a few minutes into the old man's spiel on the company's forward direction.

A final suggestive smile and then she was gone. He relaxed a little and the Finance Director resumed his overview of the company strategy, even though Dillon was already well aware of its contents—he'd received the document before his interview, and again with the job offer. Bored of the repetition, his mind wandered to what emails from Catherine might potentially be lurking in his inbox; would they be the no-nonsense, business-like approach worthy of her reputation, or would they feature innuendos like he'd just encountered.

When he was finally shot of the tedium of the Director's words, he opened his inbox with trepidation. He needn't have worried; Catherine's emails were completely professional—he would be kept busy getting up to speed to deliver all the requirements. There were sales targets to meet, efficiency savings to identify and an acquisitions strategy to draft—all set out with a ticking clock.

♒

The first day passed quickly, as did the days following, and Dillon began to feel more at ease. His other colleagues were hardworking, friendly and made him feel welcome. A few of the younger—and sometimes older— female administrative staff had sought him out, battering their eyelids and attempting flirtation; while flattered at the attention, he was here to work.

A thought at the back of his mind had begun to surface whenever other women approached him.

I don't think Catherine would be impressed if I flirted with the administration ladies.

Quite apart from ensuring that he was capable of conduct befitting a department head, somehow, despite only brief encounters with her, he already felt a sense that he belonged to Catherine Everdene—in more ways that he wanted to admit.

As Friday came around, he'd only seen her in the occasional meeting involving others; there'd been no further opportunity for her to make him feel hot under the collar. Not that he needed her presence to do that; she'd dominated his daydreams every moment that he didn't focus on work. Once in the safety of his flat each evening, any masturbation he indulged in featured his new boss as inspiration. Gone was the revolving door of imagery in his mind—ex-girlfriends, actresses, models and attractive, random commuting females from the tube. Now there was only one woman in his mind; a bossy brunette called Catherine Everdene—the one woman he shouldn't be thinking about.

The office floor emptied mid-afternoon—many of the team heading off early for drinks—and Dillon promised to join them as soon as he'd emailed his draft proposals to the first reviewers. As he reached down to grab his backpack, ready to clear his desk for the weekend, he caught sight of a familiar pair of red-soled heels in his office doorway.

Strangely, it was the view of Catherine from the waist-down that he knew the best; the shape of her legs and bottom, the arch of her feet and the four-inch Louboutin heels she favored. Thanks to her performance on the stairs, he was already used to being lower, despite his own six-foot-three height exceeding hers by at least seven inches.

"How's the report?" she asked; her words were straightforward enough, but the tone set his heart racing again—the air of authority, mixed with feminine sexuality, was a potent mix.

"Um . . . the draft is actually looking good, um . . . I was about to send it to you," he replied, stuttering over his words.

Since when have you stuttered, you fool.

Dillon was struggling to come across as confident right at this moment; all week the thought of her complete power over him had been in his dreams—or perhaps they were nightmares—it all depended on how one categorized fantasies about a ball-breaking boss quite literally *breaking your balls* with instruments designed for cock-and-ball torture.

These were new fantasies for Dillon; previously the only extreme fantasy he'd had was asking an ex-girlfriend that he lived with at university to blindfold him and tie him to the bed. While it'd been amusing, and a bit of a novelty, when they tried it, he hadn't revisited that particular fantasy in the fifteen years since.

Catherine stepped forward and leaned onto his desk; the pose allowing him a glimpse of her cleavage enveloped in a lacy bra. He could almost feel the warmth radiating from her body, and the smell of her perfume, evoked memories that he couldn't yet place.

"I am pleased," she purred. "I would so hate to have to punish you, particularly after you've been pleasing me with your performance all week."

Dillon's look of surprise brought out her sparkle-eye smile again and he found himself flushed in the face with embarrassment. She couldn't possibly have known about all the performances he'd done in private, but in his bewitched state, he thought Catherine capable of anything—even reading a man's thoughts. He stayed silent, his larynx paralyzed under her spell.

As she stood upright to take her leave, she winked. "Have a *very* nice weekend Dillon."

She turned away from him, and he let out the breath that he hadn't even realized he'd been holding. Just when he thought he was out of the woods, she spun back around. Sitting behind his desk, he prayed that she hadn't been able to spot that she'd aroused him, yet his worst fears were confirmed when she added, "You can stop standing to attention now."

Chapter Two

It took a marathon effort of courage for Dillon to return to work on Monday. His embarrassment at the events of Friday evening was acute; he hadn't been caught with an erection in an inappropriate setting since secondary school—an incident he'd chosen to forget until now.

'It's quite normal during puberty,' he recalled his very understanding, and entirely professional, teacher telling him. 'You'll soon start to look at the girls in your class instead when their bodies start to change.'

Now, he wondered if that adolescent encounter was the start of his weakness for women in authority; an irrational pondering considering the teacher had been right and he hadn't fantasized again about teachers, or bosses—until that is, he met Catherine.

Adopting as much of a confident and macho swagger as he could muster, he walked into the weekly team meeting ready to face her. Quickly taking a seat, he looked around as the Chair opened the meeting.

"Catherine Everdene sends her apologies as she will be in the New York office this week."

Relief swept over him and he noticed that the atmosphere of the room had changed; his feelings clearly shared by the other attendees. He was a little disappointed that he wouldn't get to see her for a whole week—she hadn't mentioned being away when she'd wished him a good weekend. Then again, he hadn't even asked about her weekend—her presence seemed to render him mute. However, her absence meant that he could focus on the mountain of work he needed to plough through before the day ended. As the meeting dragged on, Dillon distracted himself by planning his week; he had a date arranged for Wednesday evening.

That should clear my mind of her.

❦

Dillon found himself in a quandary; last night's date hadn't delivered on the dynamics he was now craving. Strangely, he'd been bored in the woman's company, despite it being their third date. The highlight of the evening was a lively conversation on the merits of Apple's new iPhone 5— its launch announced earlier that day—while the lowlights were too much talk about their future.

Clocking red flags in a date wasn't normally Dillon's style—at least not until after he'd slept with a woman, yet he found himself noting phrases that made him feel like he was being evaluated as a candidate for matrimony and parenthood. She was the sort of girl he would normally date—attractive, nice personality, and who ticked the online profile boxes that matched his own life plan of marriage and kids. He'd also enjoyed chatting to her online and even their previous two dates before she'd gone on holiday were fun.

Dillon had been looking forward to the evening, particularly as she'd hinted that she followed the infamous three-date-rule; he'd been hopeful that he could relieve some of his sexual tension.

After dinner near his office in Hammersmith, he'd accepted her invitation to accompany her back to her flat in nearby Fulham, even though it was a weeknight. Once there though, he'd managed only some lack-luster action on his part—and for that matter hers; despite the release of some of his pent-up sexual frustration, he didn't feel at all satisfied. He even excused himself early, blaming an early start at work.

How have I become the right shit of a guy who walks out after sex? I left before round two, or maybe even three!

He was pissed at himself for his behavior, yet it was unfair to string things out into hugs and a future, when he'd no desire to call her again; she wasn't Catherine.

Even though Dillon had made it back to his Wimbledon flat home less than twenty minutes after doing a runner—and therefore at a reasonable hour—he'd had a sleepless night. As he sat at his desk on Thursday morning, he drank a second mug of coffee, hoping that the extra shot of caffeine wouldn't only wake him up, but also snap him out of his self-loathing. However, where the coffee failed, Catherine succeeded—her sudden entrance startling him into a jittery alertness.

"I hear you've been a *naughty* boy," she said—far too suggestively for the hour of the morning.

Dillon choked on his coffee, the liquid burning the back of his throat.

Oh fuck, please tell me that she doesn't know about last night.

Knowing his date was unconnected to the office did nothing to stop his paranoia.

His look of bafflement amused her. "I'm joking," she said. Her sparkle-smile was on full display again, and the sight of it clouded his brain and made his cock twitch. "I hear you didn't join the others on Friday evening after all."

"Ah, no, I had a parcel to pick up from the Click-and-Collect point near my flat before it closed."

Dillon was surprised that he'd managed to get a coherent sentence out—his throat was still recovering from the hot coffee, and his brain was in over-drive imagining all kinds of ways she would punish him for being naughty.

"Really . . . here was me thinking that you must surely have needed some alone time after the way you were when I left you on Friday," she teased, with another wink loaded with wickedness.

Please, please, please leave my office.

Once again, Dillon found himself adjusting his trousers as his thoughts continued to wander.

"How was New York?" he asked, determined to try to engage her in a normal conversation rather than appearing only as a horny, mute fool.

Her sparkle-smile vanished, and she looked uncomfortable; he immediately wished he hadn't asked, fearing that he'd somehow over-stepped a mark and invaded her privacy.

"It was fine. Anyway that report is looking good; we should be able to present it next week," she replied dismissively.

Dillon was relieved she'd changed the topic and he suddenly felt more confident in her presence—work praise did that for him, and while not arrogant, he knew he was normally good at his job.

Just when his confidence reached its normal level, she brought it crashing down. "You *up* for that?" she asked, pausing for a second while waiting to spark a reaction in him. "Presenting that is—not *up* as in anything else!"

How does she do it to me every fucking time?

Her naughty, temptress streak was making his normal calm, and professional, composure crumble with anticipation and vulnerability; yet this newfound loss of control was something that strangely he was getting off on.

"Yes Catherine," he mumbled obediently—the agreement devoid of any confidence.

"Excellent. I shall leave you now to whatever it is you need to do," she said, with yet another sparkle-smile and wink. Then she was out the door, leaving him in an embarrassingly aroused state once more.

As soon as he could see that she'd left the floor, Dillon rushed himself to the gents—thankfully only a few paces away from his office, and therefore not requiring the passing of any of his colleagues in his compromised state.

༺∽༒∽༻

Catherine wasn't in the office on Friday, and after a busy weekend working on the report, Dillon hoped that he might run into her on Monday; the first thing he did when he arrived in the morning was email the revised report stating he wanted to run through the document with her before the Board meeting.

Not short of other things to be working on, he found ways to distract himself while waiting for her reply. He occasionally glanced at his full email inbox, but with the lack of anything bearing the sender name *Catherine Everdene*, it seemed empty.

Dillon was surprised when one of his hopeful glances towards the screen alerted him to the time—8:00 p.m. He looked out of the office towards the dimly lit open-plan area—long since abandoned by those heading home to families. Hitting the off-switch on the computer, he picked up a pile of marked-up finance papers. Keen to please, Dillon had always made an effort to learn the preferred working hours of his superiors; his diligence meant that he knew that the Finance Director was an early-bird worker who liked to read reports when he got in at 7:30 a.m.

Leaving the papers on the Director's desk offered Dillon two benefits—it would please the Finance Director, plus allow him one final excuse of the day to visit the fifth floor; while Dillon was sure Catherine would have left for the day, her office was located next to the Finance Director's. Like a lovesick teen, he would be able to smell the remnants of her perfume from her office doorway—a final reminder of her to take home for the evening.

The fifth floor wasn't as dark as the fourth; the cleaner was still working up here—saving it until last due to the longer hours of the directors, and their hard-working personal assistants. As Dillon headed across the open-plan area, he spotted a brightly lit office, with the sound of classical music escaping from its open door—Catherine was still working.

He stopped and watched her through the glass wall, mesmerized by the difference in her appearance at this hour. Her hair was unfastened from its normal style and hung loosely over her shoulders, and she'd tossed her suit jacket over a chair—warmth was now being provided by an over-sized sports jacket, most likely retrieved from her gym-bag. Seated comfortably on the office sofa, her bare feet were propped onto the coffee table; her toenails painted with a vibrant berry color polish. The nudity of her lower legs—without their normal cover of stockings and heels—gave him a thrill; surpassing the desires stirred in him when he'd been forced to look at her legs so often before.

He continued to watch voyeuristically as she read the printed document in her hands; every so often she would stop and remove the pen that she held in her mouth, highlight something important, then return the pen to its place—her action drawing his attention away from her toes and onto her glossy lips. Becoming aroused again, Dillon wondered whether it was wise to disturb her.

Do it! You've been waiting to see her all day and now you have your chance.
Just as he summoned macho courage, he saw the cleaner beat him to it.
Damn. She's brave.

The Catherine that he'd come to know wouldn't want a cleaner to disturb her—especially a female one who didn't even bother to knock first. It was therefore a pleasant surprise to him to hear friendly voices coming from the room—the volume on the iPod speakers muted by her upon the entrance of the cleaner. He stepped closer to listen, ensuring he remained in the shadows and therefore out of sight.

"Still on New York time I see," he heard the cleaner ask—her query and tone indicating familiarity.

"I'm afraid so. It might have only been a quick trip, but it was enough to throw me out completely. It hasn't helped that I didn't sleep much over the weekend with all the things I've now got to sort out for New York," replied Catherine casually.

She didn't seem at all phased by her unpolished appearance to the woman now busily cleaning her office. Dillon edged closer, glad that the cleaner had switched off a few more of the central lights before heading into his boss's office. Catherine suddenly jumped up off the couch, and he shrank back, afraid that she'd heard him—or worse, spotted him watching. Thankfully, no reprimand came—he was still invisible.

"Before I forget again, I got you these. I remember you saying before I left, that your granddaughter had given you Hershey's chocolates once and that you rather liked them. They aren't much, but I grabbed a bag when I saw them at Duty Free," she said.

Dillon watched with curiosity as she gave the older woman a large bag of chocolate—the woman showing her gratitude with a hug, and mumbled words of genuine thanks.

Here, in the after-hours of the normal office day, she was showing a side of her that was far from icy, competitive and perfect; out-of-hours Catherine was relaxed, friendly and, more importantly, kind-hearted and thoughtful. Dillon's heart fluttered—he desperately wanted to go and converse with this new, likeable woman, but some part of his mind told him that he shouldn't. To do so, would have felt like an invasion into a personality that she'd chosen not to show him for whatever reason.

Recalling her sudden change of topic when he'd asked about New York, he compared it to how she'd now openly discussed it with a cleaning lady. Dillon suddenly felt a sense of his place—that of lower than a cleaner in her estimations. Full of rejection, he quickly put the finance papers on the Director's desk and left the fifth floor.

Chapter Three

Mid-week in Dillon's third week—two days after he'd last seen Catherine—came the call; well more the modern-day equivalent—an electronic calendar invite. He was aware the Executive Board meeting was the following day, and as he'd heard nothing more from her since the previous week, he wasn't sure if he was presenting the report in its current state. Despite having been privy to another side of her personality less than forty-eight hours before, Catherine had struck him as someone who might enjoy humiliating him by giving critical feedback on his report in front of the whole Board. Yet at the last minute, she'd emailed a meeting request.

> Sender: Catherine Everdene
> Meeting Request: Wednesday 19th September, 2012.
> 20:00-21:00
> Location: My office, 5th Floor
> Subject: Board Report Review
> Dillon,
> Apologies for the late start time, but it's vital that we get
> the report perfect before it's printed for everyone (they're
> printing it first thing tomorrow morning). I'm in meetings
> all day today.
> Catherine Everdene
> Director of UK Operations

The time was inconvenient; after Dillon's perception of being rejected when he'd seen her on Monday, he'd given in to the bombardment of texts from the woman he'd slept with the week before. Still feeling guilty about effectively dumping her right after sex, he'd agreed to go on another date—dinner and a movie.

He wanted his normal dating life back; a focus on finding a woman that could make him as happy in a relationship as his parents still were. He doubted that someone as intensely seductive as Catherine, and especially with her split personality, would be the one to do that. Online woman however, did tick wife-material boxes, and he reasoned that the fumbles and flatness of the previous date might have just been first-time-with-each-other-sex nerves.

The more he convinced himself that agreeing to a fourth date was the right thing to do, the more he'd started to fantasize about how it could play out—hot, fast-paced action in her hallway, followed by her riding him in the bedroom. Strangely, it was mundane details that he found easiest to add into the fantasy. He definitely remembered the magnolia walls of her rental flat— their blandness a metaphor for the evening. He also remembered the jingle of a metal necklace hanging on her bedframe—the sound reminding him of the metal connections of a saddle and reins when riding a horse. However, the rest was vague; mismatched bra and panties, too many pillows, and an over-bearing vanilla scent similar to the smell of the local candle shop that he passed every day.

None of these details aroused him like the detailed fantasies involving Catherine; the glimpse of her lace bra—he'd pictured her wearing a full-set of matching lingerie from Agent Provocateur. Since Dillon had first smelled her floral perfume, he'd been trying to recall why he knew the scent. Now, he remembered it; the waft of climbing roses on a warm summer's evening, filling his childhood bedroom with their scent as he indulged in teenage boy curiosity—the deep breaths after his physical exertion and release pulling the floral scent further into his nostrils. While many men found musky, sensual scents a turn-on; Dillon equated the smell of roses in the air with sexual release.

Damn.

Catherine was hijacking his fantasies again, putting in a comparative appearance and leaving his arranged date woefully lacking; the desire he was trying to convince himself to feel for someone else subsided. The last minute scheduling of a meeting with Catherine that night was a sign. He sent a short text:

> 'I have to meet my boss and work late. We're going to have to cancel.'

He received an even shorter reply:

> 'Fuck You.'

The language of her reply revealed a sub-text—she hadn't used expletives in any earlier conversations or messages—had she noticed his tone change whenever he'd mentioned his boss on their last date? Sub-text or not, he suspected that there'd never be a fourth date, and definitely no frantic sex in her hallway.

He turned his attention back to the meeting request and clicked the Accept button.

What boxers am I wearing? Do I have after-shave in my gym-bag? Stop it! It's only a work meeting and you didn't care about these things this morning when you were preparing for an actual date!

All day long, he couldn't concentrate, constantly checking the clock, impatient for the day to end. At 5:30 p.m., he decided to escape for a while by heading to the on-site gym; he needed to relieve his frustration before the meeting, but if he went for the jerking-off option in the gents, Catherine would be firmly in his thoughts—keeping another part of him well and truly firm.

After a thirty-minute, fast-paced run on the treadmill, followed by an all-out fight with a boxing bag, Dillon washed away the last of his anxieties in the shower. He put on the new boxer briefs that he'd purchased in his lunch break, and then generously slapped on some of the musky after-shave he'd discovered in his gym-bag. Before dressing, he studied himself in the mirror, sucking in his stomach to enhance his six-pack.

Will she like these designer boxer shorts? Will she think I smell okay?

He wanted to please his boss beyond his work performance; even daring to admit to himself that he was actually looking forward to seeing the seductive Catherine one-on-one after everyone had gone home. Perhaps he'd even get to see the friendlier side of her that the cleaner had experienced.

At precisely 8:00 p.m., Dillon walked into the spacious, top-floor office of Catherine Everdene. The office smelled of lilies—a huge bouquet was on the side table. The smell was strong, and the rosy smell of her perfume was unable to compete. He was relieved—lilies didn't make his cock twitch.

He glanced towards the sofa and coffee table area where he'd seen her sitting on Monday, and he wished she was sitting there now. However, Catherine had already seated herself at the meeting table in front of two copies of the report, and she motioned towards the empty chair beside her.

"Take a seat and let's get started. Neither of us wants to be here at this hour, or longer than we have to be."

He obeyed, disappointed that the chair didn't offer the comfort—or intimacy—of the sofa. She immediately launched into feedback on the report, with no seductiveness to her words; they were here to work and he tried to focus—especially now that his proximity to her had allowed a whiff of her evocative perfume to reach him.

After an hour of nothing but professional dialogue, Catherine suddenly changed the topic.

"Would you like a drink?" she asked, getting up from her seat.

Immediately Dillon's heart started to race; a sense of expectation building by the second. He nodded, not caring what beverage was on offer. She busied herself at a cabinet behind the desk, and then returned to the table with two crystal glasses filled with what looked to be Scotch.

As she bent forward to put them down, her left breast grazed his shoulder and a jolt of electricity ran through him, finding a direct path to his cock; it twitched in appreciation of the spark and awoke from its slumber. Dillon downed a good portion of the strong liquor.

"Steady boy," she teased, raising her eyebrows at him, and putting her hand on his shoulder. He placed the glass back on the table, not knowing if she was referring to his large mouthful of the drink, or the increasingly large bulge in his trousers.

This is it.

She leaned closer, and he could now feel the warmth of her breath on his cheek as her lips caressed his ear.

Ouch.

A silent yelp and he rose out of his seat—an automatic reaction to her nipping his earlobe, ever so gently, with her teeth. He was fully erect now and desperately wanted to pull her tight skirt upwards, and then grab her onto his lap, but his arms wouldn't comply; his mind was too aroused by the thought of her in control and having her straddling him wouldn't satisfy his newfound need for her dominance. There was no denying she'd be able to see how turned on he was—she had a clear view of his groin.

"Shall we move to your sofa where you were sitting the other night?" he whispered, his mouth already close to her own ear. Catherine froze and he wished he'd stayed silent.

Crap, now she knows I was watching her.

His spying discovered, he reasoned that she couldn't know what time he'd been there, nor how long he'd watched, or what he'd seen. The awkward silence continued as he agonizingly watched her face, her mind comprehending the implications of what he'd just said.

"I thought I'd heard the lift open and then ping shut. Since the cleaner was in my office, and no one else was still at work on the floor, I wondered who was about that hadn't bothered to say hello." Her seductive manner had disappeared, replaced by her practical, dismissive tone; staring at him, she sat back down into her seat.

In his significantly aroused state, Dillon wasn't about to give up on his chances; he could see her flushed face, and her nipples were perkier than usual under her blouse—she was as aroused as he was. His arms regained their ability to move and he placed his hand onto her upper leg.

"Catherine, I—"

He didn't have time to finish his apologetic sentence, or seduction—in one swift move, she flicked his hand away and was standing again. They both silently stared at each other for a moment, contemplating their respective next words, or moves.

As expected, Catherine took the lead, leaning forward to nip his earlobe again—this time considerably harder. He flinched, but managed to hold in a yelp.

"Not tonight," she whispered.

She was back sitting in her seat before he could protest; the whole movement had been so quick, that Dillon wondered if he'd dreamt it. He returned her gaze, even though his eyes had clouded over with desire—endless thoughts running through his head of all that he wanted her to do to him. Despite his disappointment, embarrassment and confusion, his soul was on fire; he was completely at her mercy, desperately wanting relief from the torture—only an orgasm with her would do.

Please Catherine.

Yet she wasn't about to give in to the weepy, begging look in his eyes; two minutes later, he was instructed to go home and make the amends on the report before the next morning's deadline.

Dillon sat on the Wimbledon-bound tube physically, and emotionally, deflated; his libido sent to great heights through torment, then crushed through denial. He hadn't even self-satisfied himself after the meeting had ended—instead allowing his erection to deflate by the time he'd descended the stairs to the ground floor; all he felt was rejection.

It wasn't until later in his flat—once he'd finished the final report amends—that he allowed himself to re-live the meeting; 'Not tonight.' Catherine's words now haunted his head, but they also gave him hope.

That isn't a never.

That thought gave him a thrill, and as his rejection abated, his hard cock returned to form. As the clock struck midnight, Dillon reached a more intense climax than he'd ever experienced before—his mind imagining Catherine standing over him; telling him when to start, when to stop, when to start again and, more importantly, when to come.

Chapter Four

The Board meeting went well; Dillon was the undoubted star—possibly even upstaging the perfect Catherine Everdene; he'd caught sight of her during the CEO's praise of him, and she'd not looked pleased.

What the fuck have I done now to make her mad?

Dillon hadn't taken credit where it wasn't due, and he'd made her department look good; the Board were clearly happy with the team appointment she'd made—even if it hadn't been her that interviewed him. There was no reason she should be annoyed with him.

Surely, she isn't still pissed with me about last night.

His self-doubt, and fears of failure and rejection, attempted to erode the confidence he'd felt during the meeting.

As the day dragged on he didn't see her again, nor did she send any emails. Dillon instead found himself researching his boss; he'd read about her online before he joined the company—after all her professional reputation had scared him a little—but now he was an employee he had access to internal information. It helped that a girl in Human Resources had developed a crush on him, and he easily persuaded her to provide him with access to personnel records—since he was restructuring his section, he needed to look over his team's performance. He was aware that initially Catherine had joined the company's commercial division, and that her record would likely to be within the team's files.

I can compare her performance to the current team.

As he started to scan the file, he repeatedly justified his legitimate performance comparisons to himself to help alleviate the guilt that he felt at prying into her personal details. Dillon was fascinated with the contradictions in Catherine's personality, and was curious to find out more about her; whether that be prior history with male colleagues that might have made their way into her personal record, grievances related to her icy demeanor, or glowing performance statistics that would rub further salt into the wounds of his already deflated male ego.

However, there were no demons lurking in her records, and certainly no complaints of sexual inappropriateness or bullying. Even in a paper file, Catherine Everdene came across as perfect—an ambitious high-achiever praised by her superiors in her appraisals. It also irritated him to discover that she was younger than he would've guessed. While her looks placed her in her early thirties—flawless skin showing no signs of ageing—her position and assertive composure suggested a woman in her early forties; Catherine was thirty-five—a year younger than he was. He felt a familiar pang of jealousy that someone younger had achieved more.

'When are you going to settle down?' 'Head of Department, that's not a Director though right?' 'When are you planning on buying a property?'

The constant questions that his loved ones kept asking him sprang into his mind.

Pushing aside his own fear of inadequacy, he looked for a positive in his discovery about her age; he was reassured that he wasn't fantasizing about an older woman—especially when the majority of his single mates were starting to show an interest in much younger women. Twenty-something *girls* had become the frequent dates-of-choice amongst his mates of late; an attempt to hold onto their youth, or a rebound from long-term relationships that had failed to jump commitment hurdles. His best mate had summed it up perfectly over a recent beer—'you really do wonder whether you're with the right woman once marriage is the only thing she wants to hint about all the time.'

Dillon wasn't averse to getting married or having kids—it had worked out very well for his parents. He craved that feeling of being with someone that he loved wholeheartedly, but he'd never taken much time to think about what kind of woman that would be—his recent comparisons between date-woman and Catherine was the first time he'd called into question what he wanted. Over the years, he'd been to so many weddings of family and friends; some had just known that they'd met the right person—yet he was now their compassionate ear as they divorced—while others had fallen in love more gradually, and for the moment, seemed in marital bliss. In Dillon's circle, there was no set formula for what constituted a *happy-ever-after*—the only shining example, was the forty years of partnership that his own parents were celebrating.

He read a little more of her file; her address was a Thames-side development in Battersea that he'd read about in the *Metro* real-estate pages. He recalled the images of the amazing river views, and the modern show-home interiors; they'd cost a small fortune—even on the lower floor levels; the personnel data gave no clue as to what floor Catherine lived on, whether she was an owner, or how long she'd lived there. Searching the internet to find out her financial status was a step too far in the prying stakes—while she was driving him crazy with curiosity, he still had his sense of propriety.

Snapping his laptop shut, he resolved to stop his lust and sexual tension from taking over his sanity; he'd done well professionally today and now it was beer-o-clock.

ᶜₑₙₒ⁹

Friday 28th of September—one week, and one day, since the Board meeting. There'd still been no visits, meetings, or even emails from Catherine—Dillon's boss had gone AWOL and he'd been running the show. Curiously, no one commented on her absence, or his takeover, and for all he knew, she could have left the company.

A late summer-storm, forecasted for that afternoon, rolled in before he'd managed to leave for the week, and he cursed that he'd forgotten to bring his umbrella. Not wanting to venture out into the torrential downpour, he watched the lightning streak across the sky from the safety of his desk chair. His contemplation, however, was broken the minute that he heard heels on his office floor—the clicking sound making him far more nervous than the ominous claps of thunder outside. He swiveled around in his chair excitedly, hoping to see Catherine again.

His shoulders dropped and his smile faded; Dillon's disappointment must have been evident to his poor PA who'd also stayed late to avoid the rain. Sensing that she wasn't the one he'd hoped to see, she quickly placed an envelope on his desk and fled to the coffee room to join other colleagues who were sitting out the weather.

He opened the envelope and began to read, pleased to find a diversion from the stormy weather outside that was a direct reflection of his own muddled thoughts.

ᶜₑₙₒ⁹

Dillon exited the building from a side door; this route offered a more sheltered walk to Hammersmith tube station. He began to run through the rain, dashing across the car park to take a short cut. Just as he did, a burgundy Aston Martin braked hard, narrowly missing hitting him, but successfully spraying dirty water all over the lower half of his suit; he jumped onto the curb.

Asshole.

He didn't dare shout the words out—the driver could be any one of the senior executives. Before he could break into another run, the passenger door of the sports car opened.

"Get in," a familiar female voice yelled above the rain.

Despite the relentlessness of the downpour, he wanted to press on to the station. His unwillingness to get soaked, or even hit by lightning, paled in comparison to the fear he felt about what might await him if he got into her car.

"I'll count to three," she yelled.

That did it; the bossiness of her tone—even in this situation. Anyone else would've been friendly when offering a colleague a lift, saving them from the rain, but somehow Catherine had made it a demand—one he couldn't resist obeying.

"Mint?" she asked, holding out a packet. Dillon shook his head and the action sent a spray of water drops all over the pristine cream leather interior.

Shit.

He waited for her to comment—a reprimand, or a jest, about his soaked state—but she remained silent and focused on the road. The only sound came from the state-of-the-art audio system; the chosen track-list an eclectic mix of classical tunes and up-beat dance anthems. He noticed how similar their music interests were—another detail about her that added a tick into the pros-and-cons list that he'd started to build in his head; to date, the crosses far outweighing the ticks.

Without thinking, he began to hum along to one of his favorite tracks as he stared out the car window—only when he turned his head, and caught a glimpse of her smiling, did he realize and quickly stop. She continued not to speak, and her silence put him back on edge.

Where are we going?

He didn't dare ask aloud—not even sure if he actually cared—but they'd long since passed Hammersmith station and had taken a route that also bypassed Earl's Court, where he could have got a direct train. He'd no idea if she knew where he lived, and she hadn't asked him where he might want to go; Dillon was letting her set the agenda. Twenty minutes later, she swung a left into the underground car park of a riverside block of flats in Battersea—they were going to her place.

"Come," she commanded. Catherine, having got out of the car, tilted her head towards the elevators to indicate the direction. He obeyed her command and walked across the car park, his sodden state leaving a trail of dark water drops on the bland concrete—a path marking his walk towards his fate.

On entering the elevator, he chose to maintain a safe distance from her; Dillon had heard many a fantasy shared at the pub about elevators—the ubiquitous Hollywood stereotype had featured several times in the novels that his mate's wives and girlfriends hadn't been able to get enough of that summer. He looked across at her, desire starting to build within him as he recalled the details of the fantasies his mates had jokingly discussed.

Should I take the initiative?

He thought better of it; Catherine was all about being in control—if she wanted elevator sex, he'd be pinned against the wall by now, with her hands groping his cock. He turned away his gaze to avoid temptation, instead getting a glance at himself in the mirror.

Shit, I look a wreck.

His bedraggled, dripping suit and hair were a stark contrast to her perfection.

How did she escape the rain?

He hadn't been aware of an underground car park at the office—perhaps it was exclusively for the use of executives. It was yet another reason for him to feel inadequate—not that he needed one; standing next to Catherine in his soaked state was the only proof needed to highlight his flaws. She was the complete opposite of him right at this moment—self-assured, poised and in control—everything he wasn't.

At the ninth floor, the elevator doors opened onto the penthouse floor; Dillon had expected nothing less. He followed Catherine out into the communal hall, waiting patiently behind her as she took the keys out of her Chanel handbag, and then unlocked a door to one of the two apartments on that level. On entering, he took in the modern, sophisticated interior; behind him, he heard the door close with the ominous click of a lock. He was now a prisoner in her cage—albeit a spacious, glossy one with views towards the sights, and lights, of London; the apartment lit only by the fading light of the cloudy summer evening, and the occasional flash of lightning from the retreating storm.

Dillon was expecting an offer of a drink, and then perhaps a seduction routine. He definitely needed the drink to calm his nerves, but even a drink wouldn't have helped—for what came next surpassed any of his expectations.

"Your report was excellent and, for that, you deserve to be rewarded," she said suddenly—her posture strong and tall. Her authoritarian tone sent a rush of excitement through him, setting of the twitch in his disobedient cock.

Rewards?—a blowjob would be nice.

He struggled to envisage what she might mean regarding rewards, doubting his kind of reward would match her definition of the word. He didn't dare ask.

"However . . .," All of the rewards images running through his mind vanished as she said that word. "You did attempt to outshine me in that boardroom last week, did you not?" Her dominating stare implied she was awaiting a response to her accusation; Dillon genuinely hadn't set out to upstage her, nor even believed he had.

What am I supposed to say? I'm in your house, you're my boss and you're offering me rewards. I'm guessing if I deny it, rewards are out the window and punishments are back. How the fuck, do I please this bossy bitch?

"I didn't . . . I mean, that wasn't my intention . . . I'm sorry if you thought I did," he replied, stuttering throughout.

"Do I need to remind you of who is the boss?" she said, ignoring his denial and apology.

Remind me?—oh fuck. How exactly do you remind me?

His baffled expression gave her amusement, and her sparkle-smile only made him further confused, wondering what wicked thoughts were behind it. His cock, however, was anything but confused, responding to her domination with ever-increasing hardness.

"No . . . maybe . . . I don't know. Do you?" he asked nervously, wondering what punishment she might have in store for him for the apparent upstaging, and lack of respect for her authority.

"No what?" she demanded.

He'd clearly forgotten something in his mumble. "No Catherine. You're the boss," he replied, hoping this was the right answer.

"That's better," she said, looking pleased with herself, and Dillon hoped the threat of punishment had abated. "You're all wet."

It was a sudden statement—as though she'd only just appreciated that he was soaked, despite him having sat dripping in her car throughout the drive. While relieved that there was no anger in her observation, he was apprehensive about the hint of amusement in it.

Perhaps you could offer me a towel, or maybe a hairdryer? You know, like a normal person would do.

He wondered if she knew the concept of common courtesy.

"Take off your shoes and clothes. I don't want water dripped everywhere," she said, just as suddenly as her observation; apparently she didn't know the courtesy concept—only this freakish one.

What the fuck? Who asks a visitor to remove their clothes in the hall?

Dillon was no stranger to requests to remove his shoes; he'd lost count of how many coupled-up friends had chosen to lay pristine cream carpets when moving into a new place, yet to appreciate that cream, plus everyday life, weren't a compatible combination. Never before though, had he been specifically asked to remove his clothes—in fact, while he'd had them removed many a time by a woman in the bedroom (and sometimes in the lounge), it had happened in the heat of the moment and never was proceeded with a verbal request.

"I'm not going to ask again. Do it, or leave," she demanded; still standing facing him and not letting him beyond the grand entrance hall.

Do I run?

His thought about bolting was only a fleeting one; not only was he firmly rooted to the spot, but he was also unable to resist seeing what she'd in store for him. Besides if he ran, the punishment come Monday might be far worse. His curious mind gave him no choice but to obey. He removed his jacket, then shoes, socks and finally his shirt—his tie removed before he'd set off for his short-lived dash to the station. She stepped forward to open a closet door, and then she retrieved three hangers—one specifically for trousers.

Those too?

He looked at her—his fingers hesitating at his belt buckle.

"We don't have all night. Trousers off," she commanded, reading his thoughts; her sparkle-smiled had intensified as she admired his well-toned upper body. He quickly complied—his ego boosted from her apparent appreciation of his broad shoulders, strong biceps and defined six-pack— and he hung each garment onto the hangers she'd handed him.

Does she do this often?

Catherine seemed remarkably well prepared for hanging a wet man's suit in her hall closet; as he passed her the clothes, she hooked each item back onto the rail, then closed the closet door and turned to face him. He could sense she wanted to come forward and touch him, but she resisted—maybe it was just his wishful thinking.

"Hands behind your back," she instructed.

He stood before her in his boxer shorts—not, unfortunately, the best pair he owned—his desire clearly on show under the minimal fabric covering him. He wondered how he stacked up; his fears about inadequacy and rejection made him feel even more vulnerable. She came closer and then ran her hands downwards from his muscular chest to his abs; instinctively he breathed in, pulling the muscles taut, proudly showing off his six-pack. A lot of gym work had gone into those muscles and, for the first time in ages, he felt that he was with a woman who would truly appreciate them—he suspected she wouldn't have accepted anything less. Thankfully, she didn't appear to be disappointed and his ego was boosted even more.

Catherine stopped the journey of her hands just short of his groin, instead drawing them back up towards his chest. As they travelled, she lifted her palms off his body, leaving only the tips of her fingers, and her perfectly manicured nails, as the only things touching him. Reaching his chest, she twirled a fingernail around one of his nipples; the sensation sent ripples throughout Dillon's body and his cock jerked with anticipation—eager to get on with the proceedings.

She looked up into his eyes with an intense gaze, then gracefully raised her chin upwards, and rose onto her tiptoes for additional height beyond what her heels provided. In that position, she planted a gentle kiss on his lips; he could taste the faintness of mint. Before he could sink into a deeper kiss, she pulled back, removed her finger from his chest and wiggled it from side to side.

"Uh, uh," she tormented, reminding him that she was in charge—the boss.

Dillon stood rigid to the spot and watched her as she walked away.

Is that it? Like before? Does she get off on this?

He begged in his head that she wasn't a cock-tease, and that this delay wasn't just another game. If she tried to send him away, he wouldn't leave; he wanted her—tonight. Yet it would be wrong to force her, and just as he was trying to find words to convince her to let him stay, she beckoned him over to the lounge area where she had sank into an armchair.

Do I take the sofa, or the other armchair?

He pondered which one to choose—since she'd chosen to sit in a seat clearly for one; the sofa might be presumptuous after his faux-pas of the week before in her office.

"Stand in front of me," she commanded.

The seating decision made for him; he obeyed. Catherine was now at eye level with his waist, but she kept her focus upwards toward his face; dominantly staring into his eyes, even though she was lower than he was. He was disappointed that she wasn't admiring his enlarged manhood—now in prime viewing position for her enjoyment—and he deliberately adjusted the front seam to draw attention to it.

"Did I say you could bring your hands back in front?" she asked. Not wanting to fail her—or subjected to punishment, he immediately clasped his hands behind his back again. She never lowered her intense stare for even a second; his cock went unnoticed.

Her fingers resumed their touch on his abs, and she slowly trailed them downwards—keeping her eyes locked into his. For the most part, only her fingernails were caressing him—the mind-blowing effect was similar to a feather tickled down his body. She traced her finger over his boxers; still avoiding his unloved (and now dribbling) cock that was straining to be freed from his ever-tightening boxers.

Her fingers continued their journey down the front of his legs—one long, pointed finger only on each leg—then, once she'd reached below his knees, she dragged them around to trace their way up the backs of his calves, then his thighs. The torture went on forever—or at least it seemed that way—but finally she arrived back at the edge of his boxers. Moving her fingers more centrally, she traced her way over the outline of his cock.

Oh, yes . . . finally.

She'd been denying him of her touch on his erect cock for weeks—despite her attentions being the continual source of his erections; now her touch made him twitch with excitement, and his uncontrollable reaction brought out her wicked smile.

"Well, is it time for a short reward, or maybe a long punishment instead?" she asked, looking at him expectedly, as though waiting for him to respond.

What do those things mean? Who, in their right mind, would select option two?

He'd no idea whether the question was one he was supposed to answer. However, before he could ask her, her hands deftly removed his boxers from his waist to the ground; it had been a rhetorical question, one she'd clearly made up her mind as to what the answer should be; Dillon still in the dark as to the option she'd chosen.

He stepped out of the boxers puddled around his bare feet—now completely exposed, and his cock sprung free from its rapidly dampening confines. Her hand reached forward—the fingernail returning to resume the tracing of the lines of his body. Somehow, she managed to make her nail's seven-inch journey down his cock last nearly a minute, then another one for the return on the underside. She stopped at the head, her fingernail focused on stimulating the sensitive spot underneath; the gentle gesture drove him wild, and he desperately wanted her to take hold of him more strongly—or, better still, take him in her mouth.

His wants, however, weren't to be voiced; she gently stroked, with no firm grip and no wet mouth. Her other hand pushed between his legs, silently gesturing him to widen them. Obliging, he spread his legs about half a foot apart, allowing her hand to continue exploring beyond his sack. Soon he felt the underside of her finger massaging the sensitive spot between the base of his balls and his ass.

Please say this is the long punishment.

Dillon was struggling to remain submissive; her timeline conflicting with his natural urge to give into his desires and thrust himself forward towards her mouth—tantalizingly so close to his cock that he could feel every one of her breaths, a sensation that made the heated skin of his shaft tingle.

Unable to control himself any longer, he jerked forward slightly. Catherine raised an eyebrow, smirked a little and then, without breaking eye contact, she leaned forward; her smile morphed into an open mouth that sunk down around the head of his cock and then her lips closed down—

the coolness of her earlier menthol was a sensation he'd never experienced before. Dillon let out a groan of satisfaction, but as soon as he did, she stopped and released him.

"Quiet," she demanded.

The reprimand made him stand up straighter, and he tried to focus on anything but his imminent orgasm. A minute went by—it felt like more—before she resumed her oral torture, this time taking him much deeper into her mouth. One of her fingers returned to the sensitive spot below his balls, and the combined pleasure drove him crazy. He knew he wouldn't be able to last much longer; he could already feel the contractions in his groin that signaled he was about to come. Catherine was sucking him harder now, the tip of her tongue rolling around the head of his cock as she did.

This is it—just a second more . . . no . . .

She stopped abruptly and her fingers replaced her mouth to squeeze the tip of his cock—denying him the orgasm that he was craving. She held him this way for thirty seconds, until the pulsating in his body had started to slow, and then as suddenly as she'd stopped, she returned her mouth to suck him again. It didn't take Dillon long to reach a similar point of ecstasy, before she slowed again.

Please don't stop, you cruel bitch.

His silent prayer was answered; this time she didn't stop, and her hands moved behind his back to grab his buttocks and thrust him forward deeper into her mouth. He came hard, and when his body had released of all its tension, she smiled, swallowed his juices and looked thoroughly pleased with herself.

If this was the punishment, I don't mind at all. Do I return the favor?

He wondered if he should kneel and give her pleasure, but before he had the chance to, Catherine stood up. Taking him by the hand, she led him over to a desk. "You can sit," she said.

He immediately did as instructed; his warm, bare butt cheeks were a striking contrast to the cool leather of the modern desk chair, making him afraid that he'd leave sweat stains all over the upholstery. She opened the top drawer of the desk and withdrew three long, black, silk ribbon ties; proceeding to expertly tie the first of them around his upper body to fix him to the back of the chair. His arms were next; the second and third tie used to bind him to the chair sides—tight enough to disable the use of his arms, yet still allow some movement in his wrists.

Completely naked, Dillon was also now helpless to move. It was at this point that Catherine walked out of the room.

Five minutes passed.

Is this a joke? Will there be a camera? Worse? Oh fuck, what have I gotten myself into now?

All manner of thoughts ran through Dillon's mind as he waited in forced isolation. Finally, his silent hell interrupted by the sound of music coming into the room. Turning his head towards the sound, he saw Catherine walking towards him; a single glass of champagne in her hand, from which she took a sip as she approached. She'd abandoned her suit, and was dressed only in a red silk, and black lace, lingerie set—complete with matching suspender belt. His gaze dropped down her legs, still enveloped in silk stockings and, as his eyes reached her feet, he could see she was wearing the black, red-soled stilettos that he now favored as much as she apparently did.

His cock began to jerk back to life from the subdued state that she'd left it in; he rarely recovered from orgasm this quickly, but these were exceptional circumstances; his body had adopted a new clock—one that Catherine controlled the winding of the dials on. She sat herself on the desk in front of him.

"Champagne?" she asked, holding out the one glass.

He nodded, unsure if he were allowed to accept, but he really needed something to take the edge off his nerves. She carefully tipped the glass forward against his lips—continuing to deny him the use of his own arms; when he'd swallowed a mouthful, she returned the glass to her own lips and took another sip. The music reached a louder point of the piece, allowing Dillon to recognize it as the same music from the evening he'd watched her in her office.

"You like the music?" she asked; Dillon swore she really could read his mind—a dangerous proposition. He nodded, unsure if he was still required to obey the 'quiet' command of earlier.

"The piece is *Fantasia on a Theme of Thomas Tallis*, by Ralph Vaughan Williams." Another nod; he vaguely remembered covering it in music theory at school.

"Whatever mood I'm in, it's always my favorite thing to listen to. Whether that's when I'm working late at the office, or when I'm alone doing *other things*," she explained, winking at her last words.

Dillon was fascinated as to what she meant; he decided to be brave and ask—after all, he'd asked so few questions, "Other things?"

She smiled. "Yes, I like to use myself as the orchestral instruments," she replied casually, as though it was the most normal thing in the world to say.

He was still baffled as to what on earth that meant.

"You like to watch me when I listen to this music, don't you Dillon?"

she asked rhetorically; the seductive tone was back—more suggestive than ever—and he gulped, wondering if he was now in for the actual long punishment for his voyeurism the week before. He was now sure their earlier activity had constituted the short reward. "Now, you're going to be my audience again, only this time, I give you permission to watch."

Fuck, I'm really going to suffer for that incident.

As the strings began in the orchestral piece, Catherine leaned back onto the desk. She arched her back, and as she did, she put one hand behind her to unclasp her bra; her breasts came into view—the sight of the round flesh, and pert pink nipples, brought Dillon back to the full peak of his erection. All he wanted to do was stand up, bend over and fuck her to oblivion on her desk, but tied to the chair there was no way he could stand, no way he could reach for her and no way to caress her himself; the punishment had started.

Catherine didn't need him to touch her—this was her concert; she ran her own hand up her body towards her breast, then circled her finger around her nipple slowly, while her other hand moved down her waist to push her panties lower. In doing so, she exposed a little more of her to him; he saw that she was clean waxed. Apart from the glossy mane of hair on her head, and her shaped eyebrows, she was bare and smooth all over her body.

She began to touch herself; he could make out that lethal fingernail, which she'd used so expertly on him, now rhythmically rubbing her clit. It was true; she was playing herself like a string instrument—gently circling, and rubbing, her nipple and clitoris as the peaks and troughs of the music continued.

In his excitement from watching her, Dillon inadvertently let an audible gasp slip from his lips; Catherine abruptly stopped and sat up to face him.

"I thought I told you earlier to be quiet?" she snapped. He lowered his eyes, ashamed that he'd failed her. "That instruction still stands, but perhaps I need to assist you with that."

His eyes flashed back up to meet hers.

Assistance?

He dreaded what might be coming his way to silence him. She slipped off the desk, and once standing, she gradually slid her panties down her long, shapely legs, and then lifted each leg out of them—the action taking far longer than was necessary; deliberately slow for further torment. All she was wearing now were the stockings, suspender belt and those shoes. In one elegant movement, she bent her knees and retrieved the panties from the floor—never for a moment breaking that intense gaze that Dillon was transfixed on. The bra cast aside earlier, he hated to think what prompted the sudden need to be tidier.

Lifting her empty hand, she circled his lips with her fingers, and then pushed a single finger between them. The digit was still wet from her earlier show and, as he gently sucked on it, the taste of her only served to make him even hornier; he groaned again. Without hesitation, she prized open his mouth with the finger, and then raised her other hand that was still clutching her panties—now crumpled into a ball.

He immediately guessed her plans; she stuffed them into his mouth, gagging him. Adjusting his tongue to accommodate the garment, he savored the taste of the underwear—damp from her arousal. She smiled her sparkle-smile that he'd come to know definitely meant wickedness.

"Now you'll have to be quiet," she purred.

Interval over, Catherine raised herself back on the desk and resumed her arched back position; now panty-less, her lower region was tantalizingly on full show to him. As the strands of the music reached higher and higher in velocity, she shifted slightly and raised her legs up to meet Dillon's hands. Although his arms were bound tightly, she'd left his hands loose enough to allow him to grab hold of her ankles. He could caress the lower part of her leg, and finally touch those heels, but couldn't do much else. However, it was enough; the touch meant he could feel her body begin to stiffen, and his eyes could see her feet start to arch within her shoes.

The chosen music was over fifteen minutes in duration, but as it hit its peak, the piece proved the perfect length of time for her to reach a shuddering orgasm to coincide with it; she'd clearly done this many a time before and Dillon was grateful for her rehearsals. This had been a perfect performance; immersing him in a four-dimensional voyeurism that involved all of his senses—in only the ways she saw fit to allow.

Now Dillon understood her definition of long punishment; he was aching to deeply explore her mouth with his tongue, and simultaneously sink his cock into her glistening wetness. Her definition of long was, however, much longer than his was—it was still time for her enjoyment. Edging towards him, she reached forward and loosened the ties that bound him, and then removed the makeshift gag from his mouth. He took a deep breath of clean air as he watched her recline back for a third time onto the desk, her elbows supporting her weight and her back arched to project her breasts and pelvis towards him.

"Your turn," she said, raising her eyebrow as if to challenge him.

Finally . . .

Dillon moved to stand, ready to lean over and take her—but this was still her game.

"Uh, uh," she said, shaking her head and wiggling her finger. "Stay sitting. I meant it's my turn for some oral pleasure."

Damn.

He was desperate to fuck her now—his balls painfully swollen—but he did as he was told, leaning forward to run his tongue along her well-lubricated clit, tasting the saltiness of her arousal. He pushed his tongue deeper between the darkening lips of her labia, and the tip of his tongue found their mark—slightly entering her. She quivered with excitement and Dillon was pleased that he was succeeding in pleasuring her.

He expected her to continue in this position until her second orgasm, but Catherine had the knack for surprise; she abruptly sat up, and then slipped off the desk again to stand in front of him, pressing against his legs. She opened the desk drawer again, reaching inside to retrieve a condom packet.

"Put it on," she instructed, handing it to him.

He didn't hesitate to rip it open and carefully slip the rubber on; he was more than ready for this. However, in his haste, he'd failed to spot the condom label—a lubricant brand designed to delay a man. Catherine was definitely all about control, yet as his cock began to numb, he realized he didn't mind; he was enjoying the intensity of being under her spell and, at this moment, anything that prolonged him from coming too quickly was welcome.

She lowered herself onto him; Dillon groaned as he finally felt the tightness of her enveloping his cock after all the weeks of torture. She kissed him and, within seconds of their lips meeting, their tongues began to explore each other's mouths—deeper and deeper. She was controlling the pace, but she'd granted him the use of his hands and now he could grip her tightly around her hips, forcing her body down onto his lap with as much power as he could. As the lubricant wore off, he could better feel her strong pelvic muscles tightening around his cock, and his thrusts became more urgent.

With all the anticipation, he was worried that he wouldn't last long and would deny her an orgasm before, or concurrent to, his own. However, his fears were unfounded, for as the next musical score reached its peak; the already-aroused Catherine whimpered and shook as Dillon came to his own shuddering, noisy release.

His heart started to slow as they sat in silence; her remaining astride him. This was the awkward bit, but as expected, Catherine was the one who finally broke the silence.

"Well aren't you the star employee," she said, winking as she stood up—letting his cock slip limply out of her. Before he could respond to her bizarre compliment, she left the room.

Dillon didn't know what to do next, but grabbing his boxers and quickly putting them on seemed like an appropriate thing to do—even if she might then reprimand him on her return. Her absence was much shorter than her earlier departure; and when she returned she was wearing a silk night-robe. Her stockings and heels were gone, and her hair tousled softly around her shoulders. Catherine now looked more natural—like the night he'd watched her in her office—and, at this moment, he thought her far more attractive; although he couldn't be sure that it wasn't just post-orgasm attachment kicking in.

"Your clothes should be dry now; I put them in the airing closet," she said casually.

Dillon laughed, unable to stop himself; this was probably the most normal thing that she'd ever said to him, and it alleviated the awkwardness of what to say next. The statement had also been somewhat of a dismissal; he was to get dressed and go. He took the hint; this wasn't meant to be cozy evening for two.

Once dressed, he took his leave, but before closing the front door behind him, he looked back. Speaking with a newfound confidence, he simply said, "Thank you, Boss; Goodbye."

⌇⌇

An email ping—the sound bringing Dillon back to reality. He'd lost track of the time; the rain was still falling, but darkness had long descended on the office building—despite the British summer-time clock. He looked away from the window towards his computer screen, once again catching sight of the handwritten note that his PA had delivered earlier that evening.

Adorned with an unknown sender's elegant handwriting stating '*Dillon Oak: Private & Confidential*'; he'd opened the parchment envelope and, on doing so, had discovered the note was from Catherine. Bypassing the email system, and the awkwardness of a face-to-face, she'd sent him a story, or rather—for want of a better word—a scenario. Catching sight of him earlier in the day staring out at the rain, she'd thought he might like some inspiration for his apparent daydreaming—or so said the one-line message that accompanied the handwritten story. It was a graphic scenario, with details of how she'd pick him up outside the office; take him to her flat, and all that she'd do to him when they'd arrived.

As he'd read it, Dillon had added details in his head; she hadn't described her car, nor her apartment, and the smells, tastes and sensations were figments of his imagination; none of it was real—Catherine was still a fantasy in his mind.

The email pinged again; he checked his empty inbox, and then stupidly realized it was his personal phone alert. Glancing at his phone, his heart skipped a beat when he saw the sender—Catherine Everdene. An email from her to his personal account—with a subject line; '*Monday*'. He opened it with hopeful, rather than dreaded, expectation of what might await him on Monday, and he started to read.

> 'Dillon,
> I hope you liked my little story and I've no doubt that you've now got many images of me in your mind. Please enjoy these thoughts as an extra special reminder of me. I tried to resist writing you a story, but I couldn't help it—I thought you'd appreciate it given the few occasions we've had some flirtatious fun together.
> On Monday, I start a new job in the New York office. I've known for a couple of weeks about my pending departure, but I couldn't tell you for a number of reasons. I did want to say something when you asked me about New York, but, as it was still confidential, I changed the topic in case I let it slip. My departure is also one reason I didn't take anything further with you as this wouldn't have been fair, while the other reason was that it wasn't appropriate to get involved given our positions. I didn't want anyone to think that you'd scored the promotion (that you're about to get), so quickly through anything but your own merit, and I'm sure you wouldn't want people to think that either. There was always the intention that you'd be my replacement— we'd hired you for my role because the New York posting was essentially mine to lose; rather than to win. I was fairly well out the door when you arrived.
> You're going to do a great job taking over from me—the Board thought you very capable and the report was well received. I'm sure you have a great future ahead of you.
> On a personal matter, batter those blue, puppy-dog eyes of yours at your date and I don't doubt she will forgive you for cancelling a few weeks ago. I took the liberty of sending champagne to your flat to congratulate you on the promotion, so I hope the pair of you enjoy it.
> Take care of yourself.
> Miss Catherine Everdene.'

He re-read her last line. *Miss Catherine* were the only words he took in; the *Miss* somehow a word with so much meaning—a sexual, domineering title, but also an emotion that he was now feeling. He missed her already, despite the fact she hadn't yet gone, and his world felt like it was crashing down around him. He should've been over the moon that he was about to be promoted—a director, to finally appease his family's taunts—yet all he could think of, was that he wouldn't get to see Catherine again in person; ever.

Even though she wasn't leaving the company, the London and New York offices were entirely separate; all he'd see would be snippets from the company intranet; her picture haunting him from the homepage every time he opened the browser window. Moreover, she'd known about his date—he didn't even want to contemplate how she could possibly have known about her—and he felt gutted that she'd showed no signs of jealousy in her note; instead wishing him well.

That night, when Dillon finally made it home in a sodden, bedraggled state, he downed the bottle of fine champagne that she'd sent in the quiet, lonely solitude of his own company; a self-imposed isolation that he kept up for the rest of the weekend.

Chapter Five

"Champagne, Miss Everdene?" asked the British Airways First Class flight attendant as she held out a tray of glasses filled with Laurent-Perrier Grand Siècle champagne.

I could get used to this . . .

Catherine accepted a glass with thanks as she took in her surroundings in the spacious cabin of Britain's national airline. When she'd scored the role in the New York office, it came with higher perks—including this flight. She'd worked hard to get where she was, and now was the time to enjoy the fruits of her success.

However, despite the leisurely Sunday breakfast that she'd indulged in while waiting in the Concorde Room at London Heathrow's bustling Terminal 5, there was an emptiness inside her that no bacon and eggs—however heavenly—could fill. She was happily looking forward to her future over the pond, but she couldn't shake the thoughts she'd been having over the past weeks involving her new team member, Dillon Oak.

From the moment that she'd come face-to-face with all the six-foot-three-gorgeousness of him in the lobby—she'd sensed a reaction in him to her presence; in turn she was overwhelmed by her own magnetism to him. Unable to resist him, her confidence and natural charm channeled into a flirtation that exceeded even her own expectations. Abandoning her normal professionalism, she'd compromised herself; increasingly addicted to the feelings that she'd had when she was dominating her new employee's thoughts, and visibly arousing his body. While she'd been able to hide her own arousal—her quickened pulse, throbbing between her legs and frequently damp underwear whenever she'd imagined him touching her—Dillon's male anatomy didn't offer him the fortune of concealment.

He'd been her equal—hired by her peers to replace her when she departed, and she'd reveled in the power of managing someone as accomplished, and respected, in the industry as he was; the company had been contemplating head-hunting him for a while, but there was no suitable role for both of them. She was distinctly aware that some would have preferred Dillon over her some time ago—particularly the few female executives that would have a say in such a decision, but she'd rode out the discontent.

Since his arrival that first day, she'd banished any insecurities she had about him outshining her through imaging him naked—like people recommend to do when making a public speech. While it did nothing to help the state of her damp panties, it did work to give her dominating confidence. When she saw that she'd succeeding in ruffling his confidence through her flirtations, she ramped up the sexuality to keep the dynamic in place.

Initially it had worked, but Dillon had managed to rattle her in turn when he'd caught her out in a more casual moment, chatting with the cleaner. She'd reacted abruptly, quickly drawing her walls higher to hide any sense of vulnerability. She didn't want Dillon—or anyone else for that matter—to know how much she valued the friendship she had with the cleaner; the old woman was the only one in the office who'd never backstabbed her, and reminded her of her own grandmother who'd toiled hard at cleaning offices until her death.

Catherine's past, and things her colleagues said about her personality, were hurtful, and she didn't want him to know the weaker spots in her armor; she wanted to be admired—and occasionally feared—for her strength of character.

Not only that, but he'd also started to penetrate the hairline cracks in her carefully guarded heart and soul; his intellect, charisma and charm—coupled with his looks—were attractive to her. The more she'd flirted with him, and imagined him naked, the more intense her orgasms had been when she was alone and fantasizing about being with him; her fingers—and her rabbit vibrator—had never had so much usage in such a short space of time.

These fantasies had helped her justify her interest in Dillon as purely a sexual attraction—it had been a while since she was last in a relationship—and she pushed away any thoughts that he might be more to her than a flirtation firmly to the back of her mind.

She was annoyed with herself at the story, and follow-up email, she'd sent to him. Bored with packing up her desk—and having managed to avoid a farewell party by keeping her departure a secret—Catherine had amused (and aroused) herself by writing the story. Having passed Dillon in his office earlier, he'd looked as bored as she was.

At first, she'd been tempted to go in to see him, but resisted the urge—not knowing if she'd be able to resist taking things further. It had taken every ounce of her control to hold back the previous week, when he'd been in her office late; she'd wanted him—and he'd most definitely wanted her. If it hadn't been for him inadvertently mentioning that he'd watched her with the cleaner, she knew she would've had him there, and then, on her desk.

Instead she'd taken to the written word, and while her handwritten delivery continued her sexual domination over him, her imminent departure had made it unnecessary to continue her intimidating torment; she'd been unfair to him and, in her opinion, the personal email she'd sent him after, was too emotionally slushy. Catherine had become an expert over the years at hiding her true self, and, in only a few paragraphs, she felt that she'd exposed a caring—but much weaker—side to her character.

She now knew that her words and actions had hurt Dillon, and she hadn't been expecting him to react with such emotion. When he'd sent a reply email to her, at first she'd been surprisingly relieved as her jealousy abated—he was alone rather than celebrating with his girlfriend. However, her relief soon switched to concern as she read his reply; the content and tone conveyed a drunken, bruised male ego. Catherine felt guilty that she'd led him on so many times in the office, only to then make it worse with the story.

Her stubborn reminder to herself that he was just a horny, egotistical man—who was there to take over her job—couldn't be further from the truth; Dillon was a hard-worker. He'd not only earned a good reputation for the quality of his work, but nobody had a bad word to say about his friendly personality; he was popular with his colleagues. Never once had he validated her false belief by making her look bad, or joining in backstabbing gossip about her.

The more she'd discovered Dillon's qualities, the harder it was for her to hide behind her shield. She'd avoided him since the Board meeting for that reason; unsure if she could dominate him face-to-face any longer in the same way—all she'd wanted to do was congratulate him and get to know him better. If Catherine had stayed in London, she doubted she'd have been able to stay away from Dillon; a risk she couldn't take after everything she'd invested in making herself a success. Leaving for New York was a timely decision—one that was the best for both of them.

"Cabin crew seats for take-off," announced an unknown person over the speaker.

Catherine broke her endless thoughts about Dillon; with seven hours of flight time ahead of her, she wanted to focus on her future and not the man she was leaving behind. The plane gathered speed on the tarmac, and once airborne, she watched London—and her life there—fade behind the grey clouds that hung over the still-sleeping city. From the air, she couldn't even spot her small, second floor, riverside rental that she'd packed up and left the day before; doubting that she'd ever miss its modern, unhomely blandness, or the glimpse of the murky River Thames that she'd been able to see from the miniscule kitchen window.

Reclining back her seat into the flatbed position, she resolved to think no more of her uninspiring personal life that she was leaving behind.

Dillon Oak is London; I'm about to be New York.

⌒

The yellow taxi pulled up outside the West Village townhouse, and Catherine caught a glimpse of an excited little face peering out of a window. She hadn't yet met Madison, her best friend's three-year-old daughter, but Liddy Bradbury had assured her that Auntie Catherine had been the most discussed subject in their home for the past few weeks. As she paid the driver, she heard the unmistakable British voice of her friend.

"Hello fabulous, nice boots," remarked Liddy, racing down the brownstone's stairs to give her a hug.

Catherine glanced down at her designer boots, paid for from her earnings when she should've been saving. She briefly felt guilty that her choice of footwear wasn't the best thing to wear when visiting her friend; toddlers and Jimmy Choo boots were probably not a good match. Liddy collapsed into hysterical laughter and then pointed to her own boots—an identical pair—and Catherine's mood relaxed immediately.

Thank god, she's still the same Liddy, but damn; I'll bet she paid less for them boots over here.

She'd been worried that she wouldn't know what to say to her best friend now that they were in different stages of their lives, but thankfully Liddy seemed to be the same as she'd remembered; good, fun company, with similar interests to Catherine—especially in footwear.

The pair had met seven years before, in their first class together at the London Business School. Juggling fast-track careers with the demands of a post-graduate evening course, late twenty/early thirty-something dating, and a London social life, the women had bonded over shared histories and future priorities. Liddy was a lawyer in the corporate division for a top tier London firm, with the definite aim of being a partner by her mid-thirties. Her MBA was the final stepping-stone she needed, and the firm's commitment to letting her study showed how much value they placed on her abilities.

Three years later, the two friends had opened the finest bottle of champagne they could afford, celebrating not only their graduation, but also their respective job offers; Liddy offered a transfer to the New York office for a year, while Catherine was to head up the commercial division of the media firm she worked for in London. The pair expected a life of professional greatness.

However, like every good story, there was an unexpected twist of events;

four days after arriving in New York, Liddy had walked into a coffee shop. After bustling through the line of caffeine-starved professionals, she'd tripped over a satchel strewn by a table—spilling coffee over an unassuming American man going about his daily business. Conversation ensued (after embarrassment had abated), and by the time the coffee was mopped up, Liddy had fallen for a business and political journalist named John Bradbury who wrote for a prominent New York paper.

Liddy's path of professional greatness radically—and swiftly—changed after that. Married within months, baby a year after that. She'd created a new professional path as well, founding a small, but successful, law firm with three other mothers and a widowed father. Their children shared two nannies above the office, and it had all worked out well. Liddy's husband had written about their firm, and its unique set up, and as a result, they'd been inundated with clients who empathized with juggling careers and parenthood—or sympathized with the relatively young widowed father forced to re-think his full-time working day on the death of his wife.

Liddy's new direction was a different kind of success, but a very happy one; her life more fulfilled than she could ever have dreamed it to be. She'd achieved being partner in a firm—her own firm no less—but had also found the love and contentment absent from the original plan.

Even though Catherine was still heading down the path for the life she planned for at graduation, she was a little envious of Liddy. While she'd no interest in Mr. Right checklists—or a frantic race to bag a husband before the biological clock struck twelve—curiously, Liddy's luck in meeting her soul-mate (her words) in the way that she had, had tugged at the fairy-tale dreams of Catherine's childhood that she'd long since abandoned. Catherine had learned the hard way that emotions on display equaled weakness; falling in love meant loss of control—and loss of control meant all kinds of bad things.

"You've got Mommy's boots on," said the young girl who'd joined them. She was adorable, and her mixed American/British accent only added to her cuteness.

I think the hand on my biological clock just ticked onto one o'clock.

"I'm guessing you must be Madison?" asked Catherine, adopting the most animated voice that she could manage; it wasn't often that she spent time with children. The girl went shy, and hid behind Liddy's legs.

"Oi Miss, say hello to Auntie Catherine," scolded Liddy to her daughter. "She's come a long way from London on a big plane. Do you remember when we went on the plane to London?"

Madison nodded, but stayed behind the protection of her mother.

"Come on, stop being shy, you've been waiting to meet her all week," persisted Liddy, but the girl shook her head and ran inside.

I'm no good with kids.

Madison's shyness only served to convince Catherine that she wasn't the motherly type.

"Kids! Ignore her, one-minute she's excited, and the next she's scared shitless. She'll want to be your best friend in five minutes," said Liddy, grabbing Catherine's cabin bag. "Come inside, you must be exhausted and in need of a cuppa."

While Catherine had been fed exceptionally well on the flight—a full meal and then a quintessential afternoon tea—she'd been dying for a good cup of Earl Grey after negotiating her way through the heaving JFK terminal with her generous baggage allowance in tow. She looked down at the two heavy suitcases still at her feet, wondering which one to pick up first, or whether she could even negotiate the stairs in heeled boots with a suitcase.

Liddy's booming command solved her dilemma. "John, tired woman in heels out here—muscles required for luggage duty," she yelled.

Maybe a husband-slave has his uses . . . vibrators can't carry suitcases.

As John obediently emerged from the house, Catherine abandoned both cases at the base of the stairs and followed Liddy into the townhouse. The interior hadn't changed much in the years since she'd last been there; Liddy had chosen her to be a bridesmaid at their Central Park wedding, and she'd managed to find the time to make the journey over from London for the occasion.

"I'm sorry we weren't about a few weeks ago when you were over for the interview, but I knew you'd get the job and I'd see you soon enough," apologized Liddy; she'd already made the apology several times over Skype, but she now wanted to congratulate her friend face-to-face.

When Catherine had come over for the interview, they'd been up in the Hamptons—Liddy had married into an old-school press family with significant connections throughout New York, which had resulted in an endless stream of holiday season invitations that extended well into September.

Now that Catherine had moved here, they finally had the chance to catch up properly, and despite her long flight—and a body-clock still on London time—she spent much of what was left of Sunday filling in Liddy on all the things that had been difficult to communicate over email, or video chat at weekends.

Tellingly, Dillon didn't make an appearance in the conversation. For all her openness with her friend, she suspected that Liddy's new loved-up outlook would result in her trying to convince her that she should let her walls crumble—to allow herself to fall in love. The Liddy that she'd once known, would've told her to have amazing one-night-stand sex before she departed, but since that wouldn't have felt right either, she'd decided not to disclose anything about the man who she couldn't shake from her thoughts, even though she wasn't sure why he was still in them.

~

The following day, a jet lagged Catherine headed to her new office; it was the first day of October—the first day of her new start. She settled quickly into her new role, and her life became a whirlwind of business meetings, socializing with Liddy, and moving into a respectable West Village studio—minutes away from her friend's home.

Whenever she was in the presence of her friend, Catherine was a more approachable person; her sense of humor, charm and kindness were on show; as a result, the people around them warmed to her. She soon made connections—helped greatly by Liddy's husband—and thoughts of Dillon faded as the days went on. With her British accent to accompany her looks and intelligence, she made an attractive proposition for many men, and she wasn't short on offers for dinner companions. While a welcome distraction, they were underwhelming company; there was no spark, chemistry, or a feeling of undeniable magnetism.

Devoid of crackling sexual energy, Catherine quickly bored of dating; as the weeks went on, she focused more on the career side of her life. Although she didn't want to admit it to anyone (including herself), she'd had a secret fantasy to run into her own John Bradbury fairy-tale within her first days—converting her to the idea of destiny and fate. However, when Prince Charming hadn't magically appeared, she abandoned the whimsical dreams in favor of what she did best; charming a boardroom of executives by flirting with just the right balance of professionalism and feminine, sexual charm.

It was a focus that was to serve her well when, only four weeks into her new position, the company was bought out globally by their biggest competitor; redundancies and office closures were inevitable, and the entire management team would be out of work. As a sponsored foreigner, Catherine needed a job offer; fast.

Chapter Six

During the weekend of Catherine's departure, Dillon had swiftly followed the downing of the bottle of champagne with the consumption of the majority of his liquor cabinet. Thankfully he wasn't much of a spirits man, stocking it only for the occasional visits by his parents to the capital; once a half bottle of Scotch, and an even less full bottle of gin, were emptied, the rest of the weekend had involved staring blankly at the ceiling, or sleeping in a crumbled heap in his bed.

When he didn't show up for work on Monday, his PA had telephoned his emergency contact when she'd been unable to reach him; his drunken isolation causing him to forget to charge his mobile phones. The resulting phone call from his younger sister to his home number became his lunchtime alarm clock.

"Why aren't you at work?" she'd asked, demanding an explanation.

Not wishing to discuss the ins-and-outs of his obsession with his former boss, he'd managed to spin a plausible story about a bachelor weekend that had got out of control, leaving him under the weather.

Please don't ask who the guy is.

He would have buckled under the pressure of too much scrutiny; his lie detected. Luckily, his sister had chosen to focus her lecture on his own irresponsibility— *'Grow up. You need to create a good impression and take things more seriously. You'll be forty in a few years and still acting like you were at twenty'*—all the things he didn't want to reminded of by his younger sister. Filled with embarrassment, he finally got her off the phone by promising to call into work sick, and then work from home.

The following day, throwing himself into his work had provided some distraction—even if the memory of Catherine was more prominent in the office. He was surprised little was said about her departure; perhaps he'd missed the lion's share of gossip when he'd slept through the Monday announcement. Dillon's slight paranoia that his colleagues would link his absence the day before to her departure was mortifying; especially if they suspected he was depressed over a woman leaving him; it wasn't the masculine way to hide from the world under a duvet when you've been dumped.

Dumped.

He'd definitely had that happen in the past week. First by Catherine—

who technically nothing had happened with—and secondly, by the online woman who'd texted late that Friday evening; the contents of her first text definitely with the sub-text booty call and drunk.

He vaguely recalled replying—an inappropriate reply commenting on her performance in the bedroom, and a lack of desire to repeat it. It'd had the desired effect; he'd counted *Fuck You* at least four times in her reply.

That wasn't the worse of his stuff-ups; alcohol had shut down the part of his brain responsible for judgment. After reading the 'Fuck You' text, he'd gone on to re-read the email from Catherine on his phone. Worst still, he'd replied to it.

> 'Dear Cock-tease,
> I got your twisted story and note. Shame you didn't
> have the guts to go through with it. You would've been
> screaming from the rafters, unable to control the orgasms
> you would've had over and over again. I would've been the
> best damn shag you've ever had. If your plane leaves the
> ground without me fucking you, you will regret it, maybe
> not straight away, but one day and then you'll remember
> me for the rest of your life, because you'll never find anyone
> that could please you as good.'

He hadn't realized just how bitter he was until he'd read it back to himself, unfortunately when it was too late to retract it. He was sure that *Casablanca* must have been on the television in the background when he typed it; his subconscious had ripped off, and adapted, a sentimental catchphrase of the film. Calling her a cock-tease was also unlikely to win him a good reference if ever he needed one from her.

With many years in the dating world behind him—and several notches on his bed—Dillon wasn't new to being dumped by a woman, but the ratio of being the one to end the relationship was much more in his favor. This time, however, seemed to have resulted in more than just a wounded male ego; he felt more rejected that he'd ever felt before, with no idea what to do to get over it.

The usual plan of finding a good-looking girl for a casual encounter—either on a night on the pull, via the internet, or through a mobile app—had no appeal. The chances of finding someone superior to Catherine online, or in his local bar, were slim. There was even less likelihood of finding someone with the sexual power that she'd had over him; a power that he was craving now, and that would be hard to replicate in a one-night-stand with no build up.

There was only one way he'd known how to move on—throw himself into work and overcome the self-doubts that Catherine had managed to re-surface in his head about his abilities.

~

By the end of his first week as Director of UK Operations, Dillon had started to bounce back. There'd been no gossip that had made its way back to him on Catherine's departure, either related to any scandalous involvement she may have had with him, or why he'd been given her role so shortly after joining the company. The Board was definitely impressed with him, and colleagues accepted that his experience to date had made him the ideal candidate to take over.

His impressionable and friendly manner had also helped enormously. Catherine Everdene had been somewhat feared in the office and perceived to be someone who knew how to capture the minds of her superiors with her flirtatious self-assurance. The men who worked for her were in awe of her, while the women of the office had little to do with her; it was from the female employees where her reputation as icy bitch had originated. It was very clear that nobody in the office missed her—no one except for Dillon.

On hearing some of the talk about her, he'd wondered if he was the only one that she'd driven insane with desire.

Did others get a farewell note?

Knowing she'd tormented other male colleagues would've helped him move on, but it wasn't going to be the easiest conversation to have—it needed alcohol to loosen tongues; Dillon took it upon himself to suggest a Friday night drink, particularly as he'd missed the previous ones and was keen to appear sociable.

The night certainly brought out the stories and, as beer consumption moved onto harder spirits, the stories moved into singing. One song, or rather one chorus line of it—since it wasn't a song typically sung by grown men—was unanimously sung; *Ding dong the witch is dead*. Drunken men in chorus—just like the munchkins in Oz. Catherine wasn't liked, but for his sanity, Dillon needed to know if it was because she'd fucked with their minds like she had with him; it had been time to probe them with questions.

Again, the answers were unanimous. One of the team leaders had summed it up, "Of course all of us probably wanted to fuck her—I mean who wouldn't right? Nail the icy bitch, and put her in her place. But no one could get near her and she wasn't interested in anyone—probably a lesbian, or keeps men in cages at home for entertainment."

Despite his alcohol-fuelled haze, Dillon had felt a chill run through him at the last sentence of his colleague.

She keeps men in cages . . .

His mind had filled with a vision of Catherine standing over him; his naked body huddled in a cage.

Shit.

Even gone she was dominating his mind with her dark games, the wicked witch definitely not dead and gone for him.

I'm like the cowering lion missing courage, the scarecrow ripped apart with his brain gone, and the tin-man rusted with his heart stolen—just like in the Wizard of Oz. Why won't she just melt away from my mind?

The night hadn't delivered what he'd hoped; either he'd been singled out for her torment, or the other men weren't about to share stories about the power she'd had over them.

With very little planned for the weekend, Saturday had started with a banging hangover in bed; the sanctuary of his bed rudely interrupted when his mobile had rung.

"Have your sorted yourself out?" Despite no visual confirmation, his sister had quickly deciphered from his voice that he was once again still intoxicated; another lecture followed.

Can't bossy women just leave me alone?

Her call ended with a threat—"Get out of bed, or I will have to drive up to London and drag you out of it by your hair."

That final sentence had put yet more thoughts into his mind—Catherine dragging him by his hair out of his cage and into her bed.

Enough—time to end this!

Dillon resolved to take action and reached for his iPad; he opened a browser window and typed into the search engine 'Dominatrix + London'.

෧

At first, Dillon had been uncomfortable paying for the service of a professional. He tried a BDSM internet-dating site, but quickly discovered that his inbox became full of demanding emails from barely-legal teens trying to extort money and gifts by offering perverted conversations in return. *Tributes* they'd called it—web links to online wish lists of shoes, dresses and occasionally more mundane requirements such as course textbooks; 'Buy me this, you worthless worm,' they'd typed.

After viewing a few of their profile images, he couldn't possibly associate the word 'tribute' with them, let alone get out his credit card to send them one of their desired gifts. They repulsed him in every sense, and he definitely didn't feel dominated by their false sense of superiority. If he was going to do this, he wanted to know that he wasn't compromising; this was about a deep psychological attraction to a strong, confident feminine identity—in his case, one particular female.

Eventually he abandoned the site and started visiting the websites of professional dominatrix mistresses. Finding comfort in the frequent re-assurance on the sites that it wasn't a prostitute service, and that sex wouldn't be an option, he'd made his initial enquiry to Mistress Avianne.

Her website was very comprehensive; she offered the full spectrum of dominatrix experiences ranging from dungeon-based scenes with her donning full latex, to prim governess scenarios where she would dress a man up in a nappy. However, her main specialty was the one that had appealed to Dillon—corporate CEO role-plays with her dressed in a designer suit and black Louboutin heels.

The photo on her website was almost the image of Catherine—except this woman had darker eyes and hair, and she was no older than her late twenties. Her age contradicted the CEO fantasy a little, but he was prepared to overlook it; he'd been searching the internet for days trying to find something—or more specifically someone—to take his mind off Catherine. Even when he'd found a dominatrix bearing a resemblance to her, he'd reasoned that somehow it would help; paying someone to dominate him that happened to look like her, might change the way he thought about it—knocking Catherine off the pedestal he'd put her on.

❦

Dillon was nervous. Casting his mind back to the day he met Catherine, he realized that his nerves were a mix of re-living the feelings of that day, and his apprehension that the evening wouldn't deliver on its promise. As his allocated timeslot arrived, he pressed the doorbell of the elegant Mayfair mews house; either Miss Avianne did very well for herself, or else she was the daughter of wealthy parents who'd provided her with a nice residence in the capital. On her opening the door, and greeting him with the accent of an upper-class educated woman, he deduced that it was likely both observations were probably correct; he could see that many successful men would quite happily pay the few hundred pounds an hour for her company.

He followed her into a lounge—the decor all neutral creams, whites and beiges; plush sofas were combined with old-fashioned carver style chairs, and round tables were adorned with elegant crystal based lamps and vases of white and pale pink roses.

"Can I offer you a drink of water—I have sparkling or still?" she asked politely.

While Dillon could see a crystal decanter with liquor on the sideboard she was standing alongside, he remembered her introductory reply email that requested no alcohol consumption prior to—or during—the session. He'd desperately wanted something to settle his nerves.

"Thank you, I'll have still water please," he replied, unsure if he was meant to answer in a submissive way, even though her question hadn't come across a dominant one. She handed him a glass and motioned for him to take a seat on the sofa, seating herself in one of the over-sized carver chairs opposite.

"Now Mr. Oak, before we start, let us talk some more about what you would like to get out of this first session," she said, and Dillon flinched at his name.

I should've used a fake name.

He felt like he was in an appointment with a psychiatrist, about to bare his soul and innermost thoughts; in some ways, he wasn't far off. He debated whether to mention Catherine anonymously, and ask Mistress Avianne to role-play the story that she'd sent to him; he still had it, folded into the secret compartment of his backpack. However, he didn't want to get it out to show her; not only was it signed by Catherine, but the once pristine parchment paper was now heavily stained with a mix of spilled alcohol and his own sticky juices that had transferred from his fingers as he'd turned the pages. He'd be mortified to hand such a document to the sophisticated young woman in front of him.

Mistress Avianne was continuing to look across at him expectedly, but with patience.

I'm not surprised she's being patient—I've already paid her two hundred and fifty pounds and the clock's ticking.

Her rates were thirty minutes of introduction for a cost of fifty pounds, then two hundred pounds for the actual hour of domination—if Dillon chose to leave after the half-hour introduction, the refund would only be one hundred pounds of the total he'd paid. He'd justified that, even if he couldn't go through with it, one hundred and fifty quid was a good investment in his sanity—especially if it gave him the chance to download all that was in his head about Catherine to someone that might understand it.

In the end, it didn't take more than a minute to impart his woes.

"I had a dominating bitch of a boss; she wore shoes like yours, tormented me with spoken and written words over a month, embarrassed me when she aroused me, and then she fucked off to America before actually doing anything. Now all I do is jack off to the images of her in my head, and I can barely get it up for a normal woman—in fact, I don't even go out and find a normal woman," he said, without a breath.

Dillon looked at the woman opposite him. She was smiling, yet in a compassionate and understanding way, rather than wickedly. If she was going to be dominant towards him, she was saving it for the start of the real hour—and for another room.

"What did you most want her to do to you?" she asked gently.

It was a question that Dillon had no straightforward answer to, mainly because he didn't know what he wanted. He'd thought about Catherine doing all sorts of things to him, but he'd also thought about doing things to her too. "I don't know really, I'm new to this," he replied honestly.

"What turned you on more? Being of service to her, or being in charge yourself in the bedroom?"

That question was much easier to answer; Dillon was always more aroused at the thought of pleasing Catherine—or watching her pleasure herself. Thinking of taking the lead, and fucking her in all the traditional male focused positions, had certainly allowed him to get his release, but in a no more satisfying way than when he'd thought of other women. No, Catherine's domination had definitely aroused him far more than anyone else had ever managed to do—not since he'd first discovered the pleasurable art of masturbation in his teenage years thinking of that teacher, had he been able to go much deeper into his mind during the act.

"I want to kneel in front of her, kiss her feet and then kiss her all over. Then I want to make her come," he replied, not really believing he was finding the courage to say this to a stranger—especially one who had no certifications hung on her walls that would give him the confidence that she was bound by an oath of confidentiality.

Not that an oath would have mattered—as a client, he was decidedly average and, if Mistress Avianne's website was truthful, she had very important clients where discretion was essential. There would be no journalistic-style payday in selling the secrets of Dillon Oak, and he suspected that she'd probably make more during her career by being discreet than the tabloids might ever pay her.

"You know from my website that there is no sex involved today?" she said; he nodded in reply. "You do not touch me unless I request it, and even then it will be limited. We can include a session of foot and shoe worship, and the boundary will be just above my knee. Try higher and there will most definitely be a whipping. Do you understand?"

Another nod; her tone had switched to a domineering one and he wasn't sure if that meant he was now supposed to be silent.

"When we get into the room, you can decide if your limit is the crop, or—if you prefer more pain—I have a selection of canes. Since you're new to the pleasures of BDSM, I will create a scene for us that matches your corporate world, and I will be your boss for that hour. Does this sound acceptable to you?" she asked.

Dillon nodded a third time in agreement—thoughts of whips and canes blocking his ability to speak.

"Now, there is one more thing before we get started. It is essential that we have a safe word that is agreed. You need to be willing to use it should you want me to stop. You will no doubt want to say 'stop' many times, but you won't really mean it, because it is the natural word spoken when we feel pain; you will utter it before you have reached your real limits. Therefore, it isn't the right word for a scene. Do you know what word you want to use?"

"Catherine," he replied without hesitation. Dillon knew if he were to cry out her name, he'd want the session to be over immediately.

"Very well then—it is not often that I'm given a safe word that is a name, but if you're sure that you won't call out her name in the heat of the moment while aroused, then we will use that."

Dillon nodded again; he was sure.

Mistress Avianne stood from her chair. "Follow me," she instructed and he obeyed without hesitation.

It was a short walk back to the hall, but she bypassed the stairs leading upwards and instead opened a door opposite—the stairs to the basement; he followed her down them. At the base of the stairs was a glass door, and through it he could see an impressive temperature controlled wine cellar.

"You like fine wines?" he asked, unsure if he was allowed to ask any questions, let alone personal ones.

"My husband is a wine dealer who has been successful in the business for about thirty years," she replied casually.

"You're married!" he exclaimed; it surprised him to discover this was her marital home.

Her husband has to be in his fifties at least then, which makes him a lot older than her—lucky bastard!

Mistress Avianne seemed used to hearing such an enquiry. "We met at a specialist event many years ago, before I took on clients. He is now my slave when he is at home, but it was him who encouraged me to build a successful business out of my skill-set."

Slave at home—maybe not such a lucky bastard then.

"Doesn't he get jealous?" he asked, sure he'd never be willing to share his wife in this way, particularly if she was as stunning as Mistress Avianne was.

"He doesn't have the right to be jealous as my slave; it's part of cuck-olding him. His hard limit though is me making money out of having sex with others—I'd never do that. I respect myself, just as much as I respect his wishes," she replied.

Dillon, intrigued by their dynamic and the concept of mistress and slave, stood rooted to the spot—unsure if he wanted to do anything with a married woman.

"Would you like to see his cage?"

He nodded in agreement; his curiosity was getting the better of him as he recalled his colleague's comments about Catherine and cages. Mistress Avianne opened another door, and inside was a small metal cage. The room was no bigger than a hall closet, and there was no light fitting in it; the only light came from the hall whenever the door opened. He shivered, particularly once he saw a dog bowl in the corner of the cage with, what he hoped, was water filling it.

"I get the impression that the extreme slave scenario is not one that you're interested in?" she said, with a hint of amusement.

Dillon firmly shook his head—definitely a hard limit for him; he didn't want to go in a cage, nor drink from a dog bowl. At this moment, he wasn't sure he would want to do either of those things, even if it was Catherine commanding him to. He began to feel inexperienced and out of his depth.

"Does that mean I'm no good at this?" he asked; his insecurities were on show to the perceptive young woman escorting him through the underground rooms.

Mistress Avianne turned towards him, taking her hand off the handle of another cellar door. While she still had her compassionate and understanding smile on, she seemed to read his anxiety, yet remained firmly in control.

No wonder she has a successful husband who's willing to sit in a cage in a darkened closet for her.

"I think we will go into a different room," she said, walking a few steps further and then opening the final basement door. He'd been expecting to see the dungeon that she featured on her website, but this room resembled a normal bedroom. She sat down on the bed and indicated that he should join her. "What do you know about BDSM?"

Dillon felt like a berated child, yet she'd delivered the question in the way that a mother might when talking about a difficult subject to their child. "Very little," he replied honestly; there was no sense trying to represent himself falsely to the professional in front of him.

"Let me enlighten you then," she offered, as he sat down beside her. "Some people like the Mistress—or Master—slave scenario; it works for them. There is more humiliation involved, and generally servitude by doing household duties an extreme way while in a scene. The slave feels pathetic, but they get their needs met when they feel like that. What makes them have that need is usually unique to each individual, and it is up to them as a couple—or as a professional and client—to find out those needs and meet them. As trust builds, then they might share their deeper motivations."

She paused to let her words sink into Dillon's mind, before continuing. "Then, there are others who enjoy other ways of dominance and submission. In the lifestyle, it's commonly referred to as the Dom—or Domme—and sub; a dynamic that is more about winning over the mind, establishing control and offering more traditional servitude that worships the more powerful one. Submission normally comes from a battle of minds, rather than excessive punishment. I suspect that is the dynamic that perhaps you, and the woman you spoke of, had."

Dillon nodded; for all Catherine's torture of him, it was a mental battle of wills—he'd never felt like a worthless slave, even when she rejected him.

"Now it is up to you to find out more about what you want from this, and whether it works for you," she advised; Mistress Avianne's introduction was over.

"Thank you," said Dillon, and he couldn't help but to kneel at her feet and kiss her shoes—the action a fitting way to express his gratitude. However, this was all he wanted to say, and do, to her—her words had been worthwhile, but he was also no longer aroused. He didn't doubt that she could introduce him to all kinds of pleasurable pain—or possibly even induct him into cage play; perhaps if they hadn't had such a motherly conversation, he might well have got into it. Instead, he stood back up and added, "If that's okay, I'm going to leave now."

Mistress Avianne didn't look angry, nor offended, by the rejection of her services; he expected she often had men unable to go through with it. "That is your choice Mr. Oak. When we agreed the client fees, you understood that you would only be due a part-refund of what you have paid. I will return this to you within seven days, unless you re-arrange a session within those days; in which case, it can be used as part-payment. I trust this is acceptable?" she explained; this was her business, and she was entirely professional.

"Yes," he agreed. Although he hadn't yet experienced her dominance, Mistress Avianne was worth every penny he'd paid; he'd chosen a dominatrix well. Despite having only been there forty-five minutes, he didn't care if he'd lost money.

Mistress Avianne led him back up the stairs, escorting him to the front door. He said goodbye and never visited the mews house again.

Catherine had been the first thought in Dillon's mind every morning since she'd left; whether waking up with a hangover, or scars and bruises from the previous evening's scene, it was Catherine that he cursed as his eyes opened.

It was four weeks since her departure and he'd filled the last three of them with all manner of activities in an attempt to forget her; visiting nearly every London-based dominatrix that he'd found on the internet. The smell of latex and leather had embedded into his nostrils, he'd swallowed his own cum by force, and his sex drive had sharply increased more than he thought possible.

Yet nothing had worked; no other woman had captured his mind. On returning to his flat every evening, he'd thought about her; masturbating to the images in his mind of her until he came, then falling asleep in a heap dreaming of her.

Dillon wasn't surprised at the summons to see his boss, that he received one Monday morning in October; he knew he'd increasingly been arriving late to work, and he felt the usual high quality of his reports had dropped. He wondered if he was in for a disciplinary chat—or much worse. He nervously clenched his sweaty palms as the CEO began to speak. "Dillon, I'm sorry to say this, but . . .,"

Oh, here we go—P45 time.

". . . The company was acquired in a hostile takeover of the whole global operation over the weekend," finished the CEO apologetically.

"What?" he said in disbelief; Dillon was unprepared for that bombshell. It had been his role to focus on an acquisitions strategy, but never once had the suggestion been that they themselves were targets.

Shit. Did I miss the signs? If I'd been focused on work, rather than the pursuit of Catherine substitutes, could I have alerted the Board and saved the company?

❧

The next twenty-four hours was a blur; Dillon assisted the Board with discussions about the transition, and it was evident that very little of the management would be kept on—even in the short-term. Whole offices around the globe were being shut down, particularly in the biggest cities where DeChartine—their former competitor and now owner—had large operations of their own. As he heard the words 'New York closed' spoken, his thoughts turned to Catherine. He wasn't sure whether he was pleased that she'd be out of a job—karma for the hell she'd put him through and for leaving him—or whether he was sad and worried for her because he cared.

Will she come back?

His hopes rose that she might return to London, especially if she'd been there on a sponsorship visa. However, his concerns for her soon gave way to worries for his own welfare; the next day he received his redundancy notification—with immediate effect. Having only joined the company at the beginning of September, he had two months in post—minimum severance was all he was entitled to receive.

Thankfully, his bank balance was reasonably healthy, but Dillon was a worker with a high London rent to pay. The marketplace was a mixed bag in his sector, and the demise of the once prestigious media company he'd worked for, sent ripples throughout the industry—shareholders were nervous. His own feelings of inadequacy played in his mind.

Will potential employers hold the miss of the acquisition signs against me?

He already knew from his initial discussions with the recruitment agent who had secured him the role, that they questioned his involvement—especially as they were aware of his job specification.

Looking in the mirror of the gents' bathroom, he tormented himself with the view; the toll of the previous weeks illustrated on his face. While his work attire could hide the signs of the BDSM activities that he'd engaged in—excessive alcohol consumption had given him a puffy, dull face and his blue eyes lacked the sparkle they used to; it was time for a break.

Chapter Seven

The burgundy evening dress hugged every curve of Catherine's body perfectly. Liddy had chosen well on their shopping trip to Barneys; the dress had the right balance between feminine elegance and power. Catherine was ready to impress and had pushed the cost of the outfit to the back of her unemployed mind; her savings would dwindle quickly in New York at this rate.

It had been nine days since the buy-out, and Liddy's husband had pulled some strings to ensure Catherine could stay in New York for a little longer while job-hunting. While she'd have been willing to pack up and return to London, John hadn't had any sleep that week; his wife pestering him to ensure that her best friend would be able to stay. After arranging the extension, he'd also managed to get the three of them onto the invitation list for one of the black-tie events of the season, an opportunity for Catherine to do what she did best; win over powerful men.

Lifting her dress hem slightly off the floor to ensure that it didn't catch in the stiletto heel of her new Louboutin pumps, she followed John and Liddy into the marble hall of the grand hotel. While she'd been to numerous business events in the past month, this dinner had a notably higher class of attendees. She'd never been to such a prestigious dinner before, surrounded by the wealth that was so apparent. Old money mixed with new, older couples mixed with up-and-coming ones. It was the *Who's Who* of Wall Street and the Upper East Side.

For a moment, she felt out of her depth, but the knockout outfit she was wearing gave her strength. She donned her sparkling personality, forced a smile, and then confidently entered the ballroom for the champagne reception.

Seated at the dinner table with them were seven other individuals, making up the ten. Catherine, seated next to John Bradbury on one side, had to her right a relatively young man who spoke only to say his name.

Well he's useless . . .

Moving on, she glanced to his right and observed the couple seated beside him—both in their early fifties.

What do they do? Are they happy?

Bored husbands in powerful positions often provided an opportunity to use flirtatious techniques to get employment—as long as boundaries existed; Catherine knew how to flirt to good effect, but she'd never slept her way into a role—and she didn't intend to start now.

Opposite her was another couple; the woman was in her seventies—or perhaps eighties, but wearing it well—while he was in his fifties and was what many would refer to as a silver fox.

Is he her toy boy, or her son? They don't look alike.

Catherine pondered a little on their strange pairing, and then moved her eyes further around the table. The final couple—to Liddy's left—was also in their fifties; the husband was the owner of the magazine John had once wrote for. Catherine had already met him the previous week for a discussion, but unfortunately her skill set hadn't been something they were looking for at the publication, and it would've been difficult to secure sponsorship for her.

As the first course ended, Catherine tried to engage the man at her side in conversation. "What do you do?" she asked casually.

He looked at her as though he was about to wet himself with fear.

Seriously?

Considering that she hadn't even used her powerful charms, and had toned down her mannerisms as well, Catherine wasn't impressed.

There's no way you're a successful executive, or useful to me.

"Excuse my nephew; if you aren't a computer, he has no idea how to talk to you," said the older woman alongside him, laughing as she did. "He's trying to secure investment in whatever it is he's developed, so we brought him along tonight."

Well that explains his attendance.

"Catherine Everdene. I'm a friend of John and Liddy Bradbury . . .," she said, pausing to indicate her friends to her left. "I recently moved here as Director of Operations for a media company, but it was bought out last week by DeChartine." She hesitated, then added with a smile, "So I guess I'm here tonight to get a job offer."

Out of the corner of her eye, Catherine saw the old woman opposite her glance up at her comment, but she continued to be polite and focus her attentions on the couple she was already conversing with; the old woman could wait.

"Ah I see, you want a job and my wife's nephew wants investment. Somehow I think you, Miss Everdene, might have some more success, as you seem considerably more articulate, and might I dare say more attractive, than the boy here." The young man's uncle-in-law had waded into the conversation and clearly had little faith in his relative through marriage. Catherine deduced that this was probably the reason behind the lack of investment from the family, instead encouraging the boy to build his own entrepreneurial flair.

As though reading her thoughts, the older man added, "We aren't into all that computer stuff—nor media. Bricks and mortar—that's what made me a success. Always make money from tangible assets I say."

His wife nodded enthusiastically, and Catherine mentally crossed the pair—and their silent nephew—off the list of potentials to schmooze; she was media—not bricks and mortar, or binary code.

Second course provided her the opportunity to study the two table companions opposite her. They were regularly talking to each other, but had said very little other than pleasantries to the people either side of them, and apart from their regular glances in her direction, they didn't seem very interested in being there.

Who's the one with the power?

While her natural inclination would be to focus on the silver fox (whose attire suggested power), as a couple, the woman was showing the signs of being the more powerful one. Catherine spoke up as the main course plates were taken away.

"What did you think of the steak?" she asked, addressing her question openly to both of them; everyone else at the table had chosen the fish or vegetarian option.

"Tough," the old woman replied forcefully. "And, I doubt American."

Liddy shot Catherine a glance; both wondering if that was a sly way to have a go at the two foreigners of the table. Silence descended on the table and it was some moments before the old woman broke into hilarious laughter.

"Look at your faces, anyone would think I've just declared the War of Independence," the woman teased. Catherine stared at her, still unsure whether to join in the laughter. "I'm messing with the pair of you. This table has been dull all evening," she added; the rest of the table gave a collective sigh of relief, then erupted in joint laughter that was loud enough to cause the patrons of the next table to look over.

"I'm Emilia DeChartine, and no doubt the person you, Miss Everdene, would most like to become best friends with right now."

The woman was incredibly sure of herself and straight to the point. Catherine liked her immediately, and not only because she was the owner of the most powerful media company in the world; Emilia had a sparkle and a strength in her personality that she admired.

The woman continued with introductions, "This gentleman here is Bill Boldwood, CEO of one of our subsidiaries, and my late husband's finest prodigy."

The silver fox briefly looked up, then quickly lowered his gaze, with what—Catherine assumed—was embarrassment at the praise.

"Bill started as mail boy at just fifteen, and my husband took him under our wing and sent him to business school. Now he's one of the most respected CEOs in the country. We're very proud of him, as we'd no son of our own."

The man blushed again, and it was obvious that he was submissive to the authority of the woman at his side.

Not a real son and the husband has passed away . . .

For some unfathomable reason, Catherine had a hunch there was more to their dynamic that Emilia was letting on.

Once the meal was over and the guests had left the tables, Emilia DeChartine sought out Catherine. "Escort me to the ladies room. An old woman needs an arm to hold, and Bill here's no good when it comes to a powder room," she said—her request more of an instruction.

Catherine caught sight of the powerful CEO's eyes drop for a second when Emilia looked at him. There was disappointment in his face, as though somehow he'd failed because he wasn't able to escort Emilia to where she wanted to go. When he raised his eyes again and caught Catherine's own stare, he quickly dropped his gaze. She felt a chill from his action, and suddenly the memory of Dillon came into her mind. She hadn't thought about him in weeks.

Is he okay?

Catherine became distracted with concern for her former employee, wondering what might have happened to him in the buy-out. She'd heard the London office had severe management casualties and she felt awful that he hadn't come to mind sooner; she'd been focused on her own survival.

Her attention snapped back to reality as Emilia sat down on one of the many chaise lounges in the plush bathroom suite of the historic hotel.

If these walls could talk . . .

She wondered at what conversations might have taken place over the past few hundred years amongst New York's elite women. Now, she was the one having a conversation in the bathroom with the matriarchal head of a multi-billion-dollar global media empire.

"So you need a job?" It was a very direct question; one that Catherine wasn't sure how should be answered.

"Yes, Mrs. DeChartine, I do. I'm very good at what I do, but I should say I need sponsorship and I—," she replied, before being cut off.

"Firstly it's Emilia. Mrs. DeChartine makes it sound as if one of my household staff is addressing me. Second, I don't doubt your talents, mostly because your previous company moved you here even though the

New York executives suspected we were circling. They must have thought you might have been able to save them—idiots."

Catherine's shoulders dropped; she'd tried to work hard since arriving in New York, and certainly didn't think her efforts warranted being called an idiot.

Emilia read her reaction and quickly added, "I don't mean they were idiots for putting faith in you; you were their last resort. I meant idiots for thinking they would win over DeChartine when Wall Street loves us. Anyway, onto your third point about sponsorship—the White House loves us too—well actually, they love our money and they fear our power. When you start work with us, then a Green Card will be yours. Your previous company backed the wrong side at the last election—idiots."

When you start work with us . . .

Catherine had met her fairy godmother—albeit one with a fondness for calling people idiots. No flirtation with a powerful man had been necessary. She wondered what the job would be, and whether she'd be working for Boldwood. Thinking about his dropped stare earlier, she wasn't sure whether she could work for someone who already didn't seem able to have power over her.

Before she could enquire about the potential job any further, Emilia spoke again, "Right my dear English girl, I have to go and speak to several people that I'd really rather not talk to. Lunch tomorrow at one o'clock—I shall send a driver to your apartment building half an hour prior, as I don't yet know what I feel like eating. Since I never need to make a reservation, I tend to decide that day. We will discuss your new job."

With that, her fairy godmother was gone; Catherine felt her life about to change, even though her insecurities made her wonder why she'd been favored so quickly by such a powerful woman—one who knew very little about her beyond her resume.

∽

Exactly two weeks from the date of the buy-out, Catherine arrived at the impressive building near the Rockefeller Center, its thirty-six floors housing the headquarters of DeChartine—and all of the subsidiaries. She hadn't yet visited their offices; her previous meeting with Emilia to discuss her new role had been in an upmarket restaurant nearby. Emilia had explained that since her retirement of sorts—and her husband's death—the office wasn't somewhere she chose to spend her days. She went there only for board meetings, but mostly she preferred to video conference into them from the comforts of her home out in the Hamptons. Even the grand apartment that she'd shared with her husband now belonged to Bill Boldwood.

Catherine passed through the ground-floor lobby security with no problems; they were expecting her and directed her to the twenty-eighth floor—not the top floor by far, but she didn't mind.

I'm actually a CEO!

Emilia had asked her to take over the lead position in DeChartine New Media—a relatively small, recently established subsidiary focused on digital media channels. Still considered an emerging sector, the new company had significant growth aspirations through acquisitions of start-ups.

Aside from her extensive commercial development experience, Catherine's other skill-set had been noticed by Emilia; she suggested it was a market where she could use her feminine wiles to good effect—lull businessmen into a false sense of security by appearing naïve and seductive, and then go in for the kill once she had the information she needed.

She knows how to win over men herself I expect.

Emilia's motto seemed to be that if a man thought a woman the weaker sex, then let him think it for a bit—but punish him for it later.

Punish him . . .

When Emilia had said it, Catherine once again wondered what secrets she might have, and what her background was before she married into the DeChartine family in 1956 at the age of twenty-five.

The elevator stopped at the twenty-eighth floor and she took a deep breath before exiting onto the floor her new company solely occupied. Hers—the thought made her smile; technically, as CEO, it was her company to cherish and nurture.

She crossed the lobby to the counter; sitting behind it was a petite blonde woman with her eyes glued to her smart-phone screen. Catherine heard the distinct sound of a mobile phone bleep, and saw the young woman's eyes light up. She watched her devour each word of the text; it was obviously from a man, and based on the body language of the woman, it was a suggestive message.

Catherine wasn't amused; a receptionist shouldn't focus on a personal text when there was a visitor at the counter and, as far as she was concerned, the woman shouldn't even be using a personal mobile during office hours—it was 9:00 a.m. already and the woman should be working.

"Excuse me," she interrupted, putting all her authority into her words, making them a command rather than an enquiry. The woman noticed the sarcasm, and immediately looked up, only to then sink down into her chair at the sight of the icy woman in front of her. "You are?" Catherine asked, when it was clear the woman wasn't about to enquire as to who she was—or what she wanted.

"Faye Robine," she replied meekly, still not acting as Catherine felt a receptionist should, with a welcoming query of how she could assist; Catherine became even less pleased. This was a role requiring someone willing to fall to their knees to serve any visitors, while maintaining a professional image. While Faye had the right looks, and was showing signs of a submissive demeanor, she lacked focus and a friendly confidence.

"I'm Catherine Everdene, the new CEO of the company," she said, giving up waiting for Faye to ask who she was. "Please show me to my office."

Faye quickly did as requested; stepping out from behind the counter and grabbing her phone as she did—further irritating Catherine in the process. She led her down the hall towards the impressive, spacious CEO's office.

"Thank you—," said Catherine, turning to thank the woman and tell her that she could leave, but Faye had already headed off—her head down and her fingers rapidly typing a text message reply.

Well she has to go.

After a quick glance around her new space, she sat down and fired up her computer. The first action was an email to Janet Coggan—the Office Manager—requesting a recruitment process to commence for a new receptionist; Faye Robine could stay until a suitable replacement was appointed. Her next memo instructed Janet to instigate a 'no personal mobile phone policy' for anything other than emergency calls—with immediate effect. The *Icy Bitch* was now a CEO—and she was going to make sure that everyone knew who was boss.

Chapter Eight

Faye Robine didn't like the English woman who'd taken over managing the company—she was nothing like the nice American man who'd been running it for a while. All the office knew was the rumor that Emilia, and the Board, had shipped him off to an office on the other side of the planet when he'd failed to secure some key deals. They hadn't wanted to get rid of him; being a long-term employee he knew far too much about how the empire worked, and would therefore be an invaluable source of information if he started working for a competitor. The answer was to put his language skills to good use, and offer him a posting with much warmer weather.

He said he liked the sun, so I'll bet he's happy.

Faye remembered his smiling face, and how it was him that introduced her to the love of her life—Troy Selgent. Her mind wandered to thoughts of Troy, and the text he'd sent her that morning—the one the bitch interrupted; Faye had been waiting for that text all night, her eyes glued to her phone screen every waking moment since he'd left her small studio apartment.

She'd serviced him well; her jaw still ached from sucking his cock for ages until he'd come into her mouth—her knees chaffed from her scratched wooden floor. Troy liked making her kneel, and she did anything that he ever asked of her. He'd promised, as a reward, that he would text her details of a party.

Faye thought back to the party where she'd met him; that was the night that she—quite literally—had become his. Listening to his stories about Wall Street, practicing law and his antics aboard the yachts of his wealthy law school buddies, she'd been in awe of him. His world was so far away from hers, and she became seduced by his power and charisma. She hung onto his every word, and when no seats were available by him, she'd simply sat on the bar floor by his feet without hesitation.

That was when Troy had noticed her, looking down with a lustful gaze and grinning when she'd quickly averted her eyes towards the floor in embarrassment. At the end of the evening, when he'd ignored all the stunning, more confident women in the bar and instead asked her how close her place was, she'd been overwhelmed by a sudden love of the attention.

Back at her flat, Troy had quickly taken control and Faye had found herself introduced to the world of BDSM for the first time; blindfolded with her own scarf, another tying her hands behind her back. She didn't deny him anything he'd asked for—but he denied her completely. The evening had been all about Troy's pleasure, just as it had been ever since, but Faye didn't care; he was interested in her, and none of those other women.

Since that night, his interest had gone up and down, despite Faye trying to find all manner of ways to please him. Whenever he visited her, she did whatever he asked without question. The first time she'd felt unsure of herself was when he asked her to call him Master.

Am I his slave? Do I want to be a slave? I'm better than that surely . . .

Faye had fought the conflictions in her head, but she'd desperately wanted to be his and therefore had agreed.

Within minutes of calling him 'Master', Troy had claimed more of her, introducing her to the initial pain of anal penetration. She remembered how he'd cruelly commanded her to be quiet when she cried out at first— the lack of lubrication causing her immense pain. She tried so hardly to comply with his order, but Troy was reasonably well endowed (well in her limited experience), and he wasn't a gentle lover. When she failed to stop her cries, he'd gagged her with another of her scarves.

Only once gagged, did her body gave into his control; she'd started to feel some degree of pleasure. However, it was short-lived; the tightness of her virginal ass had made him come quickly, and as soon as he was done, he pulled out of her and walked off towards the shower, leaving her in a crumpled, undignified heap.

Faye pushed all of the bad parts of the memories to the back of her mind. Troy had kept his word from the night before, finally inviting her to a party with his friends. She'd been begging him to let her become his girlfriend in public; she wanted to show her few friends back in her home town that they were wrong about him—that he wasn't just using her. He might not be from her world as they'd reminded her, but that didn't matter. She'd read everything she could on submission to a dominant male; discovering that many confident women were submissive to alpha-males, and that their dominants did love them. Some Doms even married their subs, and Faye was sure that Troy loved her as much as she loved him.

Reading the invitation text once more, Faye remembered that morning; she'd skipped off from work at lunch break, telling Janet that she had a migraine. It was a lie, but she needed time to get ready, and she didn't want to see that Catherine woman again. The all-staff memo about the mobile phone policy had been the final straw.

Stupid English bitch; thinking she's better than everyone else is by banning our phones. I don't need her—or the boring job in her stupid company. Troy will look after me.

Getting ready for the party, she opened a cheap bottle of Prosecco; the wine soothed her nerves while she picked out the most revealing outfit in her poky wardrobe. Once dressed, she admired herself in the small mirror—crudely stuck to the wall in the narrow space between her bed and the wardrobe. The dress showed off her cleavage, and although Faye had a petite frame with small breasts, her youth meant they were perky—her nipples visible through the clingy fabric.

She finished curling her long blonde hair, then downed a second glass of wine, before racing out of the apartment towards the subway—grabbing her heavy winter coat as she left. Faye didn't want to be late for the party, but a taxi was hard to come by in this part of town and would also be too expensive all the way to central Manhattan.

An hour later and Faye had knocked back two more glasses of wine; she had rebuffed the advances of four leery men—none of them Troy's friends. She was in a bar alone and on the verge of tears, after sending text after text to Troy without a response.

Maybe my friends were right about him.

Just as she told a fifth guy to "Fuck Off,"—the elusive reply came:

'Faye, where the fuck are you?'

Faye wanted to respond with expletives of her own, but doing that would only earn her severe punishment later.

'I'm here at the bar, where are you?'

Waiting for his reply, she looked back at the text of that morning.

Shit.

She'd got the name of the bar right, but not the location; her internet search had her in the wrong bar. Quickly sending another text to apologize for her error, she dashed outside and hailed the first taxi—no longer caring at the cost.

Thirty minutes later, she finally succeeded in reaching the right destination, and she fled out of the cab, stumbling on the curb as her four glasses of wine caught up with her. There, in front of her on the sidewalk, surrounded by some of his friends and colleagues, was Troy—her Master.

The majority of his buddies had moved on to other clubs, but those that were left looked down at her with an air of superiority as she clambered to her feet. The women were all dressed in designer dresses that showed off their curves in the right way, not overly provocative like hers. Faye pulled her coat tight across her body in an effort to cover up; she suddenly felt exposed.

Troy was visibly angry, and getting angrier by the second, as his friends started to snigger at Faye as she slurred her apologetic words. He dragged her around the corner out of view of the others.

"You've made me look stupid," he yelled.

Faye's whole body dropped as she heard his accusation, and she found herself kneeling in front of him in the dark alley. "Please Troy; I'll make it up to you. I'll have a glass of water, we will head inside and you can introduce me to your friends," she begged.

Troy wasn't about to forgive her. "You really think I'm going to introduce you to them?"

"But you said—," she began to plea, but Troy placed his hand over her mouth to silence her.

"We're worlds apart. I need to start thinking about a proper girlfriend— one worthy of a Wall Street lawyer. I need a woman who's going to be able to hold her own at the sort of social events I need to go to for work. Do you really think that would ever have been you?"

Faye nodded quickly, keen to prove herself, but as Troy maintained his steely, dominant stare, her nod morphed into a sad shake of her head.

"See Faye, I knew you would be a good girl and agree with me. Now go home and sort yourself out, so that you're ready for me to visit you again sometime."

She obeyed, solemnly picking herself up off the damp, dirty alley concrete. She didn't look up at him; she didn't want him to see her tears and she definitely didn't want to see the contempt at her failure to please him that would be written all over his face. Instead, she ran.

Her friends were right; she was a casual booty call, and one that let him indulge in his dominating fantasies. If she let him, he'd no doubt keep her on the side for his pleasure for as long as he fancied her—while he probably wined, dined, fucked, and then married a woman with the right credentials. That woman would be the one to bear him children, sunbathe on yachts, holiday in the Hamptons, and live in the mansion.

Faye, on the other hand, would get the occasional gift of cheap whore- like lingerie and no-brand imitation stilettos; the most wining and dining that she'd get, would be whatever was in the mini-bar of a discreet hotel— should he wish to go somewhere other than her cramped apartment.

Even with that realization, she still hoped he would come around. 'Be ready for when I come around sometime,'—those were Troy's words, and Faye held onto them. Heading home on the subway, she tried to hide the tears that were welling up in her eyes from the other passengers. Once home though, the flood came, and she didn't leave her bed for days, ignor- ing the messages from work, firstly concerned about her, but by the end of the week informing her that the few personal things on her desk would be posted to her.

Faye was unemployed, broke and, once again, single.

Chapter Nine

"Has a new receptionist started yet?"

It was the first time that all of Catherine's management team had gathered, and she addressed her question to the Office Manager—Janet Coggan; Catherine hadn't seen the blonde receptionist since her first morning at DeChartine, and it was now Friday. Either Janet had chosen to fire Faye to show Catherine that she could take the initiative when given a difficult task, or the stupid girl had simply taken offence to the mobile phone policy and left of her own accord. She didn't care much what had happened, she just wanted a new receptionist to great visitors.

"One is starting Monday Miss Everdene," Janet replied.

Catherine was pleased; her Office Manager seemed keen to impress, and had addressed her with respect in still calling her Miss Everdene—Catherine hadn't yet decided who she was willing to let address her by her first name. It was unusual for an Office Manager to attend a senior executive meeting, but she'd noticed that Janet Coggan was able to get things done quickly in a way that no other executive had shown.

Scanning the agenda on her tablet, and visually linking names to faces around her board table, Catherine noticed a significant absence; she hadn't seen Penny Ways all week.

"Where's the Head of Commercial?" she asked, directing her question at no one in particular.

While everyone else around the table looked down awkwardly, Janet once again stepped in to reply. "She went off to the West Coast to talk to some potential clients, and has been gone most of the week Miss Everdene."

Catherine noticed the others glance at each other from their face down positions, their expressions and body language indicating that they knew something that she didn't; it was time for her to show some authority.

"Want to tell me what you're all *not* telling me about Ms. Ways?" she asked sarcastically.

Once more, the only one at the table with balls was Janet. "She travels a lot, but evidence says she doesn't bring in many deals. Always comes back with a sun-tan though," she said quickly; with three observing statements—not delivered as gossip, nor as accusations.

Janet deserves a more worthy title.

Catherine mentally noted to promote her to something that would mean more than just ordering stationery all day; she wondered if Janet had started her career as an assistant to Emilia DeChartine—her manner indicated a good training as an executive PA.

"Right," said Catherine, addressing the whole table again with a touch of exasperation to her voice. "Can anyone tell me what's happening in our commercial section? More specifically, who's actually working on the bid that a draft is due on next week?"

Finally someone other than Janet spoke—this time a woman who managed HR. "We have a temp that came in this morning to help read through a bid. He was upstairs being interviewed for something else in another DeChartine company, and since Penny couldn't read the bid today, she emailed a request to hire a temp to take a look over it. So we brought this guy down."

Catherine felt a migraine starting.

What planet are they on?

She couldn't believe that she was leading a team who thought it was acceptable to bring in some random person off the street to look over a commercially sensitive bid—with no background to the client, or the company. She decided to end this meeting before she lost her temper with the lot of them—Janet the only exception; she turned to the only person in the team who'd given her any faith.

"Janet, could you please bring this temp to my office as soon as I've had a chance to look over the bid myself. Any chance someone could fetch a sandwich for me to eat prior to the meeting. I'm not going to have time to go out and get one myself."

꙳

The terribly written bid document didn't reflect anything the company was trying to achieve; no wonder they weren't winning deals. Catherine wondered if the former CEO, or Penny Ways, remotely had a clue about the sector or Emilia DeChartine's vision for the relatively new subsidiary. The document would need a lot of revision, and thoughts of her enjoying her first-ever Hamptons' weekend faded; it was likely she'd have to abandon her trip to the clambake with Liddy in order to get a better document put together.

Taking the last bite of the sandwich that her new PA, Mary-Anne, had delivered to her desk, she checked her email to see if the HR woman had managed to find the anonymous temporary worker's resume to forward on for her perusal. There was no email; the only details she knew were that he was male, and that he'd secured an interview with DeChartine's central HR team—at least that was a consolation. It would be highly unlikely though that he'd be able to resurrect the bid in the way she wanted, even if she'd been willing to trust a temp with such a confidential task.

Still hungry, and dying to escape the office for a decent coffee, Catherine figured she'd give the guy a few minutes of grief, and then dismiss him. She was so sure that he'd be a waste of her energy, that she didn't even bother to freshen up, button her jacket or re-apply her lipstick; New York, and her first week as a CEO, were already exhausting her.

Chapter Ten

Dillon was feeling better. A week's break in the serenity of Dorset had given him the fresh air he needed, and an escape from the memories of London. It was mid-autumn, and the trees near his parent's home had already started to shed their brilliant copper leaves in preparation for winter; he'd taken this as nature's metaphor for the need for him to shed the baggage he was carrying from the past few months. It was time to get another job, but with the stigma of his incompetence hanging over him with his contacts, he wanted a change of scene.

Managing to get himself a temporary work visa, Dillon had booked a ticket to New York. In the back of his mind, he knew he'd chosen his destination with the hope of running into Catherine. He hadn't heard from her since her departure; despite drafting several emails to her personal email account to ask how she was settling in, as well as apologize for his drunken email, he'd never had the courage to press the send button. Maybe serendipity would allow him to run into her and say the words in person.

On arrival in the Big Apple, he'd settled himself in a home-stay rental that he'd found online, then set to meeting the recruitment agencies he'd spoken to from London that specialized in arranging appointments for candidates relocating. Despite the challenging market, it had taken less than a week to secure his first interview; his acquisitions research experience that he'd gained prior to the recent debacle had secured him the meeting. He was surprised therefore to discover it was DeChartine who'd agreed to see him—having only been three weeks since their take-over—but he wasn't about to turn down this apparent second-chance.

Dillon's interview day so far had been a strange one. Having arrived at the DeChartine offices at the start of the day, he'd travelled to the tenth floor where a joint HR team covered all of the subsidiaries under the umbrella of the company. After a relatively short interview, another woman had entered the room and abruptly asked him about his experience in reviewing bid documents. His short synopsis of his relevant experience was met with no more than a nod, then a request to immediately come up to the twenty-eighth floor to do at least one day's work reviewing a bid—with no guarantee of further work.

Will I be paid? Is this a test?

Dillon pushed aside his practical questions around paperwork and contract terms; this was a chance to show off his abilities and he'd no further interviews scheduled for that day. He followed the HR person out of the room and up the eighteen floors to DeChartine New Media. Given a desk without a computer, a printed copy of the bid and a glass of water, the woman had left him to work.

Several hours passed, with people coming in and out asking questions, 'Who was he? What did he think of the bid? What were his thoughts on potential clients?' Dillon chose only to ever answer the first question.

What the fuck—how the hell did this company take over ours, and these twits get to keep all their jobs?

Finally, he plucked up the courage to ask questions of his own to a rather clueless Account Manager. "What's the Head of Commercial like?" he asked; it was his understanding that the Head of Commercial had requested his involvement, but he hadn't yet met her.

I would never have let a temporary staffer near a commercially sensitive bid when I was Head of Commercial . . .

"Penny Ways? She's never here and I'll bet I could do a better job," the guy replied; Dillon detected the lack of respect in his response—he wondered who would keep on someone that was incompetent.

"What about the CEO? Doesn't he have views on her absence?" he enquired further, keen to know more about the wayward company that took over his previous employer.

"Oh, I reckon he's fucking her," the guy replied, rolling his eyes and showing an even greater lack of respect for the top man. "Well was, I should say. He's gone now, so maybe that's why Penny is AWOL!" He laughed at the thought of his ex-boss running after a man, before continuing his synopsis of the state of affairs, "A new female started on Monday, and she's a right Ice Queen. She banned all our personal mobile phones in the first few hours. I've not met her, but you might like her."

Dillon was baffled; this guy didn't know him, so why would he think that he'd like an icy bitch who banned phone use. "Why would I like her?" he asked.

"Apparently she's English," came the sarcastic reply, before the guy walked away.

Dillon's heart did a leap.

Catherine? Could she have become a CEO that quick?

He grappled with his emotions and tried to pull himself together.

Concentrate damn you.

The thought that the distraction of Catherine had lost him his last job still haunted him; he wasn't about to risk another job—especially one with the DeChartine empire.

Another hour passed and Dillon's stomach growled; it was well past lunchtime.

How do I get out of here?

He pondered on how to get out of the building with no security clearance or pass, and as he resolved to go and find someone to ask, a woman walked in.

"Mr. Oak, I'm Janet Coggan, the Office Manager," she said, holding out her hand to shake his—Dillon took it with a firm, but professional grip. "The CEO wants to see you in half an hour. Best brush up on your knowledge of the company quickly, as she isn't in the best of moods."

Shit, that sounds ominous.

"Pleased to meet you, and thank you for the head's up," he politely replied; his English accent caught her attention.

"Ah, so you're another Brit then. Well maybe that might go in your favor Mr. Oak, because heaven knows none of the rest of us have worked out what to do to get into her good books this past week. Upset most of the female staff right from the moment she arrived in our reception," she said, smiling at him.

"You don't like her?" he asked, treading carefully with his enquiry; no one had yet said the name of the anonymous CEO and he wasn't sure he wanted to know.

"I've done nothing to upset her," Janet replied. She didn't come across as arrogant, but rather someone who wasn't willing to engage in gossip.

Dillon's stomach growled loudly once again.

"You might need a coffee or something to eat before you go in. Can I get you something?" Janet's query conveyed a huge amount of sympathy.

"That would be great, if, of course, you have the time," he answered, grateful for anything to stop the noise his body was involuntarily making before he had to face the CEO.

"Coffee and a donut coming up; it's all there is in the coffee room, and it will take too long to go out and get something before you need to be in there."

Dillon nodded appreciatively; anything sounded fine to him and besides, his mind was still in Catherine mode. Janet's description of the mysterious CEO sounded too much like her scare tactics in action. He sat down, and within a minute or two, the kind woman was back with not only coffee and a donut, but also a copy of the company strategy. "Some quick reading for you—I'll be back in half an hour," she said, before leaving him in peace.

Taking the document, Dillon focused on cramming as much knowledge into his head as he could in the short time he had to prepare. With minutes left to spare, he escaped to the bathroom to run his fingers through his hair in an effort to look presentable. He was in his best interview suit, and his perspiration was kept at bay with copious amounts of deodorant and Duty-Free after-shave. Staring in the mirror, he was pleased to see the difference that the week in the country had made to his appearance; the clean air of the fields, and the stormy winds of the coastline, had faded his shadows.

Dillon was ready to meet the English, female CEO; partly praying that he wasn't about to come face-to-face with Catherine, but also secretly hoping that he was.

༅

"Ready?" asked Janet when she returned.

"Yep, let's do this," replied Dillon, quickly gathering up the printed bid and his own tablet, before following her down the hall towards the CEO's office. In the brief time since his arrival that morning, he'd slashed apart the bid. Although he didn't have an electronic copy to edit, he'd typed into his tablet at least ten pages of things that definitely needed changing, and that was even before he'd read the company strategy. Now, having quickly processed the key points of that document—in particular the vision statement by Emilia DeChartine for the new media sector—he had in his head about another ten pages of feedback.

His heart was racing through a mix of fear about the feedback he was about to deliver, but also a fear of who he was about to meet.

I can do this. Just be professional and know your stuff.

He wasn't sure how he'd conduct himself if Catherine was the one who greeted him. Adopting his most confident stride, the time had come to find out.

༅

The pair of them stared at each other—a mix of sudden recognition, awkwardness at what the first words should be, and a confusion at who should speak first. Janet sensed a tension in the air and immediately turned, practically fleeing the office.

Not used to speechlessness from his former boss, Dillon needed to fill the uncomfortable silence, "Hello Miss Everdene. I've looked over this bid and it isn't very good. I have several pages of feedback I could email to you, if they let me connect onto the network, or I could run through them with you now. I can make this a winning bid, but I need a job and wouldn't be able to do justice to this document in the few hours I've been employed for."

Catherine continued to stare at him—her silence unnerving. He'd surprised himself at the straightforwardness and speed of his words in her presence, and his request for a job. It was far from begging; he'd delivered it with a confident assertiveness that he'd never showed her in a one-to-one before, and it conveyed the value that he could offer the company in re-writing the bid.

Please say something.

He hoped and prayed that the normally in-control, and bossy, woman that he knew wouldn't take offence to the way he'd spoken.

Shit. Should I apologize? I owe her an apology.

Dillon was now even more genuinely sorry that he'd sent his last email to her, and for the first time in his life, he felt arrogant.

She still hadn't spoken.

Dillon's eyes fell, but his mind worked quickly over what to say next. He spoke again, but kept his eyes lowered, "I'm here to work Catherine. I didn't know that you were working for DeChartine—nor even if you'd stayed on in New York. I wasn't following you and I won't ever mention our last communications." Dillon hoped that the explanation was respectful and professional; he lifted his eyes to meet hers.

Her expression finally changed from the blank stare. "Very well; Janet will get you a proper computer and sort you access. I will email HR and get them to do the rest. You have a week to prove yourself." While her expression may have changed, she delivered her words with no emotion—only authority and a straightforwardness equal to Dillon's earlier remark.

He turned to go, but she halted him in his tracks, "One more thing; please address me as Miss Everdene unless I say otherwise."

Dillon hoped she'd add her sparkle-smile to the statement, as she'd so often done in London, but there was no smile this time—only a hardness to her face. Catherine looked exhausted and uncomfortable—not just with him, but in her surrounds. Leaving the office quickly, he wondered what her first weeks had been like in America—he wasn't sure he liked what becoming a CEO had already done to her.

Or was it me that did this to her?

The thought occurred to him that his own email had contributed to her hardened stance. He began to wish she were her old self; at least if she'd flirtatiously threatened him with punishment, he'd know where he stood, and what was going through her mind; this Catherine was even more of an enigma.

Chapter Eleven

Liddy Bradbury hadn't been back to their beach-house since early September. All week she'd been ringing their housekeeper checking on the progress of preparations for the coming weekend. The house didn't warrant a full-time housekeeper, but like many beach-house owners, they retained the services of a shared housekeeper to check on the property and keep it maintained when they weren't there. Now, in the lead-up to Thanksgiving, the homes began to occupy again, and their housekeeper had put in more hours; Liddy wanted to ensure Catherine enjoyed her first stay in their holiday home. She was sure that, with her friend in residence, they would have several important visitors during the weekend—all keen to meet the single, attractive female CEO that Emilia DeChartine had taken under her wing.

Since the charity dinner of the previous week, she'd been pestering her husband endlessly for details about DeChartine, and the matriarch at its head. She was curious about Emilia, but also in the potential opportunities that there'd be for her friend to meet men. Remembering all the tipsy conversations back in business school, she'd learned that Catherine wasn't the best when it came to relationships. Her fear of emotional closeness had morphed into fussiness, and an almost constant boredom with mundane men; her short attention span, and low tolerance, when it came to dating, was as legendary as her Ice Queen attitude towards most women.

Liddy wanted to change that—she'd gotten to know the witty, fun woman that hid underneath the façade and believed that Catherine could make a man very happy if she'd only allow herself to let someone get close. New York was full of high-powered men that would represent a challenge for Catherine, and who'd undoubtedly be willing to try to win her over to further boost their ego—particularly if she'd shown no interest in them beyond her initial flirtation to get their attention; the men of the city were competitive like that. It was up to her to find a hidden gem among them that would be worthy of her friend's heart.

With one day remaining before they departed for the Hamptons' weekend, her patience had run out. She'd asked million-and-one questions to John about one person in particular—Bill Boldwood. The single CEO that had sat silently at their table had fascinated her, and she suspected that he'd be attending the DeChartine clambake. When all other tactics had failed to get her husband to overcome the unwritten journalist code of not gossiping about Emilia DeChartine or Bill Boldwood, she resorted to her final trump card.

"No sex for you tonight, nor tomorrow. In fact, sex is off the menu until I get what I want. And my tongue trick will never be done again if I don't get something decent on Bill Boldwood before we head out tomorrow evening."

She'd put in her demands, and got John where he was most vulnerable; Liddy was well aware that he'd know how stubborn she could be, and that he'd never be able to hold out for sex for very long. John loved her, and he especially loved having sex with her—particularly the tongue trick that she did on him that made his orgasm feel like it would last forever.

"Okay, okay you win—but if I give you this one bit of information, I definitely get the tongue trick tonight. Like right now," John demanded.

She considered his proposition, before conceding, "Only if it's a really good bit of info, otherwise it's just good old-fashioned sex, where it isn't all about you getting off, like it is when I do my trick."

John nodded, and laid back on his pillow, ready to talk.

"Emilia married into DeChartine in the fifties. No one knows her background—what she did, if her family had money, or even where she came from. Her history before DeChartine is well and truly unknown." John glanced at his wife, wondering if that was enough.

"Keep going," she said, prodding him with her finger.

"Thomas DeChartine was thirty-three when they married, and she was eight years his junior. He was already running the company alongside his father, and rumor has it that she worked there in some capacity. He was besotted with her, and she was anything but the Stepford Wife. They were always the reunited pair, and no one linked Thomas to anyone else. When they never had kids, everyone thought he'd find a young, beautiful socialite to tempt him, especially as it was the free sixties and then seventies, but they remained together until his death about six years ago. He was eighty-three by then, and they'd recently celebrated fifty years of marriage. Can you imagine being married that long?" he joked, hoping to arouse his wife into a playful fight.

"You won't be married another five minutes, if you don't keep to the topic," replied Liddy, unwilling to give in to his taunts.

John's smile faded and he continued his tale. "So then there's Boldwood. You know the bit about him being like a son—Emilia told you that at the dinner. He's nicknamed 'the silver-fox who doesn't seem to be often seen in the hen house'." John looked at her to see if she'd registered the significance of the nickname.

"Well I knew that. I can do a web search myself you know Mr. Journalist.

There are a few pictures of women with him though, so I presume he isn't gay," she said; Liddy was curious as to why the man had never married.

"No, there doesn't seem to be any rumors circling that he prefers men—he just pretty much keeps to himself. There are some older pictures of him with sophisticated, elegant women, yet no one managed to identify them. We aren't to write about it—or so our Editor says—but the consensus is that they were escorts hired for engagements. Since Thomas died, he goes everywhere with Emilia."

"Are they—you know—a thing?" asked Liddy, remembering their closeness at the dinner.

"No, there doesn't seem to be any truth in that. He's like her son, so the rumor is that he will get a good sum when she dies—she's eighty-one now. The analysts reckon she will break up the company soon by floating it to reduce the DeChartine majority share; then she will be more philanthropic before she leaves this world," he explained.

"So why isn't Boldwood married?"

"Well . . ." It was time for John to impart the juicy stuff.

Less than twenty minutes later, John got his wish and came hard onto Liddy's awaiting tongue; his gossip had been well worth sharing and his wife had thought so too. As soon as he'd told her that it was rumored that Bill Boldwood was rather partial to bossy women, had once been seen going into a dominatrix dungeon, and that some suspected that Emilia DeChartine was once a dominatrix herself, she'd moved lower down the bed and pleasured her husband without further comment.

Chapter Twelve

The plan had originally been to head to the Hamptons after work on Friday, but a mid-afternoon call to Liddy had resulted in a change of departure to as early as possible the next morning. They all had pressing matters at work to resolve, and John suspected that the traffic might be better without the Friday evening exodus out of the city. While Catherine was disappointed to get only one night away, it was unlikely they'd have arrived before midnight anyway.

Not that she'd had much sleep; all night she'd tossed and turned—her mind racing with thoughts of Dillon. It had been a shock to see him, thousands of miles from where she'd left him, and her first week had already proved stressful enough. The problems that the company faced had increasingly become apparent by the end of the week, and she was struggling with an uphill battle to establish authority in a company where direction was lacking. When Dillon had walked into her office she'd already felt vulnerable, and hearing him so assertive had further rattled her own confidence.

Now, as the light began to show in the sky, she tried not to think about it, instead focusing on the weekend ahead as she walked towards the Bradbury townhouse. The DeChartine clambake wasn't a major occasion written into the social calendar of the Hamptons, yet it was an annual event that people wanted an invitation to attend. Unlike so many of the events, this one was very informal, and the guest list often changed each year to include only those Emilia considered within her current close circle.

Catherine recalled how excited Liddy had been when not only had she scored an invitation, but that it included a 'plus two' to allow both Liddy and John to attend. Not wanting to miss the event, and unable to find a local babysitter at short notice, Liddy even overpaid one of the nannies in her law office daycare to join them for the weekend.

Reaching the sidewalk outside their home, she discovered a weary John packing up three adult weekend bags, and six children's bags, into the back of his SUV. Catherine handed him her own bag and he maneuvered it into the small space left.

"Thank goodness you pack reasonably light. How does one child generate two more bags than four adults combined—especially when three of them are women," he joked.

"You whining about women and parenthood again?" said Liddy with a raised eyebrow, accompanied with a smile that showed her jest. She'd joined them on the sidewalk and Catherine smiled back; Liddy had pre-warned her to pack light, or she'd be holding her bags on her lap.

"I wouldn't dream of it, my dear," replied John. "Catherine, you're riding up front."

Unbeknownst to her, Liddy and John had already discussed the car-seating arrangements. While Liddy normally preferred to sit in the front of the vehicle, she didn't want Catherine to have to sit alongside her potentially irritable daughter, and the Eastern-European nanny, for the duration of the trip. Sitting in the back also meant that she'd be less likely to spill the beans about all the gossip John had shared. He'd suspected that she'd be dying to, but a car ride with a child—and a nanny that he suspected would see dollar signs in the information—wasn't the place for that kind of chatter.

Within minutes of setting off, Catherine was glad of the front seat—she didn't think she could sit that close to another repetition of Madison's chosen song; Liddy's daughter was definitely going through a singing phase, and although the words of the chorus were clear, the rest of the lyrics were rather dubious. She tried to tune out after the first four attempts, and John lowered the speaker volume in the front section of the car.

"That better?" he asked.

"Yes, thanks for that," she replied appreciatively; while his gesture certainly didn't block out the noise, it did help a little.

"How's the new—,"

"Daddy, you aren't listening to my singing. Don't talk to Auntie Catherine when I'm singing," interrupted Madison from the back seat of the car.

"Sorry darling," John shouted back, and then mouthed an apology at Catherine.

She didn't mind; there was no way she wanted to risk a toddler tantrum in the cramped car. They abandoned conversation for later, when the nanny would take Madison off to make sandcastles.

The lack of adult conversation gave her more time to think about the events of the day before. Her overnight thoughts were back; her mind once more going over every detail of when Dillon was in her office—what he'd said, and what little she'd said in response. All night she'd analyzed the meaning of every word and gesture, but now the changing landscape was giving her perspective and an opportunity to think about how she'd felt at seeing him again.

She'd been pleased to see Dillon in a professional capacity; that conclusion come to quite soon after he'd left her office the previous day. The notes on the bid document he'd emailed her later that day were excellent.

'I'll give you one week to prove yourself.'

She winced as she recalled her words to him. They hadn't been fair of her; Dillon's work in London was widely praised and she'd seen what he was capable of—she hoped that he wouldn't have taken too much offence to what she'd said.

It was imperative to her success that she could assure everyone that she was a worthy CEO and that she could take control, but a part of her wished she could show Dillon that she was human. She wanted power and control over him, but not at the expense of belittling him in the office. He was worth more than that—to her, and to the corporate world. With Dillon Oak as her second in command, she knew she'd be able to deliver the vision that Emilia DeChartine wanted for the company.

As CEO, Catherine was entitled to re-structure and the company definitely needed one. As soon as the absent Penny Ways returned, she'd get rid of her—but that might take time. There was no way though to appoint Dillon into the role of Head of Commercial while Penny was still in post. Catherine looked out at the open ocean, now visible on the horizon, and the wide emptiness of the view gave her an idea. There were no Vice Presidents in the company; the creation of two new posts at that level would solve the problem.

It was the ideal plan; Dillon could be her VP of Commercial, while she'd promote Janet Coggan to the post of VP of Operations—the woman's initiative had impressed her, and she'd retrieved her resume from the personnel file late on Friday. Janet had put herself through business school in the evenings, and while it wasn't an illustrious college, the curriculum would've taught her the most important lessons in business. Catherine admired anyone who had the ambition to invest in evening study to better themselves; she could empathize with how tough that could be.

As the first highway sign pointing to their destination came into view, she made a mental note to try to discuss the proposal with Emilia that evening; the clambake was informal, but she suspected the company owner might want a brief update on the findings of her first week. She hoped to get the green light to the new jobs for a Monday start.

"Twenty minutes away everyone," John announced; Madison was getting restless and the adults were starting to feel the need for a stretch and caffeine.

When conversation stalled again in favor of more singing, Catherine turned her thoughts back to Dillon, and the hardest question.

Should I take things beyond the professional? Do I want to?

Catherine recalled the final email she'd sent him in London and his response. She'd been honest in her email with him about all the reasons that she hadn't taken things further, and had wished him well in his new role and his relationship, yet he'd not been so courteous in his reply.

She couldn't deny though that she found Dillon attractive and that she wanted him; he was still replacing George Clooney in all her fantasies. Escaping to New York had been timely; giving her the easiest reason to avoid getting involved with him. Now he was here—every sexy bit of him—but so were the risks, and now there were even higher stakes. Embarking on a sexual relationship with him was more dangerous in their new location; it could affect both of their Atlantic careers before they'd even truly started.

There was also the remote possibility that people might suspect that they were a couple already, and that he'd come to join her—which could pose an obstacle to offering him a job. Yet Catherine was sure Janet had spotted their surprised expressions when they'd come face-to-face in her office; the last thing she wanted was for Emilia to think that she was appointing Dillon for any other reason other than what he could offer the company.

When it came to relationships, Catherine had a terrible record; they ended quickly, badly, or both—her success rate in love was yet another reason to avoid complications. She appreciated his point that he wasn't going to bring up the story that she'd given to him on her last day in London—nor the follow-up emails. Always managing to bring him to an easily compromised state with just a few well-placed words, light touches, or even sometimes only a particularly dominating stare, she'd never met someone that reacted to her as strongly as Dillon did—always unable to conceal his obvious desire for her.

Catherine had noticed that he came across as confident with the other women of the London office, and she doubted he was short of experience in the bedroom. The morning she'd returned from New York, she'd over-head two female employees talking about him; her concealed presence in a toilet cubicle had allowed her to listen to their discussion. 'I saw Dillon on a date last night. Looked very cozy and they left together. Didn't look like a first date,' the first woman had said. 'Damn, why are all the good ones taken? I had my eye on him,' the other had replied.

The memory of the conversation now made Catherine wonder.

Is he still seeing her? Are they long-distance? Maybe she's American and that's why he's here.

All of the possibilities ran through her mind; she'd encouraged him to return to the relationship, even sending champagne for them both. Thoughts of them drinking it that night, then fucking on the sofa, came into her head, but she quickly dismissed them.

He sent that drunken email that night—you don't send an email to someone else if you're happily fucking someone else.

It wasn't like Catherine to get jealous, but for some reason today she was. *Damn.*

For both of their sakes, she needed to be remain professional, because Catherine needed a friendly face on her team—someone she could rely on; Dillon Oak was the best man for that role.

c‿ɔ

"Who is he?" questioned Liddy. They had arrived, and as soon as they'd exited the car, she'd grabbed Catherine's arm and practically hauled her to the deck overlooking the beach—leaving John and the nanny to sort out the bags and their daughter.

Catherine didn't answer; this was her first visit to the Hamptons and the peacefulness of the early morning sunlight reflecting on the water captured her attention. The waves were still high from the storm the night before, but were starting to calm down. The forecast for the rest of the day, and the evening's clambake, was a good one. Being November, it was cool and Catherine pulled back on the jacket she'd kept on her lap throughout the journey.

"Think we could have a cup of tea first?" she asked; she was parched, and the earlier caffeine hit of a takeaway cappuccino on her way to the Bradbury's city home had long worn off.

Liddy didn't head inside to fulfil her request, instead taking a seat in one of the white New England Adirondack style chairs that adorned the deck. There was no shortage of outdoor furniture for enjoying the view, and with hopes of a strong brew fading, Catherine also took a seat—sinking into the pile of cushions that the housekeeper had already put onto the chairs once the rain had stopped.

"John two cups of tea please," shouted Liddy bossily; now that the housekeeper had left—once they'd safely arrived—it appeared to be the turn of John to wait on them.

"Daddy, where's my bag with the bucket and spade?" shouted Madison, wading into the list of ever-growing demands on John's time.

"The poor man hasn't even finished unloading the ten bags Lid. Can't we get the tea?" suggested Catherine, as she watched John try to rummage through the bags in search of one that might have the required items to silence his daughter. Madison was just as demanding as his wife—if not more so—and Catherine wondered how he coped with a wife, daughter and an editor.

"He'll be fine. He likes taking care of me, and for a Yank he makes a damn fine cuppa. Now stop avoiding answering. Who is he? I know there's a man. You may well have been facing forward in the car Catherine

Everdene, but I could still see that quizzical look on your face from the side."

Liddy wasn't going to let this go. Unbeknownst to Catherine, she'd been dying to tell her the gossip about Emilia and Bill, but once she'd suspected that Catherine was hiding the makings of a potentially interesting conversation of her own, she put that gossip on hold.

"Alright, alright, give me a minute. Can I at least go use the bathroom before the tea comes? Then I'll tell you," Catherine promised.

Liddy conceded—as she expected; the last thing she would want was her to stop during the best part of the conversation to go have a pee; impatience in waiting to hear a whole story paled in comparison to the suspense of having to stop for a toilet interval when you were halfway through a juicy girly chat. At least at a bar it was perfectly acceptable to follow a friend into the ladies and carry on talking through the cubicle doors. or from the next stall, but in the privacy of a home, that was just weird and an invasion of boundaries.

Catherine followed Liddy through the French doors and took in the decor. The housekeeper had known how Liddy would want the house to be ready; groceries delivered and unpacked, fresh flowers in the vases throughout and the French doors and windows opened at first light if there was no sign of any more rain. The open plan lounge, dining room and kitchen was exactly how Catherine imagined it would be; all whites, creams, pale blues and navy stripes—exactly like typical beach-house chic in magazines. She noticed several accessories and ornaments that had a decidedly British seaside look about them.

I dread to think what the excess baggage charges were on her last trip back to England.

When her friend had last been home to London, Catherine had missed the opportunity to see them, as Liddy's parents—keen to spend time with their first grandchild—had whisked them all off to Cornwall. Knowing Liddy, and her preference to spend as little time as possible with her mother, she guessed John had been dragged around every quaint village interiors store that she'd found, while their daughter was fed with every ice cream and sweet that she tricked Granny into buying her.

Liddy stopped outside the open door to the guest room; Catherine saw her bag on the bed already, and beyond it, she saw the entrance to the bathroom—inside a deep, antique roll-top bath.

Look at that bath!

Catherine desperately wanted to ask if she could soak in a bath for a bit right now, but Liddy dashed her dreams of some peace. "Five minutes and you're back on that deck, and even then that's too long for a pee. Don't avoid me girl," she instructed.

Damn, there's no getting out of telling her about Dillon.

She suspected that if she got in the bath right now, Liddy would sit right beside her waiting for her update; reducing the therapeutic benefit of the soak.

"Yes, Ma'am," she joked, saluting her friend.

Catherine went about her business, and then swapped out of the jacket into a more comfortable over-sized cardigan. She spotted a cozy pair of sheepskin-lined boots on the bathroom floor and, not caring to whom they belonged, she took off her beach shoes and stepped into them instead. It was chilly and she needed comfort for the moment; it wasn't likely they'd be going for a beach walk straightaway if Liddy's need for gossip had anything to do with it.

Returning to the deck, she saw that Liddy had moved to higher chairs, seated either side of a white wicker table; two mugs of steaming tea, as well as a plate of morning pastries, placed on it. She never would've guessed John was so domesticated—either that, or the housekeeper had left everything so well prepared that all he'd had to do was pour the tea.

Catherine hadn't had breakfast before they'd set off and was thankful for the pastry; lunch was probably still a good few hours away, and her stomach had started to rumble. Dinner the night before had been late, consisting of only a couple of pieces of toast as she frantically packed a weekend bag. Biting off a piece of croissant, then washing it down with a mouthful of tea, made her feel better. Liddy was right; for an American, John had made the perfect cup of English Breakfast tea, although she suspected he'd spent the last four years being made to practice until he'd reached this level of perfection.

Catherine looked up at Liddy and saw she wasn't eating; she was giving her an expectant waiting stare that said 'stop eating right now and talk'.

"He's British," she said, then bit once more into her pastry.

"Now I'm definitely listening," replied Liddy, intrigued at the confession; she'd been hoping for a romantic tale that would surpass her own coffee-shop love story, but the premise of someone crossing the pond to follow Catherine topped her wildest fairy-tale dreams.

"I suspected that might catch your attention. His name is Dillon, he worked for me briefly in London and yesterday he unexpectedly turned up in my office as the result of a cock-up by HR," she explained—the cock-up wasn't strictly true, but it was an easier and quicker explanation than the full details.

As much as she trusted Liddy, on the other side of the open French doors was one of New York's most prominent business journalists. She couldn't risk John knowing that her company had wayward executives, random people having access to sensitive information and no sense of how to run a company. Catherine wasn't yet aware of the details that John had shared with Liddy about how DeChartine was only reported on with praise, or wasn't written about at all. Her experience in the corporate world had only taught her that the press could be the difference between success and failure.

"It's fate!" Liddy exclaimed.

Ah, here's the married, loved-up Liddy I was expecting.

This was the reason that she hadn't mentioned Dillon all those weeks ago when she'd arrived in New York; confess that she'd felt drawn to Dillon the minute she'd met him and Liddy would map out their whole, married future. Catherine sometimes missed the friend that was so career-focused, but even then, there'd been signs that she believed in soul mates and that everything happened for a reason. The more alcohol they'd consumed on a London night out, the more Liddy could sometimes even convince her to believe in it. She cast her mind back to the nights when they'd walked back to the tube, falling over laughing as they'd pointed at random men shouting 'it's him, he's my soul mate,' and she smiled at the memory.

"See, even you're smiling because you know it," said Liddy, looking pleased with herself.

"Ah no, actually I was remembering our drunken evenings on the Southbank. Like that night where you pointed at the man with no teeth and told me that he was, in fact, a foreign prince in disguise and so obviously my soul mate," she replied, before taking another sip of tea. "So you see I have no faith in your choice of men for me!"

"I said that? God girl, what was I drinking that evening?" asked Liddy, bursting out laughing.

"Oh, I think probably a bit of everything on the cocktail menu."

The pair of them was in hysterics over the memory, and the sound of their laughter brought Madison out onto the deck.

"What's so funny Mommy?" she asked, wanting to join in the fun; then she saw the pastries and the inquisition into their laughter disappeared, replaced with the demand, "I want one of those."

"Okay pumpkin, you go ask Daddy to put jam on this one. Then go and get your bucket and ask Nanny Jo to take you to the sand. Oh, and no going in the water, it's too cold," said Liddy to her daughter, before raising her voice to shout. "Jo, no letting her get wet. I'm not having a child with a snotty nose the rest of the week."

She lowered her voice again to address Catherine, "I've got a court case on Tuesday and the last thing I want is a cold for that, and for Thanksgiving. Do you know what germ factories kids are?"

Catherine shook her head; she rarely spent time with kids, and had always chosen to grab a cab to work when it was school holidays back in London.

"You know I could almost go a cocktail right now, but it's a bit too early. Where were we?" Liddy wanted to return to discussing the more interesting details of life.

Catherine was selective with the rest of the details. Without a stronger drink, she wasn't ready to share the details of how she'd tormented Dillon in the office. She focused on what she knew about him professionally and how she was probably going to give him a role in the company. She included this last fact as it gave a good context for the reason as to why she wasn't going to take things further. It was a fair argument that would appeal to the lawyer in Liddy, but also to the side of her that knew how important career was to Catherine.

"I suppose you have a point, but will you be alright working with him every day?" asked Liddy, agreeing with Catherine far too quickly—a sign that made her a little suspicious as to why she'd given in so easily to abandoning the fairy-tale angle.

"I'll be fine. It's not like anything had happened between us," she replied, hoping that the cracks in her soul, that Dillon had started to infiltrate, had now hardened.

"Great. There are plenty of men in New York, and that brings me onto my news." Liddy's change of topic was confirmation that she had plans for her—or more specifically, had identified a potential man for her; she would never have dropped Dillon so quickly if she hadn't.

"I guess it's my turn to say who is he? I'm right aren't I—you've chosen someone for me?" She decided it was better to get straight to the point, however before Liddy could burst out with the information, John came onto the deck.

"We have visitors," he announced.

༺ ❦ ༻

The next two hours were spent entertaining others; Liddy had pre-warned Catherine that housekeepers fuelled the gossip lines of the Hamptons, and were rewarded for passing on information about houseguests that might be valuable contacts. Their first unannounced visit was from a professional couple, who had a house down the beach; both worked in new media and wanted to introduce themselves to Catherine to get a proper meeting in her diary to talk about an idea.

When they left, another couple turned up, this time to speak to John about an article he'd written the previous week, and whether he could introduce the man to one of the contacts mentioned in the piece. The man's wife had quizzed Liddy about various decorative pieces in the room, and through Liddy's answers; Catherine had discovered she'd been right about the Cornish shopping expedition. The woman was so impressed at the British-meets-American interior, that she suggested to her husband that they consider a much longer visit to Europe the following year.

Judging by the look on his face, he might think to send her alone for some peace.

Catherine hadn't warmed to any of their morning guests, so much so that she actually would've preferred to return to further inquisition about Dillon.

Even their eventual escape from neighborly visits included meeting more people—Liddy and John had arranged a lunch in a seaside village with a couple that had met at their wedding. Debra was a lawyer in the office that Liddy first worked in on arriving in New York, while Peter was a long-time journalist friend of John. When they entered the restaurant, they had a third person with them; a younger man, introduced as Debra's brother, who was taking time out from law to attend business school.

Please don't let this be the guy Liddy was going to tell me about earlier.

Despite his age, he had the American college-boy look about him, and while he was what most women might consider attractive, nothing about him aroused Catherine in any way. She gave Liddy the evil eye, hoping to telepathically communicate to her matchmaking friend that she wasn't interested. Liddy discreetly shook her head, guessing what the stare meant, and it wasn't long before both of them discovered that Debra was the aspiring cupid this time.

"My brother is taking time out from his role at the firm we both work at. He's studying at Harvard, getting his MBA. I expect when he comes back, he will be made a partner within the year," boasted Debra, focusing her words towards Catherine.

Catherine took a sip of wine as she studied her intended lunch companion. Strangely, her mind wandered to thoughts of him kneeling at her feet—either naked or in only his boxers—and the thought made her shudder.

Eugh. Have an MBA. Don't need a husband—particularly not a student who isn't even a law partner yet—but thanks anyway.

She wanted to tell Debra that she wasn't at all interested in her pompous brother, but it would be cruel for her to crush his ego in such a public way and she didn't want to offend his sister or, in doing so, hurt Liddy.

"That's impressive. I'm sure you'll succeed," she said, forcing the more acceptable words out, and then looking back towards Liddy. The knowing smile on her friend's face showed that she'd guessed the intentions of both of her friends—cupid Debra and dominant Catherine; the smile enough for her to know that Liddy accepted she wouldn't be taking things further with him.

It was mid-afternoon when lunch was finally over, and even then, Liddy had offered apologies for cutting it off early so that they could get ready to attend the clambake. Catherine observed an element of jealousy in the woman's acceptance of the excuse.

"Catherine, if you need a plus-one for the clambake, my brother has no plans for the evening, and he's rather partial to clams. He could talk strategy with you some more, and he's also a great source of warmth on a cold beach," said Debra, determined not to give up on her brother and his dating prospects.

Catherine was done with politeness; she'd passed her tolerance level when they'd gone into a third hour of pleasantries, and the young man had tried to educate her on the merits of putting together a matrix to plot the company's products.

"Thank you for the offer, but there was no plus-one invite extended to me—only an invitation to John and Liddy. Thankfully, there are plenty of people attending who have business degrees, who I can get to remind me of ways to develop a company strategy—should I have forgotten what I learned in my own MBA studies years ago. I'm also sure that a clambake will have a bonfire. I doubt Emilia DeChartine—who's hosting the event—would dare let anyone freeze and she will probably put on the biggest bonfire the Hamptons has ever seen."

The group fell silent and she didn't dare look at Liddy. "If you'll excuse me, I need to use the ladies before we go. Nice to meet you all," she added, before quickly leaving the table.

By the time she re-emerged, John and Liddy were waiting in the car. Apologetically she got in, waiting for an outburst from either of them.

Liddy burst out laughing. "Kudos to you girl for holding out so long; Debra is great but, by god, her brother is a pompous ass. I told her that you'd definitely not be interested in him, and that she shouldn't bring him along, but she idolizes the ground he walks on. I'm so sorry you had to sit through all his crap about how he could help you develop a strategy from what he has learned. At that point, even I wanted to tell him I have an MBA and that he should just shut up because he was one of the least educated at the table."

At that last bit, John stepped in to protest and remind his wife of his lack on an MBA, but Liddy wasn't about to be silenced—or let him stick up for this particular male of the species. "Yes, but you did a good double-degree and are considerably educated in life. Besides, you've gained far more knowledge about business from your work than that jerk has from a text book or lectures. Don't defend him, he isn't worth it."

John said no more; secretly pleased that his wife had validated his intelligence and praised him.

"I did wonder at the beginning if this was the man you were mentioning this morning?" said Catherine, thinking back to the morning; she now was even more curious as to who the mystery man was.

"I thought you might have thought that, but definitely no. You deserve so much better. Besides, you'd eat that guy for breakfast. He'd be a crumpled heap and you'd get bored—like when a cat leaves a mouse in dying throes once it's had enough of torturing it. You need someone far more of a challenge—and I know a potential target."

Unfortunately, the drive back from the restaurant was an extremely short one, and the late lunch meant that they'd absolutely no time to discuss the man in question. Liddy couldn't just say his name without the full context and story, or Catherine would simply dismiss it as a stupid folly. They'd no more than an hour left to get ready for the DeChartine clambake, and Liddy needed her friend to look her best. "I can't believe I'm saying this, but more details are going to have to wait. We have a clambake to get ready for."

☙

Despite the mid-November chill, there was a good turn out to the DeChartine clambake; the prestige of the event—and its timing the weekend before Thanksgiving—ensured its popularity. As Catherine and her two companions drew nearer to the gathering, they felt the warmth of the huge bonfire at the center of it. The scene reminded her of childhood memories at the British Guy Fawkes' bonfires in early November—when her parents would take her down to the village green. A lump formed in her throat; she didn't like to reminisce too much about her childhood.

Catherine's mother had died from cancer just before her tenth birthday, and her father never got over it. He'd frequently left Catherine with her only surviving grandparent while he disappeared somewhere, then tragically, he'd taken his own life after a recurrent bout of depression; she'd become an orphan at thirteen. Her widowed grandmother, having lost her son so tragically, had managed to cope for a while, but then she too had passed away—just as Catherine started university.

After that, she'd been alone; her only inheritance being the best attribute of both her parents—intelligence. With only her brain to capitalize on, Catherine had worked hard at university, and in her part-time jobs, in order to not only survive, but also to flourish professionally.

Watching the flames dance, she blinked back a tear; she remembered her father holding her hand by the village bonfire, telling her she could be anything she wanted to be when she grew up.

Would he be proud of me now?

She was succeeding beyond even her own expectations, now that she was the CEO of a subsidiary of a multi-billion dollar company—not bad for an orphan.

Catherine, however, wasn't the only early-orphaned CEO at this particular gathering; there was the mysterious Bill Boldwood.

As the trio was welcomed into the central group of Emilia's guests, Catherine spotted him on the outer edge of the gathering. Unlike his silent manner at the previous week's dinner, he was now deep in conversation with several important businessmen. As she watched them talking, she noticed that a few glanced over in her direction. She was obviously a topic of their conversation—the new female CEO appointed from out of nowhere.

Irritatingly, Boldwood didn't look over in her direction. He hadn't engaged with her at all in the week since her arrival—even to welcome her. Considering they'd met at the dinner, she'd expected a note from him—or at least his PA, welcoming her to DeChartine. It shattered her ego a little that he wasn't paying her any attention, especially as she'd discovered on the internet that he was a single male—linked in the past with women of a similar age to her.

Boldwood wasn't someone that she'd needed to use her sparkle on; Emilia had given her the job and he wasn't her superior. She didn't need his help with making contacts—people were seeking her out for business conversations; overnight she'd become a powerful woman in her own right.

As the night wore on, Liddy and John barely had a moment of time with her, although it didn't bother them—they were finding plenty of opportunities to further their own careers through contacts made at the party. Just before leaving, Catherine finally had a chance to catch up with Emilia, giving her a quick run-down on her first week. As expected, Emilia gave approval for her two new hires.

Catherine was surprised at Emilia's interest in Dillon, and worried that she may have read far too much into her brief synopsis of how he'd worked for her in London. Emilia's curiosity further piqued when she jokingly added that she needn't worry about him being a dedicated worker because Dillon would do anything she asked of him.

"Anything?" she asked, raising her eyebrow suspiciously; causing Catherine to blush with embarrassment.

⁕

"What do you know about Emilia and Boldwood?" asked Catherine to Liddy as the three of them walked along the path back to the beach-house.
"Bill Boldwood?"
Catherine nodded; she didn't feel comfortable calling him by his first name for some reason.
"Good god woman, how did you keep that secret for over a day? That isn't like you," said John suddenly, his outburst taking Catherine by surprise; she soon realized though that he was speaking to his wife, which only puzzled her further.
"We've been inundated with people, but yes, I'm about ready to burst," replied Liddy excitedly.
Catherine knew Liddy had been dying to tell her something all day—particularly before the clambake, but she thought it was about a man for her, rather than gossip.
"Well spill then," she said, stopping on the deck; she suspected that the nanny might still be awake and in the lounge.
"I'm guessing I'm the tea-boy again?" joked John, knowing his presence wasn't required for gossip-sharing, yet his tea-making skills would always earn him favor with his wife—he was rather fond of reward time. Switching on the patio-heater to provide the two women with warmth, he turned and headed toward the kitchen as Liddy began to share the secrets her husband had told her a few nights earlier.
Catherine's mind was mesmerized with what her friend was revealing.
Emilia's a dominatrix . . . Boldwood's a submissive . . .
Catherine was open-minded, and had certainly used feminine, bossy powers to good effect in recent months, but she'd never indulged in BDSM. The story she'd written for Dillon was inspired from her reading over the shoulder of a woman commuting on the train; an erotic romance novel currently in favor that summer. The pages she'd read were very explicit in what the man was doing to the woman he was with, and Catherine had simply reversed the dynamic and filled in a few male-orientated aspects to the fantasy.
She struggled to associate Emilia with the role of dominatrix—in her mind only the stereotype of latex, leather and extreme fetishes, which didn't fit the Emilia DeChartine she had met; polished, elegantly dressed and composed. She doubted Emilia would ever have been anywhere near a pair of knee-high boots, or even stiletto heels—although that was quite possibly

due to her new boss being an eighty-something woman; the absence of heels maybe being the compromise to her ageing bones.

Boldwood, however, she could believe in the role of a submissive; the lowered eyes and inability to meet her stare at the dinner party, his silence next to Emilia, and his avoidance of Catherine would all fit with the profile. If he'd used professional escorts to accompany him to parties, this might also fit with his desire to keep up a certain image.

"If he's that way inclined, why doesn't he just find a strong-minded woman who doesn't mind a bit of bondage—or the occasional use of a whip on him?" she asked Liddy naively.

"Yes, because New York socialite strong-minded women go around with labels saying *'I whip men for fun'*," replied Liddy sarcastically.

Catherine could see her point; the desire to have a man on his knees doing all manner of acts was hardly something that you broadcast. "It's a bit risky with his stature and position," she said, thinking about how her worries about Dillon were nothing compared to these revelations about Boldwood.

"I expect the media blackout that DeChartine have, gives him some protection—especially if the stories about Emilia are true," John interrupted, bringing out two cups of Earl Grey.

"Thanks John. What media blackout?" she queried, before sipping the hot tea.

"John says that journalists and DeChartine gossip is a no-go. You print negative stuff, and your career and paper are shot to shit, so any gossip stays on random blogs and stuff," interjected Liddy.

This knowledge gave Catherine some relief that she wasn't likely ever to become a topic of conversation in print. When the two women called it a night and headed off towards their bedrooms, Liddy turned and joked, "So a whip and a pair of boots for Christmas then, Miss Everdene? A gift that will help win over the dashing, mysterious silver fox that is Bill Boldwood perhaps?"

"Err, no thank you," she replied, laughing.

That night, as she got into bed, for once it wasn't Dillon that she thought of—he'd been replaced by Boldwood—the dark and brooding CEO that had ignored her charms.

Chapter Thirteen

Dillon looked over the bid document for the final time. He'd spent all weekend on it, keen not only to get it right, but also to impress his new boss. New boss—that was what he was going to make sure he only thought of Catherine as. Every time his mind had started to wander, he reminded himself that his addiction to her had caused the downfall of a company. He'd been a director for only weeks and, in his mind, he'd failed in the position; reduced to begging for a job at any level again.

Catherine had been harsh to him on Friday, but the consolation was that she hadn't mentioned his spiteful email. He cringed again at the arrogance of the words he'd used; while he'd never had any complaints—and therefore considered himself a good lover—he shouldn't have boasted. Until that night in her office, he'd never before been rejected that close to commencing a sexual act. The memories of her rejection had fuelled his drunken words to her.

While Dillon had spent the weeks after her departure doing all manner of sexually-based acts with women he'd paid, he hadn't actually had sex—penetrative or oral—since the dismal one-night-stand with the online dating woman.

In the past two weeks, since some harsh words from his sister about cleaning up his act, he'd exercised a huge amount of self-control; refraining from even the slightest daydream that might lead to him wanting to jerk off—doing that would only bring back the images of Catherine. The first thing he'd done when returning to his New York rental apartment on Friday evening, was stick notes by his bed, and in the bathroom.

'Icy bitch who nearly ruined your life', he wrote.

It had worked; nearly seventy-two hours on from seeing her and he hadn't given in to temptation—or allow himself to be aroused by thoughts of her. It helped that Catherine had been surprised to see him, and that she wasn't quite as polished in her appearance; reducing some of her power had given him the chance to keep his alpha-male mindset during the meeting.

Dillon also suspected that it was more than just her behavior that had changed him. Although he'd only explored a little of London's BDSM scene, he'd learned more about self-control, compliance and the euphoria of serving a powerful woman. These new skills were going to be invaluable if he was to prove to Catherine that he was capable of being in her team again.

As he headed towards her office on Monday morning, he was more confident than he'd ever been before at facing her. With a bid document that she'd struggle to find a plausible fault in, he donned a powerful stance to project his height and then strode forward to deliver the performance of his life.

Catherine was back to her perfect self, and Dillon was pleased to see she was wearing less make-up than usual, choosing instead to show off the color in her cheeks from a weekend at the beach.

He'd over-heard the conversations about the clambake at the coffee station when he'd got in early; several of the junior staff gossiping that there'd be less senior management at work—either all that week, or at the very least for the morning—on account of them having all escaped to the Hamptons for the event. Catherine's attendance, so early in her role as CEO, was also a topic of the conversation, tinged with hints at what got her a role so quickly. Dillon suspected that had Emilia been a man, the hints would've been even more of an accusation. He'd walked away quickly, not wanting to get involved in the debate.

She looked up at him from her desk, and he was relieved when she smiled. It was a considerably warmer expression than her glares on Friday—a genuine smile, one devoid of the wickedness that she'd so often favored back in London.

"Good morning Dillon."

"Good morning Cath—, I mean Miss Everdene," said Dillon, quickly correcting himself as he remembered her words.

Despite his wanting to be confident with her, he found that he wasn't averse to using Miss Everdene; the title sent a shiver of anticipation through him as he linked her to Mistress Avianne and all the other dominatrices he'd met.

Catherine laughed; a warm laugh that he hadn't heard before. "Oh, I was a bitch on Friday, wasn't I? I'm sorry Dillon, will you forgive me?" she said, with apologetic amusement.

"Yes of course, Miss Everdene," he replied, remaining formal and focused; Catherine's split personality had floored him in the past, and he was nervous that this was another one of her mind-fucks to take control over him once again.

"You can call me Catherine. If I'm going to have you as my new Vice

President of Commercial, it's going to look odd if you keep calling me Miss Everdene in front of everyone."

Her tone was new to Dillon; any praise from her usually came powdered down with seduction, but this was full of professional respect.

"You're offering me a job? With that title?" said Dillon, as his confidence failed him and his voice faltered with disbelief.

Still acutely aware of his recent career failure, he'd expected an uphill battle to get any work—let alone something at a more senior level. While he'd still be working for Catherine, she too had had a promotion, and therefore neither of them was stepping down a rung on their career ladders.

"It was a good bid document," she replied, matter-of-factly.

She's read it already? I only emailed it last night. When does she sleep?

Dillon had printed a copy to bring along; after hearing about the clam-bake and possible late arrivals of executives, he was unsure if she'd have had time to read the copy he'd emailed late the night before. He couldn't stop himself from grinning; an egotistical grin that formed at the corner of his mouth as she praised him.

"Such a good read in bed last night. Left me all excited . . .," she paused deliberately. "In a professional way of course, about all we could deliver the client."

And she's back.

This was the Catherine that he knew—the flirtatious, seductive tease. At the pit of his stomach, he felt a fear, one that stemmed from the sudden desire now about to cause havoc in his groin. His fear must have shown; she smiled her sparkle-smile, with all its wickedness still there.

"Relax, I'm messing with you. I want us to be a team and, more to the point, I need us to be. I have a heap of people to win over, over here in New York, and I need someone I can count on to help. Can you do that? Can you be that man?" she asked.

Dillon pondered on her request. She was messing with his head with her flirtations, but she'd no idea just how much she'd affected him, or the path of discovery that she'd set him on. He contemplated being honest with her; telling her everything that had happened since she'd left him—everything she'd caused him to do in his professional and personal life—but that was a step too far. She was offering him a job and if he confessed all his inner-most secrets, she might well show him the door and he wouldn't be able to cope with the rejection.

Catherine had told him that she wanted his skills in her team—that she needed him—and for the moment, he was grateful for that. He vowed he wouldn't let his desire for her, ruin an opportunity for career redemption.

"Yes Catherine, I can do that," he replied.

Chapter Fourteen

With the Thanksgiving break, and a constant agenda of client meetings finally over, the last Friday in November provided Catherine with a rare night off before the Christmas party season kicked in. Liddy didn't hesitate to fill the empty calendar slot with a girl's cocktail evening in Manhattan; their first one alone since she'd arrived two months earlier.

Changing in the private bathroom adjacent to her office, Catherine had decided to wear the burgundy dress she'd worn at the dinner that had landed her this job. Liddy had encouraged her to wear something to wow—*'just in case'*. It was gone seven when she emerged from the bathroom—her make-up done and only her heels left to put on. As she walked stocking-footed across the carpet to her desk, she caught sight of a familiar figure in the doorway.

She had to admit Dillon looked rather good right at that moment as he casually leaned against the doorframe. He'd relaxed over the past two weeks and his confidence in her presence had increased. Whenever jealousy over his shining performance had started to appear in her head, he'd had the remarkable timing to say something suddenly that made her look good to whomever they were meeting with. He never took credit for anything he hadn't done, and he deflected praise away from himself to remind the client of Catherine's vision for the company. She was pleased with her new hire.

The two of them still had an electric chemistry and Catherine couldn't help but add flirtatious innuendo whenever the opportunity arose; now more in playful friendliness, rather than in an attempt to knock his confidence. She was happy that they'd re-booted their relationship to something different to the London one; this time around it was more fun, and intellectually stimulating, for them both. Had the sexual tension not been an ever-present under-current, they could almost be best mates—or even brother and sister.

She'd started to let her guard down around him, and her witty sense of humor was coming through. She constantly wound him up, and although she could see that he often wanted to do a witty comeback more times than he actually did, he still seemed hesitant. She secretly wished he'd be a little more willful sometimes; it might have been fun to bring back the threats of punishment.

"You . . . you look good," he said, stuttering over his words.

"Thank you, you don't look too bad yourself—for an Englishman," she teased.

The taunt about his nationality was deliberate, and one she'd hoped would result in a witty retort commenting on her own London roots, but Dillon didn't take the bait.

"Date?" he asked, with a tone that didn't indicate he was jealous; Catherine was disappointed.

"Drinks with a friend—a female friend," she replied.

Damn. Why did I tell him it was a female?

She'd missed the opportunity to gauge if he'd react with a hint at jealousy, but his body language did suggest a sense of relief when she said female, and that pleased her. Although she'd resigned herself to the fact that Dillon had to remain a no-go zone, she secretly wanted to know she had a hold over him; that he was still hers.

"What about you? Are you going on a date?" she asked in return.

Dillon noticed she'd made a point of telling him that she was only meeting a female friend, and he hoped that maybe she wanted him to know that she wasn't dating.

"No, I'm still new here and there are loads of things to sort out. I'm moving into my new place tomorrow. Finally out of a short-stay, and all that. That way I can get my sister to send over some more stuff now that I've got a job, and all that," he replied, realizing he'd repeated 'and all that' twice, and mentioned his sister.

He didn't want to string out all the mundane details; even though they were becoming friends, Catherine hadn't asked him much about himself or his family. He did notice though that she'd looked pleased at his lack of a social engagement for the evening and he wished that he had the guts to ask if he could come along for a drink; he was keen to meet any of her friends—he'd begun to wonder if she had any.

"Yes, moving abroad takes a lot of sorting as I discovered myself," she agreed. "You have a sister? Is she older or younger than you?"

"Younger. She lives with her husband and kids near my parents down in Dorset. They have a holiday place down in Cornwall too, which I own a very small share. No other sisters or—,"

At that moment, Catherine stumbled; he was unaware that she'd been trying to discreetly step into her stiletto heels behind her desk, and she'd lost her balance in doing so. He leapt to her aid, suddenly kneeling alongside her, supporting her silky leg with his strong hands. She looked down at him, and without a second thought, he picked up the other shoe, ready to put it on her foot while she leant on his broad shoulder for balance. He had an overwhelming urge to want to kiss her delicate foot—naked but for the silky fabric on her stocking—but he restrained his desire.

It could've been the perfect moment, if they'd carried out the Cinderella and her prince scenario, but instead she chose to speak—a return to her wicked witch persona, rather than vulnerable princess.

"I so would have to have punished you if you'd been about to go dazzle a New York lady on a date," she teased.

Dillon dropped the shoe and stood up, letting go of Catherine's leg as he did so—slightly knocking her off balance.

"Please don't do this again," he pleaded; his request was full of the pain that ran deep within him from the emotional scars of the last few months. He'd been punished enough; although it had been a number of different nameless women wielding the crops and whips, the real person doing the psychological punishing was Catherine—she just didn't know she'd been punishing him.

He looked at his tormentor; there was a look of hurt in her eyes, and for the first time he saw a real vulnerability that extended beyond stumbles in heels. Maybe this dominating seduction was the only way she knew how to interact with a man she was interested in knowing better. A wave of guilt ran through him; he didn't want her to feel rejection—he knew how painful that was. He still desired her, but the last two weeks here were better than when he'd worked with her in London. On that first day he'd encountered her in New York, he'd hated the cold Catherine, but her change the following week was significant.

He'd come to realize that her initial hostile reaction towards him was down to him catching her in a moment when she felt out of her depth in her new role. It must have taken a lot of strength for her to swallow her pride and tell him she needed his help. He didn't want to fail her, but he could only be dependable Dillon if his mind wasn't constantly full of erotic images of her. Until he could learn how to balance those yearnings with his everyday need to be an alpha-male, and in control at work, he had to keep Catherine at arm's length.

"I can't be that man for you. You need me to concentrate," he explained, hoping that she'd understand. He lowered his eyes to stare into hers. While the hurt still showed in her return gaze, he could see that she understood.

"I do need you to work hard," she replied briskly. "You'd better be going and do all that stuff you have to do, and I need to get a move on to meet Liddy."

"Enjoy your night out, and I meant what I said earlier, you do look amazing," he said; his final comment had the desired effect—Catherine's expression softened into the sparkle-smile. Not waiting for a response, Dillon left her office.

~

Walking out of the elevator into the ground floor lobby, Dillon's wandering mind was awoken from daydreams of Catherine, dressed in burgundy, by the sound of a woman crying. Looking over towards the security counter, he saw a petite blonde woman visibly upset. Never one to leave a woman in distress, he walked over to offer his assistance.

"Is everything okay?" he asked kindly, yet he saw her bristle at his words and shrink backwards.

Oh shit, has she been assaulted?

Dillon read her retreat as a fear of his gender.

"You're English?" she asked, ignoring his enquiry as to her welfare.

"I am," he replied, wondering why his nationality might cause someone to recoil from him.

"Do you work here?" The woman had stopped the hysterical element of her sobs and her curiosity had taken over.

"I do," he said, unsure why his place of employment was relevant to whether or not she was okay.

"With the English bitch—the one who is the new CEO?" she hissed.

Catherine, what have you done now?

Dillon could well imagine her reducing a woman like this to tears.

"Yes. Has Miss Everdene done something to upset you?" he asked gently, ignoring the bitch part; he knew Catherine made enemies in her career—particularly amongst women, yet everything about the woman in front of him suggested that she wasn't someone that Catherine would have taken much interest in. Even if she had, she'd have been unlikely to do something that might leave her this distraught.

He looked at her attire; she'd made an effort to look seductive and Dillon thought it more likely that the poor girl was distressed over a man. Maybe Catherine had beguiled a man in some way that had resulted in his affections taken away from her—he could definitely believe Catherine capable of that.

"She fired me," she replied bluntly.

Okay, so maybe I was wrong!

He hoped that Catherine had had a good reason; he hadn't seen this woman before and, as he'd started at the end of Catherine's first week, it must have been a dismissal at the very beginning of her tenure. She could be quick to judge and impulsive to act, but he knew that she wouldn't lose an employee she thought might be valuable. "I see. This is what's upsetting you?" he enquired.

"Has anyone come looking for me?" the woman asked, again ignoring the question posed to her.

Dillon was puzzled. If the girl was upset about Catherine's dismissal of her, she wasn't showing it; there had been a total lack of emotion—anger or otherwise—when mentioning the firing.

Come looking for me?

Other than her withdrawal from his accent, he could see no signs of fear, which suggested that she didn't think someone was after her maliciously.

"I'd need to know your name to know that. I'm Dillon Oak,' he said, smiling and holding out his hand, along with a tissue. The only firing he'd heard about, was that of Penny Ways—the former Head of Commercial—but he'd seen her storming out of Catherine's office later in his first week and this wasn't her. It dawned on him that she was most likely the former receptionist; he recalled an email, announcing the name of a new receptionist, sent around that same week. As far as Dillon could gather, the only reason a receptionist would want to know if anyone had been looking for her, would be for personal reasons.

Back to the male theory, it is then.

The woman in front of him started to back away, and Dillon realized she'd guessed his curiosity.

"I've got to go," she said, retreating further. "Don't tell anyone I was here."

"But I thought you wanted to know if—,"

Before he could finish his sentence, she'd scarpered out of the lobby, crashing through the revolving doors with force into the cold night. He turned and shrugged at the security guard, and as he did so, he caught sight of Boldwood looking toward the fleeing woman who was disappearing out of view of the glass frontage. Eyeing his concerned expression, Dillon suspected that he might be the mysterious man that the woman was referring to.

"Was that Faye Robine?" Boldwood asked, turning to face them; the question directed at Dillon and the security guard.

"Yes Sir," the security guard confirmed.

"Was she alright? What was she doing here? Who did she want to see?" Boldwood asked the three questions in quick succession, all accompanied by the continued look of genuine concern. Dillon was even more interested now to see if Boldwood was who she wanted to know about.

"She was upset. She said she'd lost her job, but was more interested in knowing whether anyone was looking for her, rather than trying to get her job back," answered Dillon, eagerly watching to see how the older man reacted.

"Mr. Boldwood Sir, she was asking if Troy Selgent had visited," the security guard interjected.

"Stupid girl, ever since that man turned up she has lost her senses. Did she say where she was going?" Boldwood's concern had switched to panic.

Dillon wasn't only disappointed that the mystery wasn't solved, but now there was another man involved; Catherine's firing of this woman could still be linked to a wayward flirtation.

"No, she just went and—,"

He didn't get a chance to explain; Boldwood had ran out of the building, no doubt in an attempt to catch up with Faye.

Chapter Fifteen

Entering the crowded Manhattan bar, Catherine noticed the stares of several suit-clad men. Ignoring their *'come hither and I'll buy you a drink'* intentions, she scanned the room for Liddy. They should have met up forty-five minutes ago, but she'd come to know that Liddy notoriously arrived late. Many a time in London she'd fobbed off unwelcome attention for several precious drinking minutes while awaiting Liddy's arrival, and tonight she'd decided to delay her arrival at the bar, rather than sit alone in a city that she was new in.

Only once she received the text confirming Liddy had arrived, did she walk the short distance from her office—glad of the cold air freezing the image out of her mind of seeing Dillon kneeling at her feet earlier.

She'd nearly weakened and extended an invite to him to join them for a drink. She felt bad that he might not know people here, and would therefore be lonely; she would've been lost if it hadn't been for Liddy. She'd thought twice though when she realized how Liddy would interpret the invite; an intense grilling by her wasn't what the two of them needed—especially if alcohol sparked a flame from their sexual chemistry.

She spotted her friend at the bar, already with two cocktails ordered.

"I recognize that dress. Not spent any of your hard-earned CEO cash yet then?" she said, winding her up. Catherine tended to invest in good pieces and was otherwise frugal with her money; the importance of looking after her finances was one thing that she'd learned the hard way growing up.

She raised an eyebrow, "Do you know how expensive it is to set-up in this city and move stuff from London?"

"You're preaching to the converted on that one! Let me tell you though, it pales in many zeros to how expensive it is to have a daughter," Liddy replied.

They both laughed at the thought of them now discussing expenditure on homes, removal companies and kids; a far cry from the days when they once discussed articles on financial investments for their business degree, or how much the latest offering of seasonal fashion was going to set them back.

"So, how's the past few weeks been then—any dirt on Boldwood, and what about the new Englishman?" Sometimes Liddy was more of an investigative journalist than her husband was.

"One question at a time please," pleaded Catherine. Knowing that men would be the bulk of their discussion, she'd come prepared. "Boldwood still ignores me."

"What? Is he gay? Nobody ignores you." Liddy seemed perplexed at the thought of any man immune to Catherine's charms.

"No idea. He just keeps his head down at meetings and won't look at me."

"Okay, well moving on, the Brit—whatshisname?" Liddy wasn't about to press further on Boldwood if there was no gossip there.

"Dillon. He's settling in well. We've agreed to be friends."

"He agreed to that? What on earth has got into single men, when you're highly eligible and gorgeous," said Liddy with disgust at the hopelessness of the male species.

"Enough of the highly eligible, but gorgeous will do just fine. Yes he agreed—it was his suggestion in fact," she lied; it was a decision she'd probably pushed him into.

"Boring! Now I remember why I moved to the Big Apple. There's less dull, more go-getting men," she joked.

"Oh yes, John is such a go-getter. Go get tea! Go get bags!" said Catherine, pleased with her one-line comeback.

"Oi you, I don't boss him around," Liddy retorted, slapping out a hand.

"Really?" asked Catherine, raising her eyebrow.

"Well, err, maybe a little. Now, I'm not wasting my excellent matchmaking skills—or valuable time—on an English guy who won't go out on a limb for you. Who's next?"

"That's it. Men talk over," said Catherine, relieved the conversation was over; she didn't want to talk about Dillon anymore.

As they drank their cocktails, gossiped, rejected the advances of sub-standard men, and then drank yet more cocktails, Catherine began to loosen up. By her fourth Cosmopolitan, she was in the mood for mischief. Looking around the room and finding no one that caught her eye worth flirting with, she remembered the handful of Christmas cards she had in her handbag.

Pulling them out of the bag, she looked at the picture on the first one; a snow-covered New York sidewalk with an elegant woman walking past a prestigious jeweler, and at her feet a little white dog on a bright red lead. It could almost have been a scene from *Breakfast at Tiffany's*—had Audrey Hepburn's character not preferred an un-named cat to a dog. Catherine's wicked sparkle-smile filled her face as she looked up at Liddy.

"What are you up to Miss?" Liddy enquired nervously; Catherine knew that her expression would've given away the fact she was having naughty thoughts.

"I'm going to send him this card. Unsigned," she said, smiling smugly.

"And just *who* is him? And *why* is that card unsigned going to spark a reaction?" asked Liddy—they'd spoken of several men throughout the evening, even the tiresome Harvard-attending brother of her friend that Catherine had met in the Hamptons.

Catherine didn't reply, instead reaching for a pen and neatly writing inside the card:

'Fancy a walk at the end of my leash to buy me a sparkling Christmas gift?'

Liddy's eyes opened wide at the ballsy comment. "You're never going to send that to Boldwood, are you?" she asked. The words Catherine had chosen answered the questions about who the card was for, and more specifically, why. The rumors about his activities outside of work fitted with the line.

"I doubt he'd know it was me, and even if he remotely suspected, he hasn't shown an ounce of interest in me. It's just a little Christmas joke," declared Catherine, thinking her prank amusing.

With Dillon pleading earlier for a release from torment, she needed someone new to play with—an outlet for her flirtations. Now she had a company to manage, she didn't have time for a relationship, but it was human nature to want attention.

A sober Liddy would have seen the folly in what her friend was about to do; it was a risky thing, and they were no longer young women catching the attention of equally aged, but immature men. However, tipsy Liddy—needing some escapism from the routine of marriage, motherhood and the legal world—spurred her on.

"Send it through internal mail on Monday and that way he will be driven crazy with desire at who in the company wants to dominate him like that," she suggested.

The idea of doing it Monday would have been a good one—giving them both a chance to sober up and think twice about doing it—but the DeChartine building was less than a block away, and definitely not much of a detour for two women hyped up on cocktails and pending Christmas spirit. Giggling like schoolgirls, heels clicking across the marble, Catherine and Liddy walked across the lobby. Waving a hand in recognition at the security guard that she'd said goodbye to earlier that night, Catherine confidently announced who she was and that she needed to put an urgent envelope into the internal mailroom directly behind reception.

"Certainly Miss Everdene, I'll put that in the tray for you now."

With that, her prank was set in motion; awaiting for the arrival of Boldwood at work on Monday, and his opening of the hand-written addressed envelope marked *'Private and Confidential'* that contained a card loaded with a gun of erotic suggestion.

Chapter Sixteen

Faye Robine had spent the last few weeks in a constant haze of depression. The money had run out; she'd no savings to fall back on, and the rent on her small studio was due within days. Troy hadn't contacted her, but she was still holding onto hope that he'd tried in the past few days; her mobile phone was cut off when the credit had gone. While her priority should have been trying to secure a new job, she was bitter about the working world.

Faye had always worked for DeChartine since moving to New York eight years ago. It was Bill Boldwood who'd hired her, the CEO himself taking an interest in the appointment of a receptionist—keen to ensure that the first impression of a visit to his company was the right one. Faye had been a good employee and loyal to the firm. When the new subsidary started, she'd requested a transfer; she was keen to break into new media and hoped to be an Account Manager one day. It had never occurred to her that she didn't have the initiative needed to progress beyond her current role, and she'd made little effort to acquire additional qualifications—despite the opportunities the company offered for training. Once Troy came into her life, everything had changed; her focus was only on him. Now he'd left her and she felt lost.

This was that bitch Everdene's fault; if she hadn't distracted her that morning, Faye was sure she'd have read the message right; none of this would have happened. Pushing aside the bitterness, she'd dragged herself out of bed that last Friday in November.

Maybe he was away for Thanksgiving.

Convincing herself that he must now be looking for her, she'd headed for his office.

'Troy Selgent has left his previous role and has transferred to another New York office,'—that was all the receptionist had been willing to say, indicating that they couldn't give out any personal information beyond that.

She's just jealous.

Faye thought she'd seen her before, maybe at the office party where she met Troy, or perhaps she was one of the people who'd been leaving as she arrived at the ill-fated bar drinks a few weeks before. Her memory was hazy about both events; she hadn't even meant to be at the one where she'd met Troy. The last minute invitation by the former DeChartine New Media CEO to accompany him to a party at a Wall Street firm was fate in her mind; Faye had totally blocked out any thoughts that the married CEO may have had an ulterior motive in asking her along.

Once she'd finally given up on getting Troy's whereabouts from the prim, stuck up cow at the legal firm, Faye had concluded that he must have gone looking for her at her old work.

He'd want to tell me about his job and my phone wasn't working.

Walking into the lobby of DeChartine, she'd wondered where to go; her pass had been de-activated and it was after work hours on a Friday.

The visitor log book!

Having worked as a receptionist for so many years in the building, Faye knew Troy would need to sign in at both the ground reception, and on their floor. It never occurred to her that her thought process had one fundamental flaw; only those actually going up to their floor would have signed in anywhere. Had Troy come looking for her, he would have asked for her at the security counter—her removal from the company database would have yielded him the same response she'd just had at his firm; 'left with no forwarding details'.

Once the security guard on duty explained this, Faye had burst into tears. It was at that moment that a gorgeous man had walked out of the elevator towards her, almost making her forget Troy. The minute he talked though, she'd hated him—his accent was a reminder of the mobile-phone-ban bitch who was ruining her life.

She ran; ran from the evil-sounding man, ran from the stupid company, and ran from the CEO who hired her and who'd just emerged from the elevator. She didn't want him to see how she'd let him down.

It had been a long day; at the beginning of it, she'd made an effort to look her very best. Now, as it was nearing 8:00 p.m., Faye had been traipsing the streets of New York for nearly twelve hours in her search for Troy. Her efforts in vain, she needed to accept that the focus was now on getting money for rent. She hailed a taxi; no longer caring if it would cost her the last few dollars that she had in her purse.

Faye had a back-up plan—albeit not a good one. In the gap between leaving Troy's old office and her visiting DeChartine, she'd sat in a coffee shop staring at a business card. Madame Rose; that was all it said—there was no job title, no phone number and only a website. Faye had taken it from Troy's briefcase one day when he was in the shower. Back then, she hadn't seen him for a week and was insane with jealousy that he might have been seeing someone else; she'd opened his case to try to find his phone and had instead found the card. A web search revealed the nature of Madame Rose's business, and now Faye found herself asking her taxi driver to drive to the address of the dungeon.

She knew the address; before the disconnection of her phone, she'd emailed the contact from the *Male & Female subs required* page on the website. Drunk and desperate at the time, she'd been willing to consider anything, but then she'd hung on to the hope of Troy coming back to her for a little longer, and Madame Rose's reply went unanswered.

Now, a week later, she'd given up. Her only hope was that if she worked for Madame Rose, Troy would be able to find her via the website when he needed a sexual fix from a submissive that knew how to please him.

Madame Rose ignored Faye's disheveled appearance and smudged mascara; unbeknownst to Faye, this showed the Madame that she was desperate and wouldn't take much convincing to undertake the most explicit submissive requests. Faye wasn't visibly destitute, or addicted to drugs; her nails were still home manicured, her clothes bore no sign of street life and her face had only signs of depression from a bad-breakup, rather than malnutrition or drug abuse. She could be marketable as an attractive, girl-next-door submissive; she wasn't high class, but she'd be profitable for a time, and Madame Rose needed new blood.

With no more than a 'when can you start', Faye had a new job. While it should have been a sad moment to find herself in this predicament, she was only happy to think she might finally be on the right path to run into Troy again.

Chapter Seventeen

Boldwood stared at the hand-written message inside the card that laid on his desk. The contrast between the water-color of the festive image, against the harsh glass of his desk, somehow added more to the significance of the card; an intrusion of the colorful nature of his personal life into the sterility of his professional one.

He'd already had a perplexing weekend, deep in thought at how his worlds had begun to collide, constantly ruminating over the Friday evening with his rush to catch up with Faye after he'd spotted her running from the lobby.

When, years before, Faye had turned up for the receptionist interview at DeChartine, he'd felt an overwhelming empathy for her. He saw in her a submissive nature, one who was desperate for someone to take her under their wing and look after her. She'd graduated from high school, and while this was common for prospective employees of his company, for Faye this was an achievement; back then she'd been proud of herself.

He'd learned Faye's life had been a difficult one, and she'd beaten the statistics that indicated she was unlikely to graduate based on her demographics. Her family hadn't shown her love, and her sister had followed her mother into a profession that involved waiting on tables while scantily dressed.

While she'd remained relatively private about her prior life, Boldwood had always taken an interest in ensuring that she was doing well; more of a paternal interest rather than a sexual one, founded through an empathy gained from his own tough beginnings. Besides, Faye wasn't dominant and therefore hadn't stirred any desire within him.

Boldwood had noticed her absence the past few weeks, but initially put it down to holiday leave. He hadn't kept tabs on her as much now that she worked for a different subsidiary; he'd no reason to speak to her every day and therefore notice when she was absent.

When a third week had come around, and she was still absent from the reception desk when he visited the twenty-eighth floor, he'd enquired about her. Disappointed with the response, he immediately made the connection of Faye's dismissal with her recent focus on only one thing—or rather one person; Troy Selgent.

The name was familiar to Boldwood. He'd first come across the man in professional circles; Troy was a lawyer who wanted to go places, but was going toward them in all the worst ways. His arrogance masked with charm, he could schmooze men when he needed to, and had a number of women literally falling at his feet. It was a power that was only mesmerizing to those weaker; younger men who were desperate to get a foot into Wall Street yet lacked connections, or less attractive society women who were desperate for the attention of a good-looking man.

There was a third group of followers that Troy frequently had at his disposal; attractive, deeply submissive, young women that he treated like toys. When he couldn't find a new toy, Troy also used the services of a specialist agency—one that had the use of one of the most discreet, yet elaborate, BDSM dungeons in the city.

The dungeon was where Boldwood had encountered Troy in a more personal capacity—witnessing him leaving the premises. The agency catered for all—female domination for male and female submissives, and male domination for female submissives. While they didn't have any male Doms on their books for servicing a male sub, their website did state that the dungeons were available for private hire. The wide range of types that frequented the venue had meant that Boldwood was none the wiser as to Troy's tastes, but he suspected that he was more dominant in nature and inclined towards females.

Boldwood had also heard the rumors about Troy's past. His mother, for whom he'd inherited the Selgent name, had been a famous model in the seventies, and if the gossip was true, she'd been the mistress of one of Wall Street's biggest tycoons. With the absence of no other suspected father, Troy was most likely the love child of the liaison.

Some months after he saw Troy exit the dungeon, Boldwood had run into him at DeChartine. At the time he h'd felt as if his heart was in his mouth—Troy was the type who would turn up to blackmail him. Thankfully, Troy had shown no obvious recognition of him, and instead he witnessed the obvious flirtation of Faye towards Troy, picking up immediately on the undercurrent of a sub and her Master. His heart, only moments before practically in his mouth, had sunk; this wasn't what he'd hoped for Faye; she needed a strong man to take care of her, and he thought that she'd make an excellent submissive for a loving Dom—Troy wasn't that man.

This was a thought that was proved correct that previous Friday evening. Boldwood had caught up with Faye, but hadn't spoken to her. Having successfully hailed a yellow taxi immediately after she'd departed in one, his driver had kept on their tail for the short journey. Once out of the taxi though, Faye was twenty paces in front and didn't respond to his calls of her name. Only when he stopped, about to shout louder, did he recognize his surrounds. There in front of him was the discreet entrance to the agency's dungeon.

Although he'd arrived there by accident, his paranoia was acute. The media were ever present, and a few years before he'd been photographed entering the dungeon. Emilia, knowing his true nature, helped cover up the scandal and he'd never intentionally risked a visit again; the time he'd seen Troy leaving was a one-off slip. He still occasionally used the services of Madame Rose's best Dominatrix, but the agency prided itself on its discretion and they'd found a suitable alternative private venue, only to be ever be used by him, and his choice of companion.

Boldwood had desperately wanted to stop Faye from going in—to protect her from what lurked inside. No good could come of her visit. At best, she was there looking for Troy; she might well find him, but in a compromising position. At worst, she was there for work.

He suspected that even if the worst-case scenario hadn't been her intention for the visit, Madame Rose would soon make it so. She was an expert in reading a person, and if she sensed the desperation in Faye for money and attention, she would recruit her. While Madame Rose had excellent retention of the best dominants, and treated them well, many young submissives burned out quickly, or those clients coming to dominate them bored of the same subs for sessions. Submissives often descended into full sexual service within weeks, and months later, Madame Rose cast them off—often leaving them to find their own way on the harsh streets of the city.

The thought distressed Boldwood all weekend; he didn't want that life for Faye, but he hadn't found a way to help her avoid it. If he contacted her offering money, she might take it the wrong way and think he wanted something from her. If he offered the money by being honest with her and telling her what he saw, she'd know that he knew the place. He needed to be careful.

Boldwood looked down once again at the card; evidence that he hadn't been careful enough. His desires to submit ran deep, and even though he was worried about his true nature coming out, he couldn't help but be aroused at the image now in his head; a well-dressed female Domme walking him naked on a leash through a shop filled with diamonds that he'd buy for her to wear. It was the ultimate submissive fantasy for him, complete with the humiliation of voyeuristic sales-men watching him paraded in front of them.

He had to find out who sent him the card.

Chapter Eighteen

Bill Boldwood was ten minutes late for the meeting on the twenty-eighth floor. His tardiness was unusual, and Dillon could see Catherine growing irritated at having to wait for him—especially as his presence was vital to getting the right input into the acquisition bid. None of them was aware what could be holding him up; they were oblivious to the fact that Boldwood had barely got any work done in the past twenty-four hours, instead starting intently at a Christmas card on his desk. One day on, and the mystery was consuming him—a constant distraction with all manner of fantasies now running through his mind.

"I think we will get started, if—," the sudden entrance of Boldwood interrupted Catherine's introduction.

"I'm . . . err . . . Sorry I am late," he stuttered. It wasn't like him to forget how to speak and Dillon noticed his confusion; Boldwood was scanning the faces in the room, and banging into chairs as he struggled to move around an empty one. Something was bothering him, and as Dillon turned back to concentrate on Catherine and the meeting, he noticed a glimmer of her wicked smile.

No! She wouldn't—or would she?

He hoped Catherine wasn't stupid enough to intimidate such a senior figure. Throughout the meeting, he watched Boldwood and Catherine; the former kept his head lowered—lost in his own thoughts, while the latter tried to illicit his attention whenever she could.

Shit, she would.

As soon as the hour-long meeting was over, Boldwood quickly left the room and hurried down the hall. Dillon closely followed, watching the man in front focus his attentions on opening a handful of letters in his hand. Flicking one over, he suddenly turned and walked straight into Dillon; his downward stare preventing him from seeing him

"Sorry," he muttered, then went back to his letter reading.

"No problem, I know how it goes when you're absorbed in work," replied Dillon. He hadn't had the chance to speak to Boldwood since Friday's encounter and he was still curious about the upset woman in reception. He hadn't dared raise the incident with anyone—especially not with Catherine—but he'd discovered that Faye's dismissal had been down to a mobile phone incident on Catherine's first day. A dismissal seemed harsh to Dillon; a warning or disciplinary might have been a better action, especially as the policy—and Faye leaving—had caused bad feelings towards her from the employees.

Just when he thought Boldwood wasn't going to mention the incident, the man looked up and said, "This is actually a letter for Miss Everdene. I apologize, I think the addressed envelope covered up the name and all the mail sorting boy saw was CEO."

"New mail boy needed then!" Dillon joked; he was keen to relax the agitated man standing in front of him.

"I started as a mail boy here. It is a demanding job," replied Boldwood without humor, his agitation growing.

Shit.

Dillon tried to work out what to say to salvage the situation.

"The letter is from Faye Robine," said Boldwood, changing the topic. He held out the letter to Dillon who took it, relieved to move on from his stupid remark, but also for the opening to ask about Faye.

"Did you catch up with her?" he asked; it was an innocent question, but could have been crossing yet another personal boundary line.

"No, sadly I didn't," replied Boldwood, not quite speaking the truth. "But I fear for her. She's very vulnerable and this letter only reiterates my fears."

Dillon looked down and skimmed through the words—*new job, new home, going to marry her partner*—it all seemed good news and he couldn't see anything that constituted a need to worry.

"Is there something amiss in the letter?" he asked, remembering Boldwood's comment about 'that man'.

"Quite apart from the fact that she has omitted the details of her new job and home, I don't believe that Troy Selgent would ever marry her." The hint of disappointment and sadness was evident in Boldwood's voice, but Dillon suspected that there was more to it than he was sharing.

"Besides," continued Boldwood. "There's no point to Faye sending such a letter to Miss Everdene—it isn't a letter to HR accepting her dismissal, nor is it providing forwarding details for paperwork. It's just a delusional letter, one to boost a failing self-esteem and not so much designed to show Miss Everdene that she doesn't need her job, but one to convince Faye herself that things are going well for her."

Dillon could see the logic in his argument, but where women were concerned, who knew what went on in their minds sometimes.

"This Troy, how do you know he won't marry her?" Dillon had never heard anything about the man before Friday and, to his knowledge, he hadn't been a DeChartine employee.

"She doesn't offer him opportunity to further himself, and Troy is all about that. Faye would have only ever been his mistress, and either he's become bored with her, or she did something that he needed to distance himself from until the heat died down. If he's told Faye he intends to marry her, I expect it was hollow words designed to get her to do something," explained Boldwood.

Dillon listened intently and made a mental note that if ever this Troy did come looking for Faye at reception, he'd ensure he was sent on his way; he hated to see women mistreated. He quickly pushed aside his memory of how he'd treated the last woman he'd dated before leaving London; that wasn't the normal Dillon, it was one driven crazy by Catherine. Until such a time that he felt he could date a woman without the shadow of her hanging over a potential relationship, he'd decided to focus solely on work.

"I hope it works out for them. Thank you for the letter. I'll get it put into the personnel file as I don't think it needs any specific action." Dillon needed to get on; he was late to meet Catherine for a working lunch.

"Before I go, can I ask if you've seen this handwriting before and know the hand?" asked Boldwood.

Know the hand? What is this—Victorian England?

Dillon chuckled in his mind at the propriety of Boldwood, who was holding out a Christmas card that he'd retrieved from under the letters and board papers in his hands. It was an odd enquiry, particularly as Dillon was so new to the company and Boldwood was aware of that. Glancing down at the card flicked open to the message, Dillon's heart sank and memories of his own personal torture came flooding back—the handwritten story.

There was no mistaking whose hand had penned the short, one line message that left nothing to the imagination; it was Catherine's handwriting. She was up to her old tricks, only it seemed she'd escalated her BDSM wordsmith repertoire to include a crawling, leash and collar submissive fantasy—set in the snowy streets of New York.

"Catherine Everdene's handwriting," said Dillon before he could stop himself. He'd rejected her advances since his arrival in New York, and she'd moved on; his curiosity back in London led him to try to discover whether she'd tormented others back in London, but his investigations had never yielded any evidence to suggest so. Yet now the truth was on display in a card in front of him.

It was a very personal message, and he was surprised that Boldwood chose to show it to him. The thought crossed his mind that the enquiry was part of an intended disciplinary, but there seemed to be no anger in his question about the handwriting. He heard only curiosity and arousal; a tone he understood well from his own desires for Catherine, and Dillon felt gutted that the man in front of him was looking to discover the sender for a very different reason.

Not wanting to face his potential rival for Catherine's attentions any longer, he quickly turned and left Boldwood without another word.

Catherine could sense that Dillon was annoyed with her, but she didn't know what she'd done to warrant any irritation. He'd been late to their post-meeting working lunch and had nearly bitten her head off when she'd asked what had delayed him. He'd gone straight into questions about the meeting, citing that the reason for his delay was irrelevant and discussing it would only further intrude into the lunch. Their stunted conversation had continued for the whole half an hour, silence descending whenever they stopped talking to eat; Catherine didn't like it.

"Are you wearing an invisible gag? Perhaps some lacy knickers stuck in your mouth?" she teased; the reference to her gag of choice in the story she'd once sent him was deliberate—she wanted to prompt a memory.

Her joke didn't go down well; Dillon bolted out of his chair.

"What have I told you before about keeping it professional? I'm not your toy to play with whenever you feel like it."

The outburst was loud, and even though the closed door and the sound-proof windows would have blocked the words, Catherine could see that several people had spotted Dillon's abrupt move out of his chair, and his obviously angry body language; they were now watching them through the glass.

"Dillon, keep your voice down and sit." Catherine was stern with her tone, but this time it didn't work.

Ordinarily, Dillon would have complied immediately, and with contrition, but he wasn't going to give in to her instruction; conceding only to lower the volume on his next comment, "You want to mess men around with your notes and stories, fine go ahead. But pick one to be your toy, your boy, your partner—whatever it is you want from a man. Stop this leading us on with no intent for anything to happen, or any consideration for our feelings."

There was considerable buried emotion in Dillon's voice; Catherine noted his hurt and rejection regarding a few months earlier. She'd only ever sent Dillon a story, and now the card to Boldwood; there were no other men. The *others* he was referring to could only mean that he knew about the card—and its contents. She knew that if he'd seen it, he'd have recognized her elegant fountain-pen cursive; she suspected that he may well have kept her story and re-read it on occasion.

"How did you know about the card?" she asked, hoping that, by mentioning the card in the singular, Dillon would realize that there was only one other incident. If she asked what he meant—or what men he was referring to—it would imply there were several men she was conversing with at present.

Dillon did pick up Catherine's implication, and the thought of only one other incident and man in her life strangely calmed him a little. For some reason he was no longer jealous of Boldwood—the feeling he'd had earlier in the hall abated. He'd never seen any chemistry between Catherine and Boldwood, and the way she'd just asked him the question about the card—rather than asking him about how he knew about her and Boldwood—seemed to imply that this was yet another of her pranks rather than a hidden relationship.

"He showed it to me. He wanted to know if I recognized the writing," he replied.

Catherine was on the edge of her seat, and one of her wicked sparkle-smiles was forming. "And you told him what?" she asked.

"All I said was that it was your handwriting," he replied truthfully.

Her smile widened; she was playing a game and now Boldwood had upped the ante.

"Catherine, be careful. I don't think he's taking it as a prank."

She looked back at him baffled. "It's a bit of Christmas fun—he will know that. He's always so serious. Besides I've heard the rumors about him, so it's just my way of saying have fun at Christmas."

Dillon sighed; Catherine was one of the most intelligent women he'd ever met, yet she could be so naïve sometimes. He wondered if she really thought that men were so superficial and could laugh off every comment made about their deeply personal nature. He'd observed that she liked to keep people at a distance, but he still didn't know her back story and why she built the walls the way that she did.

An ex-lover? Fiancé that jilted her?

Right now though he didn't want to fight with her; he could see her stubbornness was starting to kick in and he had a lot of work that needed to be completed that afternoon.

"Okay. I'm just saying tread carefully, and know what you're getting into if you take it further," he advised, before turning and quickly leaving her office; providing Catherine with no opportunity to answer back.

Chapter Nineteen

Bill Boldwood debated where to put the Christmas card. He wanted to look at the image on the front as often as possible, and read the note inside, but he didn't want anyone else to read it.

He uncharacteristically felt safe that Dillon wouldn't discuss the contents of the card with anyone. For some reason he trusted the new man, and he'd been going out of his mind trying to work out who sent it. He hadn't intentionally singled out Dillon to ask—it was more a case of he was the only one he'd run into. Nor was he suspicious as to why Dillon would know Catherine's handwriting; after all, he'd become her right-hand man in the past few weeks. He'd put Dillon's strange facial expression, and stiffened body language, down to surprise at the phrase in the card; he'd expected him to comment on the actual words when stating whom it was from, but he hadn't said a thing.

Maybe he felt awkward at seeing such a sexual reference sent by his superior, or perhaps he knows her perversions and it doesn't bother him, like Emilia ignores mine.

Eventually Boldwood settled on putting the card back on his desk. Few people came around to his side of the desk, and he wanted it close to him.

For the rest of the week his productivity dropped significantly. The suggestive image on the card—now prominently in his view—constantly led him to daydream and now he had a real person to put in the role of his Domme when he fantasized. He was glad he had an empty calendar that Friday, allowing him the chance to escape into his private office bathroom on several occasions, but unlike many men, Boldwood didn't indulge in jerking off; his interests ran to the more extreme.

In the privacy of the small room, he tightened the self-administered chastity cage that he'd locked himself into some months before. Another near miss with the media had made him vow to curb his urges until he found a loyal and dedicated Dominatrix that he could truly belong to—a powerful, bossy woman that would allow him to indulge his desires without risk to his position.

As he looked in the mirror at his contorted cock squashed behind the metal bars, for the first time in ages he felt hope that he'd finally found that woman. A woman called Catherine Everdene—who, by her own written words, had shown that she wanted to own him.

c‿ꙮꙮ

Catherine had avoided Dillon for the rest of the week; she didn't like being reprimanded by anyone—least of all him. He was wrong; wrong about her messing men about, and wrong about Boldwood's interest.

It's harmless fun. How could he think there would be deep emotions involved from only a one-line card?

Three days had passed since Dillon had told Boldwood that she was the one who sent him the card, and she'd heard nothing from Boldwood. He'd never paid her any attention, and surely, if he was interested in her—or suddenly attracted to her because of her bold gesture—he'd have made contact.

She thought about Dillon's words; the warning to think before doing anything further. She wondered whether he meant more cards, notes or even stories like those that she'd sent to him, or whether he was referring to an actual sexual relationship with Boldwood.

Boldwood and I?

Catherine laughed at the thought of sexually dominating the greying CEO. She didn't deny that the thought of power aroused her, but she didn't feel attracted to Boldwood at all; her interest had all been in the challenge of getting him to notice her.

As the office emptied promptly on Friday evening—her employees keen to kick off the first weekend of December festivities—Catherine turned off her desk lamp and put on her winter coat. Heading toward the door, she halted—startled by the sudden appearance of Boldwood.

"Hello Miss Everdene," he said; there was an erotic, suggestive tone to his voice, and he'd addressed her as Miss Everdene, rather than Catherine as he usually did. Considering he had seniority, there was no need for formality. She hoped that it was just a gentlemanly gesture; they were alone for the first time since they'd met. Despite her warm coat, she felt a chill run through her body—not of arousal or fear, but dread that Dillon may be right.

"Hello Bill," she replied, deliberately choosing to use his first name to try to draw the conversation away from anything untoward.

"That's a nice coat Miss Everdene. It reminds me of the one in the Christmas card scene."

Shit.

The tactic hadn't worked. Catherine's palms went clammy; she was rarely nervous, but he'd used her formal title yet again, complimented her on her attire and brought up the card—all in the space of a few words. There was no awkwardness in the way he was addressing her—a stark contrast to how Dillon had responded to her seduction and domination banter when she'd first met him. It was clear that Boldwood wasn't new to the role of submissive—the gossip was right; he used no suave masculine tone that a man would normally use to chat up a woman, he only focused on complimenting her.

"Thank you, the coat is from one of my favorite London stores," she replied, deliberately avoiding mentioning the card; had she said that she was glad he received it, she thought that the comment would make it worse.

"The color suits you, and it falls at a nice length to show off your ankles to their best Miss."

Catherine froze at his response; her surname dropped from his addressing of her, and he'd looked at her feet with lustful eyes as he complimented the coat length. Dillon had been right to caution her; she was out of her depth, but her ego was strangely betraying her fear and enjoying the compliments from this powerful man.

"Bill, about the card—please don't read too much into it. It's my sense of humor and Christmas spirit at play," she explained, hoping he would understand, and not be embarrassed by his behavior.

Boldwood stared at her, looking a little disappointed, but wasn't going to be discouraged, "I don't know that I read anything into it that wasn't there. You're a strong-minded attractive woman, who knows how to get the men around her to do her bidding. I appreciate that in a woman, and I think our tastes—all of them—are very similar. We would be a good match."

Fuck!

Catherine didn't know how best to respond to his suggestive remark about similar tastes. "We work together Bill," she said bluntly.

"One very good reason as to why we would be perfect for one another. It is difficult for me to find the right woman that I can fully trust. Our working situation gives me confidence that both of us would get the secrecy and mutual understanding that people like us need. Neither of us would want to risk the company's reputation to discredit the other."

Boldwood had an answer for everything, not even remotely considering the possibility that she might not actually be interested in pursuing a BDSM relationship with him—or anyone.

Like us?

Catherine felt uncomfortable at the suggestion that she was different to other people. While she'd always had an open mind—and had indulged in some fun bondage play many years before—she'd never really pursued an active interest in BDSM until the recent mind-fucking domination she'd used on Dillon so effectively. The continued presence of Boldwood in her office was un-nerving her, and Catherine decided it was time to make her excuses to leave.

"I have to go Bill, I'm already late to meet a friend," she lied, hoping that would detract him from following her. "We will talk again another day. Have a good weekend."

"I will Mistress, and I look forward to our next talk," he said, bowing a little before taking his leave.

Catherine winced at his use of the word 'Mistress' and his eagerness for their next meeting—his words continuing to haunt her for the rest of the weekend.

Chapter Twenty

Monday morning and the start of a fresh, busy, week; one in which Catherine wanted to forget everything that had happened the week before. Dillon being right about Boldwood annoyed her, but she'd managed to assure herself over the weekend that the whole thing would blow over. When she'd arrived at work, there was nothing in her inbox, or on her desk, and that was confirmation to her that everything would work out.

"Morning Catherine," said Dillon, coming into the boardroom for the weekly meeting. It would be all hands on deck this week to finish the first round bid document; only three companies of ten would make it through to the lucrative client's final bidding stage, and Catherine wanted to end her year on a successful high. Dillon seemed relaxed and she wondered whether to mention Boldwood's reaction to the card, but then she thought better of it.

He would only say 'I told you so.'

Once the rest of the team sat down, she ran through the list of things to do that week, and then asked for final questions.

"Is Bill Boldwood going to be further assisting on the bid?" asked a member of her finance team.

"No. Is there any reason you feel he should?" Catherine replied, slightly unnerved as to why he was mentioned.

"I saw him come in Friday evening, and I heard he's since cleared several things in his diary this week to make space for meetings with you," the curious finance man explained.

Shit, what's Boldwood up to now? Nosy buggers, why don't they mind their own business and work for a change?

The curiosity in the Finance Manager's question stretched beyond a work interest, and now others around the table gave her a look—keen to find out if there was anything going on between Boldwood and their own CEO. She looked at Dillon, hoping to read his reaction, but he continued to look down at his tablet screen.

Catherine took charge, asserting herself with all the confidence she could muster, "No, Bill Boldwood isn't on the bid team. He was here on Friday to pass on a personal message from the owner of DeChartine, Emilia, who is away for Christmas. I'm not sure where you've heard the information about meetings, but I can assure you that my diary doesn't have any such meetings and I can bring it up on the screen now, should you still be questioning that. In addition, I'd like to remind you all that discussion of the contents of CEO's diaries for anything other than the setting of your own meetings isn't appropriate."

The team asked no further questions, and Catherine departed the boardroom.

Her timing was awful; just as she crossed the hall, Boldwood stepped out of the elevator. In full view of her team members that had followed her out of the boardroom, he held up a bag of takeaway lunch.

"Miss Everdene, I suspected that you might be working hard on the bid today, and took the liberty of bringing along a lunch for you," he said, his head slightly dipping into a bow.

Oh, fuck, fuck, fuck. He's a fucking CEO, not a fucking lunch delivery boy.

While Catherine appreciated the many occasions when employees had brought her back a lunch takeaway—especially the British-style fish and chip packs that Dillon had recently discovered in a cafe nearby—this was different. She heard the hushed whispers from behind her. It was impossible to dismiss Boldwood so publicly, but she was concerned about the gossip that would ensue.

"Thank you Bill, we shall go to my office for our working lunch," she said, and then turned towards her office—her back to the team so that they couldn't see her face. Boldwood followed eagerly—far too eagerly in her opinion.

He's like an excited puppy on its leash, being taken for a walk to the park.

Catherine shuddered at the thought and the continued influence of the card. Once inside the privacy of her office, Boldwood closed the door. She noticed Mary-Anne, her PA, walking past and glancing in—no doubt heading for the staff coffee room to regale the other employees that had missed his arrival.

"I've been thinking about you all weekend Miss Catherine," he said; he'd seated himself in the lowest chair he could find in the room. Her unease grew as she looked at him; unlike Dillon, he didn't look visibly aroused, but still the thought of him masturbating to her image all weekend made her queasy.

"I'm sorry that I dominated your thoughts." It was a bad choice of words, and once out of her mouth, she knew it.

"It's your domination that gave me those thoughts Mistress," he said, with a lowered voice, filled with adoration to the point of idolization.

"Bill, I don't think I would please you." Catherine mistakenly took his lack of his visible arousal to be a sign that he wasn't sexually attracted to her.

"It is I that should be pleasing you Mistress. My pleasure is in your pleasure."

There was no dissuading Boldwood from his pursuit to become hers—Catherine oblivious to his continued certainty that he could bring out her dominating side to make her his perfect Domme.

His statement though had sparked her curiosity and stroked her ego; she liked the thought of a man who was all about pleasing her. "How does that work?" she asked.

Boldwood looked up at her, his enthusiasm spurred on by her curiosity, "My focus would be on pleasing you. Anything you wanted—gifts, service and sexual pleasure. Your orgasms would be the only ones that are important."

Catherine liked all of those thoughts in principle—especially the importance of her orgasms—but she wished that the person suggesting them wasn't him. He was handsome in the silver-fox way, but she didn't feel any chemistry with him.

"I've never met a man who didn't think of his own orgasm within a few minutes," she retorted with a laugh, then stopped; she was embarrassed that she was talking this openly about sex with a colleague senior to herself.

"Well I would not Mistress. You would take ownership of my key as well," he replied indignantly, ignoring her laughter.

"Key? What key?" she asked; now Catherine really was confused. She'd never heard a man's cock referred to as a key before.

Perhaps it's a euphemism—a key going into a lock, represents a cock penetrating a woman.

Catherine was way off, and Boldwood's reply even shocked her open mind.

"The key to my chastity cage; as my beloved owner, you would now hold it. I have managed to keep it safe without ever giving in to my overwhelming desire to unlock it and find release. I wear it all the time and have done for many months. Would you like to see it?" he said seriously, already reaching to undo his belt.

"Fuck no! We're at the office for fuck's sake," she yelled a little too loudly; she didn't normally swear, but her surprise at his lack of propriety and shame had rattled her. She now bitterly regretted sending the card—the prank that had started this madness. Reporting him was out of the question—it would end her job—besides she was just as responsible, if not more. The thought of a chastity cage didn't turn her on at all, especially not if used for anything beyond a fun, short game between two consenting adults. A self-applied device, fitted for months, gave her all sorts of concerns about his sanity—as well as his hygiene.

"Quite right Mistress, as ever your wisdom and concern for privacy endears me to you more," he said, not put off by her shout. "I shall leave you to your lunch Miss Catherine—that is, if you would please release me from your service for the moment?"

To her relief, he was now standing.

Release you? Fuck yes, GO!

"Yes Bill, thank you for the lunch. Please leave."

While Catherine prayed that her stern dismissal would get him to take the hint that she wasn't interested, it seemed that a dismissive stern tone was exactly what turned Boldwood on even more; he bowed before he turned and left.

⁂

"FUCK!" Catherine shouted loudly—far too loudly considering her door was open. Dillon, who was walking past with a coffee, heard her outburst and rushed in. Catherine could see the look on his face—the one that said he thought she was hurt, or was in need of saving; she knew he liked to play the knight in shining armor.

"Shut the door Dillon," she instructed.

Her briskness made him hesitate in the doorway. "With me inside the room, or outside?" he asked.

"Inside you twit," she replied. She knew she was being insulting, but she was highly agitated and in no mood for Dillon to finally start showing some wit. She watched him contemplate leaving her to her bad mood—she wouldn't blame him if he did—but was glad when he thought better of it, instead closing the door and taking a seat.

"What's wrong? The bid?" he asked innocently; unbeknownst to her, Dillon already knew that it wasn't likely to be work. He'd come from the coffee room where the topic of gossip was all about Boldwood, and he really didn't want to have to lie to Catherine if she asked him what people were saying.

"Boldwood is what's wrong. He wants me to be his Mistress," she replied, deciding it was better to get to the point, even if there was a risk of *'I told you so'*; Dillon was the only one she could talk to about his.

"He isn't married though," he said confused; he was thinking of the usual use of the word mistress, but then the penny dropped. "Ah. You mean that kind of Mistress."

He went quiet and she waited to see if he was going to start lecturing her. "Boldwood seems a good man. Besides, you do have a flair for domination and seduction. He could be a good match for you. You must have been attracted to him to send the card," he eventually added.

Why isn't he jealous? Why isn't he telling me off?

"I told you it was a joke. And I don't need a fucking man in my life," she said angrily; she'd told Dillon it was a prank, so why was he now telling her that Boldwood was good for her.

"Fine, but I'm just saying that you got yourself in this situation and now you seem to want my advice. When I give it to you, you yell at me. Maybe you just want me to say that you're the damsel in distress and that I will sort it all out for you. Is that it?"

She'd never heard Dillon angry before and it made her own temper increase. "I didn't ask for your fucking advice, I only told you he wanted me to be his Mistress. Does that sound like me asking you if I should? Am I the type of person that needs your permission? I'm your superior."

Her questions were rhetorical and Dillon stayed quiet, waiting to see what she said, or did, next.

When a few moments had passed, her posture and voice dropped as she asked, "Are they talking about me and Boldwood?" Catherine looked at him inquisitively, hoping he would answer honestly.

"Yes, you know they are," he replied quietly, his head lowered to avoid witnessing her reaction.

"What are they saying?" She wanted to hear him confirm it—to tell her that they were all speculating how she got the job, and whether Boldwood would be a frequent visitor on the floor.

"The usual; how you got your job, whether you're a couple, the age gap, all that kind of thing. But no one suspects his more niche interest in you." Dillon had summarized the gossip, but he hadn't hid the truth.

"Niche interest? What exactly are you insinuating by that?" Her voice rose again, annoyed at Dillon's calmness.

"You said yourself, that he wants you to be his Mistress, Dominatrix or whatever it is you want to call it," he replied, his own voice rising once again; she could tell he was getting exasperated by her.

"And you an expert how? My giving you endless hard-ons, jerk-off inspiring stories and flirtatious one-liners somehow makes you the fountain of knowledge on the topic," she said sarcastically; she doubted Dillon had experienced any BDSM prior to meeting her and, since she'd done such a sterling job in dominating his mind, she doubted he'd ventured away from her. However she was about to be proved very wrong; his revelation would shock and hurt her more than he'd ever know.

"I think I well and truly experienced every facet of that world when you left London. The marks have only just started to fade on my body, but I'm not sure the scars it left on my mind will ever fade—particularly those that you left," confessed Dillon, finally telling her just how much she'd affected him.

"You did what?" Catherine could feel her anger moving away from the Boldwood issue, and focusing all of its force onto Dillon.

"When you left, I went to every Pro-Domme I could find. I wanted you gone from my mind. I started out with the ones that reminded me of you, but then I moved onto harder extremes. You don't need to know the rest." Dillon delivered his confession calmly, and Catherine read that as a sign of unfeeling and hatred towards her.

"You're fired," she said bluntly.

The startled look Dillon gave her in response to those two words showed her that she had her control back. "WHAT?" he shouted.

"Don't fucking shout at me. You heard what I said, clear your desk and get out of my company this afternoon. I don't ever want to see you again. I'm not responsible for you, or what you've done, and I'm not taking the blame for your actions."

Catherine could see he was pissed off at her words and his dismissal.

"Did I blame you? Yes, I fucking well did. I liked normal before you. Me equals alpha male. Women I date are nice normal women—not ball-breaking seductresses like you. Then I met you, and you rocked my world as no one had before. *I* didn't want to fuck you, I wanted *you* to fuck me like there was no tomorrow. I wanted to kneel at your feet, to kiss them and never let you go, but you never let me. You just went and fucked off over here, leaving me unable to do normal anymore. So I went and found Catherine imitations who would whip me until I cried out your name and then they'd stop. But guess what? None of it worked. I never felt satisfied, even if I did more extreme things. So finally, I stopped; I escaped back to my countryside childhood home to find me again, and then just when I thought I was back on track, I run into you again. My fucking bad luck. So go on, fire me. See if I give a shit. But don't fuck with Boldwood too. Try and learn your lesson for once and don't hurt any more poor guys who might actually be feeling something for you."

Dillon didn't wait for a response to his sudden, long outburst, instead opening the door of her office and storming out, slamming it behind him. Catherine sank into her chair. Once the tears started to flow, she couldn't stop crying.

༺✦༻

Three days passed and she hadn't heard anything from Dillon. Catherine knew where he was though; an email had come through from Boldwood only hours after their argument, stating that he'd taken Dillon on for some work. She wondered what he'd have said to Boldwood; she herself hadn't yet told anyone about his dismissal and therefore he may have used the excuse that he'd resigned. Boldwood hadn't put anything inappropriate in the email—a fact that she was grateful for. She hadn't had any further advances from Boldwood since Dillon left.

Has Dillon said something to him?

Dillon's words were constantly distracting her from the focus she needed to put into work. She was devastated at his criticism, as well as his confessions. It hurt that he thought about her in such a negative way, and she was oddly jealous of all the activities he'd partaken in after her departure. The act of paying professionals didn't sit that well with her, but she didn't want to judge him—particularly now that she'd spent ages on her laptop scanning the web to find out more about ProDommes and what he might have done with them in London. The absence of full-sex had relieved her, but she still felt guilty over what she'd done to him, and said to him earlier that week. She wanted him to come back, but her stubbornness prevented her from apologizing, or begging for his return.

As the week ended, her distraction—and the lack of a commercial lead— had led her to miss things in the important bid documents. By Friday, her team was updating her on events on the West Coast that could derail their bid. She couldn't leave the office to fly out there, and she desperately needed someone she trusted to meet with key players. There was only one person she needed—Dillon Oak.

At first, Catherine asked members of her team to go and find him, but they all came back with the same response; 'he says he doesn't work for you anymore'. Not accepting that, she sent them right back upstairs, with a demand that he come back. When that didn't work either, she was left with no choice. Keen to avoid running into Boldwood, she sent Dillon a text:

> 'Please don't abandon me. I need you. You're the only one
> that can fix this. I can't do it without you.'

Catherine waited, looking hopefully at her phone every few seconds. Fifteen minutes later, Dillon appeared in her office doorway. She jumped up, wanting to apologize, hug him, whatever it took—but he stepped back from her.

"I'll fly to LA tonight. I'm not doing this for you Catherine. I'm doing it for me. I worked hard on this bid too. It's not fair to everyone else to let something in the past dictate the future of so many others," he said with the same tone he'd used when he'd first walked into her New York office and asked for a job.

Now he didn't want the job long-term—he just wanted to fix what he'd left unfinished. Dillon was still being the knight in shining armor, only now he was there only to save the people, and not their Queen.

Catherine nodded; she understood she'd hurt him deeply earlier that week, taking the razor that was her stubborn personality and slashing his heart, mind and soul with it.

"Thank you Dillon." It was all she could say, and she meant it whole-heartedly.

Chapter Twenty-One

Thanks to the hard work of all of her team, the bid was starting to get back on track. Professionally speaking, Catherine was cracking the whip to all of them—as well as to herself—keen to avoid personal distraction. She'd managed to avoid Boldwood, and Dillon was still out in Los Angeles. While she was communicating with Dillon, the calls were entirely focused on progress updates, and the emails were brief and to the point. At least he was back; she prayed that the few days back in his job would convince him to stay on, as she knew that Boldwood didn't have a senior vacancy suitable for Dillon.

Another person that she'd been avoiding was Liddy; she hadn't returned her friend's calls in nearly two weeks—unsure of what to tell her about all that had happened. The last time they'd spoken, she'd told Liddy that Boldwood had received the card and that he'd been enlightened as to the sender by Dillon. At that point, it was an honest status update; Boldwood hadn't mentioned the card to her directly. Now that the situation had changed, she didn't know how much to divulge.

Eventually Liddy decided to take a different tact to using the phone. On the Thursday, she showed up at Catherine's office for the first time—having previously only got as far as the lobby on that fateful drunken night out. Bearing a takeaway lunch for two, Liddy was cleared to come in by Mary-Anne, and the first Catherine knew of her presence was when she was in the doorway.

"Avoiding me?"

Catherine looked up from her laptop to see the raised eyebrow glare of her best friend.

"What are you doing here? Did I forget a lunch?" she asked with surprise; it wasn't like her to forget things, but her recent distractions could have caused any number of out-of-character mistakes.

"Well I brought lunch, and perhaps the reason you didn't know about our lunch was because you clearly haven't listened to my voicemail messages; all nine I left for you!" There was humor, rather than annoyance, in Liddy's comment, but there was emphasis on the number of messages she'd left. Catherine was well aware that none had included a specific lunch invite, only a 'we must catch up.'

"Lid, thank you for lunch, but I'm not sure I can spare much time though, I've got a massive bid to finalize that we've got to submit in the New Year." Catherine had loads of time for the bid document, but agreeing to lunch would mean time for Liddy to grill her face-to-face.

"Twenty minutes. You can spare your best friend that at least. I need to talk to you about Christmas," Liddy insisted.

Catherine relaxed, even if Christmas was also a topic she'd been hoping to avoid. Liddy would never buy her excuse that she was returning to London to see family and friends; knowing that she'd either go back to spend it alone, or she'd stay in New York alone and then pretend to others that she'd been away with her family.

"It's our turn to host the Bradbury Christmas, which means I also get control over the guest list. So madam—without any of your excuses—you're cordially invited to spend the day with us." Liddy's most pretentious voice, adopted for the last line, made Catherine laugh.

There would be no getting out of it, but she actually didn't mind. She hadn't wanted to ask Liddy what she was doing, having known that in previous years she'd always been at one of John's many relatives for Christmas Day—either in New York, or up in Boston. The last thing Catherine wanted was for Liddy to go to great lengths to try to get her single, orphaned friend invited to her in-laws. If Liddy was the hostess, she felt more comfortable going along.

"I accept your invitation, and enough of the madam!" she replied, helping herself to some of the sushi that Liddy had brought.

Just as she'd stuffed a salmon and rice morsel into her mouth—rather less than elegantly—Dillon appeared in the doorway. She nearly choked on the sushi, a rather poignant reminder of all the times that she'd caused him to choke on his coffee back in London whenever she'd appeared from nowhere.

He hadn't been due back until the following day, and Catherine was hoping to have had time to prepare an apologetic speech designed to encourage him to return to working for her. He'd managed to catch some LA sun, no doubt from client meetings held in outdoor restaurants, and he looked good—too damn good—despite a few signs of tiredness.

"Oh, apologies, I'm disturbing you. Mary-Anne had said you weren't in a meeting," he said with his British stiff-upper-lip politeness on show, and she could see Liddy had instantly guessed who he was. Dillon was considerably better looking than she'd given him credit for when she'd described him to her friend, and despite Liddy's happily married status, Catherine could sense her about to unleash prime flirt mode.

"Oh you're definitely not disturbing us. Have some sushi. I'm Liddy, and you must be the Dillon I've heard so much about." It was a stretch of the truth; although he'd been a topic of conversation, Liddy's statement implied that there had been much more discussion.

Good old match-making Liddy.

"I've had lunch, but thanks. Yes, I'm Dillon," he replied bashfully, reaching out his hand to shake; had Dillon not been so damn English polite, she expected he might well have made his excuses and bolted. "You're a friend of Catherine's?"

Damn. The ever-curious Dillon has come to join the party.

"Best friend, right love?" replied Liddy, turning to face her.

Catherine nodded, "We met at business school in London years ago, but then Liddy abandoned me to fly off to New York for a year, only she got married and is still here four years on." Catherine had regained her voice, and despite the awkwardness and anticipation in her tone, she couldn't hide the obvious camaraderie and shared past that she had with her best friend.

"And a good thing I am, otherwise I'd be in London and it would be you who had abandoned me. Not to mention of course, that it was that husband of mine that got you this office. Well, at least that's what he likes to take credit for." Liddy was laughing as she informed Dillon of her husband's involvement in the invite to the dinner where Catherine had met Emilia.

Catherine watched him; his face showed that he was fascinated to learn all of this information about her background. She was unaware that he was thinking how fortuitous it was that he'd managed to get an earlier flight back to New York; therefore having the chance to meet a friend of hers, but also grateful that her presence had softened the atmosphere for his first proper face-to-face with Catherine since the fight.

"So Dillon, are you off back to London to anyone special, or family, for Christmas?" Liddy was fishing, and Catherine knew it.

As she wondered how she could subtly cut Liddy's line of questioning off, Dillon responded, "My sister and her husband wanted me to come home for a week over the break. They're going to Cornwall for Christmas and New Year alone with the kids, as my parents are taking an extended trip abroad for their fortieth wedding anniversary. But I haven't been here long, and there's loads of work for a bid to do right into January, so I will probably just do something last minute."

Catherine's heart leapt; he'd talked about work beyond today, and she wondered if it was an indication that he might be persuaded to stay on.

"Well, how about a last-minute invitation to the Bradbury's Brit-American Christmas Day party? British new-comers to New York especially welcome," asked Liddy happily.

Catherine could see Liddy was pleased with her opportunity for match-making, and she wished she'd told her earlier about the current tension between the pair, and the dismissal of Dillon from the company. Now that Liddy had the single, gorgeous Dillon in her view, Boldwood was all but forgotten. She rolled her eyes and stared at Liddy, almost pleading with her to retract the invitation. Once Dillon had politely declined the invitation, she would have to update her as soon as he'd gone. However, she was to be disappointed, for not only was Liddy in a willful mood, so it seemed, was Dillon—the 'thanks, but no thanks' response that she'd expected him to give in the circumstances wasn't forthcoming.

"That sounds great. Let me know where, when and what to bring," he said, smiling at Liddy, before turning to give Catherine a look of defiance.

The few days in Los Angeles had given him a strength and confidence. Little did she know, but he'd come back determined to focus on work and not let her personal issues affect his career. Dillon had decided that if she wanted to create her own downfall that was up to her, but he could do well at DeChartine, and there was more opportunity here in the new media company than if he joined at a lower level within Boldwood's company.

Through Liddy's revelation, he'd now become aware that Catherine had secured the role by networking at an event that she'd been invited to by John Bradbury, and now he wanted to meet the prominent journalist himself. Dillon was going to that Christmas party—whether Catherine wanted him there or not.

"If you could leave us now Dillon, I will catch up with you later on the bid," said Catherine and Dillon took the hint, saying his goodbyes to Liddy.

Just as he was leaving, he turned back towards Catherine. "I'm staying on." It was three simple words, but it was all he needed to say.

Catherine nodded with a straight face; it was all she could do, a smile would be the wrong way to respond to the words delivered so bluntly.

"What did you do that for?" asked Catherine, glaring at her friend once Dillon had gone.

"He's gorgeous. I must remember to buy mistletoe." Liddy was being mischievous now; no wonder Madison, her three-year-old daughter, was a constant source of amusing outbursts.

"Liddy—" warned Catherine.

"What? He'd be alone otherwise and you know as well as anyone what that's like. Dillon will be company for John. They will get along like a house on fire. Stop being a miserable Scrooge." Liddy wasn't about to retract the invite and Catherine would just have to suck it up.

The two finished their sushi with no more talk of Dillon or anyone else, focusing on the finer details of Christmas shopping—Catherine trying to ascertain what her friend might want as a gift. The twenty minutes well and truly up, Liddy stood to leave; Catherine followed suit, intending to walk her to the elevator to ensure that she didn't head for Dillon's office. However, even as they took the straight path to the lobby, they did run into Dillon. Liddy gave him a wink and he smiled in response, widening his grin further when he saw Catherine's scowl.

Willful bastard, you're only doing it to wind me up now.

Reaching the elevators, she thought that she was finally safe from Liddy's meddling, but then the elevator opened and Boldwood stepped out. He looked at Liddy in recognition; he'd seen her at the dinner where he'd met Catherine, and again at the Hamptons clambake. On facing Catherine, he immediately lowered his eyes from her awkward stare and mumbled a hello.

"Bill," she said in response to his greeting, hoping that Liddy would hurry up and step into the empty elevator. Once more, she was disappointed; Liddy was still in mischief mode—overdosed on Christmas spirit, or was being a wicked elf programmed with the sole purpose to find her a Christmas gift in the form of the male of the human species.

"Mr. Boldwood, are you looking forward to Christmas? Cards up, presents wrapped, Christmas Day plans finalized?"

Catherine suspected Liddy had led with the cards query deliberately, especially as she'd managed to avoid telling her anything about Boldwood's reaction to it.

Boldwood looked surprised at Liddy's forwardness and familiarity. "I don't really do Christmas much. In previous years, I've often spent it in the company of the DeChartine family, but Emilia is on a cruise with a recently widowed school friend, and so I will attend a charity lunch and then relax at home. However, yes there is a card up." He looked at Catherine briefly as he mentioned the card, strangely not at all embarrassed by the fact he'd let slip that there was just the one card up.

Catherine felt sorry for him in some ways, he seemed unhappy and lonely, and her card had filled a void. Liddy wasn't one to leave someone alone at Christmas if she could help it, and before Catherine could stop her, she'd extended the Christmas Day invitation to Boldwood.

Oh, shit.

"I will most definitely try to drop by for the afternoon or evening festivities after my lunch. Thank you so much for your British hospitality. I am coming to appreciate the thoughtfulness of British women." Boldwood's response was formal, but there was a strange excitement to it and his last words about British women were weird.

Catherine froze as he spoke, and when it was obvious that he wanted to speak to her alone, she realized that she wouldn't get a chance to enlighten Liddy, who was now looking like she was regretting her rash invite. Giving her a quick hug, she whispered, "Will tell you later." Then she practically pushed her friend into the next elevator that opened.

She stood in the lobby facing Boldwood, hoping that he would quickly address whatever it is he wanted here, rather than having to go to her office with him. When he held out an envelope of bid papers for her attention, she took it quickly and then started to retreat.

"Thank you Bill, you could have sent it internally," she said putting a sense of dismissal in her tone; a look of rejection took over his face.

"I wanted to hand-deliver it as it's for your attention only. Are you walking to your office?" he asked over-eagerly. Catherine felt the now familiar chill through her spine, as she realized that there was likely to be something other than bid documents in the envelope.

"Ah no, Dillon has just returned from Los Angeles and I'm late to meet him. He's agreed to stay on here," she explained, quickly using Dillon as an excuse. Boldwood nodded; his disappointed look in his lowered eyes for the missed opportunity of a lunch, rather than at the loss of Dillon from his team.

"I will leave you then Miss Everdene," he said, before turning and heading back upstairs. He'd used her title again, and she saw the new receptionist giving her a knowing look. She frowned back at her, and the young woman immediately focused back on her computer screen.

Catherine returned to her office. She wasn't due to see Dillon for another hour, but she needed time to gather her thoughts. Opening the envelope, she was relieved that Boldwood hadn't accompanied her. Although there were bid documents inside, there was also a large red envelope.

She opened it, finding inside a Christmas card with a similar undertone to the one she'd sent. The cover image showed a man kneeling at a Christmas tree putting gifts underneath it, with an elegantly dressed woman standing alongside adjusting the final baubles. The symbolism was evident but the handwritten message on the inside of the card left nothing open to interpretation.

'To all of our future Christmases. BB x'

The message wasn't the only thing inside the card. Three smaller envelopes each contained gift vouchers—one for an expensive lingerie company, another for a designer shoe store and the final one for a specialist erotic toy online retailer. Each voucher value had three zeros after the first number, but before the dot, resulting in thousands of dollars' worth of Christmas gifts.

She dropped into her office chair, completely deflated and with no idea what to do about Boldwood. She might well have been flattered, and not at all concerned, had there only been a card with no undertone—or even if there had been a lower value gift voucher to the shoe store. Colleagues at that level might give each other cards and gifts of reasonable value, and with often a PA charged with the gift buying, it wasn't unusual for a gift to be a retail voucher.

The lingerie, toys and the card message however, left no room for innocent interpretation; she'd captivated Boldwood's attentions, and he was set on becoming her submissive.

Catherine thought about Liddy's extended Christmas invitation to both of the men in her life; the Christmas Day festivities, that only twenty minutes earlier she'd been looking forward to, were now something she was dreading—a day with two men that she'd created chaos with through her own naïve and stubborn actions.

Please let there be endless wine . . .

Chapter Twenty-Two

Dillon was up early. With his parents soaking up the sunshine in Asia, and his sister hosting a family and friends gathering in Cornwall, he'd started the obligatory Christmas morning calls at a ridiculous hour of the freezing New York morning. The call to his mother and father was brief—reception on their mobile in Thailand was patchy—and they knew nothing of his background with Catherine Everdene. They were pleased that their son had made some friends in New York to spend time with on Christmas Day.

His sister wasn't so easy to shake off though; her concern elevated to the max when she discovered that he'd be spending the day in the company of Catherine and her friends. It was his brother-in-law's loud shout from the kitchen—an Aga versus turkey disaster—that saved him from further chastisement from his younger sister. He regretted confessing to her that Catherine had contributed to his wayward state of a few months ago, although he'd never shared the explicit details beyond an office relationship gone wrong.

Having done the family calls, texts to friends, and a Facebook post of Christmas cheer to everyone he knew around the world, Dillon got himself ready for the Bradbury Christmas. Liddy had followed up her verbal invitation with an email telling him to bring only himself, and to come at any point of the morning; lunch would be at 1:30 p.m. He was keen to offer his help if he could, and had settled on 11:30 a.m. as a suitable time to arrive. Although the invitation hadn't requested anything, he'd picked up a couple of bottles of red wine, a bottle of champagne, chocolates for Liddy and, having discovered they had a toddler, a handful of crudely-wrapped storybooks about princesses; the saleswoman had assured him they were bestsellers.

Dillon was glad he'd set off earlier as snow was starting to fall in the city and he was going to have to walk; taxis were hard to come by. Arriving just before noon, he was welcomed in to the bustling front room where John's family had seated themselves in every available spot. A few children—including Liddy and John's daughter—were playing with their new electronic gadgets, looked on by the disapproving grandparents who had opted for more traditional toy gifts.

"You made it. John have you offered Dillon a drink?" said Liddy who had appeared from the kitchen; John rolled his eyes at his wife, and then smiled at Dillon. He'd already introduced himself, offered the drink and was about to attend to serving it when Liddy had interrupted.

"Merry Christmas Liddy, and yes, John is getting me a glass of champagne. These are for you, and this is for your little one," said Dillon, handing over the bags of wine, chocolates and the books. He leaned forward and kissed Liddy on the cheek as an additional festive greeting, and she returned his embrace.

"Oh you didn't need to do that, but thank you. Our daughter, Madison, is in digital heaven this morning having got a real iPad from us—don't ask—and her grandmother brought her a child's learning version too, but she will love the books later, especially when batteries need charging, so save them for then," she said gratefully.

Her batteries—or the iPad's?" Dillon joked.

"Both! Take it you know toddlers?" replied Liddy, laughing.

"Two nieces, one nephew, and all under ten—my sister has the patience of a saint."

"I think we will definitely stick with the one," interjected John. "She's enough of a handful."

"Go and find a perch somewhere in the lounge, or if you'd probably prefer, John and I are in the kitchen, so you can come and chat with us at the breakfast bar."

Liddy seemed keen to talk to him prior to Catherine's arrival, and he wondered why she hadn't yet arrived. He'd thought she would have come earlier to help with the preparations, and he hoped that her delay wasn't because she wanted to avoid him.

He followed Liddy into the kitchen, where John was pouring his champagne. "Cheers," said John handing him the glass. "So you work with Catherine?"

"Yes, it's my second stint working for her. I joined the same company she worked for in London back in the summer," he replied openly; it was easier to answer a man's questions, as they were rarely looking to find out any secrets, although he was aware John was a journalist.

"Was it a nice surprise to come across her in New York?" Liddy wasn't so discreet with her line of questioning.

Dillon wasn't sure how to respond; in truth, he didn't know whether it had been a nice surprise, or his worst nightmare. In the beginning, it hadn't been too bad, but then his knowledge of Catherine's antics with Boldwood had distracted him once again. They were back at the stage of colleagues who put up with each other, but they'd never discussed Catherine's firing of him, or the conversation that had instigated it.

"It was unexpected," he answered honestly.

"Maybe you're destined to work together?" Liddy's question was one he'd no obvious answer to, and he was relieved when John came to his aid.

"Excuse my wife, but she became a believer in fate when she met someone as great as me in a coffee shop on her arrival in New York." John looked fondly at his wife, and then gave Dillon a quick summary of how they'd met.

It was a serendipitous meeting; Dillon thought back to all of his online dating and bar pick-ups, and he was envious of the couple. His connection to Catherine was unexpected, but it definitely hadn't been a meeting followed by a quick blossoming of love through some dates, engagement and then marriage. It had just been a hell of longing, desire and rejection; a relationship that kept having ups and downs, and was currently at lowest point.

"Catherine is very driven, as am I, so we make a good working team," answered Dillon, acknowledging Liddy's earlier question by focusing on their professional working relationship. "I know very little of her outside of work."

Liddy jumped at the opportunity to enlighten him, and Dillon could tell that she was now thankful that her friend had chosen to delay her arrival. "She's driven yes, and it can be hell working for her I expect. She's quite the private person and is very different outside of work with her friends."

"What about her family?" he asked, noticing that Liddy had omitted them from her overview. He'd overheard Catherine say to a colleague that she wouldn't be returning to London to visit family.

"They have all passed away. Catherine's been alone since her teens. Her mother died from cancer when she was nearly ten, then her Dad took his own life a few years later. She lived with her Gran for a while, but then she died too. By eighteen, she was on her own, and spent so much of her time working hard at university, and in part-time jobs, that she had no time to make many close friends. Those friends back home that she made, mostly at boarding school, all have their own families now, and so she's distanced herself. I think I'm it, so it hit her hard when I left. It's probably why she pushed for the New York job."

This insight into Catherine's childhood saddened Dillon, despite his current hardness towards her. He'd come from a happy, solid family and had developed life-long friendships in school and university. His only exposure to broken homes and devastating losses had been vicariously through those friendships. As he stared at the bubbles rising in his glass of champagne, he thought about how this all would have affected her. He couldn't imagine what would happen if one of his parents had died and the other had taken their own life rather than live without their partner, especially abandoning a daughter in the process. No wonder she was so externally strong and determined not to show emotion around men. It would also explain her message pleading with him not to abandon her—just as her father had done when he committed suicide.

"I didn't know any of that, she never shares anything about herself," said Dillon, hoping that by telling Liddy this, she might encourage Catherine to open up more to him.

"No, she doesn't. It's all about not letting anyone in I guess. It took me a long time to get to know her, and I'm a woman. Even then, I still don't know what goes on deep inside her head, or more importantly her heart, but I do know she isn't really the Ice Queen that everyone thinks she is. It's just an act."

Dillon nodded, he understood the business world and how Catherine might not have succeeded in the way that she had, if she'd focused on gaining pity and sympathy through using her childhood story.

"I did see her be nice—once," he said, laughing a little to provide a lightness to the conversation.

"Oh?" Both Liddy and John were curious, and he regaled them with the memory of seeing her talk to the cleaner.

"Yeah, that sounds like something she'd do. The grandmother she lived with was a cleaner. She really is a different person if she doesn't see you as a threat. Catherine is quite the entertainer as well when she's in a good mood. Hopefully we will see that Catherine today."

Dillon was hopeful that some champagne and festive goodwill would let him see the friend that Liddy knew and loved. He could tell that Liddy liked him and was playing cupid, but strangely, he didn't mind.

"Which Catherine are you hoping to see?"

No one had heard the bell go announcing Catherine's arrival—John's brother-in-law, who was braving the snow to take a cigarette break on the front stairs, had let her in. She'd entered the kitchen just in time to hear the last words that Liddy had said to Dillon.

Liddy squealed an almost childish sound, and dashed around the breakfast bar to give Catherine a massive hug. John was already pouring the champagne, knowing that Liddy would only tick him off if he didn't. Standing up from his stool, he took her the glass and gave her a hug and kiss on the cheek in a warm greeting. Dillon watched her from his stool, unsure if he should also rise and greet her. He desperately wanted to, especially after hearing her sad life story.

"No hug for me Dillon?" she suddenly asked; her sparkle smile on in full force, with a hint of wickedness.

He immediately obliged, keen not to disappoint her. It was the first real embrace that they'd ever shared and the closest contact since the months before in London, when she'd nipped his ear in her office. He could smell the rosy perfume on her neck, and felt the softness of her cheek as he kissed her. The intoxicating mix that was Catherine went straight to his head— and his groin—and he quickly added a distance between them, returning to his stool with the safety of the breakfast bar protecting his modesty.

She took up the stool alongside of him, her loose red wrap dress riding up provocatively as she did so—revealing the lace top of a black stocking. The style of the dress also provided a gape around her cleavage and, from his side view, he could see her matching black lace bra.

Oh fuck, look what Santa has brought me.

Dillon took a gulp of his champagne; he'd need Dutch courage to get through the day.

"I come bearing gifts for you all," she said, putting three small bags on the counter, and then with her long, perfectly manicured finger—adorned in festive red polish—she pushed each bag towards its intended recipient. Dillon was surprised to see he had a gift, and was disappointed that he hadn't thought to get her anything.

He watched Liddy open hers first—a designer clutch bag in the latest seasonal color. John went next and was delighted with his state-of-the-art digital pen—particularly as it hadn't yet been released; Catherine had procured it via a client.

Dillon rather apprehensively opened his bag, unsure of what Catherine might have chosen for him. First, he found the Christmas card envelope and he hesitated, worried that he might be getting something akin to Bold-wood's card. Opening it though, he was pleasantly surprised to find the card's cover image was a British scene—a snowy thatched cottage similar to ones in the Dorset village where he grew up in. He opened it to read the message written inside.

> *'From acorns, mighty oaks grow. They can withstand the strongest storms and still flourish, steady when weaker trees bend and need propping up.'*

It was a strange, poetic Christmas message that didn't make much sense. There was no oak on the card image, and he could only assume that it was a reference to his name and the storms they had weathered; was she the weaker tree?

Putting down the card, he looked into the bag; inside was a small box, embossed with the stamp of a famous London jeweler. On opening it, he discovered a set of intricately carved silver cufflinks; the carving on each was an acorn—indeed a reference to his own surname—and Dillon realized that she would have had them sent over from London before their fight. It was an immensely personal gift, filled with thought, and was perhaps a sad premonition about their stormy relationship.

"Thank you Catherine. These are . . .," Dillon didn't know what word to use, and instead leaned over and kissed her cheek once again; afraid he might actually choke up after hearing her background story, and now on receiving this gift.

Although she allowed him the kiss, she seemed even more awkward at this second one; the greeting kiss was fitting in the circumstances, but now she clammed up at this showing of gratitude. She couldn't keep his eye contact for more than a second, and quickly took a mouthful of champagne before turning to Liddy and John to start Christmas chatter.

They too had a gift for Catherine; a gift that not only again made Dillon feel thoughtless at not buying her anything, but also because the sparkling Jimmy Choo heels that they'd brought for her—and had sent in advance— were on her feet. He hadn't even noticed them when she'd come in, not thinking to look down at her feet assuming that she'd donned snow-worthy shoes like most sensible people.

Now that she'd pointed them out and discussed them, he couldn't stop staring down at them; a view of stocking top lace and sparkling stilettos. If only he could have a view like that every Christmas or—better still—wake up to look at her smile and naked body in his bed each year.

Sitting alongside her, he almost felt that they were there as a couple—a happy couple sharing a Christmas morning with another happy couple. It was a pleasant fantasy, if not for the tortuous nature of it; he didn't have Catherine—only the alluring view of her more sensuous preferences. He needed a distraction; any more of this and he'd need to excuse himself to the bathroom for some relief.

Dillon never would have guessed that it would be a three-year-old girl that would come to his rescue; keen to see what food goodies she could steal, Madison had come into the kitchen.

"Auntie Catherine, come and dance with me," she said; she hadn't spotted Catherine arrive, nor Dillon for that matter. "Ooh, I like your shoes, can I wear them?" Dancing was all but forgotten.

"You most certainly cannot young lady. They were a present to Auntie Catherine from you. You don't ask to wear a present you gave someone do you?" scolded Liddy; Dillon expected that she wasn't about to let her daughter break her neck in the shoes, or break the heel of a thousand-dollar pair of sparklers, but she'd covered up her concern well.

Madison looked perplexed, replying, "But Mommy, I didn't buy shoes for Auntie Catherine, I made her a necklace." She turned from her mother to study Catherine's neck; indignant to her mother's suggestion that she'd brought Catherine shoes. "Where's your necklace Auntie?" she asked.

"Here it is," replied Catherine, withdrawing a multi-colored beaded necklace from her clutch, and then putting it around her neck. She adjusted it so that the clay-baked, glitter-covered star shape was at the front. "I didn't want it to get wrecked in the snow."

The young girl looked happy, and Dillon looked on with amusement. The scene he'd just witnessed, and now the sight of Catherine in a nursery-made necklace, had succeeded in subsiding his arousal, but now in its place was a different feeling, and he was back to picturing what a life would be like with Catherine at his side; this personal moment was providing a different context to that possible life.

"Now *Little Miss Shoes*, how about Auntie Catherine gives you *your* Christmas present?" said Catherine, addressing Madison with a friendly, over-animated voice that endeared her to everyone in the room—especially the young girl. Her eyes lit up, first at the new nickname, and then at the idea that a Christmas present was looming.

"What is it?" she asked excitedly, bouncing up and down in her reindeer-antlered, sparkle slippers.

Catherine didn't make her wait, pointing to a larger red bag at the base of the stool, and Madison ripped it open; retrieving a toddler-sized shoebox. As she lifted off the lid, Dillon saw the most sparkly shoes that he'd ever seen; the silver sequins caught the light and sent holographs around the room. Designed for children, the low heel was as safe as a heel could possibly be, and the base of the sole had Cinderella embossed on it in the same style that many shoe designers adopted for their own signatures. Auntie Catherine's gift was a well-appreciated one and the youngster gave her a huge hug that Catherine returned with equal love and affection.

Catherine continued to surprise him throughout lunch, and Dillon was pleased that Liddy had seated him alongside her. Her personality around the people at the table was unlike what he'd seen in her before, and he listened with enthusiasm as she made jokes and enquired about the lives of Bradbury family members.

While she was polite to their own queries as to her background, she noticeably changed whenever the focus was on her. In a boardroom, she relished the chance to shine—as she did at events designed for networking, but here in a family atmosphere, he could tell she was on guard. A streak of her icy coolness came out whenever he asked her anything, and by the main course, Dillon had made the decision not to be the one to pose her any questions.

Dillon's biggest mistake of the lunch came when John's mother asked Catherine about her own parents. Before she had a chance to answer, he'd reached under the table to squeeze his hand on her thigh, a gesture meant to be a private show of support—but one that made her flinch and abruptly retort, "They died when I was young."

She glared at Dillon, and then across at Liddy, and he realized that she'd now know that Liddy had betrayed her confidence in revealing her childhood past. All the guests were sensitive to her mood from that point onwards, and the rest of the lunch focused on others. As they moved onto coffees or aperitif spirits, Catherine had only just started to lighten up a little, when rescue once more came from Madison; the three-year-old showing remarkable timing when it came to putting the festive spirit back into Catherine.

"Auntie Catherine, can we dance in our sparkly shoes now?" she pleaded with the innocent hopefulness of a child; she was oblivious to Catherine's mood.

Dillon had expected her to politely decline, but instead she rose and took the girl's hand, following her into the larger playroom off the dining room. Madison turned up the stereo, and chose a different song on the iPad that rested on the dock; for someone so young, she was proficient in the use of the device—considerably more than he was. Liddy, John and Dillon followed to the doorway and watched the two of them twirl around the room.

Dillon was dumbstruck by the new side of Catherine that he was witnessing; he'd never been able to picture her with children, but it came naturally to her to interact in such a playful, innocent way.

The next song that came on was much more upbeat—more akin to something played in the clubs; unlikely music for a young child to dance to—or something Dillon would expect Catherine to either. All of them were therefore shocked to see first Madison copy the bum-wiggling moves of the music video, and then Catherine start bending her knees and taking on the twerking actions; her well-toned thighs and rear lent themselves easily to the energetic moves.

"Err, hello Madison, where did you learn that, and as for you Madame Catherine, look at you go," said Liddy, unable to know what to think about seeing both her three-year-old daughter, and her thirty-five-year-old friend, dancing around the playroom like club-going teens; the scene was both amusing, and slightly disturbing, with the obviously sexual moves.

Dillon couldn't take his eyes off Catherine—a fact noticed by Madison—

and by the time the next, more up-beat folk song had started, she'd decided it was time for others to join the dancing.

"Mr. Dillon, you come and dance too," she said, holding out her little hand, and he looked at Catherine—silently asking her permission to join them.

Catherine looked hesitant, but then she smiled and said, "She won't take no for an answer, and she can be even more demanding than I am!"

Dillon laughed; the alcohol and Christmas spirit was relaxing them, and although his dancing skills weren't up to her standard, he stepped onto the makeshift dance floor that the playroom rug provided. Catherine knew the song—The Lumineers were one of her favorite bands, and as the chorus came around, she started to sing along, *'I belong to you, you belong to me, you're my sweetheart.'* She playfully pointed to Dillon on the *'you'* and herself on the *'I'*, and he was reminded that in so many ways he did belong to her—but he was doubtful that she'd ever be his.

Catherine looked so happy, and he spotted Liddy secretly snapping pictures of them on her mobile phone, and made a mental note to ask her for copies before he left. Liddy tried to encourage Dillon and Catherine to pose together for another photo, but her request killed the lightness of the moment; suddenly conscious that there was a camera present, as well as her matchmaking friend, Catherine called time on the dancing and headed towards the drinks table.

Dillon left her alone for a while, taking the opportunity to use the bathroom. In the solitude of the quiet upstairs, he stared outside at the falling snow. He hadn't had many white Christmases—but the ones that he'd had, all involved his family and were pleasant memories. He racked his brains to remember how old he would have been for each of them, and whether they were ones that Catherine would have experienced with her parents. As he knew her age, he calculated that there must be at least one, or two, that she would have had with them before they died. Deciding to take a wild chance, he headed downstairs.

Spotting Madison, he started his plan; "Would you like to build a snowman?" he asked her, hoping that Liddy and John wouldn't mind them going outside for a bit. His hunch that the girl would like the idea was correct, and she excitedly ran for her snow-gear. "Catherine?" he said, turning to her. "It's not often we get a white Christmas in England these days, and it's always fun to do something childish now and then."

Dillon was skating on thin ice, rather than snow.

"These shoes aren't really snow-worthy," she replied, trying to find an excuse, but even Dillon could see that she was tempted; it showed in her eyes.

"I saw you arrive in some pretty impressive snow-boots and coat. Those heels only came out of the bag in the hall," interrupted John's brother-in-law, who waded into the conversation to reduce her excuse.

"And I've got thermal leggings you can borrow," added Liddy, also spotting the opportunity for what it was—she was keen to help Dillon see how much fun Catherine could be.

Excuses over with, fifteen minutes later all of the children—accompanied by Catherine and Dillon—were in the small garden of the Bradbury brownstone, rolling ever-increasing balls of snow to form their snowmen. John threw Dillon a bag of carrots, with enough snowmen noses to appease all the children. While Catherine wasn't the most proficient snowman-maker, she didn't stand back from the challenge.

Dillon looked at her pathetic attempt. "Um, Madison, what do you make of Auntie Catherine's snowman?" he asked. Catherine could tell he was taunting her, and she glared at him; a glare that suggested a punishment was coming his way—rather than an outburst of anger.

"He looks funny," replied Madison giggling, and all the other children joined in the laughter. Dillon was grinning; not at all worried that she might decide to punish him while surrounded by company. He was wrong; the punishment came hard and fast—a snowball that was hardened by her tight grip before she threw it. He had his back turned to her when she took aim, and it came as a surprise; at first, he thought one of the younger boys had thrown it.

Turning he saw Catherine staring at him with her wicked sparkle-smile, and another snowball perfectly formed in her gloved hand. He didn't have time to form one of his own before the second one hit him—this time on his muscular upper arm. Catherine was laughing at him now and he reached down to grab a handful of snow of his own, yet was reluctant to throw it; he had quite a strong arm and he didn't want to harm her. She must have had the same thought, as she started to run towards the safety of the patio stairs, still laughing.

"You can't catch me," she taunted.

All the children were watching the playful adults, and Liddy had joined John at the door to watch the spectacle. Rising to the taunt, Dillon ran after her. It wasn't difficult to catch her; what to do with her when he did was going to be the question, but just as he caught up to her, she slipped on the step and fell backward. Dillon lunged forward and managed to grab her, despite the handful of snow still in his hand; his arms awkwardly wrapped around her, her back hit hard into his chest and her head clashed with his shoulder.

Somehow he turned her, providing the opportunity for her to regain her footing on level ground, and she looked up into his face. It was one of those moments where they were face-to-face, snowing falling gently around them. If they'd been alone, it would have been the perfect Christmas moment for a kiss, but both of them were acutely aware they had an audience that included several, very curious, children.

"Kiss her Mr. Dillon, like the prince always does," encouraged Madison, clapping her hands with glee.

Catherine broke her stare into his sparkling blue eyes, and looked away embarrassed.

"I'll help you up the stairs," he said, ending the moment; he wouldn't be able to resist kissing her if they stayed there any longer. Together they walked up the stairs, Catherine still a little unnerved by her slip and moment of weakness. She hadn't let go of him, holding onto his arm for support, and it was only once they were safely inside that she released him.

Once they'd removed their coats, changed their shoes and had a glass of warm mulled wine in their hands, Dillon sat down on the lounge chair near the fire. He was surprised when Catherine—now back in her stockings and heels—came and joined him in the small space left on the same sofa. There were other free seats, and he wondered whether she was attracted to the fireside, or to him.

"Thank you," she muttered quietly. It was a humble form of gratitude and Dillon wasn't sure what she was thanking him about; he looked at her, directly meeting her eye contact, and saw there was a sadness in her eyes, mixed with happiness—a confliction of her emotions.

"You're welcome. It was lucky I was there to catch you," he replied, assuming that was the heroic act referred to; he smiled at her.

"Yes, but my thanks went beyond that. Thank you for LA, for the bid, for staying on, for having the guts to tell me things that needed to be said—but especially for the whole snow thing just now," she explained in a quiet tone.

He sensed her vulnerability and desperately wanted to put his arm around her and offer his support. He wondered whether to say why he'd suggested the outdoor fun, but before he could broach the subject, she spoke once more.

"I remember the Christmas when I saw snow for the first time. I was five, and my Mum's parents had convinced my Dad to take us up to their Scottish house for Christmas. Normally Dad would only drive us there in summer, because he was paranoid we'd end up snowed in and then he'd have to spend weeks with his in-laws. Grandpop was insistent we make snowmen in the garden on Christmas Day. I remember the carrots; my Mum was spending so long trying to find perfectly shaped carrots that we were all getting too cold waiting. I get it from her you know—the perfectionism . . .," Catherine hesitated, but then continued when Dillon didn't say anything in jest.

"We had this big snowball fight after Dad made fun of the carrots thing. Mum threw one at him and that started it all. That was the best Christmas I can remember. We didn't go to Scotland anymore after that as Grandpop died the following year, and Grandnan moved to a nursing home in Edinburgh. It was the only snowy Christmas I ever had with my parents."

Dillon spotted a tear in her eye. "I'm sorry if I brought back painful memories," he said apologetically.

"It's always painful on holidays, but sometimes it's good to be reminded of the nice memories. That's why I said thank you," she replied, nudging her arm to his in a gesture of friendliness. Dillon began to think that he was finally making progress with her, but his dreams of togetherness suddenly disintegrated with the arrival of another guest.

"Catherine. Dillon." It was the unmistakable accent of Bill Boldwood; Dillon hadn't known that the man was invited, but he sensed that Catherine did; she sat bolt upright and put distance between them.

"Bill," she said, smiling at him. It wasn't quite the sparkle-smile that Dillon had become accustomed too—but it did have a warmth to it that he hadn't seen her show Boldwood before. He rose off the sofa, keenly aware of the distance that she'd created on the chair.

"Bill, can I go and get you a drink? You can take my seat near the fire—you look frozen from the cold," offered Dillon, realizing that Boldwood had most likely walked a great distance in the snow to get here on a Christmas afternoon.

The man looked pleased at the invite, and accepted the offer of the warmed mulled wine. Strangely, he didn't take the spot on the sofa, instead taking the cushion from it and placing it on the floor in front of the sofa, and then sat at Catherine's feet. Dillon's previous concern about Boldwood's intentions seemed correct, but if she was at all concerned, she wasn't showing it—nor did she look surprised at his action.

Leaving them to their conversation about his charity lunch, Dillon headed for the kitchen. He couldn't watch any longer; witnessing Catherine and Boldwood sitting there together hadn't only wounded his ego—and stirred up his old fears of rejection—but a realization had hit him like a ton of bricks.

Without a doubt, he was in love with Catherine Everdene, and he knew he would do anything to make her happy—even if that meant giving up his spot beside her to free it up for a wealthy man who was equally besotted with her.

Chapter Twenty-Three

It had been a busy January, with all hands on deck to get the bid done; Catherine was proud of the work her team had done. They'd been successful in winning the client and, now that it was the first week of February, the pressure was on to deliver all of the year's objectives. The endless work hours had given everyone a useful distraction from the troubles in their personal lives and to Catherine's relief, throughout the first month of the year, Dillon and Boldwood had also both immersed themselves in work.

It was in the early hours of each morning, as sleep evaded her and insomnia took over, that she was free to ruminate about Christmas Day; a day that had been full of mixed emotion. Surprisingly, she'd enjoyed the first hours of the festivities more than she initially expected to, for the most part relaxed and happy with Dillon's presence. His suggestion to make a snowman was a good one, despite the memories it stirred up, and it had provided her with a way to open up to someone and briefly let them in.

Skimming over the confusing thoughts in her mind about the slipping on the stairs incident—the flutter of her heart when Dillon caught her and looked deep into her eyes, and how she'd wanted him to kiss her so badly—she remembered how Boldwood had interrupted their later conversation. If he hadn't turned up, Catherine was worried about just how much she might have revealed to Dillon about the weaknesses and vulnerabilities that came from her painful, and lonely, childhood. There was also the chance that they would have ventured into the awkwardness of discussing the dismissal conversation—something they'd so far avoided.

Dillon was a good friend whose company she enjoyed, and she was determined never to hurt him again. As the days of January had progressed, she'd held back on the temptation to flirt with him to avoid the risk of upsetting him; she needed him in her friend zone, especially with everything she was dealing with at work, and with Boldwood.

Boldwood's arrival on Christmas Day was unwelcome, even if he did have an invitation. Catherine had hoped he wouldn't come, but when he did, she didn't want to show her disappointment to her hosts—or the Bradbury relatives. Boldwood was another CEO in DeChartine—one of higher standing no less—and she didn't want to embarrass him with a public rebuff, even if his presence undoubtedly gave the impression that they were personally linked.

She'd worried that there might have been whispers about how she was apparently there with two men—at lunch many had assumed Dillon was her partner—but he hadn't openly shown a loving affection towards her in the presence of anyone aside from Liddy and John, or the young children. Boldwood, however, had been quite open about his infatuation with her, and when he'd sat on the floor alongside her leg, his behavior had freaked her out. She had the generosity to keep her feelings hidden though, not wanting to play up any rumors that anyone might have heard about him; it wasn't that odd to sit on the floor—two other adults were seated on cushions by the fire due to the lack of sofa space.

To her relief, Boldwood didn't openly embarrass her with use of inappropriate titles, nor did he ask about her gift from him. She hadn't used the vouchers prior to Christmas, and had since chosen only to redeem the shoe one during her post-Christmas sale expeditions with Liddy; the lingerie and toy vouchers were safe in her home desk drawer. Boldwood had commented on her Christmas shoes, and looked disappointed when she mentioned they were from the Bradbury's, realizing that they'd not been purchased with his money.

At least he brought me a gift, which is more than Dillon did.

The lack of a gift from him irked her, especially considering how much effort she'd put into his present—the idea having come to her when reading a magazine from London. Dillon had only been working with her again for a few weeks and she'd been looking for ways to reduce the guilt she felt about sending him the story and leading him on. It had never once occurred to her that such a personal gift might well do the actual opposite of assuring him that she thought of him as only a friend. However, his emotional reaction to the cufflinks had made her see that he might have feelings towards her, and she'd felt uncomfortable when he'd given her a second kiss of thanks on the cheek.

Being annoyed with his lack of a gift for her was an unfair criticism—it was only a few weeks before that she fired him; he wouldn't have known that she was going to give him a gift. What he had done though, was provide her with the gift of a cherished Christmas memory—a priceless gift in many people's estimation—and that thought left her as confused as ever as to what she felt for him.

One thing was certain; Catherine had added to her New Year's resolutions that she would focus on work that year, with relationships strictly off the agenda, and she knew of no man who could change that.

Dillon had been avoiding Catherine whenever he could; since the events of Christmas, he'd been back at the point where he couldn't stop thinking about her. He was jealous of the attention that Boldwood was giving her; his constant visits to their floor to praise her work on the bid, and the regular flower deliveries were the talk of the office. Everyone seemed to be waiting for some sort of announcement that Catherine and Boldwood was officially an item.

Catherine was quiet on the topic, and he noticed that she was very reserved in both his company, and that of Boldwood—her sparkle-smile rarely on show. In some ways, Dillon was glad that she was no longer yelling at him, or asking him for advice on her personal affairs; but in another way, it meant that he was less likely to be able to hate her. Hating her might be a solution—reducing the feelings that he felt for her and the jealousy that was poisoning his heart.

At the end of the first week of February, as Winter Storm Nemo raged towards the city, all thoughts of avoiding Catherine went out the window when her safety was in jeopardy. While she'd been sensible enough to heed the warnings and send her team home early; her relentlessness to focus on work had resulted in her staying back to finalize negotiations with East Coast on a project—with no regard to her own journey home for the weekend. Knowing how stubbornly independent she could be, and would, in all likeliness, attempt to get home late in the blizzard, Dillon stayed back too, watching for her departure.

As expected she stayed until late, and as soon as he saw her head towards the elevator, he rushed into the lobby.

"Mind if I join you?" he asked, his sudden appearance startling her. "I might need you to hold me upright looking at the weather outside, I'm useless at ice-skating."

His joke was deliberate; he knew Catherine too well to know that she'd decline any offer of assistance to get her home, yet she might take pity on him.

Catherine raised an eyebrow at him and he suspected she'd seen through his ruse. "I guess we can't have you injuring yourself," she replied.

The two boarded the elevator, and Dillon pressed the ground floor button without another word; his mind though was on overdrive—this was the first time they'd ever been alone in an elevator together, and she was the one who'd written an elevator scene into her story.

"How are you parents—are they back from their travels?" she asked unexpectedly, breaking the sexual tension and his wayward fantasies of pining her against the elevator wall; Catherine had never really asked him about his family and he was surprised, and flattered, that she'd remembered that they'd been away at Christmas.

"Yes, they arrived back home last week. Spoiled all of their grandchildren with gifts from far-flung destinations, and they seem to have caught the travel bug as they've booked another break already."

"Are they coming here?" she enquired, and Dillon hoped that meant she might be interested in meeting them.

"Sadly they don't seem to want to come to New York," he replied, laughing nervously; he didn't want to give away his disappointment at their lack of interest in visiting him. He suspected his sister was responsible for discouraging them from coming to see him due to Catherine's presence, and he didn't want to risk upsetting his boss by revealing that detail.

"That's a shame. I bet you miss them."

Dillon wasn't sure whether to admit he missed them terribly; it would seem like driving a knife further into her heart considering that at least his parents were alive. "At least I will see them at some point this year," he finally replied.

Just as she opened her mouth to say something, the elevator abruptly stopped and the mains light went out. They were in darkness for only a second before the dim emergency light flickered on.

"Shit, the storm must have kicked the power," he cursed, studying the control panel. Picking up the emergency phone, he failed to get a response. "I'm afraid we might be here for some time."

He didn't know what else to say; he was all out of save-the-day heroic ideas now that the phone had failed, he didn't know who to call on his mobile, or even know if his frantic waving at the security camera would be noticed.

Catherine, however, looked remarkably calm, sitting down on the metal floor of the elevator and typing a quick text into her smartphone. "I've alerted emergency security. The phone and cameras in here don't work in a power-cut – didn't they tell you that in the induction?"

Typical that she's in control and I don't know what I'm doing.

Dillon watched her take out warm, woolly-lined snow-boots from her large carrier bag. Replacing her heels with the warmer footwear, she looked up and caught his stare.

"You said we'd be here a while and my feet are cold," she said, justifying her actions. "I hate being cold."

"Fair enough," he replied and joined her on the floor; he didn't care about her change in footwear; he was only relieved that she was at least a little sensible, even if her coat looked woefully thin for the New York winter.

"We should be okay—that is as long as neither of us needs the bathroom!" Dillon was trying to be practical and reassuring, while also making light of the situation; not that she appeared to need his efforts to calm her.

Catherine laughed; a hysterical laughter that made him think that maybe he was wrong and she might already be losing her mind in the confined space. "What's so funny?" he asked.

"The bathroom comment," she replied, trying to stop laughing, but failing dismally. "But I can think of one way to solve that!"

"How would you do that?" he asked, baffled at her laughter and comment.

"I shouldn't say this . . . please don't yell at me . . . but Boldwood—,"

"What about Boldwood?" he interrupted, trying not to sound jealous at the mention of the man.

"He's into that," she replied, finally managing a straight face.

"Into what exactly?" Dillon didn't have a clue what she was on about considering they'd been talking about using the bathroom, and now that she was laughing hysterically again, he was more concerned. "Stop laughing and tell me; what is he into?"

He suddenly felt protective; for some reason feeling that she needed protection from whatever Boldwood might be subjecting her.

"Water-sports," she said looking at him as though she was trying to read his reaction.

His face fell; he'd read about water-sports during his experimental phase back in London, but it was something that he'd never tried.

"You and he are obviously getting close then," he commented, resigning himself to the fact that if she knew this level of detail about Boldwood, it was likely they'd crossed the line into a sexual relationship.

She stopped laughing. "He sends me these text messages where he tells me things, and suggests things, but I don't reply. You have to believe me."

"It's none of my business what you do in your private life," he replied bluntly, trying to hide his disappointment.

"I swear nothing has happened and I'm not involved with him." There was a desperation in her denial.

"So you haven't done that?" Dillon didn't really want to know—the jealousy was welling up inside him – but his curiosity won over.

"I told you that we haven't done anything. Why won't you believe me? I don't want a relationship. I . . .," Catherine hesitated, as though unsure what to say. "I don't love Boldwood—nor will I ever fall for him—I'm not even attracted to him."

Even if she wasn't telling the truth, he was relieved to hear her words; it must have shown in his body language, because Catherine relaxed too.

"He says he wants me, but I don't know what to say to him because he just won't let it go, and anything I've said to put him off is almost like a further attraction. It doesn't even seem to be an ego thing where he wants to win me as a challenge, but instead it's like he seems to get turned on by me saying no," she explained.

Dillon didn't reply, and she quickly added, "I don't mean he'd attack me—you know the 'no' word being a turn-on—he'd never touch me without me saying yes; that's the rules he says. He's into chastity and that's why the whole no thing is arousing."

Unbeknownst to Dillon, she'd left out the bit about the chastity cage; that would have been too much of a betrayal in the trust Boldwood had put into her. "I haven't told anyone else about this, but I needed to talk to someone, and I trust you."

He could see she was being genuine, and now he did completely believe her when she said that she wasn't involved with Boldwood—at least not from her perspective. She needed protection, not only from the perverted CEO, but also from her own naivety.

"You need to find a way to be clear with him that you don't want what he is offering. The words you're using must be the wrong ones, so he needs to know that you aren't playing a waiting game with him that feeds his chastity fantasy. I don't want to be harsh, but you do have a tendency to not know how to do that. You . . .," he paused, knowing that he had to speak the hard truth. "You like the attention of a man, and I think you never really let go of that, which some might say results in leading on a man." He winced as he said it, and waited for the indignant outburst that he was expecting—but it didn't come.

"I will tell him. I will try to find the words," she said quietly, staring at the floor as she took onboard his reprimand.

He prayed that she'd be able to find the right words, for her own sake as well as for Boldwood. The situation couldn't continue, yet he suspected she would procrastinate for as long as she could, mostly out of fear of hurting someone, and that the outcome might affect her working environment.

They stayed silent for a few minutes—no sound coming from anywhere else; the building was eerily quiet. Catherine shivered and he draped his own scarf around her. She leaned against his shoulder and looked up into his face with a smile. Dillon felt an energy flow through his body—an instant reaction to her touch—and despite their intensely personal conversation about Boldwood; he was slightly embarrassed to find he was still capable of being easily aroused in her presence.

"Did you try it in London—water-sports I mean? You knew what I meant by it didn't you?" Catherine's question surprised him; she seemed curious, rather than asking through a judgmental accusation, and he was relieved, yet still wary as her mood could swing in a second.

"Yes I know what it is, but no, I didn't try it," he answered, glad that he was able to be honest; he would have hated to lie to her, but if he'd tried it, he would have been far too embarrassed to tell her that he had.

"It didn't appeal?" she asked; she appeared to have no reservations in prying into his sexual fantasies. He contemplated changing the topic, but was worried that if he did, she might think he had things to hide. Even though he wanted to attempt to keep it professional, he had an overwhelming need to answer anything that she ever asked. His heart and soul wanted her to know him intimately, with no secrets between them.

"Not in that sense. I'm not sure if several of the things that I did really appealed to me when I did them." As he said it, he realized that he hadn't explained himself well, resulting in the wrong impression. He was still confused about what he'd experienced in those weeks of experimentation.

"You didn't like being submissive?" Catherine was even more inquisitive, and there was a hint of disappointment, despite her rejection of Boldwood's inclination.

"No, in some respects I didn't." He still wasn't conveying what was really going on deep inside his mind.

"It didn't turn you on?" she asked with surprise. "I always thought being dominated aroused you." She gave him her sparkle-smile, her wickedness returning as she relieved the memories of all the times she'd given him a hard-on.

"Yes it did, if what you're asking is did I have an orgasm during all the scenes?" he paused when he saw jealousy and disappointment flare up on her face. "I'm a man and so it's quite an easy achievement, but it doesn't mean that it deeply turned me on, or gave me a true sense of satisfaction. Once the initial novelty wore off, I couldn't keep doing it. I realized that there were so many things that I was curious about trying, but I couldn't bring myself to try them with strangers."

He'd finally found the words to express his deepest thoughts.

"You were afraid people would find out if the strangers told?" Catherine's focus on people finding out made him wonder if this was something Boldwood may have mentioned.

"No, it wasn't that. They were all professionals and I was small pay dirt compared to their clients, unlike Boldwood probably would be. It was just that it was so intense and intimate. Things like watersports for instance—I couldn't let my mind get into the headspace to get the sexual arousal from it. I'd be constantly thinking all these questions like where's she been, or who else is doing this with her. You know—weird thoughts that were distracting and ended any arousal that I might have got from it. I do get why some guys could do it with strangers, because it's about humiliation, and there are some who want to be humiliated by women in general. Then there are some guys who idolize the one they love and want to be put in their place only by her, plus have a kinky sex life within their relationship. I guess I'm that type, because I admit I'm curious, but I wouldn't go to those dungeons ever again."

Dillon was shocked at how honest and open he'd just been with his boss, especially now that she was gazing deep into his eyes. He'd let slip the *l-word* in his confession and he feared that she was studying him for some indication that she might be the one he idolized.

Please don't ask me.

Dillon knew that he'd never be able to convincingly lie to her. He was desperate to break her stare before she could succeed in reading him, but if he lowered his eyes, she would know his thoughts. She also might follow his gaze down towards his groin where his erection was, for the moment, concealed by his adequate winter coat.

While there was no electricity in the building in the traditional sense, Catherine and Dillon had plenty of electricity between them, just as they'd had since the first day they met. The sexual tension was filling the small elevator by the second, and he was praying for all kinds of release; mostly wishing the elevator would release from its trapped position.

"Lay down," she said suddenly, not breaking her stare as she took command.

As though she'd hypnotized him with her demand, he didn't hesitate to succumb to her power—laying his body across the elevator floor and resting his head onto her knees. He re-established eye contact with her from his new lowered position.

What does she want me to do? What's going on in her mind?

The questions raced through his own head, remembering Liddy's words that even as her best friend she didn't know what went on in the depths of Catherine's mind. Dillon desperately wanted to be the one to find out—the sole one to unlock her secrets.

She continued to say nothing, not moving any part of her; the intensity of her stare burned through him, searing its mark deep onto his soul. Dillon raised his arm from his side and tentatively placed his hand on her thigh. He waited for a reprimand—like the one she'd given him at

Christmas lunch—but when she remained silent and still, he took it a step further, pushing up her coat and dress a little, just enough to enable him to slide his hand under the fabric and onto the silkiness of her stockings. She didn't speak, move or break eye contact; her stare was providing him the encouragement and silent permission to continue.

His hand slid further up her thigh, over the lace of her stocking top to reach her bare skin. Dillon's body was in an uncomfortable position—his left arm pinned under his weight and his right arm engaged in the activity. There was no way to adjust his position, or his heavy coat, to relieve the pressure on his trapped arm, or the tightness in his trousers. He didn't want to ruin the moment—as he'd once done before in London—and so he continued with the advance of his hand, choosing to ignore the pins and needles sensation in the other one.

As he reached the lace of her panties with his fingertips, excitement began to show in her eyes; they had that sparkle that he now knew well, and even though her mouth hadn't broken into a wicked smile, he suspected she was enjoying herself. The wetness of her arousal was seeping through the lace onto his fingers, and Dillon savored the moment, wishing he could taste her.

"Keep those fingers moving," she prompted when he'd hesitated for a little too long. He quickly obliged her command, obeying her wish by pushing aside the gusset of the garment and rubbing the smoothness of her skin. Although he had no view, Dillon had confirmation that the full-waxed character in the handwritten story was based on her; this was a female hygiene detail he remembered vividly.

Dillon was gentle with his touch, focusing one finger on finding her clitoris. She moved for the first time since he'd begun to touch her, a gentle rise of her body as he found the right spot, followed by a slight widening of her legs—well as much movement as she could with his weight on them. He responded to her by rising a little—the action allowing her to widen her legs more, and for him to release his left arm from under his body. Shifting his upper body further over her legs, he rested onto his left elbow and cradled his head in his hand for support. His new position allowed him greater movement of his right arm—essential if he was going to give her pleasure with the use of his hand.

"Don't stop," she assertively instructed, with a sense of impatience.

Dillon complied, resuming his rubbing of her clit with his finger for a few moments, before switching to use his thumb. As he established a rhythm, he slowly inserted a finger inside her. She let out an audible breath and he felt her body ever-so-slightly push down onto his finger, welcoming him in. He continued, maintaining his thumb and finger thrusts at an even pace, massaging the mound of nerves on the outside, as well as the most sensitive front wall of her vagina.

If there were eight-thousand nerve endings in a clitoris, and a fabled g-spot, he was determined to stimulate all of Catherine's eight-thousand-and-one most sensitive places in order to prove that he could bring her to the shuddering orgasm that he'd boasted that he could in his drunken email a few months before.

It was working; Catherine's body was responding more to him now—her pelvic muscles squeezing around his finger, and her hips pushing forward to meet the thrust of his hand. He added a second finger to penetrate inside her and the result of the extra width covering more of her sensitive front wall brought out a whimper in her. Wondering if he should push deeper, Dillon opted to go with variety; on every second thrust, his fingers sank deeper, while on the alternative he focused on the spot an inch inside. She gasped, and her flushed face involuntarily clenched—the alternation choice was clearly working.

Dillon was also seriously aroused—the front of his trousers increasingly getting damp from his own pre-cum. He wanted her to unzip him, and then grip him with her dainty hands, or even just stroke him with her long, manicured fingernails. He didn't dare assume that she might go further than that, however much he desperately wanted her to take him in her mouth, or let him sink his cock deep into her.

He shifted his body, hoping that would give her the chance to see his stained trousers under his coat. She immediately picked up the not-so-subtle hint—for the first time looking away from his eyes and down to his groin. Lifting up her left hand, she undid his lower coat button and pushed the coat open. The wet patch on the upper part of his left trouser leg was growing in size, pulled tightly over the bulge created from his cock tilting to one side.

Catherine didn't speak—quite possibly from being incapable of speech—for Dillon hadn't stopped with his rhythmic thrusting of his fingers and thumb. His digits were making the most of being in the place that he wished his cock could be; he'd never before wanted to be somewhere so much. There was a chance he might have an orgasm just from the pleasure he was giving her—it would be a first if he did—but he wasn't about to find out, for Catherine was in a generous mood.

Deftly managing to undo his belt, and then his zip, with one hand, she tried to push his trousers and boxers downwards. He lifted his hip and upper thighs slightly off the ground to assist her, but his cock was determined to stay hidden—its aroused state preventing his underwear from moving. Sliding her hand under the cotton, Dillon finally felt the softness of her fingers—contrasted with her sharp nails—touching the bare skin of his groin, and then his sensitive cock. She gripped hold of it and pulled it from the constraints of the garment. He let out a groan—unable to contain himself after the months of sexual tension between them—then tensed as he dreaded her punishment for his sound.

Dillon was lucky; she was too engrossed in her own ecstasy to silence him, or to let go of her hand on his cock. She tightened her grip and then matched the rhythm of the thrusts inside her. He was going faster now, keen to please her, and was getting more excited through his own sensory pleasure. He wanted to hold on as long as possible, but as soon as she started to shudder with the first waves of her orgasm, he finally let go.

The earth, quite literally, moved. As Dillon groaned and spurted his own release onto the elevator floor, and Catherine let out a moan of pleasure, their sexual electricity brought on the return of mains power. The lights flashed on and the elevator jolted into action, heading downwards. There was no time for post-orgasm recovery—they were both breathing heavily, and Dillon was naked from the waist to knees—but the elevator had only lost power on the fourth floor, which now meant they were seconds away from the door opening on them both, exposing them to anyone in the ground floor lobby.

Hurrying to their feet—still flustered from their exertions—Dillon turned to face the back of the elevator while he pulled up his trousers, hoping that his coat would protect his modesty if he weren't quick enough.

Catherine had spotted the visible evidence of his ejaculation. "Dillon, step on it," she said urgently; he followed her eyes and pointed finger downwards towards the floor, and managed to put his foot over the small white puddle just as the door to the elevator opened revealing two security guards looking in. He shuffled his foot, hoping his snow-boot would smudge and distort his bodily fluids into something less recognizable.

There was no possible way to wipe it up without attracting attention; they were going to have to walk out of the elevator calmly, and promptly, if they weren't going to create further suspicion, especially as the guards were already smirking. He knew she'd be mortified at the gossip that may result, especially as people were already linking her to Boldwood.

Catherine stepped out first and walked straight forward without engaging in conversation. After one final shuffle of his foot, Dillon followed, deciding not to look down to assess the effectiveness and possibly alert them to the floor. Catching up with her, he walked alongside in silence. This was the most awkward post-coital moment he'd ever experienced.

"Well that was timing," said Catherine as soon as they were out of earshot. Dillon wasn't sure whether she was referring to the elevator restart, the quickness of their moves to avoid embarrassment, or their concurrent orgasms—all of them were good timing.

"Yes" he replied, with a simple word of agreement to whatever she meant.

"If I'd had more time, I would've got you to clean up your mess, like they would have done in those dungeons!" She grinned wickedly as she imparted her belated threat.

Dillon shuddered; the elevator floor was filthy and it was already enough of a punishment to forcibly be made to clean up your own cum off a floor with your tongue.

He tried to think of a suitable response, but Catherine changed the topic quickly—her post-orgasm bonding wearing off.

"Let's not ruin this with over-analysis—I'll go home, and you'll go home. We will have a nice weekend, and then come to work Monday with no mention this ever happened. Okay?"

She was rejecting him yet again, and her words were like blades digging into his already deep scars. He didn't want to argue with her—arguments with Catherine came at too much of a cost.

"Have a good weekend. Get home safe." He managed to get the words out strongly, with no emotional cracking, and turned to walk as fast as he could towards the revolving doors, keen to get physical distance from her before she could spot his disappointment that she didn't want more to happen between them. Experiencing Catherine's intimate touch was like a drug, and now he was even more addicted to her.

Chapter Twenty-Four

Dillon's quick get-away was thwarted by the elevator technician—the far-too-cheerful young man blocking the exit. "Where exactly are you guys heading?" he asked, over-hearing Dillon's last words to Catherine to 'get home safe'.

"West Village," replied Dillon.

"I doubt it—not unless you have some serious wheels—because nothing is moving out there, and the trains are cancelled," said the technician.

"Well we can't stay here all night," protested Catherine.

Dillon looked out at the deep snow, already banked up a foot deep against the full-height lobby glass. With hindsight, he should have at least tried to convince Catherine to leave much earlier and work from home; her dedication to work might mean they were stuck here for the night—or perhaps even longer depending on the weather.

"How did you get here?" he enquired, noticing that the technician had only just walked through the doors.

"We have a snow-vehicle for emergencies, and I was dispatched over here to get you out, but I see the generators finally took over. I did think DeChartine had an impressive back-up system, so it surprised me when I got the text to the emergency number. It's only used when the power hasn't come back on for over a half-hour."

Dillon raised his eyebrows at Catherine. "Was that your text?"

"What's the point of an emergency number if you have to wait a half-hour to use it?" she said shrugging her shoulders. "Anyway, how do we get one of those snow-vehicles?" She gave the man her best flirtatious smile.

It appeared to be working; his cheeks blushed and he scratched the back of his neck while he pondered a response. "I shouldn't really offer, but now that you're out of the elevator, I can get to my next job quicker. It's out your way. It might be a tight squeeze, but—,"

"That's great, thanks," interrupted Catherine, already hurrying towards the doors and the relentless blizzard beyond them.

"I guess we're going with you then! Thanks mate, much appreciated," added Dillon, signaling for the technician to go in front of him.

The snow was belting down, and Dillon climbed into the front of the vehicle to squeeze alongside Catherine. There was really only room for two in the cabin, and he pressed tightly against her body to allow room for the technician. Keen for a distraction away from thoughts of her body next to his, he focused on small talk and providing directions to their Good Samaritan.

After only a few blocks, the dispatch radio crackled into life, and the technician picked up the responder; their ride was going to be cut short due to several people, including children, trapped in an elevator in the opposite direction to where they were headed. Instead, they would have to walk the final few blocks themselves to reach Catherine's place. Dillon thanked the technician for his help, slipping a twenty-dollar-bill into his hand in gratitude.

Once they were standing on the corner, Catherine's willful independence returned. "I'll be fine to get home from here. Your place is the other way and it's late." She started to step away from him, attempting to wade her legs through the deep snow.

"Listen you stubborn woman, if you think that I'm going to leave you to walk alone at this hour, let alone in this weather, you can think again," said Dillon forcefully; this was a non-negotiable command of his own. For all his submissiveness towards her, he was still a gentleman—and a practical, safety-conscious one at that.

"Fine," she replied indignantly. "Keep up then."

⌇

Dillon was sure that Catherine wouldn't have made it home alone; on more than one occasion during the hike back to her brownstone, she'd stumbled in the heavy snow. The storm was still gaining force.

We should have stayed back at DeChartine where there was back-up power.

Looking at Catherine now, he was worried about her; the forecasters had been right about the storm's severity, and it was taking its toll on her under-dressed body. Her face had icy crystals forming on the surface, blown onto her by the wind, and her lips were tinged blue. Her thin gloves were barely concealing the uncontrollable shiver in her hands, and he dreaded to think what her legs were like under the silk of her stockings.

Why doesn't the stupid bitch bring leggings to work on a day like today?

He was concerned that she didn't take more care of herself in a sensible, rather than aesthetic, way. By the time they reached her apartment, she wasn't even able to undo the clasp of her bag to retrieve her keys; her fingers too numb for the dexterity of action required.

Following her inside, he was relieved to see that she had an open fireplace in her small apartment; they both desperately needed warming up, and the power was still out. In the dim light that his mobile phone screen provided, he saw that the interior was homely and not at all modern like his own contemporary rental.

Spotting a candle and matches on the fire hearth, Dillon headed towards them to light up the room; the candlelight giving off a fragrant glow once lit. Before he set to making a fire, he wrapped Catherine in several blankets and seated her on the couch; her freezing body was only marginally warmer than the iciness he had felt when, as a curious boy, he'd sneaked a touch of his deceased grandfather in the open casket.

"Thank you," she whispered, her teeth still chattering.

Dillon returned to the fireplace, concentrating on bringing warmth to the small space. His breath was icy in the room, and he guessed the power had been out for several hours in this area.

Thank goodness she has a good supply of dry logs and kindling, even if she can't dress warmly.

Catherine was an enigma to Dillon, but his priority was on ensuring her safety, not on working out her bizarre contrasts. Once he lit the match and tossed it onto the kindling, it didn't take long for the light of the flames to start dancing around the small room; the warmth would soon follow. In the brighter light, he scanned the room and spotted the kitchenette.

"Do you have a kettle for the fire, or maybe even just a solid handled saucepan?" he asked.

"There's a cast-iron pot by the stove," she replied.

Retrieving the pot-for-one, he filled it with water. He intended to put his boy-scout skills to good use; boiling water on the fire would mean he could make them both a cup of tea to warm them from the inside. Taking up a seat alongside her on the couch, he waited for the water to boil. Not asking for permission, he draped his arm around her to help warm her with his own body heat, ignoring the voice in the back of his head that was reminding him of her earlier post-coital dismissal in the lobby.

To his surprise, she laid down, resting her head into his lap. He could feel her cold face on the top of his thigh—even through his thick suit trousers—and he gently stroked the icy cheek that faced upwards. They sat for a while in silence, and as the warmth returned to her body, Dillon's urges began to stir once more.

Not now . . .

Her head was in a crucial spot, and any arousal would be detected immediately; he wanted to be her savior—not a horny devil intent on sex.

Catherine, however, never missed an opportunity to play; she'd felt his stirrings and now began to rub her head ever so gently, almost innocently, against his groin. The proximity of her face, mouth and her mind to his most private, intimate area was intoxicating. Only hours before, she'd used her hands to great effect, but that was nothing compared to the torture of this.

She moved her head and, without a word, unzipped his trousers for the second time that night. Until this point, he hadn't yet been fully erect, but his twitching intensified as he burst out of the zip. Catherine lightly kissed the head of his cock, and the coldness of her frostbitten lips reminded him of the menthol in her original story. He couldn't stop himself from ever-so-slightly rising upwards, pushing his cock harder against her lip; a plea to coax her into opening her mouth wider to allow him to warm the inside of her with the burning heat of his engorged member.

Her lips parted, obliging his gesture, and she sank her head further down the shaft of his swollen, warm cock. Once she'd taken all of him deep into her mouth, she sucked her way back up and then removed her mouth, instead planting gentle kisses on his equally swollen blue balls. His genitals were recovering from the bitterly cold wind that had risen up from the sidewalk as they'd trudged through the snow, but now he could finally feel the return of sensation to the area; he groaned.

"Quiet," she snapped, finding her reprimanding voice that had eluded her earlier in the elevator.

He stilled; the memory of the story gagging scene as vivid in his head as if he'd only read it only for the first time a few moments ago. He wanted the story to come to life, but he didn't want her to stop and find a makeshift gag right now, especially considering it was dark and still cold in the room.

She resumed sucking his cock; up and down, she went, with her tongue swirling around the head making him twitch with pleasure. Dillon no longer felt the cold that had ravaged his own body; finally, warmth was taking over—not from the flames in the grate, but from the fire inside his soul and his body.

Despite his earlier release in the elevator, he knew he wouldn't last long. Faster, and faster she went, and Dillon could feel the tightness of an impending orgasm deep within him. Ignoring the risk of being gagged, he let out an even bigger groan as the waves of ecstasy ran through him. A final thrust upwards into her mouth, and he let go—shooting his load towards the back of her throat.

Catherine released him and looked up; her wicked sparkle-smile had returned, as had the pink color to her lips. Saying nothing, she rose up from her laying position and straddled over him. As much as he wanted to please her, he couldn't manage a second time so quickly—especially as it would make it a third in under two hours—and he silently hoped that she wouldn't lower herself onto his lap; his cock and balls were too sensitive after orgasm to take any weight.

To his relief, she stayed in the higher position with her eyes staring down into his. This was the kiss moment; he could see that same intensity that they'd shared on that Christmas afternoon in the snow. He'd wanted Catherine for five months now, and although they'd exchanged a thousand kisses through their eyes, now all he desperately wanted was to kiss her lips, taste her and explore her mouth with his tongue.

He reached up to run his hands through her hair and pulled her head downwards towards his own face, gently raising his lips to meet hers. When she didn't resist as they locked into the embrace, he gave into his desires and opened his mouth further, ready to meet her tongue.

It wasn't only Catherine's tongue that greeted him; the distinctive taste of his own cum over-powered every taste bud on his own tongue—Catherine hadn't swallowed and now she was dribbling his own juices into his mouth. The experiences in the dungeons of London came flooding back into his mind and he contemplated recoiling back from the taste. It was only a split-second thought; his desire for Catherine took over and he returned her kiss with full force and intensity, subduing his gag reflex. The more passionate they became, the greater the build-up of their bodily fluids inside their joined mouths. Catherine had embraced the continual snow-theme that seemed to be bonding them; managing to surpass the playful Christmas snowball thrown at him, with a far more wicked and kinky snowball during this blizzard.

❧

"You can stay," she announced suddenly, breaking the embrace of their lips. Dillon swallowed the fluids in his mouth, and she watched with amusement at his pained facial expression—no doubt fighting the urge to gag.

"I'd no intention of going out into this snow at this time of the night," he replied, when he'd regained his composure. He had a point, and while she wasn't sure what to do with him now—especially after two incidents that she shouldn't have allowed to happen—she didn't want to risk his safety by demanding that he leave.

"I only have the one bed, so do you think you can behave?" It was a stupid thing to say considering what they'd just done.

I don't even want him to behave . . .

"The couch will be fine, and it's warm here by the fire," replied Dillon, looking uncomfortable; she was still straddled over him and staring into his eyes.

Slightly disappointed that he'd accepted the couch so easily, she dismounted him, taking up the place on the couch alongside. He was right, it was warm this close to the fire, and her bed would be cold. Huddling under the blankets might have been bearable with Dillon's body heat beside her, but she'd ruined the chance of that with her teasing. There was no way she could seduce him now without giving off mixed-messages.

Turning her attention towards the fire, she watched the bubbles of the water in the cast-iron pot; the liquid was boiling and she suddenly had a craving for a good cup of English tea.

Keep calm, tea solves everything.

She laughed at the thought of quoting a tea-towel strap-line.

"What's funny about me sleeping on your couch?" he asked.

"Nothing at all, I was laughing at something else," she replied.

He's always so paranoid.

"If you must know, I was thinking about the stupid 'Keep Calm and Have a Cup of Tea' saying—the boiling water reminded me of it."

Dillon's face relaxed. "Oh shit yeah, sorry I'd forgotten about the water. I'll make the tea.

Before Catherine could say that it hadn't been a reprimand, he jumped up off the couch and headed for the kitchen in search of mugs, teabags and milk; she guessed he'd been glad of a suitable distraction.

"That would be nice . . . tea-boy," she teased; the way he'd diligently set out undertaking the task of getting her a good brew reminded her of the well-trained John Bradbury. It might be nice if she had someone to wait on her this attentively; even her PA rarely offered to get tea or coffee unless there was a meeting. Thinking about servitude, Catherine's mind wandered to Boldwood.

Would he make a cup of tea for me?

She tried to imaging him making a cup using the makeshift fire set up that Dillon was using, but failed to see him in that role—or even, for that matter, in a kitchen doing it the traditional way. Nothing about that man struck her as normal, and he was far from a good boy scout. All she could picture was a chastity cage, and she shivered from that thought.

Dillon raced to her side with the hot tea when he spotted her slight shake. "Are you still cold?" he asked with obvious concern.

"No, I was just—," she stopped herself; Dillon looked so keen to be helpful and caring that she didn't have the heart to mention Boldwood right now. "Just hungry," she added.

It was a quick save, but it was also the truth; her stomach was rumbling and it had been lunchtime when she'd last ate something.

"Do you have bread?" asked Dillon. "I could make toast using that iron fork by the fire."

Catherine smiled and nodded in response, strangely enjoying their little camping adventure in her small apartment.

For the next hour, the two of them sat contently watching the fire, drinking tea and eating the slightly burnt toast. Catherine leaned against him as they laid on the rug in front of the hearth, and her eyes started to close.

"Sorry about the toast," he said apologetically. She opened her eyes again, but didn't get up—nor turn to look back at him behind her.

"You did a good job with what you had." It wasn't the first time that she'd noticed that Dillon often found fault with his skills.

"Yeah, but I should have been more focused on watching it cook, rather than be distracted."

Catherine guessed there was more than just burnt toast on his mind; his self-reprimand was loaded with ghosts of past-doings.

"Dillon, I've been meaning to talk to you for a while about something. The DeChartine acquisition wasn't your fault at all. You need to accept that no one saw it coming, not even those here in New York."

After a few moments, he responded, more quietly spoken than before, "If I'd been focused, I would've seen it—that was my job to see it—and I failed." There was a steely determination in his words; anger at himself that he wasn't ready to let go of.

"No," she said, rolling over to face him. "You wouldn't have seen it. It might have been your job to do acquisitions, and notice things, but no one can notice something that was so well hidden that even the majority of DeChartine didn't know about it. There were external people involved at the highest level of politics, and it was a deal done for all kinds of reasons other than just business. I only know this because I was thinking like you are now and Emilia had to give me the same pep-talk that it wasn't my fault, and was in no way a reflection on my competence."

"I was still distracted though," he replied, not willing to let himself off the hook.

"Whips and chains will do that," she joked, unwilling to get further into the conversation about their relationship and the workplace. She rolled back towards the fire, and pulled a blanket over her. "Now get some sleep. Goodnight Boy-Scout."

"Goodnight Boss," he replied.

⸎

Catherine woke abruptly; the mechanical sound of grating by the snow-plough that was clearing the street outside, now that the heavy snow had stopped, ripped her from her pleasant dream of being curled up with a man wrapped around her. Only it wasn't a dream; the mechanical sounds mixed with the sounds of breaths from Dillon's sleeping body beside her. The fire had long reduced to ashes and, despite the warmth of the blanket and his body heat, she was cold; even with power restored, the central heating had yet to make an impact on the icy room.

She quietly got up to look out of the window at the whiteness that had enveloped the city; the pristine snow made it look much cleaner than the grimy reality of a major city. She turned to look back at the slumbering heap on her rug, and struggled to decide what to do about the events of the night before. Dillon had fulfilled his emailed promise to give her an orgasm to remember; the elevator foreplay had been memorable. Once he'd started to touch her with his rough hands and amazingly talented fingers, she hadn't been able to find the willpower to stop him—her mind blank to all of the what-ifs.

With all the drama of the past months, she'd relished a moment of pure, unadulterated pleasure; Dillon had been there at the right moment to give that to her. Now though, it was the awkward morning after, and this wasn't just a one-night-stand where there could be a good-bye and a never-see-each-other-again assurance. She did need to file it as a one-off though—two consenting adults that had released the sexual tension that had built between them. Dillon would surely agree that it was for the best; he was a competitive, hot-blooded, lustful alpha-male and would no doubt have experienced plenty of casual flings in his past with no regrets.

In her mind, she reasoned that now that he'd fulfilled his desire for her, the challenge was gone; he'd walk away happily with his ego intact. They had no chance of a proper dating relationship, and besides, Dillon had told her in his outburst that he dated normal women that weren't like her; a son of a happily married couple wouldn't want an emotionally stunted woman like herself; incapable of the warm love needed to sustain a relationship. All they ever did was have a rollercoaster of fights that involved them ripping the shit out of each other's personality flaws—that could never be a healthy relationship.

Dillon stirred and rolled over, smiling at her when he noticed her in the window light. Catherine was determined not to be a needy girlfriend, nor a bitch. She'd walked out of the elevator determined to show him that she wouldn't read anything into what they'd done, and while it would have been easier to keep to that if the weather hadn't had other ideas for them, she now needed to be strong. It was time to break the illusion; no dreamy breakfasts in bed or, in this case, on a rug by an extinguished fire—the ashes were a metaphor for their own passionate night.

"The snow has stopped. You can go home," she said abruptly. All hopes of her not being a bitch faded.

Dillon wiped the sleep from the corners of his eyes and stretched out his body to relieve the aches of sleeping on the hard floor, not comprehending her instruction.

"I'm meeting Liddy and I need to go shortly," she added, trying to find an excuse to get through this quickly; she reasoned that providing an escape plan of her own would avoid a prolonged debate. "Have a shower or whatever, and you can lock the door on your way out."

Before Dillon could say a word in response, she grabbed her handbag and coat and, still in the clothes of the day before, she headed out of the front door—there was no way she was sticking around with the temptation of him in her shower. Catherine was unsure what Liddy was doing on a snowy Saturday, or even if she'd be home, but right now even a café was more appealing that an awkward morning in her apartment with Dillon.

All she wanted was space and distance from the man that was confusing the hell out of her; questioning everything that she wanted for herself.

Chapter Twenty-Five

The first few days of the week passed without comment from Dillon or Catherine on their encounter—either their pact not to speak of it was sealed in concrete, or Dillon was just avoiding her. He'd barely spoken to her at all since she'd rushed out of her apartment the previous Saturday, and Catherine felt guilty that she'd handled things so callously.

It was a tough time of the year to keep emotions in check; the lead up to Valentine's Day that coming Thursday had romance infiltrating everyday activity. Even the local coffee shop baristas were asking men if they'd remembered to get their partners a gift, before trying to upsell them a branded coffee and chocolates basket.

Catherine was taking some of Dillon's words to heart; his advice about Boldwood—and setting him straight was welcome—especially as the man's attentions had increased in intensity and number. Since Christmas, Boldwood had been constantly enquiring as to whether the shoes she was wearing were purchased using his voucher and, when she continually told him that they weren't, he decided to move onto replacing the voucher with actual gifts. So far, that week, he had called onto their floor each morning to ascertain her attire for the day and then, by lunchtime, a pair of designer heels perfectly matching her dress or suit was delivered.

By mid-afternoon coffee each day, he'd made his second visit to her office to see if she was wearing them. On Monday and Tuesday, she didn't change into the gifted footwear, hoping to discourage him, but it only served to increase his focus. By Wednesday, when a matching handbag arrived too, it was time to put her last-ditch plan into action.

⁓

Boldwood knocked on her closed office door.

"Come in," she shouted and deliberately sank deeper into her chair to reduce her dominating presence. She'd planned this meeting, and today's delivery had only given her strength, even if it was the most gorgeous Jimmy Choo handbag and matching heels that she'd ever seen—the color complementing her suit perfectly.

Boldwood entered, and his look of surprise told her that she was on the right track. She was no longer wearing her suit, nor the shoes he'd sent her. In fact, she'd swapped her attire for a shapeless, inexpensive and badly manufactured dress that she'd found on a sale rack the night before in a shop that she'd never normally set foot in at her age. On her feet were bland, black ballet-pumps, her face was stripped of all but the barest of make-up, and her hair was in a messy ponytail.

"Hello Bill," she said in the plainest manner she could manage.

"Hello Catherine, are you okay?" He hadn't used anything but her first name, and she was pleased. They were alone, and normally that had meant the use of a title such as Mistress, Miss Catherine or something else. Even in company, he tended to use Miss Everdene, and he'd never called her Catherine before that she could recall.

"Yes I'm fine Bill, why do you ask?" She acted as though nothing was unusual about her appearance, even if she felt uncomfortable in the drab clothes. Her changed appearance this afternoon was solely for Boldwood's benefit—or rather, to his dis-benefit.

"You've changed you clothes. Was there something wrong with them? This dress doesn't suit you, and it doesn't match the shoes or bag I sent." He was flustered; Catherine was creating havoc with the way things should be.

"No, I just like this outfit and wanted to be more comfortable today. It's more what I'd normally wear back home, and I wanted to get back to feeling English again," she said casually. While she felt a little guilty for lying to him, if her plan worked, it would be worth a little white lie.

Sadly, her intentions didn't have the desired effect, for once Boldwood got over his initial shock, he returned to his infatuation of her—in whatever guise she chose to wear.

"I understand Mistress. I thought perhaps you were displeased with the gifts I sent you but, as ever, it is entirely your decision what to wear."

Shit.

She realized that the depth of his infatuation went well beyond her appearance; she was going to have to find the right words—just as Dillon had told her that she would; she hated it when he was right.

"Bill, this needs to stop—the gifts, the servitude, and your obsession with me. I'm not the person you think I am," she said, trying to be sympathetic and caring, remembering Dillon's advice that a stern tone would have the opposite effect to what she needed to convey.

"I have displeased you. How can I make it up to you?" he asked, keeping his head lowered.

"Damn it," she shouted in exasperation; Boldwood flinched, then dropped to his knees, head lowered so that his chin touched his chest.

Double shit, get up off the fucking floor.

She waited a moment before speaking again in a more sensitive way.

"Bill, I never asked to be your Mistress. The card was a practical joke—a badly thought out joke—but that's the kind of person I am. I don't think, and you need someone that isn't going to make that kind of mistake. You need someone that will have your interests and welfare foremost in their mind, and that's not me."

Catherine had done her research; fascinated about the mind of the submissive male since Dillon's disclosure, and Boldwood's advances, she'd studied up on domination and submission on the internet. The only way to break Boldwood's delusion would be for him to accept that she didn't want him to change his need to be submissive, but that equally she couldn't become the dominant he'd need her to be; he needed to understand that they weren't the right fit.

"I think you could. You could learn and we could be happy," he replied desperately; he'd come the closest that he ever had to finding the perfect person to relieve his loneliness, and he didn't want to let her get away.

"I don't want to learn Bill," she persisted. "I want to be me and I can't do those things to you that you would want me to." Catherine put as much sincerity as she could muster into what she was saying.

It wasn't the whole truth; reading the online information, she could imagine herself as a Domme, but it was true that she couldn't do the things to Boldwood that he wanted. Being a Domme wasn't the wrong role for her, but Boldwood wasn't the right submissive; when she met the right person, it would be different.

Dillon.

She quickly dismissed the idea that maybe she'd already met the right one.

"I think I understand, but please will you think about it some more, and think about everything—I would give you everything I have—it would be yours—the money, the houses, me. You would never want for anything and you would never have to do anything if you didn't want to. Even—," he hesitated, not sure if he really wanted to say the next bit.

"Bill, I—," she tried to interrupt his pleas.

"Even sex," he said cutting her off to finish his own sentence. "You wouldn't have to have sex with me if that was what's holding you back."

Catherine was shocked; nothing made sense to her.

He can't be serious? What man is willing to give up sex, yet give me everything else and let the whole world see that?

"You can't really be willing to give up on a fulfilling sex life for me?" she replied with bewilderment.

"I would—because I would get a sense of belonging that I yearn for, by belonging to a beautiful, sensual woman such as yourself, and I would be at your servitude. If you didn't want me to be the one to pleasure you sexually, I would let you find a way to achieve that—even if that meant cuckolding me. It would be my honor to be yours." Boldwood was looking at her pleadingly, yet with serious conviction in what he was saying.

What the hell can I say to this guy to put him off?

Catherine was getting desperate herself; with no intention of ever accepting his proposal, she needed time to work out how to deal with this additional revelation and incorporate it tactfully into her refusal. He was never going to give up easily and she'd run out of options in how to convince him how wrong she was for him. The last thing she wanted was for him to think she was rejecting him because she was judging his sexual persuasion.

"Okay Bill, give me some time to think, but you must believe me when I say my answer is unlikely to change."

Boldwood nearly burst into tears with happiness; his obsession with her taking over. "Thank you Miss Everdene. I eagerly await your response."

"You can go now," she said sternly, knowing that he would obey immediately and leave her alone if she did. He complied with her request, leaving the room with a skip to his step.

⁓

Four hours later, and Catherine was still staring at her computer screen blankly. She hadn't come out of her office all afternoon, not wanting anyone to see her disheveled state in the outfit that she loathed, and yet she hadn't found the motivation to change back into her suit; Boldwood's continued advances had her questioning her whole persona. Only when she was sure that everyone would have left for the day, did she finally find the courage to venture out of her office.

The lobby was deserted—the new receptionist having long gone home. Catherine walked towards the counter, noticing the display screen still on.

Hello people, save the planet and the company's money please.

Reaching over to press the off-switch, she snagged her dress on the edge of the desk. The vile garment had several loose threads and one had caught on the rough laminate, threatening now to pull apart the hem.

Bending over the desk—rather inelegantly—she fiddled to release the cotton strand; the only thing on show to anyone who might venture into the lobby was her shapely bottom, albeit blurred by the shapeless cut of the sack she was wearing. It was an unfortunate position to be in, for she sensed a person had approached behind her.

Please let it be a cleaner, or else at least only Dillon working late.

Before she could extricate the hem, she felt a hand run over her butt cheek.

"Mm, what I could do with that ass," murmured an unknown American male.

Definitely not Dillon, and probably not a cleaner. Fuck!

She stood bolt upright, not caring if the awful dress ripped further; she didn't know the voice, and certainly didn't recognize the shape of the hand assaulting her butt-cheek.

"What the hell? Get your hand off me," she yelled, turning to face the stranger.

He stepped back, holding up his arms in mock surrender, his face showing astonishment at seeing Catherine in front of him; she guessed he'd been expecting someone else.

"Following the lady's request, I surrender," he replied with his suave New York accent.

"Just as damn well. Now who are you and what are you doing here?" she demanded.

Catherine had definitely never seen him before, and dressed in the expensive suit he was wearing, he wasn't a cleaner or security; there was no reason for him to be on their floor after hours.

"Troy Selgent," he replied, holding out his hand for her to shake it. "I'm a lawyer for the company and have worked here before."

"You're not a company lawyer," she said suspiciously; she'd met all of the DeChartine lawyers and they hadn't made any new hires recently.

"Yes I am, but we haven't had the pleasure of meeting. I've been at another client for a while. You're a temporary receptionist here? He was looking her up and down, seemingly pleased with what he saw—Catherine blissfully unaware that he was bored and looking for a new submissive playmate.

"No I'm definitely not a receptionist—temporary or otherwise—just as you're definitely not one of our lawyers, and we don't bring in outside help. I'm Catherine Everdene, CEO of the company."

She was pissed at the audacity of his suggestion that she was a receptionist, even if it was an understandable mistake given her position by the counter and her less than commanding appearance.

"My mistake," he replied jovially, once more looking over her, but this time taking more time to study the dress and shoes.

Under the continued scrutiny of his sexy grey eyes, she felt the need to justify her appearance; she wasn't dressed in a manner that anyone knowing her by reputation would expect her to be. "My suit and shoes were damaged earlier in a coffee incident, and I had to borrow some in haste to get me home," she falsely explained, hoping he'd believe her.

I'd fire any employee that turned up wearing this sack-of-shit dress, but as he doesn't seem to have a clue of who I am, he won't know that.

The man in front of her changed his tune; she saw an increase in his stature and a wicked look in his eye. She knew that look—one she'd perfected to use when seducing a worthy opponent.

"I see. Although now I think that I should get to meet you when you are yourself, as I think you'd be a stunner," he remarked, his smile widening to reveal a perfect set of veneered teeth.

He was all-American college boy charm—not unlike the lawyer that she'd met in the Hamptons—but he had something else; a sexy allure that she was struggling not to be aroused by. The longer he stood there staring at her, the more embarrassed she was by her appearance.

"You need to go, Mr. . . .?" She couldn't remember his name, or even if he'd said what it was.

"Troy Selgent, but you, *my lady*, can call me Troy—or *anything* you like for that matter." He handed her a business card and smiled, a salacious grin as he emphasized the 'British lady reference' and 'call me anything' parts.

"Well, Mr. Selgent, thank you for this, I will file it under legal contacts never to use. Now, if you don't mind, it is time for you to leave as we're locking up the office."

"You're leaving too? Can I take you for a drink? Perhaps via your place so you can change into something that you haven't borrowed?" Troy had a cheeky forwardness, threading his invitation to a drink with playful sarcasm.

"No thank you, I will be leaving later, but I can get security to accompany you out if you need help finding your way?" she asked with a slight hint of a threat; his assertiveness made her a little uneasy and she was alone in the office with a strange, over-flirtatious man late at night.

"I can take a hint, but I will be seeing you again soon Cat Everdene," he said with a wink, and before she could step away, he leaned forward and kissed her cheek.

Startled, Catherine slapped his cheek hard in response. "It's Catherine, not Cat, and you need to go," she yelled, fuming at his insolent boldness.

"Feisty lady—such an unexpected turn-on—well *Catherine Everdene*, it's been an experience." Troy waved a hand in an over-animated farewell, before departing into the elevator.

She watched him leave, staying in the same spot to watch the electronic display confirm that he'd descended all the way to the ground floor. While her intuition told her that she shouldn't trust Troy Selgent, he'd certainly stirred up something else in Catherine, irritating the hell out of her in the process.

Chapter Twenty-Six

Troy Selgent was in a good mood despite not succeeding in his original intention; he'd started his day with the hope of finding Faye. After not hearing from her for months, he was craving some scenes with his favorite submissive. In truth, he hadn't thought of her before today as he'd been too busy with his latest two conquests; a politician's daughter and another petite blonde who was remarkably similar to Faye.

He'd initially been optimistic that something serious might have arisen from dating the politician's daughter—she was definitely marriage material—however, unfortunately for him, the relationship had ended when her Daddy had found out. Troy was not heart-broken; her allure only ever linked to her social standing—he'd only benefit if he were an approved partner.

The other girl met the criteria for his more secular tastes—petite, anal-virgins willing to be submissive. She'd entertained him for a while, but he'd begun to bore of her needy texts and far too many hard-limits.

It was Troy's need for an open-minded and willing submissive that led him to look for Faye again. However, instead of finding her, he'd come across a far more interesting proposition—Catherine Everdene. At first, he had the thought that she'd be the perfect woman to pursue for more traditional dating—a way to raise his social standing and have a beautiful, intelligent, powerful woman at his side, especially considering the DeChartine political connections. Then, as his mind went back over their encounter—her assertiveness and her lack of succumbing to his obvious charm—his ego kicked in; Catherine would be the ultimate challenge. Troy wanted to not only win her affections, but also sexually dominate her.

Troy didn't doubt for a second that he'd succeed—his confidence rarely failed him when women were concerned. Since he'd arrived home at his over-priced apartment that night, he'd read everything he could on Catherine Everdene—the internet providing a wealth of information on her career. As he surfed, he finally found the goldmine in the images search—she'd been linked personally to Bill Boldwood, with rumors circling of a secret relationship.

Although DeChartine had managed to keep Boldwood's secret safe from media exposure, they hadn't been able to protect his proclivities from Troy.

He'd met Boldwood through Faye, and when the older man had told him to leave her alone, he at first suspected that Boldwood fancied her for himself. Never one to back down, Troy had stood up to him in that conversation, and in doing so, he hadn't seen a dominant man fighting over a submissive, instead he'd witnessed an empathy and concern for Faye.

Once he had the suspicion, Troy's eagle eyes had scanned Boldwood whenever he saw him take a seat; chastity devices required some adjustment of trouser fabric to conceal their shape whenever a man sat down, and it didn't take long for Troy to recognize the action. If Catherine was in a relationship with Boldwood, it was highly possible that she was into domination, especially if she always behaved in the way she had earlier that night. Troy didn't want a Domme, but he relished the challenge in trying to switch one.

He spent the night formulating his strategy to win her favor; it would take the old-fashioned approach of romantic seduction under the cover of Valentine's Day. Boldwood might have money and power, but his age went against him and, according to the internet, they hadn't yet openly gone public with the relationship. Troy would win Catherine before that announcement ever happened.

By the next morning—Valentine's Day—his plan had begun. He handed a small box and message card over to the florist, and chose a dozen red roses to accompany his gift.

⁕

Catherine had been dreading the arrival of Valentine's Day all week.
Please God, don't let Boldwood send grand gifts.

The thought had crossed her mind to send something to Dillon—at the very least a card after what had happened the week before—but then she reminded herself of all the trouble cards seemed to cause, and dropped the idea. Arriving early to her desk, she concentrated on getting ready for the team meeting.

"You have a delivery Catherine."

Her heart sank at the now familiar announcement by Mary-Anne, and she looked up to stare at the huge bouquet.

When will he just quit it!

Setting the vase down, Mary-Anne handed her the small white box, wrapped in a red ribbon to match the flowers.

"Thank you Mary-Anne, you can go—oh, and Happy Valentine's Day"; Catherine wanted privacy before she opened the box—she never knew what to expect from Boldwood.

Once she was alone, she pulled at the ribbon end, and the bow slid undone. Lifting the lid, she looked inside—expecting lingerie, or an erotic toy. Never in her wildest imagination did she expect stain remover.

It was the most unusual gift—the small bottle indicating its usage on coffee and tea stains. She was baffled.

When did I spill coffee in front of Boldwood? What the hell is he thinking now? Am I supposed to pour coffee on him for a kinky thrill?

Her mind went back over all her recent interactions with her colleague, and she scanned the label to check that its usage didn't also cover other, more questionable, stains that might arise from watersports. She took the bottle out, and spotted a handwritten note underneath; it wasn't Boldwood's handwriting.

> 'This is so you never have to wear that hideous dress again—a beautiful woman like you should wear clothes that show off your figure. Instructions: (1) spill coffee again; (2) sprinkle this on stain, and then rub under water; (3) dry; (4) put nicer clothes back on. There, no need to send clothes to outside help, no loss of nicer dress, no need to borrow someone else's sack and pass it off as an actual clothing garment someone might wear.'

Catherine turned the card over—Troy had penned the note on the back of another of his business cards. She couldn't help but laugh at his sense of humor—his words flattering and amusing her.

She sat daydreaming about him, with her chair facing the window, and was oblivious to the arrival of Dillon when he came to ascertain why she was late for the team meeting.

"More flowers from Boldwood?" he asked, interrupting her dreams of Troy's smile and the thrill it gave her to slap his face.

Catherine swiveled to face him and Dillon detected a giddy guilt, almost as if he'd just walked in on a child hiding a stolen cupcake. "Actually no, these aren't from Boldwood," she replied happily.

"You dealt with him?" he replied, trying to hide the jealousy that was now returning with force. He banished thoughts about who her newest admirer might be, or the hurt he still felt over her abandonment of him the previous Saturday; he'd sat waiting in her apartment for nearly two hours for her to return, even jerking off in her shower to the scent of her rosy perfume, before giving up and going home.

"I tried, but I don't want to talk about that now," she said dreamily, still staring happily at her flowers.

"New guy?" Dillon hoped she wouldn't confirm his worst fears.

"It's just flowers—everyone's going to have them today. We women get flowers for Valentine's Day, and you men spend your money on them." She was definitely in a good mood, and he hadn't seen her act with such girly happiness at a romantic gesture before—not that he'd found the courage, or time, to do anything romantic for her before today.

"Well enough of the romance and flowers, because it's team meeting time *Boss*," he joked, making one final attempt to get her undivided attention with his emphasized, flirtatious 'boss' comment, but she failed to take the bait.

"Okay, I'll be there shortly. You can head off without me."

Disappointed, he quickly headed out of the room, and as he did so, he concealed a small box into his suit pocket. In Catherine's ecstatic state, she'd failed to spot that he'd come into the office with a telltale aqua-blue box with white ribbon; Dillon had brought her a Valentine's Day gift. He'd avoided the more obvious heart shape, instead selecting a necklace from the Tiffany Christmas range—an exquisite snowflake that would remind her of childhood memories, their recent Christmas and even the snowstorm the week before.

Once again, he felt only rejection; his gesture would go unappreciated and his love for Catherine unrequited.

⌇

The team meeting progressed quickly; everyone was in high spirits due to Catherine's good mood and the love infiltrating the building; Dillon the only quiet, reserved person at the table. After the meeting ended, Catherine headed out of the boardroom with a smile on her face, engrossed in reading an email that had come through on her tablet.

> 'Spilled any coffee this morning? Did the flowers startle you into coffee spillage? I hope the stain remover worked and you've not been forced to strip!!!'

Troy was definitely a charmer, and she couldn't resist the chance to flirt back in response.

> 'I get flowers regularly, but spill coffee rarely.'

She waited with anticipation to see if he'd respond—the comment about regular flowers designed to goad him into jealousy. Not that she'd lied—Boldwood frequently sent flowers and she'd made up the coffee spillage excuse.

> 'Yes, I see you do—there are flowers everywhere and I can't see a spot of coffee on that black suit—but then again it's black, so it's hard to tell.'

Catherine looked up from her phone after reading the message; the words suggested he was here, otherwise he couldn't have known about the presence of several bouquets of flowers dotting nearly every female's desk—nor the color of her suit.

Sure enough, the far too gorgeously tempting Troy was leaning against the reception counter, a beaming smile on his face. He seemed almost surreal—the flashy veneers only adding to his falseness—but the latest receptionist was gazing up at him with doe eyes, even though she already had a dozen pink roses on her desk.

He's like the wolf in Grandma's bed, and something tells me I'm Little Red Riding Hood.

Troy Selgent was definitely a ladies man, yet that only added to Catherine's magnetism to him; the challenge to tame him was far too tempting.

"Don't you work?" she asked sarcastically, secretly flattered that he'd dropped by; any thought of potential gossip from those coming out of the boardroom behind her was far from her mind.

"I do. Taking the most stunning female CEO in New York to lunch is very hard work, and I begged my firm not to send me, but you're quite the prize client and they commanded me to step up to the challenge."

DeChartine didn't need a legal firm—both of them knew it—however his words were a well-calculated personal, and professional, compliment to her. It was highly unlikely he was here at the request, or even knowledge, of the firm he worked for, yet his confidence impressed her, and she was oddly aroused at his mention of begging, and submitting to commands.

"Well, I'd hate to get you into trouble with your firm, especially as I prefer to hand out punishments to *bad* boys," she purred, giving him her flirtatious, wicked sparkle-smile, not caring who might have overheard her inappropriate comment.

"Oh I expect I could be bad, and I expect I'm *bound* to find myself in trouble during our lunch—excuse the bound pun," he replied, winking back. He was laying the charm and innuendo on thick and fast now, knowing that to have a chance with her; he was going to have to play her game for a while. "Shall we?" he said, holding out his arm, ready to escort her into the elevator.

"I'll get my coat Mr. Selgent," she replied, kicking herself that she'd agreed so easily—giving into the charms of a man wasn't something she liked to do, but she'd found herself unable to say no.

Troy remained in the lobby and, when Catherine was out of earshot, he spoke to the doe-eyed receptionist. "What happened to Faye Robine?" he asked, keeping up his smiley charms.

"She left—quit, fired—I'm not sure." The girl didn't really care about her predecessor, other than whoever she was, she'd given her a reason to speak to the charming, gorgeous, smoky-grey-eyed man in front of her.

"That's a shame. If she ever returns, could you give her my business card? It has all my details on it, including my mobile. You could call me some time and let me know if you hear about Faye, or maybe just a call to ask about anything. I'm a good listener," he schmoozed, flashing his toothy, over-shiny smile again.

It never occurred to the girl to tear up the card, despite the fact that he'd just invited Catherine out in front of her, and asked about Faye; also her boyfriend, who sent her the pink flowers, was momentarily forgotten.

Before the receptionist had the chance to give him her own number, the elevator opened and Boldwood stepped out holding a bouquet of white roses. He froze when he saw Troy, an angry expression sweeping over his face.

"What the fuck are you doing here? You leave our receptionists alone," he yelled with nothing but rage in his voice. Boldwood rarely swore, and the receptionist's doe eyes switched to a look of fear, particularly with the strong expletive and the warning about receptionists.

"Hello Boldwood," said Troy nervously. His smile had faded, not out of fear of Boldwood, but out of concern that he might say something to Catherine when she returned from getting her coat.

At that moment, Dillon exited the boardroom. He took in the scene—one scared receptionist, one shady-looking newcomer and Boldwood holding a bouquet, visibly shaking with contained rage. It was more drama that he'd ever seen in the lobby, or even when he'd unwillingly watched British television soap opera Christmas specials with his family. Only the receptionist was an employee of the company he worked for, and therefore he felt a responsibility—as a senior executive—to identify what was going on for her sake.

"Is there a problem?" he asked, looking at them all in turn, and then finishing his tour at the face of the receptionist.

"Um . . . well . . .," the poor girl was struggling with what to say. "Mr. Selgent came to take Miss Everdene to lunch and he's waiting for her here in the lobby. Mr. Boldwood just arrived and um . . .," she was looking at Boldwood as though unsure what to reveal about the senior man's outburst.

Dillon frantically tried to remember where he'd heard the name Selgent, his mind blurred by hearing that—whoever he was—he was here to take Catherine out to lunch. He wasn't aware that she was due to meet a client or business associate—typically that would have been mentioned in the team meeting—yet he didn't recall that being where he'd heard the name before. He wondered if the mystery man was the sender of the flowers, and perhaps Boldwood's anger related to his jealousy.

"Bill is everything alright?" he asked, hoping to ascertain what the receptionist had been unable to articulate.

"No, it's not fucking alright," hissed Boldwood, spit escaping from his lips.

Dillon had never seen the man in a rage, nor heard him swear before—he was normally docile and well mannered.

"This is Troy Selgent—you know the one who did a number on Faye. He's here again chatting up our receptionists and—," Boldwood suddenly stopped, realizing what the receptionist had said to Dillon. He turned towards Troy. "You're taking Miss Everdene to lunch?" he asked, disbelief and anguish replacing the anger in his voice; his face showed the disappointment of a crestfallen man.

"I am," replied Troy smiling cockily from knowing that he would win this battle.

In this state, Boldwood was no longer a risk—he could fob off anything that the old man tried to tell Catherine. However, he didn't know anything about the new man that had come into the lobby, who spoke with a British accent like Catherine. Neither Boldwood, nor the receptionist, had addressed him by his name, and Boldwood's comments suggested that the British man knew about Faye, and therefore Boldwood's version of Troy as a person.

"We haven't met, I'm Troy Selgent," he said, holding out his hand to the man who was playing hero. "I used to date Faye Robine who worked here. Unfortunately, it didn't work out. She just vanished after saying she'd found someone else. That's women, hey! I didn't catch your name." Troy continued to hold out his hand to shake, hoping that his false excuse to explain Faye had worked.

"I hadn't said it, that's why. I'm Dillon Oak, the Vice President of Commercial," Dillon replied, not extending his hand to accept the shake. He might have been more courteous had Troy not lied about Faye, but now all he wanted to do was protect Catherine; his polite British reserve going out the window in favor of protective alpha-male in a cock-swinging contest. "I did have the opportunity to briefly meet Miss Robine and, at the time, she seemed quite keen to contact you, but as you say—women." His last words were sarcastic, laying down the gauntlet for a male challenge.

Troy didn't have the chance to accept; Catherine had returned to the lobby. The infectious smile she'd been wearing all day disappeared when she caught sight of all three men in the lobby, and the flowers in Boldwood's hand. She read each of their faces—arrogance in Troy, disappointment in Boldwood and stoicism, mixed with jealousy, in Dillon.

"Well quite the lobby party," she joked, trying to break the atmosphere with humor.

None of the men spoke in response—all three not wanting to be the first one to upset her.

Troy eventually broke the stalemate.

"Shall we go Cat?" he asked, holding out his arm for her to take.

Catherine held back on reprimanding him once again on the incorrect use of her name; although she hated it, in front of Boldwood and Dillon wasn't the place—she didn't want to give them further ammunition for the likely protests about her dating someone else that would come from them both later that day. She stepped towards the elevator, but didn't go so far as to take Troy's arm—not wanting to add further insult to injury. She was acutely aware that Boldwood would take it badly, and although Dillon appeared indifferent, she suspected his male ego wouldn't take kindly to her dating another—especially so quickly after their snowstorm indiscretions.

"We can only have a very quick lunch . . . to talk business," she said loudly, hoping that would take the sting out of the situation, but as she waited for the elevator to open, Boldwood grabbed her arm.

"Catherine, please don't go with him. He's bad news and definitely no good for you," he pleaded. There was desperation in his voice, but she could also hear the genuine concern for her welfare. Somewhere, deep inside her, her intuition agreed with him, but her stubbornness about not letting people tell her what to do overrode his plea.

"Bill, please let go of my arm. This is only a business lunch and when I return, we can speak then," she said softly, gently releasing her arm from his grasp. "Dillon . . .," she turned to face her friend. "Could you take Bill to lunch please?" There was a pleading look in her eyes; she hoped that he'd be able to handle the crisis.

"I will," he answered, without any sign of emotion; now wasn't the time for openly criticizing her choices with the receptionist watching.

Boldwood walked away from her. As he passed Troy, the arrogant new-comer leaned forwards, and with a whisper only audible to Boldwood, he dealt a final blow, "White roses are a sign of humility—rather apt choice of yours, don't you think?"

Flaring up at the taunt, Boldwood raised his arm holding the flow-ers—ready to bring them crashing down onto Troy. Dillon hadn't heard what Troy had said, but he did read his triumphant expression; he lunged forward to pull Boldwood back and spare the CEO from a scene, and Catherine from further controversy. "He's not worth it Bill, let them go."

Catherine watched the scene unfurl from the elevator, torn between stepping out of it and calling time on the lunch, or instructing Troy to hurry up. However Troy quickly joined her just as the doors began to close and the pair travelled down in silence.

When they reached the ground floor, he pulled her to one side of the lobby. "You're a strong, intelligent woman who works hard, and you need a man that can make life outside of work fun—an escape from the day to day. I'm that man, but I don't want to complicate matters for you. I understand if what happened upstairs just now has you questioning that, and if you'd rather cancel the lunch I had all planned—then you can say so."

There was sincerity in his statement, yet his intentions were far from honorable; he suspected Catherine would always want to stand her ground, and he was betting that she'd let him take her to lunch, if only to show that she wouldn't give into the wishes of the men upstairs.

"Are you questioning taking me out?" she demanded; Troy had been right about how she would react—Catherine was on the defense.

"Of course not, I'm giving you the choice. If you want to make the choice to have lunch with me—knowing that others would prefer to make your choices for you—then we shall have lunch," he replied, deliberately choosing words to use her willful nature to his advantage.

"Well Mr. Selgent, I suggest you take me to this grand planned lunch," she said assertively, challenging him to live up to what he had promised.

Troy smiled, took her hand and led her out of the lobby.

❦

Dillon had spent the best part of an hour calming Boldwood down and in that hour, he'd learned more about Troy. In Boldwood's distressed state, he'd been less discreet about his own personal life as he revealed more about Troy's activities—inadvertently divulging details about his own forays into the BDSM underground scene. Dillon wasn't judgmental—he could hardly be when he'd visited dungeons himself—but he didn't share his own history with Boldwood.

He was shocked and saddened though when he discovered Faye was now working as a professional submissive, selling her body for use in all manner of ways as one of the agency's no-limits girls. Dillon felt sorry for her; while he'd paid for the services of professionals, they'd willingly chosen to become a Dominatrix, but there was more scope for exploitation of professional submissives, especially if full-sex was on offer. Although he'd only briefly met Faye, he'd noticed she seemed desperate, and therefore vulnerable.

Faye and Catherine were worlds apart, yet underneath Catherine's strong personality, she liked attention and was naïve in her stubborn actions—often leading her to make bad choices. While he doubted she would give in to Troy's attentions as easily as Faye had done—nor suffer the same fate as her due to their different financial and educational circumstances—he knew that she was heading for a broken heart with Troy if she let him get close. It was going to be a difficult talk, but he was the only one who could save her from a lot of hurt and pain; she would dismiss Boldwood's desperate pleas.

'She has returned.'

The internal electronic message from Mary-Anne popped up on his computer screen; two hours had passed since Catherine had left for lunch, and he'd requested her PA to alert him to her return; he wanted to talk to her, and check she'd arrived back safely.

Dillon took less than a minute to be at her office door.

"Catherine," he said, announcing his arrival. She was staring at the flowers, and a bottle of coffee stain remover that sat alongside them; she didn't bother to look up as he came in, or when he shut the door.

"I was wondering how long it would take you to turn up when I got back," she said, her reply lacking friendly warmth; they both knew a fight was inevitable. "How is Boldwood?"

There was compassion in her question, and for all of Catherine's icy bitch stubbornness, underneath she did care about people.

"He's worried about you, and so am I. What you need to understand is that this isn't about your refusal of Boldwood, nor is this about you and me. This is solely about Troy and that he's the wrong man for you," he explained; he needed her to understand that Troy was bad news and somehow stop her from stubbornly digging her heels in just to be defiant.

Catherine laughed. "Bullshit, it's everything to do with the pair of you. You can't deny that you're jealous."

He tried to stay calm. Admitting he was jealous—and that Boldwood was too—would only reinforce Catherine's argument and do nothing to focus on the real issue; Troy. Telling her about Faye would be unlikely to help—she'd only distance herself from being anything like the former receptionist. There was also the risk of implicating Boldwood if he mentioned Madame Rose. To get through to Catherine, he needed to find any source of doubt deep within her intuition and bring that to the surface.

"Catherine, I want you to ask yourself—how did you meet him? What was he doing here? Who was he here to see initially? What did he say to Boldwood when you were in the elevator? Why did Boldwood tell you he was bad news?" he said, trying to appeal to her inquisitive nature.

She stared at the flowers, and he hoped what he was saying was starting to sink in.

"You know we're right," he added.

She glared up at him, and he cursed himself for letting that last phrase slip out of his mouth.

"Of course, men are always right. They always know what's best," she yelled, now pissed off. "Now tell me Dillon, since you're such an expert on Troy being bad, what makes a good man? Everyone says that my father was a good man, but what kind of man thinks it's right to avoid a grieving daughter for three years? How is a man right when he chooses to take his own life, rather than choosing to live a life with his daughter that loves him?" Tears started to flow down her cheeks.

Dillon stepped forward to comfort her, but she pushed him away.

"I'm sorry Catherine. You shouldn't have gone through what you did as a girl, but investing your time in a man who isn't going to love you isn't the answer. It's only going to make things worse."

"Oh fuck off with your constant caring and wise words. What, do you think that you're that man—or that Boldwood is?" she said, trying to put distance between them by picking a fight.

"You really know how to go for someone's jugular, don't you?" he replied, failing to hide his hurt. "I know you don't want me, and I know you don't want Boldwood, but either one of us would treat you a million times better than Troy would, and that's my point. If you don't want either us, fair enough, but do yourself a favor and find someone other than him."

"You don't even know him," she said, stubbornly defending Troy, even though she knew very little about him, other than the fact that every man seemed to hate him.

"I know of him, and I could give you the details that I've heard, but you might think I was setting out to discredit him to further my own cause. I have, however, given you the questions for you to answer yourself," he explained, and then turned to go.

"Did I say you could leave?" she demanded. Their conversation had come to a natural close, but she didn't want him to go without her say so.

"What else do you want to say—insult me some more, accuse me of bad-mouthing the men in your life, maybe ask for my advice on how to break Boldwood's heart, or perhaps tell me to go take care of the exes you've left in your wake while you head off for a date with someone else?" He struggled to hold back from telling her how fed up he was with her bullshit. "Or maybe you want me to finger you up in your private bathroom like I did in the elevator, so you can relieve your boredom?" His patience was wearing thin, and he'd definitely said too much.

Catherine was seething at his outburst. "You're fired. Get your stuff and get out."

Dillon laughed; he was angry, but was surprisingly able to respond calmly and clearly. "Catherine, I have half a mind to resign, but because professionally that doesn't serve me well, I won't be. You have no legal grounds to fire me, and you'd never involve HR anyway because it would embarrass you to bring up us. Therefore, I'm staying. You'll calm down, and I suspect you'll even apologize within days. I'll remain your second in command, and I expect the one you will still turn to whenever you have a professional—or personal—drama. Right now though, I'm going back to my office, I'm getting on with work, and I'll leave you to work out what the hell you're going to do with your fucked up love life. I've told you my views on it, but if you do choose Troy—or even if you don't—you need to speak to Boldwood."

Dillon didn't allow her to respond, storming out of her office after delivering his demands.

Sitting quietly back at his desk, Dillon ruminated over the argument while staring at the aqua-blue box that housed his Valentine's gift for Catherine. He was angry at her hurtful behavior. His male ego wanted to go back and tell her that he was resigning after all, but the words about her father stopped him; he could see the pain of abandonment from her past, and he didn't want to prove her right that men always leave. He'd failed though in his duty to protect her from Troy, and he still wanted her to see that the man was bad news. It was time for a last ditch resort; he opened his email application and typed a one-lined message.

'Catherine needs her best friend right now.'

Chapter Twenty-Seven

Liddy Bradbury had returned from court exhausted; keen to have a glass of wine as soon as she got home. Thankfully, she wasn't venturing out for Valentine's Day—John had taken her away the previous weekend to avoid over-priced babysitting and loved-up crowds; plus she'd had a busy week with a corporate trial.

Taking out her Blackberry to see what time he was going to be home, she spotted an email from Dillon Oak. It was a cryptic email—the subject line had the one word 'help', and the body was only a single line message; no context, no 'hello', 'goodbye', or 'thanks' and not even his name.

Since Christmas Day, Liddy had guessed that he cared a great deal about Catherine, and she noticed that he didn't appear to be one to gossip. Working in the law, she was able to spot the nuances in what people chose to say—or not say—and the motives that people had for the things they did; Dillon was reaching out for her help and he wanted to be impartial—and anonymous—in doing so.

Texting John to say that due to an emergency, she'd be delayed home, Liddy headed towards the DeChartine building.

Catherine hadn't answered any calls, returned emails, nor come out of her office; she wanted to be alone. Troy had sent four texts—but even those had gone ignored. As 5:00 p.m. arrived, she contemplated leaving the office for the sanctuary of her apartment, and a hot bubble bath. As she scrolled through her phone—ready to dial for a car—Liddy opened her office door.

"Fancy some single girl wine?" she asked, holding a bottle in one hand and two wine glasses in the other; single girl wine was a tradition they'd partaken in during their business school years whenever they were alone on Valentine's Day.

Catherine smiled appreciatively. "You're married, and I'm not your wife!"

"True on both counts, and sadly you're not my type, but I've had my fill of cock this past weekend, so now it's girl-on-girl time," she replied with mock sauciness.

"Watch it! I'm so done with men right now, that I might just take you up on it," joked Catherine, laughing as she accepted the glass of wine that Liddy handed to her.

"Well, how about we just settle on talking," said Liddy seating herself on the comfortable office sofa.

Catherine joined her and began to regale her with all the details about Boldwood, Dillon and Troy; surprisingly she didn't hold back on anything—relieved to finally download to someone she trusted.

"No wonder you've not returned my calls, or seen me for weeks!" Liddy exclaimed with wide-eyes at all she'd heard. She tried to work out where to start with the questions; Catherine hadn't specifically focused on anything particular that might have been the trigger for Dillon's plea for help. Although Liddy was now aware of the elevator and snowstorm affair, she didn't believe Dillon would resort to the message for selfish motives; it was unlikely he was asking her to convince her friend to choose him. His message conveyed concern—more likely related to Boldwood, or the new man in Catherine's life. Her legal mind quickly assessed all the facts;

Dillon's email was sent today, Boldwood's been showering attention on Catherine since before Christmas, and Troy's been around two days; Troy Selgent is the trigger for Dillon's outreach message.

"So this Troy, what are your thoughts on what might happen there?" she asked.

Catherine didn't say anything to begin with, apparently gathering her own thoughts.

"He's different," she replied finally, shrugging her shoulders and then gulping more wine.

"Okay, he's different, but that isn't what I asked. What do you think might happen?"

"We went to lunch, he sent flowers, and he is sending texts asking to see me again. I guess it would be like what normally happens—dates, dinners, sex," explained Catherine.

She really didn't know what would happen, but what she did know, was that it would be different to Boldwood propositioning her into a bizarre mistress/slave set-up, or the up-and-down/will we-or won't we situation with Dillon; those two relationship scenarios weren't normal.

"You said normal. When do you do normal?" teased Liddy.

"Maybe that's why he's different. I want someone who's charming, fun and who isn't looking to change me. Someone who knows what they want," she replied, looking dreamily at the flowers on her desk.

"Fair enough; if you really think that Troy is someone you want to see more of, then I won't say anything to put you off—but go into it with your mind, as well as your heart, open, and remember to never stop listening to your own intuition. Don't listen to anyone else's opinion," Liddy advised, knowing her friend would appreciate her supportive words; while Dillon may only be jealous of Troy, she had a hunch it was likely to be more than that; she would start discreet enquiries via her legal contacts—and her husband—to get the bigger perspective.

"It's early days yet, I've only just met him, but I will look after myself," promised Catherine.

"Good, glad to hear it, now how about we go back to my place for dinner? It won't be anything special, but it saves you being alone, and you'd be saving me from being ravished again by that loved-up husband of mine," offered Liddy.

Catherine suspected Liddy would have enjoyed every moment of her weekend alone with her husband, yet she was appreciative of the gesture. "Well if I'd be saving you from a horny man, I couldn't possibly refuse!" she replied, standing to fetch her coat.

Walking across the lobby, they came across Dillon waiting for the elevator. He smiled knowingly. "Hello Liddy, aren't you going out with John this evening?"

"No, not tonight," she replied. "Friends before husbands."

She winked back at him; her statement a coded message to him that she'd received his email. He chose to nod in response rather than say the wrong thing and potentially alert Catherine to his involvement in her visit.

Their elevator journey was silent, however as Dillon and the two women parted in different directions outside the building, Catherine turned back towards him.

"Have a good evening," she said; there was no animosity in her words, and while she could have left them unsaid, Catherine didn't ever want the last words of the day that she said to him to be angry ones. She wasn't sure what decisions she was going to make regarding men, but somewhere—deep inside her—she always had the urge to make things right with Dillon.

"You too—enjoy yourself," he replied, genuinely meaning it; thanks to his intervention, he knew he was leaving her in safe hands with Liddy—even if it was just for that night.

Chapter Twenty-Eight

Three weeks had passed since Valentine's Day. Catherine and Dillon, having slipped back into a professional relationship, were keeping things amicable. Boldwood had eventually taken Dillon's advice and significantly reduced his contact with Catherine. At first, he'd argued, insisting that he must convince her of Troy's true nature and, in doing so, prove that he would always look after her.

Using all of his inner strength—and pushing away his own anguish and jealousy—Dillon had managed to talk Boldwood around by reminding him of the wisdom of patience; making him understand that pushing her would only make her more willful, and determined to get her way. In the end, he'd even used Boldwood's fantasies to manipulate him to comply—the waiting, her in control, and the cuckolding. Together, all of those methods had worked; to Catherine's relief, apart from the occasional email to say he was at her service if required, Boldwood had gone silent—no gifts, and no visits.

Troy, however, was anything but silent. Rather wisely choosing to avoid the DeChartine offices, he'd met with Catherine on several occasions for dinner. He'd deliberately kept things very vanilla—traditional dates and alpha-male flirtation—but whenever she'd playfully asserted her dominance, he'd responded in an equally flirtatious manner that subtly indicated that he'd be willing to submit to her control sexually—should it advance to that.

Unbeknownst to Catherine, Troy had no intention to become her submissive—his ruse was a means to an end. He wanted only the prestige that she could bring him through their relationship and, more than anything, he wanted power—in the bedroom, and outside of it.

Catherine reveled in the attention, and the more time she spent with Troy, the more Boldwood had retreated. It was all a positive change from a few weeks ago—with much less drama. Dating a man outside of her company—and the wider DeChartine—was far less risky for a major fallout that would have an impact on all areas of her life.

Nonetheless, there were two major hurdles to overcome. The first was the constant niggling doubt she had about Troy—that deep unsettling feeling that came to her in the night when she couldn't sleep; she kept hearing in her head the questions Dillon had asked her to consider.

'*Who was he here to see? What did he say to Boldwood? Why is he bad news?*'

The second hurdle was sex; Troy hadn't yet invited her to his place—nor asked to come to hers. They were stuck in a power struggle as to who would take the lead. Even after six dates, the furthest base they'd reached was a chaste kiss on the cheek at the end of the evening. She was attracted to him, and she felt a giddy flutter of excitement in her stomach whenever he kissed her, yet so far there was none of the electricity, or over-whelming desire, that she'd hoped there would be when she met the one.

Catherine tried hard not to compare Troy with Dillon—the two were totally unalike—their accents an excellent metaphor for how oceans apart they were. With Dillon, she had amazing chemistry, but a relationship with him would be far too complicated and risky. Troy was someone she was easily having fun with, and although her inner judgment wasn't immediately identifying excuses to stop anything from happening, it was screaming at her to 'watch out'.

Keen to move on from her endless inner deliberations, she decided it was time for her to take things to the next level.

'Dinner tomorrow. My house. 8:00 p.m.'

She'd kept to a short, instructional text, rather than a question.

'I'll bring wine—and pajamas. Oh, wait . . . I don't wear any!'

The sub-text of her invitation clearly received, she found herself over-come with teenage excitement; it had been a long time since she'd prepared for a date where it was known that the outcome would be sex. She'd also never cooked a dinner for a date before, but to her relief she discovered that there were plenty of enterprising chefs in the West Village catering for people like her; with minimal effort needed on her part, a dinner—that would appear convincingly homemade—could be delivered and set-up moments before Troy's arrival.

When 8:00 p.m. Friday came around, Catherine was elated that the last thirty-six hours were finally over; she'd planned (and re-planned) her out-fit, menu and bed linen choices at least four times, and her indecision had stretched into what sexual activities she might instigate. Catherine didn't know whether to live up to the dominance she'd so far shown Troy—or whether she should let him lead.

Wanting to be prepared for anything, she finally used Boldwood's gift voucher. She did feel guilty to be using his gift in this way, but reasoning it would otherwise go to waste—and that Boldwood had suggested she could have sex with other men—she'd chosen to spend it regardless.

On answering the door in a slinky black dress, Troy gave her a look of approval as she let him in, and on entering, he set the wine, and his laptop bag, down on the table. Before she had the chance to thank him for the wine, he pushed up against her body—pinning her to the wall—and kissed her hard.

Desire filled Catherine's body—she was aching for an orgasm after the sexual tension they'd built up to over the past few weeks. Aroused by his sudden dominance, she let him sink into a deeper kiss; his tongue exploring her mouth and his hands ran down the sides of her dress. As they reached her thighs, he grabbed at the material to pull it upwards.

Stop, stop, stop.

Catherine pulled back from his kiss, and used her own hands—already placed on his chest—to push him backwards. The voice inside her was screaming to go no further, even if it wasn't clear as to whether her reluctance to relinquish sexual dominance was the stop sign, or her intuition about Troy.

"Dinner's ready," she said breathlessly; it wasn't like her to care about dinner, but she needed an excuse to explain her withdrawal.

Troy looked annoyed—he was aroused and made no effort to hide the impressive erection tenting in his casual trousers.

"I would hate to spoil the meal you've spent a lot of time on," he said chivalrously, unwilling to ruin his chances—for sex that night, and for his longer endgame.

"Sit," she commanded, directing him to the small table for two in her studio. He obeyed, and they proceeded to flirt their way through all three courses as they'd done in restaurants—only this time, Troy frequently ran his foot up and down her leg.

Once dinner was over, they retreated to the couch—where only a month before she'd snowballed Dillon. The memory added an awkwardness to the atmosphere; while Troy was unaware of Catherine's couch-history, something was missing between them—neither of them knew what to do next, and she lacked an overwhelming desire to jump his bones.

"Would you like a fire?" she asked, hoping he might offer to light one in the grate as Dillon had done.

"I think we can make our own heat," he replied suggestively. Catherine blushed, yet she was disappointed that they wouldn't have the romance of the flames. If this was going to work, she needed romance, cheeky banter and foreplay—rather than cheesy one-liners, or him going alpha-male on her pinned up against the wall.

"About earlier, when you arrived in my apartment, is that what you like?"

she asked, blushing again as she asked; it was unlike her to be embarrassed when discussing sex.

"You mean did I want you then and there—or that I didn't wait to be asked?" he said, understanding her question perfectly. Catherine was naïve to the research that Troy had been doing on her, and mistook his insight to be a sign that he could read her mind.

"Both," she replied, although she already knew the answer to the first one—his arousal had confirmed he wanted sex on arrival.

"Yes, I wanted you—but I've wanted you from the first moment we met. As to being asked, that isn't really my style. I don't mean I don't respect a woman who says no, but I'm not a man who derives his pleasure from chastity."

His final line wasn't a blatant admission that he knew about Boldwood's preferences, but it certainly alerted her to the possibility.

"You're not interested in me for my dominant personality?" she asked, relieved that he wasn't only seeing her as someone to fill a role.

"A strong, intelligent woman—who knows what she wants—is attractive, but I don't get sexual pleasure from being told what to do. There are many other ways to give and receive pleasure—for the benefit of both," he replied.

Catherine pondered his answer, unsure what to ask next. The thought of a man in charge was a very different prospect to her, although mutual pleasure was always welcome.

"Do you want me to show you?" He stood up as he said it, holding out his hand for her to take.

"Yes," she found herself saying; the time for over-thinking was over; Troy was taking the lead, and she didn't want to wait any longer.

Once they'd moved from the couch, Troy undid the zip at the back of her dress, letting it fall to the ground. Catherine shivered at his touch—as well as from the cold.

We should have lit the fire.

Standing behind her, he kissed her neck as he undid each clasp of her new basque.

"Take off your panties, stockings and heels," he instructed, stepping back to watch.

She complied—albeit a little reluctantly, and once she was completely naked, Troy tied a silk blindfold around her head, and then firmly gripped her arm and led her to the bed.

I'm going to trip. I want to see where I'm going . . .

"Lay down," he commanded.

A sense of anticipation now started to drive her every move and she obeyed. Devoid of her sight, she could hear him retrieving items from his laptop bag—a bag she now doubted contained a computer. The rummaging noise stopped, and he returned to the bed. Taking hold of her left arm, and raising it at a forty-five degree angle above her head, she felt him tie her wrist firmly to the bedpost. He repeated the move with her other wrist, then she felt the mattress depressing downwards as he made his way to the lower part of the bed.

Troy's fingers briefly caressed her legs, and then, taking each one in his firm grip, he completed shackling her to the bedframe; Catherine was naked, blindfolded, spread-eagled and restrained by her wrists and ankles.

What's he going to do next?

No longer in possession of clothes, sight or movement—her sense of control didn't want her to let go and enjoy the surprise of the unknown. She didn't have to wait long to find out his next step; earplugs were suddenly stuffed into each of her ears, and the blindfold was adjusted over them to hold them in place. They were an odd item for seduction, but served the purpose of removing another of her senses—all she could hear was the internal sound of her racing heartbeat.

Troy touched her again, dragging his strong finger all over her, stopping to tease her most sensitive spots.

It's like my story in reverse . . . no, stop thinking about the story . . .

Just when she thought the teasing would go on forever, his fingers entered her—two fingers inside and his thumb stroking her clit.

The elevator . . .

She desperately tried to erase from her mind all thoughts of Dillon—how he'd done the same thing to her—but it was much harder to forget him when she couldn't see Troy.

I need to see him—his grey eyes, his teeth—or hear his American voice

"Stop, I need the blindfold off," she pleaded, not wanting to have to say why she needed her sight back.

Troy ignored her request; although she couldn't hear if he'd said anything, his continued thrusts relayed his unwillingness to comply. Despite the turmoil in her mind, Catherine's body responded to his touch—her body moving involuntarily into an arch even though she was bound tightly into position. Her mind though could only imagine Dillon's hand between her legs, and she bit her lip to stop herself crying out his name.

"Troy, I said stop," she repeated, more forcibly this time.

Abruptly the thrusts stopped and her breathing started to slow; she tried to calm herself.

"Thank you," she said, mistakably thinking that he'd complied with her request.

After a moment, just as her breathing had returned to normal, Catherine felt the blunt force of objects forced inside her simultaneously—the penetration, completely unexpected, made her wince at the intrusion into her body. The buzzing sensation on her clit suggested it was her own rabbit vibrator—or one similar—filling her vagina, but the anal butt plug was definitely not hers—not even something from the bag of goodies she'd brought with the Boldwood voucher.

The sensations spread through her lower body, and her nipples perked up, only then to be bit by the sharpness of a metal clamp. She cried out at all the pain—and pleasure—taking over her.

Troy evidently didn't want her to make a sound; as she couldn't hear orders to be quiet, he'd decided that the best way to gag her, was with his own body. His fingers prized her mouth open, and within seconds, she was choking on a full mouth of his cock. Her orifices filled in every way possible—now she'd escalated to no ability to speak, move, see or hear.

Denied seeing Troy undress, her only indication of the size of his cock prior to this, was his earlier arousal contained in his trousers—now she was struggling with the full length and girth of him in her mouth—he was bigger than she'd guessed. Bizarrely having him inside her mouth was the diversion she'd needed to stop thinking of Dillon—the size and taste of Troy provided a differentiation.

She tried to tense her legs back together to reduce the sensation of the rabbit ears, but it was useless—her ankle bonds were too tight. Troy continued on—faster and faster—with the simultaneous thrusting of the vibrator, butt plug and his own cock, and Catherine had no choice but to give up control; her body was submitting as it headed to a climax. She futilely tried to control her gasps; worried that she would gag as his cock hit the back of her mouth.

Just when she thought she could take no more—unable to breathe and about to climax, Troy withdrew himself from her mouth, and pulled out the toys concurrently. She felt the warm sensation of liquid dribbling onto her face, and despite her repulsion at the degrading cum-shot, she was relieved to avoid the risk of her choking from the deep throat action.

Her own pending orgasm—likely to have been intense due to the multitude of sensations on her body—was cut off the moment he had his release. She wanted more, but Troy had rolled off her body and she sensed his body laid next to her on the bed. He didn't untie her wrists or ankles—nor remove the blindfold—and she laid there for what seemed like an eternity; her naked body fully exposed, with his sticky juices running off her cheek.

"Troy?" she asked, wanting to connect with him—she didn't like the silence, or her lack of control from being bound.

His finger probed one of her ears to remove an earplug.

"What?" he mumbled irritably.

"Are you going to untie me?"

"Don't you want more?" he replied, sounding more annoyed than flirtatious.

"Well . . . maybe . . . but you need time to recover, so can't you untie me for a bit—or at least take the blindfold off?" she requested; Catherine was agitated, and had no intention of laying there for anything more than a minute—certainly not for however long it took him to recover from his selfish orgasm.

Initially he didn't respond—not wanting to give in to her—but he silently reminded himself of the endgame; Catherine wasn't just a one-night-stand to fuck and forget, even if the kinkiness of the sexual encounter had failed to deliver all the highs that he normally got from taking control. Reluctantly he removed the blindfold and gave her a fake smile. "There you are gorgeous, is that better?"

She smiled back sarcastically, and looked upwards, motioning with her head towards her tied wrists. He took the hint—untying each in turn—yet left her ankles tied, returning to rest his head on the pillow. She reached down to untie them herself—despite the awkwardness of the stretch with her legs still spread wide. Once she was free, she used a tissue to wipe her face, before looking at him laid on her bed—he was naked, and she took time to study his previously unseen body. He kept himself reasonably fit, yet he was less muscular than she'd imagined he'd be under his suit, and while his flaccid cock was large, it was roughly comparable in size to Dillon.

Damn it, stop with the comparisons!

With Troy not paying her any post-coital attention, she couldn't stop herself from thinking about Dillon's longing stare after she'd given him a blowjob to remember. She stood up from the bed and went to the bathroom to compose herself. Washing her face clear of the remainder of Troy's cum, she looked at her reflection in the mirror. Staring back at her was a woman she didn't want to be—a woman not in control, with her mind wandering to things in her past. Drying her face on the towel, Catherine took a deep breath.

Troy was still laid on the bed with his eyes closed—bordering on sleep. Creeping quietly towards him, she retrieved a pair of handcuffs out of her bag of purchased tricks; she didn't have time for silk-tie bondage if she was going to restrain him. He didn't stir—or open his eyes—as she approached.

Catherine was fortunate that he'd chosen to lay in a position that showed himself off—his arms raised above his head. Silently clipping one of the cuffs to the bedpost, she snapped the other end quickly around one of his wrists. Troy's eyes flashed open, and he tried to jerk his body upright, but the cuff kept him down on one side.

"What the fuck?" he shouted, visibly unimpressed at her seduction game plan.

"My turn," she announced, dangling the other pair of cuffs in her hand and smiling seductively at him.

Troy wasn't sure how to react—he'd never allowed anyone to tie him down. A sense of fear ran through him—with everything he'd done with women in the past, he wondered if he'd messed with the wrong one; one who was now about to teach him a lesson. It was an irrational fear that stemmed deep from his own insecurities of humiliation—thoughts that she'd planned this as revenge, along with help from Boldwood, Dillon, and Faye, briefly ran through his mind.

"This isn't how it works," he said sternly, trying to remain in control, rather than have to plead.

"Really?" she said, with as much seduction as she could muster. "I thought you said this was about equal pleasure, so now I'm returning the favor."

She wanted him to be attracted to the assertive woman that she felt most comfortable being; although she'd wanted normal before tonight—and had flirted with the idea of a dominating man in her life—once she'd experienced his version, she wanted her control back.

"Now stop struggling, and enjoy."

Troy stopped trying to free himself—his futile attempt only made the cuff dig painfully into his wrist. He contemplated grabbing her when she advanced toward him, but Catherine was a step ahead, and—as though reading his mind—she placed the handcuff keys on the dressing table before she took the final steps towards the other side of the bed.

He had no choice to obey her—she wasn't going to release him, and he couldn't tell her the truth that he didn't ever want to submit. If this only way to get closer to Catherine—and benefit in the long-term—he would have to give in for a while.

Once Catherine had attached the other handcuff to his wrist, she snapped it onto the bedpost. However, she stopped short of shackling his ankles as he had done to her. Starting at his neck, she kissed his body gently, so beginning her seduction of him. Troy took a while to arouse in response to her seduction, but as her kisses neared his groin, his cock hardened and his hopes rose that she would go down on him again—just as he'd forced her to do earlier.

However, she quickly moved away from his aroused cock; although she'd so far only removed his ability to move, he watched her pick up the blindfold.

"No blindfold," he said threateningly.

"Fair enough," she replied, heeding his warning and putting it down. "But, you will be quiet."

Rising up onto her knees, she put her legs either side of his face—as close as they could go with his arms in the restrained position they were in. Lowering her body, she rubbed herself onto his lips to queen over him. Still wet from her earlier arousal, Troy detected the faint taste of rubber, transferred from her vibrator, as he reluctantly licked her clit. He hated giving a woman oral—at least he did in this queening manner—previously he'd only gone down on a bound woman as an initial torture to arouse her before repeatedly denying her an orgasm.

Therefore, it was a relief when Catherine stopped long before her orgasm. He didn't have the patience for a woman to come, and he'd never had the desire to perfect the skills of bringing a woman to a quick oral climax. She retreated further down his body, and then hesitated, as though contemplating her next move, and abruptly she got off the bed. For a moment, Troy hoped it was over so that he could go to sleep, but instead she reached into a bedside drawer and withdrew a condom packet.

Typical in control woman.

Sliding the condom onto him, Catherine then wasted no time in mounting him. Troy responded by lifting his hips to thrust deeply into her. Despite his arm bonds, he found that he was free to assert a degree of control over the sex and he prayed she wouldn't suddenly decide to bind his ankles. Knowing that he was topping her—even though she was riding him—Troy came quickly, groaning as he did.

Not wanting to let him win, Catherine slapped his face as she tried to keep him inside her until she brought herself to an orgasm. He however had other ideas, and bucked his hips upwards with sudden, brute force; Catherine lost her balance and his limp cock slipped out of her to fall back onto his body.

The whole evening—particularly the sex—had left her wanting. Both of her orgasms had been cut short, and she hadn't even had the chance to fake something the second time around. Laid beside him once she'd undone his cuffs, and listening to his snores, it dawned on her than any of the pleasure had been from the stimuli of her own vibrator and the butt plug. While Troy had been inside her mouth, and had briefly kissed her body, the only real element he contributed to her arousal was the eroticism of cutting off her sense of sight, sound and movement—something that any man could do to her, particularly if he was directed to.

Troy had fooled her with his technique; a false sexual prowess with no real skill, and in her mind, this wasn't a sustainable connection. There was no real intimacy between them, and no real bond created; Catherine was lacking an orgasmic high that would make her want to repeat this. She definitely couldn't sleep with him there; she wanted him gone from her apartment, and her life.

"You're snoring," she said loudly, hoping to wake him. When that failed, she kicked him, and reluctantly Troy stirred.

"What the fuck did you do that for?" he yelled.

"I said you were snoring," she repeated.

He blinked in the faint light of her bedside lamp, "I was asleep."

Well obviously, people don't snore when they are awake.

"It's keeping me awake," she said. Catherine was picking a fight, hoping that might make him leave. It was still relatively early—certainly before midnight—and therefore a respectable hour to send a man home.

"I snore, get used to it," he said, rolling over onto his side, to face away from her, and her unwanted bedside light.

Troy didn't seem to have any intention of leaving and alarm bells rang in Catherine's head.

Get used to it? The sex wasn't that great—he'd have to agree about that—so why the fuck does he want a repeat?

Troy didn't strike her as the sort of man to fall desperately in love so easily; post-sex oxytocin bonding definitely wasn't supposed to be an alpha-male thing.

"This was a one night thing." Catherine put all of her icy bitch assertiveness and domination into the six words; even the dumbest of men would have got the hint and felt either rejected—or relieved—depending on their own thoughts about the sex they'd just engaged in.

Troy rolled back towards her. "Oh, I think I could convince you otherwise," he said grinning—yet there was no flirtatious attempt to grab and seduce her.

"You know how to operate some sex toys. Big deal, I can do that," she replied; if he wasn't going to go willingly, she was going to have to go for the metaphoric jugular—his male pride.

He sat upright in response to her taunt; Catherine wasn't going to be an easy conquest.

"You want me to fuck you up against the wall until you're a screaming heap?" he asked.

The line he delivered should have been full of sizzle, but to Catherine it sounded flat and like something from a bad porno movie—dirty talk needed to stir up a deep longing that made her pelvic muscles clench in anticipation, her legs go weak, and her panties dampen with arousal.

"No, I want you to go home," she said, wishing he would finally get the message.

Troy raised his eyebrows at her, and half-heartedly ran his fingers up her naked thigh. She slapped them away—the only shiver they sent through her was one that told her that she was cold and his fingers were warm. His demeanor changed at her physical rebuff; he was angry.

"Well fuck you then. You weren't so hot yourself," he yelled, rising off the bed and then pulling on his trousers.

His criticism of her performance stung a little, although it helped that Catherine knew that not only was it the truth, he was speaking from his rejected ego—just as Dillon had once done.

Catherine didn't care; he was finally leaving.

Ten minutes later, she had her apartment—and more importantly her bed—all to herself once more. As she settled down to sleep, her final thought was a resolution to avoid men for a while.

Chapter Twenty-Nine

For the first few days after his evening with Catherine, Troy filed the encounter as a bad one-night-stand. Knowing that he'd never be willing to submit to domination by her—or by any other woman—he gave up on the idea of anything more; even if she was the ultimate show-wife prize.

Sitting down with the newspapers, he browsed the social pages to eye up potential dates. His shoulders sank when he spotted a wedding announcement; his half-brother was engaged to a stunning New York socialite.

Troy had always been in competition with his half-siblings—even though the rivalry was one-sided; he'd never officially met them and he doubted that they knew, or cared, about his existence; their late father's long-standing secret affair, with Troy's former-model mother, was an undiscussed topic.

He'd always wanted his name and photo to be a regular feature on those newspaper pages; his goal was for those privileged bastards to see that he was just as successful as they were—professionally and personally.

Thoughts of Catherine entered his mind; her rejection annoyed him. While he was willing to let go of all the other women whose daddies had intervened, letting Catherine reject him was a wound to his ego that was unbearable to contemplate; Troy needed to win her over. Knowing that to succeed, he would need to find a way into her heart, he resolved to set about finding any emotional chinks in her icy armor.

❧

A week had passed since Catherine had chucked Troy out of her apartment, and she was relieved that he'd made no further contact. She'd kept their break-up a secret, not wanting Dillon's *'I-told-you-so'*, or renewed attention from Boldwood.

The fifteenth of March was a sad day for her—the anniversary of her father's suicide—and she focused on finishing work tasks so that she could escape on time for quiet solitude in a hot bath.

On returning home, she was surprised to find a boxed bouquet of white lilies outside her apartment door; no one in New York knew the significance of the date—nor was there anyone alive back in England that would remember.

Once inside the safe haven of her apartment, she nervously opened the accompanying card.

> *'Thinking of you today, because I know what it's like to lose a father through abandonment and death. I'm here if you need to talk. Troy.'*

A tear slipped from the corner of her eye—she didn't know how Troy had come to find out about her father, but none of her walls could prevent her from being appreciative that someone had reached out to her today. She typed a short text:

> 'Thank you.'

Moments later came a reply:

> 'No problem.'

By the time she'd poured a large glass of wine, a second follow-up text had arrived:

> 'Come away with me tomorrow for the weekend. How do the Hamptons sound?'

The beach always had an appeal, but the Hamptons were too much of a reminder of the clambake and Boldwood; she doubted Troy would be enough of a diversion to erase those thoughts. She texted back:

> 'Maybe some other time, or place.'

His reply:

> 'Brunch in the city tomorrow?'

Troy was persistent—she had to give him that—and a brunch couldn't do much harm, nor have a sexual context if they met there.

> 'Okay. Goodnight.'

The compassion of someone who understood loss was hard to resist, and Catherine resolved to give Troy the opportunity of a second chance.

౿ ౬

Another month passed, and the bitterly cold New York winter had finally relinquished its hold on the city – the flowers of spring filling the *Big Apple's* green spaces. At weekends, Catherine had explored most of the city's parks while having brunches, or late lunches, with Troy.

During their dates, he opened up more to her about growing up with his mother, and coping with the rejection of his father, and in return, she cautiously shared the details of her mother's death and her father's suicide. Any reservations she had about how Troy had come to find out the date of her father's death, she pushed to the back of her mind; she was only flattered that he'd sought to find out more things they had in common.

Although they were becoming closer, neither of them had instigated sex again—the choice of dates during the day was a way to avoid it. The one time Catherine asked if Troy wanted to come back to her apartment, he declined, stating that he was enjoying getting to know her.

At first, she thought it was nice, but as Easter passed—and May rapidly approached—Catherine wondered where their relationship was heading. She was enjoying the company, yet the sexual spark was lacking, and she didn't want to waste time with someone that she wasn't interested in a future with.

Make—or break—time had come.

ⅽⅇⅺ

Finishing their Saturday lunch, Catherine broached the issue. "Your place is nearby isn't it? Can I see your apartment?" she asked; she studied his face, assuring herself that there was a hint of lust in Troy's eyes.

Catherine was unaware that Troy had been getting his sexual release elsewhere—and not through jerking off with his own palm.

"Okay," he said, shrugging his shoulders—devoid of the enthusiasm that a man about to have sex would normally have.

She was curious to see where Troy lived; his apartment was located relatively close to her own place, but in a more contemporary area. On arriving, she wasn't surprised that it was a modern bachelor pad—kitted out with high-spec gadgets—but the apartment was considerably larger than her own place. As she walked through the open-plan space, she wondered where the money was coming from to pay for it—Troy wasn't a partner in the law firm, and he'd already implied his father never gave him a dime in life—or in death.

"Nice place," she said, looking around for the bed. "Where's the bedroom?"

He grinned, and beckoned towards a hallway. Catherine headed down the hall, seductively motioning him to follow. She wanted to be in control this time, but she suspected she might need to lull Troy into a false sense of security after the handcuff incident.

Once in the bedroom, she kneeled at his feet and reached up to unzip his trousers. Troy's cock began to harden with her attention, and he grasped it with one hand—leveraging it out of his boxers towards her mouth. His other hand reached behind her head and grabbed hold of her ponytail, yanking her forwards. She had no choice but to open her mouth and take his length.

Troy was strong, and she gave in to his direction by compliantly sucking him up and down, her tongue twirling around the tip of his cock. Her hands took hold of his balls, gently kneading them to heighten his sensations. His thrusts become more frantic as she continued—his hand pushing her forward to the point where it was painful.

Catherine could feel the pressure of his impending orgasm travelling up his shaft, so she withdrew a little, but maintained her tight suction around the head to ensure that she caught every drop; she had no intention of a cum-shot to the face again.

Troy groaned and sank onto the bed, and with a sly smile, she stood over him and firmly kissed him, dribbling his fluids onto his tongue—just as she'd done to Dillon. The outcome was very different though; Troy recoiled and spat out the sticky mess onto the sheet.

"You bitch," he yelled, continuing to spit in an over-dramatized reaction to her snowballing surprise.

Catherine's doubts about him re-surfaced. His angry outburst was one hard limit, but the difference in his reaction was such a contrast to Dillon's passionate desire and compliance, that she knew—without a doubt—they had reached a relationship breaking point that couldn't be resolved.

"I never would've taken you for a vanilla," she remarked sarcastically; a retort against his bitch insult.

"Far from it, but I've told you before, no woman controls me, and I will never be made to swallow my own cum—nor yours for that matter," he replied, full of angry repulsion at what she'd tried to make him do.

While Catherine wasn't hung up on the idea of a man swallowing his own ejaculate, she wasn't about to give up a man giving her oral, or relinquish her control to anyone.

"Fair enough," she said, grabbing her bag and heading for the door.

"I hope you find a nice, compliant woman who's just right for you. It's been . . .," she struggled for something to say in farewell. "A revelation."

With that, she left, leaving Troy gulping down copious amounts of water to rid himself of the bad taste of his semen—and her rejection.

Chapter Thirty

Catherine walked into the lobby on Monday morning to a dagger-like stare from the receptionist. It wasn't usual to get a smile from her, but not since Catherine's first morning at DeChartine—and the encounter with Faye—had a receptionist glared at her with open hatred.

Dismissing it as nothing more than the woman having her own problems—or a bad time of the month—Catherine headed for her office. Mary-Anne looked petrified to see her approaching, and her paranoia returned, especially as she'd been in a good mood of late and, as such, couldn't think of anything that she might have done to upset everyone.

"Morning Mary-Anne, do you have my papers for the team meeting printed?" she said, not daring to ask what was wrong with everyone.

"Um . . . yes Catherine," she replied, handing her a folder. "You have Mr. Boldwood in your office, and . . .," she hesitated, as though thinking twice about saying something. "Congratulations."

Catherine looked at her blankly.

Congratulations for what, and what's Boldwood doing here?

She hadn't seen Boldwood for over a month, and a sense of dread spread through her mind.

Shit, what's Boldwood done to warrant congratulations?

There was no reason for celebration on any deals, but she wasn't about to look clueless in front of her PA.

"Thank you," she replied, managing a faint smile before bolting into her office and closing the door.

To her relief, Boldwood didn't drop to his knees, nor even lower his gaze, but he was visibly distressed. Even in his panicked state, he still managed to address her with his own desire for formality.

"Miss Everdene, are the papers to be believed? I thought based on our previous conversations that we had an understanding, so surely this would have warranted you telling me the truth to my face before the world knew. You deserve much better than him—can't I get you to change your mind?"

His ranting plea did nothing to enlighten Catherine on what was going on. The morning was turning out to be a headache; she wasn't in the mood for cryptic games. Her phone beeped and she looked down at the text message from Liddy; initially glad of the interruption, the words only served to add to her baffled state.

 'OMG, Why didn't you tell me??? Drinks Miss!!!

 P.S. Congrats, and when do finally I get to meet him.'

Catherine began to think that someone was playing an April fool on her—albeit a few weeks late. "What the hell are you talking about Bill—is what in the papers to be believed?"

"If you're not even going to do the decency of telling me, I will go," he said without explanation.

"Tell you what? What the—," Before she'd the chance to quiz him further, Boldwood had stormed out of her office towards the elevators.

She sat down at her desk to call Liddy, but only managed to scroll down to her name, when Dillon came in and shut the door.

"This is an unexpected development," he said, equally as cryptic as Boldwood had been.

"What the fuck is with everyone today?" she yelled; Catherine was getting angry through frustration at her ignorance. "What's unexpected?"

Why can't everyone just get to the point?

"Your engagement," Dillon replied, looking at her accusingly as though she was deliberately being evasive.

Is this a joke?

Catherine rubbed her head—her migraine was getting worse.

"My engagement—who the hell am I marrying?" she said.

Dillon knew when she was putting on a defensive front to remain private, but no one could mistake her surprise as anything but genuine.

"Your engagement to Troy was announced in the papers this morning," he explained, wearing as much of a baffled expression as hers now; he'd read the news in several reputable broadsheets.

Catherine laughed at the absurdity of the rumor. "You believe newspapers?" she retorted.

Dillon looked as though he didn't know what to say, and she sensed that he was struggling to believe her denial, but finally he gave more context. "It was Troy that was quoted in them—rather than a source—and he has the announcement on all his social media as well. He proposed to you over the weekend, you accepted and the wedding date is set for this August before he moves into a political career. Even you can't deny that it's come from a fairly credible source—well as credible as a person like Troy is."

Catherine didn't respond to his taunt about Troy's credibility, instead firing up her computer to see for herself. He watched her searching the internet frantically for the details.

"I understand if you wanted to keep it quiet, and I know you're more private than he is. I also accept that I wouldn't have been high on your priority list to tell, especially as I warned you off him," he said quietly, trying to show that he was supportive, rather than upset.

"Shut up Dillon," said Catherine, not wanting to listen to his self-pity when she was concentrating on reading the search results to find out what the hell was going on.

Dillon's temper flared up in response to her insulting reply, "Well that's hardly fair, when I was trying to be understanding."

She didn't react at first—her eyes scanning the media report—but after what seemed like an eternity to him, she looked up and asked, "You believe this rubbish? You honestly think I would do something this rash?"

Although Catherine often denied it, she was aware Dillon knew her better than anyone else did; it hurt to think that he believed her capable of something this stupid—an engagement to Troy this fast was beyond even her impulsiveness.

"The story is fairly factual, and he's tweeting about it—why would he make it up?" remarked Dillon, calming a little and forgetting the earlier insult as his curiosity into what was transpiring took over.

It was a fair question, yet one Catherine couldn't answer; she'd ended things with Troy the previous Friday, and although she'd badly wounded his arrogant ego, she couldn't work out why the bastard might resort to this—even to bolster his pride.

Do I have painkillers, or better still, vodka? Is it wine o'clock?

Her headache was intensifying, and for the second time that year, she was going to have to reject a man more forcefully so that he would get the message into his thick skull. This time though, there was a public aspect to the rejection, and Troy wouldn't take public humiliation well.

Catherine considered what to tell Dillon. Sparing him the details of how her relationship with Troy had panned out—she didn't want another lecture about giving men the wrong idea—she kept it simple.

"I didn't know about the engagement," she said, hoping that her friend would recognize the honesty in her admission. "I will come and find you later to tell you more but, for now, could you let me make a private call?"

Dillon nodded. "I truly hope you resolve things," he said.

As he left her alone, Catherine prayed that he was right.

೭ don ೨

Troy Selgent let his phone go to voicemail; it had been ringing off the hook and he'd taken all the calls—except for those from one particular caller; Catherine had diverted to his voicemail four times in the past ten minutes. He didn't plan to ignore her forever, but he knew this wasn't a conversation for the phone—Troy wanted to see her face when he won this power struggle.

Exiting the elevator, he smiled mischievously at the latest DeChartine receptionist. Despite her earlier daggers towards Catherine, her natural reaction to Troy was to return a smile. He hadn't got far towards Catherine's office before he came face to face with Boldwood. The rejected suitor had returned to the twenty-eighth floor in search of Dillon, and when he hadn't succeeded in finding him, he was headed back to Catherine to try once more to reason with her.

Boldwood glared furiously at him and shouted, "What will it take to make you change your mind—name your zeros and I will write a check." His desperation was evident as he pulled out his checkbook.

Troy sniggered back at him, "Always out to save the ladies, aren't you Boldwood. Yet we both know that you're not the white knight that people might think you are—more the dark horse, wouldn't you say?"

He laughed before continuing, "I'll bet you love to be ridden around like a pony, whipped by your rider until you were really going for it."

Boldwood's face reddened from a mix of embarrassment and anger. The receptionist—not wanting to be present for another one of the men's duals—made a hasty retreat for the coffee room.

"Miss Everdene deserves better than you. I could love her far more than you ever could," said Boldwood despairingly.

"Oh I don't doubt that you think you love her, but could you make her happy old man? You see love is about making someone happy. Would you really be willing to let her go to allow her to be happy?" Troy was taunting the distraught man, and if Boldwood hadn't been so enflamed with jealousy and hatred, he might have asked the same question to Troy; instead he took the words as a test of his love for Catherine.

"Yes I would," he said, opening his checkbook and rapidly signing away a considerable sum of money. "Take the money to make her happy. Marry her and treat her right. Buy her the ring she deserves."

He held out the check, imploring Troy to do the right thing either way.

Troy stepped forward to take it to study the zeros, whistling when he saw the amount. "Impressive show of love," he said, folding the check and lifting it towards his shirt pocket. The move, however, was only for added drama. Seconds later, he ripped it up, emphasizing his action by doing it in slow motion. "Oh I know how to make Catherine happy, and it doesn't involve money. Money might have been all that you could have given her, but you see old man, I know what she really wants and how to give it to her. I made her wail with ecstasy when I tied her up. You read her all wrong, because what she wants is a strong man who will make the decisions. She wants to be the one to beg for more."

Troy stood erect opposite Boldwood; his height surpassing that of his broken-hearted, and defeated, rival. "Now if you'll excuse me, I have a fiancée waiting to be of service to me," he gloated.

છે

Even the closed door of Catherine's office didn't prevent the shouting from being overhead in the hallway. Troy had confidently strolled in to see her as though nothing was amiss, and she'd launched into him the minute he entered the room.

"What the fuck is wrong with you?" she screamed; while waiting for Troy to respond to her calls, she'd firmly placed him into the insane category—somewhere that she hadn't even rendered Boldwood.

"Nobody rejects me," Troy replied, looking smug.

"Well I do, and I have. What part of *it is over* didn't you understand on Friday?" Catherine emphasized her question slowly to drum it into him; she didn't want a relationship—let alone an engagement.

"Cat, we're getting married and you will be mine," he said, not about to be deterred; Catherine Everdene ticked all the boxes he needed in a wife—prestige, beauty and money. Having her would spark jealousy in every man that didn't have her, and in his world that was powerful; his half-brothers' wives weren't nearly as good a catch.

"Stop calling me Cat and you didn't even propose! Why do you want to marry me?" she asked. It wasn't that she doubted that a man might want to marry her one day; it was just that there was no obvious reason as to why Troy might want to.

Troy shrugged. "The challenge and the rewards," he answered honestly, not caring at his lack of romance.

"Do you have a screw lose? What makes you remotely think I would agree to marry you now you've admitted your daft reasons?"

"You will agree, otherwise you will have to go public with the denial of our engagement—embarrassing yourself in the process. And, if that doesn't make you agree, I have pictures of you tying me up with handcuffs and sitting on my face," he said smugly.

Oh, fuck.

Catherine sank into her chair, horrified at his confession. There were loads of naïve things that she'd done in her life, but letting Troy blindfold her was a moment of recklessness she was now going to live to regret.

This is what happens when you relinquish control—especially to someone you don't trust.

The thought that he might have taken photos, or installed a camera, while he had her blindfolded and restrained, had never crossed her mind. He'd set her up right from the start—always with selfish intentions to further himself through their union. Dillon and Boldwood were right about him being bad news, and she bitterly regretted not listening to them—or more importantly—to her intuition.

Determined to try to salvage the situation, she offered what little she had in terms of money, but Troy only laughed at her attempt.

"Ah dear Cat, you're going to have to learn not to fight me. Besides, your pitiful admirer Boldwood offered ten times that amount for me to leave you alone, then—when that didn't work—he offered me the same check to take you off his hands. Told me to buy you a ring, and make you happy. See, no other man knows what to do with you, or how to control you, but I, on the other hand, know exactly how to get you to fall for my charms and make you submit. I'll bet you're even willing to beg me to marry you now, in order to save your precious reputation and career."

Catherine wasn't about to beg, but she was out of options. For the sake of everything she'd worked for, she nodded.

"I will marry you," she said sadly.

❦

The embarrassment at her activities with Troy prevented Catherine from discussing her situation with Dillon—or even Liddy. She was intensely private when it came to her sexual exploits, and if she confessed to Liddy, she'd no doubt involve her husband in an effort for him to set things straight with his journalistic peers about the engagement.

Troy scared her, and she knew if she told Dillon, he wouldn't only think badly of her, but he'd sense her fear and then try to protect her. After his engagement-in-the-media stunt, she had no idea what Troy would be capable of doing if he felt his plan to marry her was being threatened by outsiders. If he could find out about the date of her father's death, and about Boldwood's secrets, she was determined not to put Dillon at risk—Troy would destroy him if he found out the details of his submissive past with Catherine and the London dungeons; she had to protect him—as he would her.

Catherine wasn't ready to give up though, determined that it would never reach a point where she actually married Troy. Going with the theory that it was wise to keep your enemies close, she decided that now she had agreed to the engagement, Troy would no doubt move in with her and she could search for the photographs and destroy them.

This nightmare would end; she would win.

Within an hour of accepting Troy's warped proposal, her new fiancé had emailed all of the employees of DeChartine New Media—and several of the executives from other DeChartine companies—inviting them to an engagement lunch the following day.

As she scanned the congratulatory email sent from Emilia's personal assistant—her fairy godmother was away on a cruise—her humiliation was complete; she was publicly engaged to an asshole and all because she was worried about her career and reputation.

Chapter Thirty-One

Catherine was outraged as she watched the drunken revelry of her team, despite it being a Tuesday lunch hour.

Seeking out the organizer of the impromptu, and unwelcome, celebration, she grabbed Troy's arm and hauled him into a corner of the bar.

"Are you trying to get me fired?" She yelled above the bar noise—chants of 'kiss, kiss, kiss' coming from the more inebriated of the party attendees.

"Stop being such a boring bitch Cat, have a drink," he slurred in response, having drunk enough champagne for both of them.

"It's a Tuesday lunch time. These people—and me especially—should be working," she replied.

Catherine, embarrassed by his behavior, was worried at how it would reflect on her if the lack of decorum on display during work hours reached back to Emilia. Boldwood hadn't attended, however Dillon was watching from a quieter corner of the bar with a soda in his hand; he clearly wasn't amused. Catherine's fears about him replacing her, as she'd felt in London, came into her mind—especially now he was disappointed with her about the engagement. His ego had taken a hit when she'd rejected him for Troy—was now the time for his revenge?

Dillon caught her stare and hurriedly put down his soda before leaving the bar. Catherine's shoulders dropped as she turned her attentions back to her irresponsible fiancé.

"I need them all back at the office by one," she demanded; it was already twelve-forty-five.

Troy glared back at her, before he raised his champagne flute in defiance. "Ladies and gents, I propose a toast to your CEO—and my soon-to-be wife—Catherine Everdene, who's just agreed to an open-bar for the afternoon."

His loud announcement, greeted with cheers, left Catherine no choice other than to smile at her team; this wasn't the time—or place—to contradict Troy publicly. Mouthing a 'fuck you' at him, she stormed out of the crowded bar into the open air of the sidewalk.

Catherine had no intention to return to the party. Any attempt to demand the return of her employees would only goad Troy further into defying her, and would alienate her from her team who wanted to celebrate. Walking slowly back to the office, she cursed how her life had become such a complicated mess in the last year.

As she wallowed in self-pity, her ruminating was interrupted by the ping of a RSS alert—Twitter was on meltdown.

Quickly opening the Twitter app, her eyes scanned the notifications for the cause; it was glaringly obvious.

> @AP The Associated Press. Breaking: Two Explosions in the White House and Barack Obama is injured.

The tweet, issued at 1:07 p.m. (EST)—less than a minute ago—was already re-tweeting. She rushed out of the elevator, thankful that security hadn't yet gone into lock-down and shut it down—she had no desire to be stuck in that elevator again, alone with memories of the night with Dillon.

The lobby of DeChartine New Media was deserted and an evacuation wasn't needed; right now her team were oblivious to anything that wasn't champagne, or Troy. She tried to stay calm despite her panicked thoughts of another 9/11; she'd only been in her mid-twenties back then—and safe in London—but she remembered the chaos in the media company she'd been working at.

Scurrying towards her office, she caught sight of Dillon frantically multi-tasking at his desk; he was on a telephone call and typing messages on-screen. As she listened, she heard him say the most welcome words he'd ever spoken: "hacked Twitter, President is fine."

Cutting off the call, he looked up. "Have you heard?" he asked.

"Only just, but you said it's not true?" she replied, hoping for further confirmation.

"No it's not true, but for us it's still chaos. I've started to notify all of our clients on social media security. The Dow Jones has already taken a drive, and we need to get ahead of this. Even when the market recovers, the doubts on new media security will have an impact on shares in our sector," he explained.

With admiration, Catherine listened to the focused, in-control man in front of her.

"Are the team back?" he asked hopefully; they needed all hands on deck.

Her eyes dropped toward the ground. "Troy started an open bar when you left," she mumbled apologetically. "What can I do to help?"

To his credit, Dillon didn't reprimand her. "I haven't contacted these ones yet," he said, handing her a printed copy of their biggest clients. She didn't waste time justifying the antics of Troy; instead, she took up a seat at his office table, and began to make calls on her mobile phone

Half an hour later and the situation had calmed down. The Associated Press had removed the offending tweet within minutes but, for a short time, the S&P 500 Index had dropped $136.5billion in value. The fall-out on their sector—due to the concern of Wall Street on the immediacy and impact of social media channels—was only just beginning. Through the combined efforts of Dillon and Catherine—and their quick, professional response to their clients—DeChartine New Media had weathered the storm, positioning themselves well to take advantage of the potential work-streams that would arise from the chaos.

Boldwood's company, they'd heard, didn't ride out the dip so well. In his distress at Catherine's engagement, Boldwood had been unreachable all day and his team lacked direction; they'd dumped some stocks too quickly and made substantial losses. Catherine knew she was the cause, and without Dillon, her company may well have faced the same fate.

"After that scare, I need a walk outside. Come with me?" she asked; she needed some fresh air to clear her mind of worry and guilt, but she didn't want to be alone with her demons.

"Sure, I could do with a coffee," Dillon replied, standing up from his chair and reaching for his coat. "You don't want to find Troy and see if he's okay though?"

"Not particularly," she admitted sadly. "Besides, if he's surrounded by an adoring audience and is downing free congratulatory drinks that I'm apparently paying for, I'd only get in the way. For someone that supposedly has political aspirations, you'd think he'd give a damn about a presidential bomb-scare, but then again, the guy is full of shit."

Catherine made no effort to hide from Dillon the fact that she was pissed at Troy.

Dillon hadn't spoken to her again since she'd told him the day before that she was unaware of the engagement, and he was none the wiser as to what had transpired. He'd heard the argument in Catherine's office—it had been hard not to—but always a man of integrity, Dillon had ushered away the curious employees, asking them to give their CEO some privacy.

Although she'd said at the time that she would find him later and explain the situation, the only explanation that had come was the engagement party invitation from Troy; Dillon didn't want to contemplate the make-up sex they must have had in her office for Troy to get her to calm down and agree to marry him.

"For a future bride, you don't seem to be all that happy?" he asked cautiously.

Catherine walked away, avoiding answering the question that he'd already guessed the answer too. He followed her to the elevators, and they headed downstairs in silence.

When they reached the lobby, she finally spoke, "Shall we take a walk in the park? The sun is coming out a little."

Although it was late April—and still reasonably cool—Central Park was in blossom.

"I think we've earned some time off," said Dillon, not wanting to raise the issue of Troy, or her missing team, again unless she did.

Reaching the park, they headed for a coffee stand and Dillon ordered two large cups of strong coffee. Pointing towards an empty bench under a blossoming tree to indicate where she would be, Catherine left him waiting for the beverages. When he joined her a few minutes later, they sat sipping coffee in silence, listening to the sounds of the city. Central Park was relatively empty for the time of day—the city a little spooked with memories of 9/11 after the false tweet.

"Dillon, thank you for everything you did today. It means a lot, and I need you in my corner," she said after a while.

"You have Troy to support you now," he replied sadly, continuing to stare upwards at the sky.

"There's only one corner he's in right now—the naughty one," she retorted with a hint of frustration.

Sitting so close to Dillon, she felt him shift uncomfortably on the bench; the wooden slats depressing as he adjusted his legs. "I didn't mean that kind of naughty corner," she added hastily. "I just wish he would...,"

Piss off and leave me alone . . .

Catherine couldn't tell Dillon what she wanted Troy to do; it would mean confessing everything about the situation and she was embarrassed at her stupidity and lack of control. A slight breeze gently shook the tree above them, and a shower of pink blossom fell onto Catherine's dark brown hair.

"You have cherry blossom in your hair," said Dillon, glad to be able to find a reason to change the topic from Troy and corners.

He was expecting her to flick it away quickly to preserve her polished look, yet surprisingly she smiled and looked upwards into the tree, allowing more petals to drift down onto her face.

"I love cherry blossom; it reminds me of my home," she said wistfully. "There were so many cherry trees in our garden that it snowed pink in April."

"Is that—I mean was that—your parents' house?" he asked hesitantly, afraid that he might be back into not-to-be-discussed territory; it seemed rude though to ignore the comment.

"Yes it was; I lived there until just after my mother passed away, and Dad stayed there sometimes after that. When my father died though, the bank sold it to cover the final mortgage payments—life insurance goes out the window when you take your own life," she half-heartedly joked. "It was the early nineties, and they didn't get much for it I don't think, but I heard it sold recently for several million. My school fees were covered by a trust fund left by my mother, but other than that, Gran had to take care of me."

Dillon saw her eyes starting to well up, and wondered how he could find a happier, common ground, rather than lay on sympathy—Catherine would hate him feeling sorry for her.

"I like apple blossom, because that reminds me of the orchards around my childhood home in Dorset. My parents sold it and moved to a village house closer to Dorchester when my sister and I finally left home," he revealed.

"I would love an orchard in my garden. A quiet place in the countryside maybe," she said, wistfully gazing up again at the trees above her.

Dillon noticed the sun's rays light up her blue eyes with a natural sparkle—rather than the frequently used wicked one. He contemplated asking whether she meant the English countryside, or somewhere here now that she was engaged to an American, but before he could find a way to bring up the issue of Troy, she asked, "Do you miss Dorset or London?"

"Every day," he replied, with no need for time to think about the answer; he missed home.

"Would you go back?"

"New York was always a temporary thing—originally I intended to come here for a few months, but I will probably go back to London in a year or two."

"Not Dorset?"

Dillon thought for a moment, not sure how much he wanted to tell his boss about his long-term dreams. "London is fine for work, but I miss the fields, the little lanes with thatched houses, and the coast. When I've had enough of working in media, and know what I could do with myself away from the capital for money and to keep boredom at bay, then I would probably find a house, get a dog, a wife and maybe a few kids."

He looked at her for the last part, unsure how she would react to his idyllic, domesticated future.

"Dog the priority after the house—a wise choice," she joked. "Is that what you always wanted to do—media I mean—not the house, dog, wife and kids," she said, smiling nervously at her intrusion into his private plans.

"No, far from it actually. Don't laugh, but I wanted to study history and literature at Oxford. Although, what I'd have done with that degree, who knows. I probably still would've ended up in media," he admitted.

"Never would've guessed you a history-buff bookworm," she teased.

"You said you wouldn't laugh," he scolded, nudging her arm playfully.

"Never said that—it was you that said 'don't laugh', and I don't recall being given the opportunity to agree, or disagree, before you told me your initial degree plans," she retorted; Catherine was enjoying their banter—Dillon was amusing when he had the courage to tease her.

"Okay, fair enough, you win. Yes, I was a history book nerd, but then the dream was shattered when I missed a few grades right at the end. Worked for a bit in odd jobs, even serving fish and chips through the summer—then I took a gap-year holiday. When I returned to England, I studied media and business at a university up north, and after that, I moved to London with the girl I was dating. That ended soon after arriving, but I had a job and so I stayed in the capital and was there until I came here to New York. So that's me—but what about you and media?"

"At least now I know why you're so good at bringing me fish and chips at lunchtime," she said teasingly.

"Yes, that I can do. Toast bread—maybe not so well," Dillon replied, grinning. "Now stop avoiding my question. Did you always want to be the shining star of media?"

Catherine looked down at the pigeons hovering around their feet. "No, media was definitely not in the original plan. I wanted to be a doctor when I was little, like my father." She looked up at Dillon's surprised face at her admission. "Yes, the Icy Bitch once wanted to help people—and don't laugh at that, or I'll wipe that grin off your face," she threatened, her wicked sparkle-smile making an appearance.

"Not laughing . . . much . . .," said Dillon, trying to keep a straight face and hold back his chuckles. "What happened to change your mind? Realize you'd have to nice to people? Discover that you couldn't actually threaten to tie patients up, or whip them if they didn't want to take their meds?" He was teasing, but he regretted his words when her sparkle-smile faded.

"When Dad took an over-dose, he left a note that said he could never forgive himself for not being able to save my mother, or to help with her final pain. He didn't think he'd been a good enough doctor—or husband. I found the letter in Gran's possessions when she died, and I was afraid that I might end up the same. I couldn't cope with the thought that I might not be good enough to save people, so I rejected my place in medicine, and avoided loads of other options too like veterinary science. I wouldn't even do law because I was afraid I'd lose cases for my clients. In the end, I figured in media you might miss deals, but no one was going to lose their life—or be banged up for it. I became an expert in avoidance of anything that I might not be good at—even relationships."

Catherine's revelations spoke volumes about her behavior, and Dillon didn't know what the best thing would be to say to help her overcome her fears. "You're doing well in your career, and you haven't avoided relationships. An engagement is a commitment, and maybe you and Troy will have kids. I've seen you be great with little Madison," he said eventually.

"I'd probably be a terrible mother—I'm always working—and I really, really, doubt Troy would even come close to winning a father-of-the-year award. As for the engagement, it's a commitment that I need to honor—so can we leave it at that?" she pleaded.

Dillon respected her wishes by asking no more about Troy and the engagement, and finishing the last mouthful of her coffee, Catherine stood up.

"We'd better be getting back. The others might finally have returned, and you should go and see if Boldwood needs help. Your assistance would be looked upon favorably by the Board."

Dillon nodded, and for once he didn't feel that she was dismissing him, or was sending him to Boldwood to do her dirty work; this time Catherine was thinking of his career and the opportunity that Boldwood's distraction had offered Dillon to show how worthy he was to be a CEO in his own right.

Chapter Thirty-Two

The next five weeks became an endless battle of wills between Troy and Catherine. After the engagement party—or rather in the early hours of the morning after it—he'd turned up drunk at her apartment and announced he was moving in. Every rebuttal she gave, from the first moving-in argument, to all the arguments following—Troy met with the threat of exposure and published photographs.

She loathed his presence in her space—and her life—and was secretly glad at all the nights when he didn't return to her apartment. Wherever he was, whatever he was doing, and whomever he was doing it with, she didn't care—all that mattered was that he wasn't snoring alongside her, or drunkenly attempting to have sex with her. Apart from their initial one-night-stand, and the April blowjob/failed snowball kiss, they had a non-existent sex life together; Troy, she suspected, was definitely getting his kicks elsewhere.

Catherine was more miserable and lonely than she'd ever been in her life, and had even contemplated a return to England to escape Troy. Even then, she knew that if the photos surfaced, her career would be over—unless she moved to Timbuktu, or better still, Mars.

As Memorial Day weekend approached, she longed for a break from Troy and her apartment; his clutter was everywhere. Under the guise of a pre-wedding girl's break, Catherine called Liddy and asked if she could join them in the Hamptons.

"Sure," Liddy replied. "Although it won't be just us girls and John, because we've already invited Dillon up for the weekend. Would that be a problem?"

In truth, Catherine thought it might be, but she needed time without Troy, and wanted to be with friends rather than alone.

"No, it doesn't bother me," she lied.

When she told Troy that she was spending the holiday weekend with friends, he simply shrugged and replied, "Whatever Cat." He'd never expressed an interest in meeting Liddy or John, even when he'd discovered what John's professional was; she knew that her decision to go away was the right one.

Packing her back on the Friday evening, Catherine had something to look forward to for the first time in months.

c҈e҈n҈o

Arriving at the beach-house, Dillon was relieved to get out of the car; four adults, and a toddler were too many bodies for such a small space, although once Catherine mentioned that during the clambake drive Madison had sang all the way, he was thankful that the child had slept through this time around. He breathed in the ocean air—another happier scent from his childhood.

"It's calming isn't it," said Catherine as she joined him on the deck to admire the view. "This is only my second trip, but I love it here."

"You never know, maybe you and Troy will buy a place here," he replied; Dillon had never re-visited the conversation of a month before when Catherine had mentioned she wanted a countryside home. Now he was curious about the Troy situation.

Where was he, why do I never see them together and why isn't she spending the weekend with him.

Liddy had only asked Dillon whether he minded Catherine joining them, and knowing that he didn't like Troy, she assured him that Catherine would be coming alone.

"I might buy one for myself," she replied bluntly. "Let's go and have one of John's nice cups of tea—Liddy has trained him in the art of the perfect British cuppa."

"Sounds good," said Dillon, resolving not to pry further into her first remark about the solo house.

The rest of the day was enjoyable—Catherine's mood completely changing in the presence of her friends. On many occasions, Dillon found himself forgetting all that had passed in the last five months—it seemed like only yesterday since the enjoyable Christmas morning he'd shared with the three companions he was with now—the four could easily be mistaken as two couples spending the holiday weekend together—one toddler in tow.

Unlike the clambake weekend, Catherine's presence to neighbors had gone unannounced—a last-minute plan to attend ensured that there were no intrusions by engagement well-wishers.

The time spent with her was bitter-sweet for Dillon; the more he watched her happy—laughing and joking, playing sandcastles with Madison, or even kicking water at him playfully as she waded through the shallows in her sundress—the more he could picture her in the future he wanted for himself back home. He wished that he was the type of man that might selfishly fight for her, but Dillon's stoical nature would never let him ruin an engagement—however much of an odd arrangement there seemed to be between Troy and Catherine.

By Sunday evening, the sea-air had restored Catherine's glow and Dillon couldn't take his eyes off her. When everyone said their goodnights for the evening, he headed for the bathroom with the image of a laughing, happy Catherine frolicking carefree in the shallow tide in a practically transparent dress—the wet material increasingly clinging to her shapely frame as the waves splashed it.

As his mind wandered to the curves of her body, he silently gripped his stiff cock in his palm to relieve himself of the sexual tension that had built up within him over the weekend. His eyes closed as he jerked his hand more forcefully, losing himself in the fantasy of Catherine's touch, just as she'd done in the elevator during the snowstorm. The more aroused he was, the more the fantasy seemed real—her arm wrapped around him from behind, her hand clasping his, her breath on his neck, her erect nipples against his naked back.

"Catherine," he hissed, unable to stop the words slipping out.

"Shush, someone will hear. Let me help you, but stay silent," she whispered.

"Fuck," Dillon shouted, anything but silently, as he tried unsuccessfully to let go of his cock and turn around.

Catherine's hand stayed clenched around his fist, and her body pushed into his from behind, stopping him from moving from his compromised position; Dillon hadn't worked out how to fasten the strange latch on the guest bathroom door properly, and Catherine had snuck in.

In any other circumstances, Dillon would have lost his hard-on through shame and embarrassment, yet Catherine's touch and boldness only turned him on more. He groaned with desire.

"Catherine, you shouldn't be doing this . . . we shouldn't be . . .," he hissed as she tugged on his hand and cock. "Troy—,"

"There will be no mention of him," she said as she silenced Dillon by reaching her other arm around him to place her hand over his mouth and gag him.

He submitted to her surprising strength, and she resumed the mutual jerking of their wrists—the added grip bringing him closer to the edge. She kissed his upper back, occasionally nipping at the softer spots between his muscles. When Dillon let himself go, he came hard and copiously into his hand, but she didn't release her own hand, instead she pushed his palm upwards as he let go of his cock.

"I believe I owe you a clean-up command—I can't have you leaving a mess like you did in the elevator, and my February snowball didn't count."

The humiliation of being caught masturbating, and then her grip on him, had sent Dillon into the highest level of subspace he'd ever encountered, and he didn't hesitate to follow her command, particularly as her other hand had left his mouth and was now tantalizingly caressing his butt-cheek, poised to slap him hard if he refused.

"Good Boy," she whispered. "You've made me all wet now, so perhaps it's time to get you to clean me."

There was no denying that Dillon was eager to go down on her in gratitude—oral pleasure was a skill he'd yet to show her how he excelled in—but his conscience snapped him out of his submissive state.

"You're engaged to someone else—pull yourself together. How many boy toys do you need?" he snapped, the words coming out more bitter and hurtful than he'd intended; Dillon was angry with himself for letting her again seduce his body—as well as his mind. He winced, expecting she would retaliate with fire, yet when he turned to face her naked body, all he saw was the sad disappointment of rejection.

"Just the one person who really wants me would be fine," she said dejectedly, then quickly hurried out of the bathroom before Dillon queried her melancholic state.

Confused as to whether to follow her, or what it might lead to if he did, Dillon washed his sticky hand, then splashed his face. Choosing the safer option of returning to his room, sleep evaded him that night—tossing and turning as he wondered what the hell was going on in Catherine's life; how he could help her resolve it, and whether he should even get involved again. The time had come for Dillon to make a decision about Catherine; he'd been balancing two jobs for the past month, and Emilia's offer to move him into a more senior role within Boldwood's company needed serious consideration—it would give him a way to ease out of Catherine's life.

❦

Arising out of bed early from his sleepless night, Dillon wanted to return to the city that morning. There was urgent business to attend to in Boldwood's company; the work would provide a valid excuse to avoid spending another tortuous day in the presence of out-of-office Catherine—particularly after their midnight encounter in the bathroom.

Finding an acquaintance that was driving back to the city after breakfast, Dillon made his apologies to Liddy and John while Catherine was in the shower.

❦

"Where's Dillon?" asked Catherine as she took up a seat at the breakfast bar. "Still sleeping?"

"No, he left for the city about ten minutes ago. What did you do to the poor guy?" John joked.

Her face reddened with embarrassment; Dillon would surely never had said anything about what had happened—even to a mate.

"I . . . err . . . nothing," she lied, hoping to avoid further scrutiny.

Liddy stayed quiet, glancing towards John as though telepathically communicating a request for him to go and find something to do elsewhere.

"Okay, I was joking. He said he had some urgent stuff for Boldwood to do, and so he went back with one of the executives who was staying nearby," said John, looking over at his wife to see if he was off the hook.

Liddy gave him a little nod, then a flick of the head to indicate he still needed to disappear.

"Anyway, I'd better go and wake our kid. She will need wearing out today if we stand any chance of peace in the car-ride home."

Catherine smiled knowingly; Liddy's glances had motives as transparent as an Emperor's new clothes, and she definitely appreciated John's intention to spare them a drive filled with Disney songs.

"Did Dillon say anything?" she asked, as soon as John was out of earshot.

"Apart from what John just told you about work, he didn't say anything else. But he did seem keen to be gone before you came out of the bathroom," replied Liddy.

"He didn't even say goodbye," she said wistfully.

Catherine was hurt at the blatant snub, yet she was feeling guilty that she'd put him in an awkward situation again—he'd been right to reject her advances; Dillon should be putting himself first and move on from her treating him like her toy or using him whenever she needed attention.

"Do I dare ask what happened between you? If anything did, that is," asked Liddy handing her a plate of toast.

"It was nothing," she protested, albeit unconvincingly. "Can we drop it?" She bit into her toast.

"Ordinarily I would say okay, but Dillon's a good guy and I like him. It is obvious to everyone—except you—that he loves you and is as jealous as hell about Troy. While you definitely have had that *happy in love with my fiancé* vibe this weekend—that fiancé you've been loved up on hasn't been Troy."

"I'm not in love with Dillon, nor is he in love with me. He's all alpha-male bossy when it comes to telling me exactly what he thinks of me—and my behavior—and the only thing he sees in me are my faults. Anyway, alpha-males fight for what they want," she insisted trying to convince

Liddy and herself that what she was saying was true; in her opinion if Dillon did love her, he would be fighting for her harder, and he wouldn't have rejected her advances last night; alpha-men wanted to win.

"Bullshit, Dillon is one of those rare guys who want to see someone they love be happy—even if that means being unselfish, or not letting their ego get the better of them. What's he supposed to do? All you do is push him away with flirtations. First, it was Boldwood, and now you're suddenly engaged to Troy. Even I'm confused, and I've known you years," replied Liddy, wanting to slap her friend in the face to wake her up out of all her bad decisions.

Catherine stubbornly chewed on her toast, delaying having to answer.

"Are you happy?" Liddy asked, taking on a friendlier, gentle tone.

Catherine's reply was a barely audible whisper, "No."

"Then why are you marrying Troy? You need to tell me what's really going on. Are you pregnant?"

"Fuck no. I've only slept with him the once, and that was terrible." Catherine cursed that she'd revealed the extent of how bad things were.

"Now I really go back to my first question. Why the fuck are you marrying a man you not only don't want to spend time with, but you don't even want to shag!"

Catherine sighed, and took a deep breath. She needed to come clean and confide in at least one person—it might as well be her best friend.

"Because Troy took pictures of me the only night we slept together. I didn't know he had . . .," she hesitated about giving the details, but lawyer Liddy would only ask. "I was blindfolded, so I didn't know. When I ended our fling that night, I thought that was the end of a bad night. Then he started pursuing me again, and we talked lots. I thought I might be falling for him as we talked about family, but then . . .," she stopped to have a mouthful of tea. "Then we tried again—you know, the sex thing—and it didn't work, so I ended the relationship."

"That's when he told you about the pictures?" asked Liddy, trying to work out what Troy's plan was.

"No. First, he announced an engagement in public and it seems I was the last to know. He hadn't even asked me to marry him. When he did, I refused—not caring if it meant public embarrassment at the retraction. That's when he said he had the pictures and would release them anonymously online if I didn't marry him."

Liddy looked at her in sympathetic horror. "Why does he want to marry you? And before you go psycho on me, I don't mean why anyone would want to marry you—because they would—I mean what's his motives, as that's not love."

"Prestige, money, trophy-wife in DeChartine to help with political aspirations—who knows—but he has affairs on the side, I know that."

"What a bastard. I'm so sorry Catherine." Liddy put her arm around her friend, before releasing her inner lawyer. "We will start a blackmail case and get you out of this, don't you worry."

Catherine sniffed, and shook her head sadly, "He says he has that covered. Apparently the pictures were taken in such a way that it looks like I'd set up cameras in my apartment, and the images expose him more than me. I stupidly had handcuffed him to my bed, and it would look like I was a kinky dominatrix, and that he was a conquest that I used until I was bored. With a public ending of the engagement, then the release of the pictures, it would appear that I was humiliating a man to end his political aspirations. He would get public sympathy."

"The guy sounds like a fucking asshole. No wonder Dillon hates him. I shouldn't say, but he's talked with John about him. They found out stuff about his past, including that he's the bastard son of a well-known Wall Street tycoon. It's all hearsay, and we didn't want to make it sound like we were all against you. That's the only reason we didn't say anything. If we'd known what he was doing to you, we would have said something."

"I knew the bit about his father—well Troy's version of it anyway. Is there anything else I should know?"

"He likes women . . .," Liddy said hesitantly. "A lot of women."

"That's also no great revelation. He's rarely home."

The more Catherine opened up to Liddy, the more she realized the engagement façade had to end.

"What are you going to do?" asked Liddy; she was coming up blank—the legal angles were exhausted.

"I don't know how to end it—not because I love him, or want him—but I don't know how to minimize the fallout."

"Can DeChartine help? They can usually cover up stuff."

"I don't want Emilia, or Boldwood, involved in this. Troy would destroy Boldwood, as I think he knows stuff about him. There was a fight in reception on Valentine's Day that suggested Boldwood knew him. That was the day you came around later, but I didn't tell you about the fight."

Liddy fiddled with her fingers. "I have a confession to make. I was there that day at Dillon's suggestion to come. He never said why, he just emailed to say you needed help. Please don't be angry at either of us."

"Typical Dillon—I think he hated Troy from that first meeting, especially considering it was only a few days after the snowstorm. I guess he hates him more now after talking with John."

Liddy suspected Dillon had never told Catherine that he'd known things about Troy beforehand, and she wasn't about to expose him to blame. "Can he help now?"

"No, I don't want him finding out about the pictures. Despite all I've done, he'd still try and protect me and I don't want him in Troy's line of fire. He's safe while Troy knows nothing of my involvement with him beyond work. If he suspected Dillon had feelings towards me, it would be the weakness that he'd manipulate. I don't want any of Dillon's secrets to be at risk, or him brought into my scandal at work. I can't do that to him—he doesn't deserve it and I've fucked up his life enough."

At that moment, John returned to the kitchen with Madison trailing behind.

"Auntie Catherine, are you coming to make sandcastles? Daddy says Mr. Dillon has gone home," asked Madison, her puppy-dog stare dissolving even the toughest resolve about avoiding sand under one's manicure.

"Of course I am," she replied, and then she turned back to address Liddy. "I will work something out."

Chapter Thirty-Three

The intercom for Catherine's apartment buzzed and Troy waited a moment before answering it, "Yes."

"We're here for Master Troy," came the reply.

"Come upstairs and wait at the door," he instructed.

Troy was making the most of Catherine's decision to go away; tonight's visitors were the third submissive order that he'd placed with Madame Rose that weekend. The betrayal of using Catherine's apartment to entertain his conquests only heightened his arousal. He secretly wished that she'd arrive home while he was still fucking them—retaliation for her continued resistance to submit to him in defeat. He doubted that he would ever achieve the level of domination that would let him involve Catherine in a threesome, yet even her watching him with another woman for only a second was a cuckolding that fitted into his fantasies. However, tonight was all about fulfilling that fantasy in another way.

He heard the knock on the apartment door, and he picked up two leather collars and leashes, reading to shackle the two submissives waiting eagerly on the other side of the door. Opening it slowly to build anticipation, he first saw the slender brunette dressed in a suit and heels, before his gaze moved to the young petite blonde, with long curly hair, who was wearing a cute and innocent pink dress.

The women matched exactly the description he'd given Madame Rose for what he wanted for the evening—even down to their attire—a brunette resembling Catherine, and a blonde. What he hadn't appreciated, was that in describing what he wanted the blonde to be like, he'd inadvertently described his former sub, Faye; the very girl who was now standing in front of him.

∞

Faye flinched at the sight of the dominant man in front of her; she'd become accustomed to all manner of sights on the other side of doors that she'd knocked on over the past months, but seeing her former Dom in front of her hit her hard. She contemplated running—just has she'd run from him the previous year in the alley, but this was the first work she'd had in a week.

Just think of the rent. Madame Rose will fire you if you don't.

Faye knew she'd lose another job if she dared turned down a client, even under these circumstances.

He's just another client—he doesn't care, just like they all don't.

Saying nothing to acknowledge that she knew him, and oblivious to his engagement, she ignored the obvious signs that they were in a female's apartment; instead Faye compliantly knelt on the ground ready to be collared once more by her former Master—now nothing more than a client.

When Faye said nothing in recognition, Troy saw an opportunity to avoid an argument—the brief concern of why she was working for Madame Rose, and the thought of sending her away, quickly dismissed from his mind. The only thing that was certain was that he wanted Faye, and now that he knew the levels that she'd sunk to, he was revisiting the thought that she'd be more willing to be his long-term submissive on the side now—without wanting more from the arrangement like she'd once done.

He proceeded to collar both women, and then yanked their leashes. "This way," he said, pulling them towards the bed.

"Take off your clothes," he commanded, looking only at Faye; she obeyed.

Troy had had many of his dominant desires fulfilled that weekend, but this was his finale; a fantasy where he dominated a Catherine-look-alike at the same time as his favourite kind of submissive—a petite, innocent blonde. As he watched Faye undress, he debated about how this should now unfold. In front of him was his actual favourite submissive, and there was also a fiancée substitute; he wondered what would arouse him more—Faye higher than Catherine in dominance, or Faye knowing her place as the second woman in his life. The decision was a difficult one; Catherine needed to be taught who was boss, but having Faye service Catherine—rather than the other way around—was closer to a likely reality.

"Dominate her," he commanded, this time facing the brunette.

Faye's eyes widened; she didn't want to be here to serve another woman—especially one that looked like her former bitch boss—but if it meant pleasuring Troy, and therefore satisfy her client—she would have to do it. Her initial doubts about being submissive to Troy were fast fading; hearing her Master command her to strip had reminded her how much she missed him.

The brunette leant down and kissed Faye, who was now kneeling at her feet; a soft kiss at first, but when she saw Troy lick his lips with desire, and his cock harden with arousal, the brunette deepened the kiss. Faye didn't resist, responding with equal hunger as she saw Troy's obvious pleasure in what he was watching; his voyeurism was making her incredibly horny.

Starting to get carried away, she moved her arms upwards, to run her hands over the clothed breasts of the other woman.

Stopping the kiss, the brunette straightened to a dominant stand, and slapped Faye hard across the cheek. "Did I say you had permission to touch me?" she commanded.

For a submissive, she was acting in the dominant role remarkably well, and the scene was better than Troy could ever have imagined it would be; pre-cum was already seeping from his erect cock. The brunette spotted the wet stain forming on his trousers and smiled seductively in response, before turning her focus to the whimpering Faye at her feet.

"Kiss my feet," she ordered—Faye complied, keeping her hands behind her back to avoid further reprimand. The brunette removed her jacket, blouse, skirt and then her bra. "Move slowly upwards," she said, once again directing her borrowed submissive.

Obeying, Faye kissed up one of the woman's legs, skipping her panties to move up to her naked breasts. She looked across at Troy, and he gave her a little nod, offering her permission to caress and suck the engorged nipples of the brunette.

Faye quickly became engrossed in the task Troy had set her, and he could see she was aroused by it—he knew all of her body language intimately. She was a true sub—even when being dominated by another woman. The brunette dug her fingernails into Faye's own nipples, and drove her heels into the girl's exposed peach-shaped bottom, resulting in a quick yelp from the hapless blonde.

The heels must have hurt.

Many a time Troy had pinched Faye's nipples with his fingers, or a clamp, and she'd only groaned with pleasurable pain.

"Serve me now wench," the Catherine-look-alike yelled, grabbing hold of a handful of Faye's blonde curls, then pushing her down between her thighs.

The statement was a little too contrived porn-speak for Troy's liking, but as he hadn't asked to be sent a dominant woman for the evening, he ignored her inexperience. Faye obliged the brunette—it was hard for her not to with the forceful hand pushing her down and the heels digging into her. Still kneeling, she worked her tongue up and down the woman's now naked clit, occasionally dipping the tip of her tongue into the aroused woman—drawing a groan of satisfaction out of her as she did.

Laying back on the bed, the brunette arched her hips forward, giving Faye full access. Troy watched as his submissive brought his dominant, replica fiancée to a mind-blowing orgasm, and then he decided it was time for him to join the party.

"Get on all fours," he instructed, facing Faye who was still kneeling in front of the brunette.

She knew what was likely to follow that command—he'd make her suck his cock for a few minutes to lubricate it a little, and then he'd take her strongly from behind—either vaginally or, more often than not, anally. Troy reluctantly moved his gaze from Faye's tempting rear, and the red-soled heels digging into it, to gaze at the brunette. She was smiling from her climax, sitting upright with her legs lifted off the floor.

"Faye," Troy commanded, using her name for the first time since she'd arrived, making her smile in response. "You will resume serving Catherine until she comes, and don't stop at all even if I do come."

Faye's smile faded and she hesitated; Troy had called the brunette Catherine—a name she'd hated since her last day at DeChartine. Her momentary lack of compliance resulted in punishment—a hard slap landing on her bottom.

"Don't defy me Faye," he demanded.

She obeyed reluctantly, leaning forward to start her task of pleasuring the bitch in front of her. Troy grabbed hold of the brunette's ankles and pulled her forward onto Faye's awaiting tongue. As he did so, he pushed his hard cock deep between Faye's butt cheeks. He hadn't indulged in his favourite past-time of anal for months—not since he'd last had Faye—but now it was time to make her dance to his desires.

Faye winced, and let out a whimper, the sound reverberating on the brunette's already over-sensitised clit.

"Lick me harder," begged the other woman—her plea a mix of dominance and submission.

Troy didn't bother to silence either of them—he was too full of his own ego and a delusional belief that he was successfully dominating the two women of his life. As he thrust his cock deep into Faye with renewed vigour, he never stopped staring deep into the brunette's eyes as she succumbed to the pleasure that the blonde was giving her.

Faye was helpless in the scenario—trapped between the legs of the pretend Domme and the strong body of the Master behind her. For the first few seconds of Troy's thrusts, her face had slammed into the stomach of the brunette, but the other woman had responded by grabbing hold of her hair and pushing her back into position. While thoughts that this was all kinds of wrong were running through Faye's mind—that it was humiliating servicing a bitch like Catherine—her body didn't protest. It felt good to have Troy inside her again and she could tell that he was enjoying it; she squeezed her buttocks around the base of his cock—anxious to please him further.

The action worked; Troy let go of the brunette's ankles without hesitation—causing her legs to drop to the floor—and he grabbed hold of Faye's waist to pull her deeper onto him. Faye withdrew her freed face from the wetness between the brunette's thighs. Now it was just Troy and his sub interacting; the Catherine-look-alike forced to watch on—and the scenario aroused him even more.

At that moment, the door opened; Catherine was home and Troy's greatest fantasy was about to come true.

∽

Silence descended on the room, and the anonymous brunette pulled her body away from the other two, huddling up at the top of the bed and putting a blanket over her naked body.

"Stop fucking that bitch," Catherine eventually yelled, trying to command Troy to stop; the bastard didn't listen. Even if she'd delivered the line with the appropriate, dominating authority, it wouldn't have mattered—Troy was in control now, and there was no way he was stopping until he'd climaxed. He already had one submissive woman completely at his mercy—kneeling on all fours in front of him and impaled on his cock—her whimpering testament to the power he had over her body, and he strongly suspected that he'd finally defeated Catherine's attempts to dominate him. If he ignored her command to stop, he expected she would resort to begging him to; the battle of wills between them had reached its finale.

The only sound in the room was Faye, rapidly nearing an orgasm with nothing to gag her cries.

"I said stop," Catherine repeated, trying once more to end the horrific scene in her apartment; Troy continued to ignore her, and the only control she had left was to attempt to shut the blonde up.

She grabbed hold of the riding crop that she saw on her bedside table and brought it down hard. The leather ripped into the girl's back, but the whipping only made the blonde whimper even more—she was clearly used to punishment and derived pleasure in it. Troy became all the more manic in his thrusting as her action played into his fantasy of another woman whipping his beloved submissive.

Catherine couldn't bear the sound of Faye any more, yet blocking her ears would be giving up and she refused give Troy that satisfaction. Spotting the stupid girl's panties, or perhaps the brunette's—it didn't matter—and remembering the scenario she'd put into her story for Dillon so long ago, she picked them up and reached forward to shove them into the girl's open, wailing mouth. It worked to drown out the noise, but the gag only further excited the pair still openly fucking in front of her. Catherine started towards the door—desperate to flee— but as she reached it, Troy found his release, and she immediately froze at his cry.

"Faye."

That one word made Catherine's body shake with anger. She needed no time to compute Troy's outburst; the name brought back the memory of an uncompliant blonde receptionist called Faye. She turned to look at Troy, and he smiled back at her, unashamed at what he'd done. His was a wicked smile, with none of the cheekiness she used to torment men—this was a smile of pure evil, which spoke volumes; Troy believed he'd won.

The blonde's head was lowered towards the floor, maintaining the natural submissive position. Catherine walked over to her and roughly grabbed her hair to yank her face upwards. She stared intensely at the face looking up at her. Despite the thinner, gaunt face, it was one she recognized; the pathetic eagerness to please a man that she'd seen on the receptionist's face that first morning, came back to haunt her.

'What was he doing here—who was he here to see?'

Dillon's questions about Troy's first visit to DeChartine returned to the forefront of her mind.

'What I could do with that arse.'

Troy's first words to her were finally making sense—especially as she was now looking at him with his cock still deeply embedded in the receptionist's ass. Catherine sank onto the bed, and the brunette she'd so far ignored, fled off it.

"Have to say Cat, your riding crop domination skills just now were far more convincing than the Catherine-look-alike's ones were. Perhaps you could step in to replace her in round two of the threesome?" Troy grinned as he delivered his taunt about the scene's purpose, and the indecent proposal for her to join in.

Catherine glared at him, and then at the brunette. She hadn't thought anything could be worse than catching your fiancé fucking another woman in your own apartment, but knowing that he'd gone to such an elaborate fantasy in getting someone who looked like her to dominate her former receptionist—clearly an old friend of his—took him to a whole new level of fucking bastard.

"Get out," she hissed, her demand full of loathing, yet directed at no one in particular.

"I said get out bitch!" Again her command didn't hit a target—there were two women in the room other than her.

The brunette, not previously acquainted with anyone in the apartment—including Faye—was unwilling to disobey; she wanted away from this scene, even if she hadn't yet been paid. Her departure left Troy and Faye in a standoff against Catherine.

Rising to her feet, Catherine lunged forward at Faye, slapping her hard across the face.

"Get the fuck out of my apartment, my company and our lives you stupid worthless whore," she yelled, her temper at a level she'd never reached before.

Faye felt winded—the slap hurt, but had hit her nowhere near as hard as the words 'worthless whore' had. All her feelings of not being good enough, and of being used, and abused, surfaced.

"Troy loves me," she protested defiantly.

"My fiancé loves you?" said Catherine, laughing at the naivety of the girl—the absurdity of Troy wanting a receptionist over her.

Faye spun around to look at him, "You're marrying her—the woman that fired me?"

Her deluded defiance was replaced by anguished, desperate sobs. Troy shrugged and didn't answer. Faye—not wanting to look at the woman she'd been dumped for any longer—hurriedly collected up her clothes and ran naked from the apartment; dressing in a communal hallway—even with the risk of being seen—was considerably less humiliating than the scene she'd just participated in.

Once she'd dressed, Faye rushed down the stairs and out into the street; stripped of what little of her dignity she had left.

※

Catherine and Troy stared at each other; no words spoken to kick-start the war that had been brewing since the first night that they'd slept together. If Faye hadn't been his ultimate weakness, Troy would have continued to ruin Catherine slowly, but now that he'd been caught, one of them would be defeated tonight; in Troy's mind the woman in front of him had finally been broken into submission.

He was only partially right; Catherine was broken, yet would never submit to him.

"I want you to leave," she said, trying to come across as calm and in control.

Troy sniggered, "I'm not leaving you. We're engaged."

"It's over Troy. Agreeing to the engagement was a mistake."

"You don't want the fall out of this, and you know it," he replied, standing his ground and determined that he'd appeal to her career pride.

"I want you to leave the house now and go wherever it is you want to go, but don't ever come back. I will send your stuff tomorrow by courier," she replied, pretending that she was concluding a business deal—the absence of emotion gave her control.

"Cat, you know I have the pictures," he said as his arrogance started to give way to desperation.

"Release them then. I will put the country's best PR team on stand-by, while my legal team will find—and subpoena—every woman you have wronged. Ruin me and I, with the help of an army, will take you down with me. Just know this—I will never submit to you."

Troy looked uncomfortable; Catherine was proving to be stronger-willed than he'd bargained for, and there was no sign of a crumbling self-esteem. "Come on Cat, let's work this out. You and I'd be a great political team."

The desperation in his voice surprised her, as did his sudden eagerness to compromise; her eyes narrowed as she studied his pained expression.

"You don't have any photographs, do you?" she asked.

Troy's hesitation gave her all the confirmation she needed that her suspicion was correct; he had no leverage.

"You conniving little shit—you have five seconds to get the hell out of my apartment. Go and join your whore—you're even more worthless than she is, so you'll make a great couple," she hissed and picked up the riding crop again, heading towards him and threatening to strike.

Troy readied himself to dodge her blow, but she passed him and opened the front door, and then threw the crop into the hall. "Go I said, and take your toys with you."

Catherine wasn't sure what eventually convinced Troy to go—she suspected that it was her invitation for him to go and find Faye that provided the catalyst. As soon as he was gone though, the strong front that she'd faked crumbled, and she crumpled to the floor in a devastated heap. Long into the night, Catherine cried the tears that she'd held back for years.

Chapter Thirty-Four

The rain fell hard the following day, gridlocking the streets of New York. Catherine had found her resolve in the early hours of the morning; dressing for work and concealing the evidence of her tears with as much concealer as her face would hold; the rain prevented the feasible use of sunglasses to cover her eyes. Leaving the apartment early, she figured that she could be in the safety of her office before anyone saw her arrive, and could then blame the puffy, panda-eye look on an all-nighter at her desk.

The plan would have worked if she hadn't had one of New York's most dedicated employees on her team; Dillon had been in the office since arriving back in the city the day before. As Catherine stepped out of the elevator, she walked straight into him as he was heading out for a caffeine hit.

Dillon knew the difference between staying up all night working, and the signs of puffy eyes from tears—Catherine's face showed the latter. Knowing her well enough to know that asking what the matter was would be taken badly, he decided to adopt the covert shoulder-to-cry on approach.

"I thought I needed coffee, but you look like you need it more. Want to come with me and get some?" he asked.

If Catherine suspected his motives, she didn't show it; with a meek smile, she stepped back into the open elevator, "Coffee would be good."

Travelling down to the ground floor, she broke the awkward silence. "You've been in the office since yesterday?"

"Yes, pretty much. I had a few hours of sleep on the couch in the office, but otherwise I was working on some stuff for Boldwood."

Catherine nodded, knowing that he was working hard for both companies. "Madison missed your sandcastles yesterday. I don't think mine were quite up to scratch—a bit like my snowmen," she meekly joked, trying to laugh in spite of her sadness.

"Sorry about leaving so suddenly. Something came up and a colleague drove me back," he said, trying to apologise; he felt guilty that his early departure might be the reason that she was so upset.

The elevator stopped at another floor and a cleaner stepped in, silencing them for the rest of the journey downwards—neither wishing to discuss personal things in the presence of others. When they reached the ground floor, they headed out of the lobby towards the coffee shop on the corner; both huddled under Dillon's large umbrella.

"Catherine," a female voice shouted out from behind them.

They both stopped and turned, trying to see through the falling rain who was the owner of the voice.

Neither of them ever found out why Faye had shouted Catherine's name—she could have been there to yell at her, or she could have been there to apologise; her reason was a mystery she would take to her grave.

The truck-driver didn't put his foot on the brake in time—the rain added too much to the braking distance for the weight of his vehicle. By the time he saw a woman run out into the wet road, it was too late. Dillon and Catherine watched in horror at the scene unfolding in front of them. Although screams were all around, Faye never had the chance to make a sound; she never saw her fate skidding towards her.

"Catherine, stay there and call 911," yelled Dillon, running out into the road; he wanted her to stay on the pavement safe from traffic, and from seeing the woman he thought that he recognised. There was little chance that she would have survived being hit that hard and, as he neared her, his worst fears were confirmed; he'd been right on both counts—the bloodied body in front of him was Faye.

The rain was already washing the blood away from her face and body as it continued to flow from her wounds. Dillon looked down in sadness at her lifeless body; she was much thinner than he'd remembered from his brief meeting with her the year before, and he recalled Boldwood telling him that she'd been working as a submissive prostitute since being fired from DeChartine and dumped by Troy.

"Oh god," said Catherine, covering her face with her hands; she'd abandoned the umbrella to follow him, and was now standing soaked above him as he crouched beside Faye. There was disbelief in her eyes—much more than from shock alone at seeing a dead woman, and Dillon realized that she too had recognized Faye.

"I saw her . . . I know her . . . I . . .," Catherine was in shock, muttering hysterically, and Dillon stood up to wrap his arms around her.

"She was the receptionist when you started," he said quietly, hoping that Catherine had never been enlightened as to Faye's involvement with Troy—nor would she ever find out now.

"Yes, but . . .," she hesitated, and Dillon's heart sank as he suspected that there was more to her pained look. "I saw her last night," she said, blank of emotion.

"Where?"

"She was at my apartment when I got home from the Hamptons. She was there with Troy, and another woman, and then there was a fight."

Catherine left out the details of the scene she'd walked into; she didn't need to explain, Dillon had worked out the overall context of what had happened.

"Catherine, this isn't your fault. Even if there was a fight, that was last night. You weren't fighting with Faye right now, and you didn't push her into the road. She walked across the road without looking. You weren't driving the truck that hit her."

Dillon needed to get her to realize that this was an accident; Catherine had to focus before the police arrived and she said something stupid to absolve her guilt. He held her tighter, and she relaxed into his strong arms, burrowing her face into his muscular chest as she started to cry.

"Shush now, it will be alright. I'm here. There's nothing we can do for her now. She's at peace. I'll protect you from Troy," he said, soothing her with his assuring words.

"No!" A cry of anguish came from behind them.

Dillon let go of Catherine and they both turned towards the scream. Troy was only steps away, and he crumpled to his knees next to the lifeless body of Faye.

"Faye, wake up. Faye, you stupid girl, wake up!" He was leaning over her body, shaking her to try and desperately revive her. Nothing was going to bring her back; her injuries would have instantly been fatal.

They watched helplessly as Troy did everything to try to resuscitate her. When the paramedics and police arrived on the scene, he finally gave up and faced Catherine; his face contorted with grief-stricken anger.

"You—you did this you bitch. You didn't want her to have me," accused Troy, lashing out—his scathing words cutting deep into Catherine who was already blaming herself.

She stepped back in horror, unable to find words to answer him while part of her agreed with him; she was responsible.

"Faye walked in front of a truck from the other side of the road to us," Dillon explained, stepping in front of Catherine to defend her from Troy. "We didn't even know she was here."

Dillon was mostly telling the truth; they'd only just been alerted to her presence by her shout, and even then they hadn't confirmed that it was Faye due to the low visibility in the rain.

"I'm so sorry . . . I didn't see her . . . she just ran out into the road," muttered the truck driver who was standing motionless nearby; seeing Troy, his guilt got the better of him and he was trying to apologize.

Troy ignored him, his sights set on blaming Catherine, and vowing she would pay for this.

"She did it," he repeated, pointing his finger at her and ensuring that the police were watching. "Everything that happened to Faye was her fault, because it all comes back to her."

Troy dug the knife further into Catherine's own self-doubt, rendering her speechless. There were tears falling from her eyes, disguised from view only by the falling rain.

"That's enough Troy. If you really want someone to blame beyond this being an accident, then blame yourself because you did this to Faye," yelled Dillon, standing up to him, but being careful with his words; Catherine was within earshot, and this wasn't the time—or place—to avail her with all that he knew about Troy and Faye's history.

However, it was too late; she'd heard him speak and, despite her distressed state, she'd comprehended what Dillon had said.

"You knew about them?" she asked with bewilderment. "Dillon, you knew about Troy and Faye and you didn't tell me? How long have you known? Is that why you told me those questions I should ask?"

This betrayal of trust was one she wasn't expecting, but now his questions really did make sense; he didn't just suspect Troy was bad news—he knew the details, even back then.

"You know I tried to tell you that day Troy first took you to lunch. You didn't want to hear, and you just kept looking at the damn flowers he'd sent. I didn't want to interfere with your happiness after that," he replied, trying to get her to understand things from his perspective. He stepped towards her to take her back into his arms, but she retreated further away from him.

"Catherine, please don't run away from me. I'm not the bad one here," he pleaded, hoping she would see reason.

She shook her head at him. "You were supposed to be my friend. You were supposed to protect me—that's what you always seemed to do. This—," she pointed down at Faye. "This is what happens when women let themselves be deceived by men. I won't end up the same. I'm just fine on my own." Stifling her sobs, she ran towards the shelter of the DeChartine building's lobby.

❧

The day passed in a blur of statements and private solitude. Catherine avoided Dillon, and once the necessity to remain at the scene passed, Liddy came to collect her. Boldwood, once informed by Dillon, wanted to run to Catherine's aid—an idea that Dillon discouraged.

Troy stayed at the scene only until the final removal of Faye's body; the police hadn't required statements from him as he hadn't witnessed the incident, and he told them that he'd take care of the business of Faye's affairs—unwilling to reveal her address due to its link to Madame Rose.

Prior to arriving at the scene of the tragedy, he'd been to see Madame Rose in search of Faye, and now—only a few hours later—he found himself back there in the small room that she'd rented behind the establishment. Faye had few possessions, and he looked around at what remained in memory of her life—the most prominent items being a photo of himself, cut from a college yearbook, and a few childish gifts that he'd given her.

He'd failed her; Faye would never have been the wife that could provide him with social status or money, but she was the only person who'd ever truly loved him, and she was the one he always went back to.

He fell to his knees, crying as he cradled a small pink teddy bear, emblazoned with the word *Faye* across its stomach.

Chapter Thirty-Five

It was 10:00 a.m. on a Wednesday morning; Catherine should have been at work, yet here she was sitting silently in a lounge armchair at Liddy's house—her hands wrapped around her millionth mug of tea. She'd remained in the chair all night, staring out of the window at nothing in particular in the street.

She didn't notice the visitors approach; Boldwood had given up waiting at the office, and when he'd failed to find Catherine at her apartment, he'd headed for the Bradbury home. As he reached the corner near their brownstone, he caught sight of Dillon walking in the same direction.

"I have to see if she's okay," he insisted, unwilling to let Dillon talk him out of it any longer.

Dillon nodded understandingly; he was there for the reason that he too cared about Catherine's welfare.

Arriving at the house, Liddy greeted them in hushed tones in the hall.

"Can we see her?" asked Dillon, speaking for the both of them.

"Yes, but I don't know what she'll be like, or what you're all going to say. She feels you have both betrayed her in keeping back details about Troy, even though I confess I'd told her over the weekend that Dillon had concerns. She'll come around though. It's just her way—attack first before she has time to consider everything."

The men followed Liddy into the front room and Catherine turned her attention away from the window.

"If there's anything we can do to help with the company Catherine, you only need to ask," said Boldwood.

It was a strange thing to lead on, particularly considering that he'd been neglecting his professional life of late, but it was the right thing to say to break the ice; Catherine always put work ahead of everything.

"Thank you Bill, the offer is appreciated. I know that the company will be in safe hands with you both; however, I will be at work tomorrow as there's no need to drag this out. Faye was no relation of mine," she replied calmly.

"Are you sure?" Boldwood was floundering now—he'd been keen to be of service to her.

"Yes I am. I've lost focus of late and let my personal life take over. It's time to make some changes."

Dillon looked at her with concern—would she try to fire him again in retaliation? Catherine seemed determined to get back control and not let men walk over her.

"Troy will no longer be involved in my professional, or personal, life. The engagement, and the relationship, are off. I ended it Monday evening—before yesterday's tragedy—however after his accusations, I emailed him confirmation that it was over and that his personal effects had been removed from my apartment into storage. Last night my locks were also changed. Security at DeChartine has been informed that he's banned from the building." Catherine delivered her update with professional assertiveness, and with no sign of emotional weakness.

Dillon breathed a sigh of relief, as did Boldwood—both men weren't sorry to see Catherine relinquish the strange hold that Troy had had over her. While Dillon's relief was more for her wellbeing and state-of-mind, Boldwood suddenly had a renewed purpose—she was single again.

"A wise decision Catherine. You need a man worthy of you that will treat you right," Boldwood said eagerly.

She glared at him, "Bill, it was my decision to end things with Troy, and it's the right one, but you must understand that I don't need a man—nor do I want one. If I've learned anything in the past twelve months, it's that nothing good comes of letting myself be distracted by the attentions of men. As I told Dillon yesterday, Faye's unfortunate accident only confirms my opinion."

Boldwood's hopes were dashed and, deep inside, Dillon also felt a pang of disappointment; he still loved her, but he was glad that Troy hadn't destroyed her strength. He hoped that one day she'd find someone that was worthy of her heart—a man who would crack it open in the right way and never smash it to pieces as Troy had attempted to do. He didn't know if Catherine was merely putting on a brave face; she must have believed herself in love with Troy—she'd never have agreed to marry him if she didn't—and therefore she must be hurting behind that tough façade of hers.

John and Liddy joined them in the lounge, bringing with them trays of tea and coffee. Before anyone had a chance to thank them, the lively tune of John's mobile filled the morbid room with a happier sound. Recognising the number as the offices of the paper, he excused himself—technically he was working from home.

"Hello," he answered; his greeting then followed by a long period of silent listening. Gradually his face began to change into a sad expression—one that Liddy had rarely seen on him during a call from the office—business news didn't warrant such anguish, even if the stock market was falling. "I understand. You can pass on the message that she's here at our house."

John put down the phone and focused his attention to Catherine. She returned his gaze; as the only female in the room that didn't live here, his last comment to the unknown person on the line had to have been about her presence at the Bradbury home. She prayed that, as her friend, John would surely not let a reporter come to interview her—even if Troy had been up to his tricks with the media again.

"Catherine, there's no easy way to tell you this . . .," he paused, trying to find the strength to say the words. "That was a colleague in the news section, who's at a police scene. He was out jogging this morning and found possessions that belonged to Troy on the Brooklyn Bridge. Amongst the items was a note with your name on it. He called me out of concern, as he knew you're a friend of ours. The police were going to be heading for your apartment, but they're now on their way here."

Catherine stared in disbelief at the words she was hardly hearing.

"He wouldn't have jumped," said Liddy in shock.

"He would," replied Catherine without hesitation; she sat emotionless, the memory of her father's suicide painfully brought back to the here-and-now.

"But why? It makes no sense," continued Liddy, still unable to believe it. However, in the room she was the only one who doubted that Troy would commit suicide—everyone having different reasons as to why they thought it was true.

While Boldwood didn't believe that Troy would grieve for Faye to the point of suicide, his own obsession for Catherine led to a ridiculous empathy that Troy may have reacted badly to her emailed rejection letter.

John felt that Troy's actions had nothing to do with love—or even revenge—and everything to do with him being a coward, who didn't have the balls to rebuild his career and connections on his own two feet now that Catherine had stopped enabling his sudden ascent to power.

Dillon was of the opinion that Troy would never jump through grief, but he'd seen the look of loathing in the man's eyes towards Catherine; Dillon believed that Troy would resort to anything to inflict maximum pain on her in revenge, and suicide was a particularly personal attack.

Catherine shared Dillon's view.

Apart from Liddy, everyone kept their opinions on Troy's motives to themselves, and it wasn't long before the squad car arrived outside the brownstone. When the police entered and asked if they could speak to Miss Everdene alone, none of the four adults with her moved.

"Anything you need to say to me, you can say in front of my friends. We all know why you're here," said Catherine, who was secretly glad of the support, even though only a short while earlier, she'd said she didn't need anyone.

"Certainly Miss Everdene, as I understand, you've been made aware that we're led to believe that your fiancé—Troy Selgent—jumped from the Brooklyn Bridge in the early hours of this morning. The note that was at the scene does indicate that he was intending to take his own life, and his shoes, jacket, wallet and phone were left in a pile on the bridge. We have started a search, of course. It was fairly early this morning that the items were spotted on the bridge by a jogger—who I understand is a colleague of Mr Bradbury." The male officer spoken with compassion, trained to deliver news such as this.

"Can I see the note?" Catherine enquired. There was no emotion in her question, as though she was an impartial detective or journalist, rather than a grieving loved one.

"That isn't possible, as it's sealed as evidence. We do have a digital image of it, although I'm not sure you would want to read it, particularly at this sensitive time." The female officer had read the note, and would want to be spared of its contents if she were in Catherine's position.

"Catherine, please don't let him get to you. You shouldn't have to see such an atrocious thing," interrupted Boldwood, who was determined to step up and fulfil the role of her protector.

"I want to see it," she insisted, ignoring Boldwood's pleas.

The male officer handed her his phone—the image of the note displayed on the small screen.

> 'CATHERINE—YOU DID THIS. YOU TOOK
> EVERYTHING FROM ME—YOU & YOUR ENDLESS
> NEED FOR CONTROL. YOU KILLED FAYE & NOW
> YOU'VE KILLED ME.'

"For a man who's in the last, desperate moments of his life, his handwriting is steadier than he ever wrote before. Nice to see he also used capitals for maximum effect—particularly as he was always more of a lower-case, text-talk kind of guy," said Catherine casually, reading through the note for a third time.

The officers didn't know how to answer; dealing with a response like hers was outside of their training.

"My father was a more eloquent man," she continued, a tear sliding down her cheek. "His final words were love."

Both officers looked confused, as did Boldwood. "A man on his deathbed is sure to say different things to one taking his own life," he said compassionately, wanting to connect with her. Boldwood had no knowledge of the contents of Troy's note, and his blame of her—nor sadly of her father's tragic end; still deluded with the idea that Troy had acted out of a desperate love for her.

"My father took his own life because he couldn't live without my mother, and his note was full of the guilt he still felt inside about her death. His words were those of a depressed, broken-hearted man, but these words—," she held up the phone screen to everyone in the room, even though they couldn't be read from a distance.

"These are the words of a man who was unable to love anyone, and who only wanted to blame everyone for everything that was wrong in his life. Troy was a narcissist and if he was hurting—he wanted to make damn sure everyone hurt more. His note was about revenge, not love."

Catherine was angry at Troy, for although she felt sorry for Faye, she wasn't going to be blamed for her death. She handed back the phone to the officer.

"Can I see it?" Dillon politely asked, having previously remained silent since arriving at the brownstone; he looked towards Catherine to seek approval.

"Show it to him."

Taking the phone, Dillon scanned the screen to read the vile words, and then passed it onto John who was standing next to him. Boldwood—too lost in comprehension of the suicide of Catherine's father—didn't ask to read it.

"I'm sorry to ask, but we may need to ask Miss Everdene to come to the station later to answer some questions. We have no reason to believe that it's anything other than a suicide—despite some of the words in the note—and without the lack of further evidence, or a body, there's nothing else to indicate foul play. However it's procedure," said the officer gently, knowing that it was always a thin line when asking relatives to attend the station for questioning in a death enquiry.

"You can't honestly think that Catherine had anything to do with his death," said Dillon defensively, worried that they were interpreting Troy's use of the word 'killed' as an accusation that need to be investigated.

"Catherine Everdene has a solid alibi. She's been here since yesterday. I'm her lawyer, and there are insufficient grounds for an investigation," added Liddy, wading into the defence of her friend. Although she'd yet to read the note, she'd heard the officer give a likely timeline based on the rain; Catherine was in the clear of involvement.

"As I said, there's no evidence, other than the note," replied the officer calmly. "We do know his state of mind due to yesterday's accident involving Faye Robine, and we also have an email that Miss Everdene sent him yesterday, which indicates that you'd severed all ties."

"Surely that email proves that Catherine had told him she wanted no more to do with him," said Boldwood, resuming his protector role.

"Some would interpret it as that, but others might ask if they met later to discuss the contents of the email face-to-face. Mr. Selgent didn't respond by email, and there are several hours unaccounted for."

Even from beyond the grave, Troy was trying to destroy Catherine's reputation by setting her up; his note had provided doubt and the only thing more that he could have done was leave a weapon at the scene.

"What now?" asked Catherine, looking at the officers with concern that she might be investigated on murder charges.

"What now, is that they're on a fishing expedition—you have an alibi," interrupted Liddy.

"I suggest they go fishing for a body then," Catherine remarked—a bad joke strangely distracting her from the thought of a future in prison.

"Miss Everdene, we will continue the search and investigation," said the female officer kindly, dismissing the inappropriate joke as due to shock. "We do need to ask though that you don't leave the city, and I understand that you're a British national?"

"She is, but until she's an official suspect—which will never happen as she *has an alibi*—she is free to do as she pleases," interjected Liddy again, reiterating the alibi statement.

"You have my word I'm not leaving, because I have a company to run. More importantly, I'm innocent of any crime," Catherine added.

The officers nodded and, after thanking everyone for their time, they left the brownstone.

Catherine turned to Dillon and Boldwood, "I'd like to be alone now and you both have companies to run. Dillon, you're in charge of mine until tomorrow."

"No problem. Get some rest and take care of yourself," he replied, before turning to say goodbye to Liddy and John.

"I'm staying," said Boldwood, not rising from the chair. "You need support."

"I have Liddy's support here, and I also know that I have your support—just as I have Dillon's—and that means a great deal. However I need your support to be back at the office," insisted Catherine sternly, knowing that her tone would be one that Boldwood would obey.

"Very well, as you wish Miss Everdene," he replied with a lowered gaze, and then he reluctantly left her.

Chapter Thirty-Six

Nearly three months had passed with no news of the fate of Troy Selgent. The police had long given up the search for his body, and it hadn't washed up further down the Hudson. John had called in every favour he could with the news journalists, but they hadn't been able to shed any light on Troy's mysterious disappearance—apparently it wasn't unusual for a body never to be recovered.

The investigation had never been progressed beyond that of suicide; there was no provable motive for murder, and Catherine hadn't stood to benefit from his death; on all accounts the police believed that she'd have had sufficient support—legally, financially and emotionally—to remove Troy from her life without resorting to killing him. The more they'd looked into his character, the more that the police believed that he'd stood to lose enough in the ending of the engagement, to warrant taking his own life—particularly considering his relationship with the deceased Faye Robine.

Ever since she'd been informed of his apparent suicide, Catherine had spoken little of Troy; Dillon and Liddy both feared her silence had more to do with her childhood, than grieving for him. When Liddy finally dared ask her if Troy had known about her father, Catherine had confirmed that she'd given him the barest of details.

On hearing this, Liddy had come around to Dillon's opinion that Troy had deliberately chosen suicide as a final revenge against Catherine, but she was still curious as to why—if that was the case—Troy wouldn't have taken an overdose of anti-depressants as her father had done. The lawyer in Liddy was still suspicious of him, and the lack of a body only added to the growing theory she had that Troy had possibly faked the whole thing, and was alive somewhere laughing his arrogant ass off.

One person, who definitely didn't think Troy was still alive, was Boldwood; he'd once again upped his interest in Catherine and was determined to be the one to give her support, reasoning that eventually she'd come to appreciate it and let him serve her.

Dillon was increasingly becoming worried about the older man's mental state—Boldwood was neglecting the most basic of work duties and he'd frequently walked in on him visiting lingerie and shoe websites during the working day. As tactfully as he could, Dillon asked Catherine if she'd resumed receiving gifts from Boldwood.

"I did a few times, about a month after Troy disappeared. I asked him to stop, but when he didn't, I started to send them back to the store requesting they refund him," she replied, with no inquisitiveness as to why Dillon was suddenly asking; Catherine had shut herself off from everyone, with no interest in anything other than work. More driven than Dillon had ever seen her before, he chose not to press the issue to avoid an argument.

೦ⅇ⌒ಎ೦

Towards the end of the August, Emilia DeChartine invited her most senior executives to an extended weekend in the new home she'd rented in the Bahamas. Getting on in age, Emilia needed warmth and it was the ideal location for a DeChartine strategy away-day break. Five of the DeChartine companies' CEOs were attending—including Catherine and Boldwood, and Emilia had extended the invitation to Dillon in recognition of the work he'd been doing across two of the companies.

Emilia laid on a private jet to take everyone south; Catherine and Dillon hadn't flown in such luxury before; a novelty they would remember. Flying over the Hudson as they departed, Catherine looked down and wondered where Troy had finally come to rest.

They would've been married by now, and although she didn't miss him, the thoughts of all that occurred—and what might've happened in the future—gave her nightmares at night, and a strengthened resolve to stay single.

೦ⅇ⌒ಎ೦

The trio of Catherine, Dillon and Boldwood enjoyed their stay in the sunshine—their woes of the summer briefly forgotten. There were smiles all around, and Catherine gave both men plenty to think about in their alone time after she donned a bikini on the beach and by the pool.

On the final evening—after they'd all plotted and planned strategic directions for DeChartine—Emilia suggested a night out at the local beach club. Cocktails being too good an opportunity to pass up, they willingly accepted.

The evening was a fun one, with alcohol lubricating their minds. Catherine laughed at jokes and Dillon saw the friendly, mischievous woman that he'd glimpsed at Christmas, and again on Memorial Day weekend. He was tempted to give her the snowflake necklace gift that he carried around in his bag, but feared it was too soon after Troy's disappearance to make a move.

In their high spirits, the foursome failed to notice a solitary figure watching them from a corner in the club bar with a growing annoyance.

In visiting the Bahamas, the DeChartine team had gate-crashed the refuge of one, very much alive, Troy Selgent.

Chapter Thirty-Seven

Troy was surprised at how easily it had been to get to the Bahamas unde-tected. When he'd moved in with Catherine, he'd fully intended to continue his sessions with professional submissives—albeit avoiding Madame Rose's dungeon for fear of running into Boldwood. These extra-curricular activi-ties required cash, and Troy had therefore kept a decent pile on standby in his apartment safe. Combining this with the small sum that he'd found in Faye's personal effects, he'd managed to anonymously make his way down the East Coast, and then charm his way onto the yacht of an acquaintance; blackmail—using knowledge of the man's rather more extreme sexual pref-erences—helped to silence him.

He'd staged his suicide with precision, ensuring that until he was alone on the bridge, he didn't place the items. He also changed his attire before leaving the spot, keen to appear as a jogger should anyone study CCTV images. He suspected there would be more scrutiny if the line of enquiry moved to murder, but his knowledge of the law led him to believe that without a body they were unlikely to take that route. Catherine would hire the best lawyers and investigators if they did accuse her, but his intention was only to cause doubt—and therefore endless suffering for her.

Once in the Bahamas, he'd continued to profit from his blackmail by working as a lawyer for his yacht-owning acquaintance. The arrangement was mutually beneficial—the provision of a home and sufficient resources to survive under a different identity, in return for off-the-record legal assis-tance with his questionable business practices.

Troy had found he had to do little to conceal his identity through his appearance, apart from dying his hair, going unshaven and wearing coloured contact lenses. No one had recognised him, and his ego never allowed him to consider that it was more due to the fact nobody had taken much notice of him during his life back in New York. To his annoyance, even the announcement of his disappearance was barely reported; he sus-pected the DeChartine media influence was protecting Catherine.

Now the heartless bitch was here, laughing and joking with the very people protecting her, despite the fact it had only been three months since his supposed death.

Why isn't she grieving? Why isn't she consumed with guilt about Faye?

The more Troy had watched her from his hiding spot, the angrier he became. Boldwood was still crawling at her feet desperate to be of service, and that Englishman was standing beside her—as stoical and loving as ever before, in his own reserved British way.

This isn't how it was supposed to be—we should be married by now; this should have been our honeymoon time; I should be fucking her senseless in a hotel room, knowing that I won.

Troy thought back to the emotionless words in Catherine's email to him on the day of Faye's death. It had come through while he was still there in Faye's room, invading his private memorial to the only woman that he'd now realised that he'd wanted to have keep hold of—the only woman that would have willingly let him dominate her for always. The anger at her emailed intrusion had been the catalyst for him to contemplate revenge. At first, he'd wanted to kill Catherine, but Troy didn't want to go to prison and killing her wouldn't have made her suffer long enough.

In the end, Faye gave him the inspiration for his plan; in her purse, he'd found a faded image of herself on a sunny beach with her parents—it had reminded him of how Catherine had told him about how her father had taken his own life in grief.

An overdose didn't suit his plan—he didn't intend to die for real—but there were ways to commit suicide that could feasibly result in no body. While the method wouldn't be a complete stab into her heart, a suicide by any means would make her suffer.

Yet the happy, laughing woman here in a Bahamas bar wasn't suffering; the time had come for a new plan.

Chapter Thirty-Eight

The sunshine had done everyone good. It was the first time Dillon had seen Catherine with a sunny glow, and the feelings he felt for her had only intensified; they were never going to go away, but he assumed that he'd never win her affections—she'd made it quite clear she didn't want, or need, another man in her life.

While out in the Bahamas, Emilia had enquired about his love life, but he'd jokingly deflected the question with a remark about all the work that Emilia was giving him, and how it meant he'd no time for a relationship. She'd nodded understandingly, and if she'd noticed him briefly looking towards Catherine as he'd said it, she was gracious enough not to pursue her query further.

When Dillon and Emilia had a moment alone, they'd discussed Boldwood, but he chose to be cautious in his response—he knew Emilia was concerned about the man, but he didn't know how much she was aware of his obsession with Catherine—or his sexual inclinations. She asked to be informed if he'd any significant concerns about Boldwood—reiterating that she was concerned for him personally, as well as professionally.

When they'd first returned from the trip, Dillon's own concern remained at the same level as prior to their departure, but as the summer gave way to the fall, he saw a new enthusiasm and dedication in Boldwood; unfortunately not a dedication to work.

෴

It was an odd shaped box—a rectangular shape, which might have contained long-stemmed roses if the weight hadn't indicated something heavier. Dillon had seen it delivered to Catherine's office a half-hour earlier, and his curiosity got the better of him; he headed to her office, anxious to see if Boldwood was sending her gifts again.

He looked down at the object; Catherine hadn't stopped him from coming into her office, nor had she hurriedly concealed the box—or the contents. Inside was a highly polished wooden object—a strange sort of bow shape with two wing screws at either end. On closer inspection, he saw that the shape was in fact two thinner shapes screwed together, and in the centre was a small rectangular hole. He recalled seeing a similar object sitting on a shelf in Mistress Avianne's basement room back in London.

"I don't know what it is," said Catherine, looking blankly at him. She handed him the handwritten note.

> *'I failed to protect you. I am humbled in my failure and must endure maximum pain when you punish me Mistress.'*

She continued to look quizzically at Dillon as he read it, keen to see if he could shed some light on the mysterious object—or Boldwood's words.

"I believe it's a humbler—which is probably why he used the word humbled," he replied. Dillon's mind was racing; his own sexual fantasies suddenly conflicting with his concern for Boldwood's out-of-control obsession.

"And it's used for what?" she asked with curiosity, despite the greater issue that the item presented in what she was going to do about Boldwood, this gift was something unusual.

Dillon closed the door, keen to avoid anyone walking in. Returning to the desk, he picked up the humbler. "I've seen one before, but I haven't seen it used," he said as he started undoing the screws, his technical mind in overdrive; Catherine watched on with fascination.

"I believe a man is expected to be on all fours. You place the two parts of the shape behind the upper part of his thighs. Then . . .," Dillon paused for a moment, slightly embarrassed at the conversation and simulated demonstration. "The person using this on the poor man pulls back his scrotum so that his balls are stuck the other side of the gap. Then, you screw it tight, your boy is trapped, and voila! You whip, gag or peg him—or whatever else you want to do while he's down there. If he tries to move, he gets excruciating pain."

Dillon was acutely aware that he'd sped up all the words as he'd spoken, and that he'd switched from an anonymous torturer to using the words 'you' and 'your boy'; talking Catherine through the humbler's usage—and touching it—had aroused him considerably more than he expected it would. He didn't dare look up at Catherine, choosing to focus his eyes instead on the controversial device, and fiddle with the screws nervously.

She remained silent and, keeping his head lowered, Dillon raised his eyes to glimpse at her. She was looking at him wide-eyed, with the slightest hint of a sparkle-smile forming at the corners of her mouth—despite the obvious pink blush in her cheeks. He tried to think back to recall if he'd ever seen her blush. Not knowing what to say next, he quickly put the humbler back into the box.

"You have a hard-on," said Catherine with amusement, breaking the charged silence, yet only building the sexual tension more; it was now Dillon's turn to blush.

"Damn, you spotted that," he replied nervously. It was useless denying it, he was definitely sporting an impressive erection—the distinct shape in his trousers unable to be hidden from view.

"Kind of *hard* not to—if you'll excuse the pun!" Catherine was really amused now; he hadn't heard her flirt with him like this since Memorial Day weekend in the Hamptons. She picked up the wooden object, her polished nails a stark contrast to the brown wood. Dillon's cock twitched with excitement at seeing her holding the contraption.

"You like the thought of it?" she asked, glancing at his groin as she did.

"Well you've already noticed that it would appear that perhaps I do. What about you? Do you like the thought of using it on someone?"

It was an inappropriate conversation between a boss and an employee—especially considering the offending item had been sent by a mutual colleague, and a more senior one at that—but the chemistry between Dillon and Catherine couldn't be contained when moments like this occurred.

"Sort of," she answered cryptically; she was aroused by the thought of using the humbler—it appealed to her sense of sexual power.

"Meaning?" Dillon couldn't stop himself from asking; he wanted to know her thoughts, desperate to know if she was coming around to the idea of taking Boldwood as some sort of sexual slave to be punished.

"I could see you strapped into it quite nicely—it might stop you from arguing with me so often," she answered, her wicked smile returning; Catherine really was imaging Dillon at her feet—completely at her mercy—with his bare bottom cheeks facing her, and his balls tightly constrained. His endless lectures of her conduct had driven her to exasperation and, even though he'd always been right, she'd wanted to punish him in some way. She'd never found a constructive way to playfully re-exert her control whenever she'd had to accept that he'd been right—or that he'd said words that she needed to hear. Discovering the humbler, and thinking of whipping him in a fun—but careful—way, offered her a solution.

Dillon's eyes glazed over, deep in his own fantasy of Catherine standing over him with a riding crop while he was clamped into the polished wood. He'd experienced the sensation of the crop before at the mercy of a professional, but even real lashes hadn't sent him into the sub-space that he was now entering at only the thought of it being done by the woman he loved. If the risk of discovery in her office hadn't been so high, he probably would have fallen at her feet at this moment—pleading with her to punish him instead of Boldwood.

"And Boldwood?" Dillon forced his name out, trying to get back to the issue at hand and away from thoughts of being whipped himself.

"Well, I don't think I could take you both on at once! Besides, there's only one humbler." It was a joke, but a bad one; Catherine was attempting to make light of the difficult discussion she needed to have with Boldwood.

"Catherine, be serious," he scolded, snapping fully out of his sub-space daze.

"I know," she replied sadly, her voice stripped of humour. "No, I honestly couldn't use this on Boldwood."

Dillon was relieved for his own sake, but he felt for the soon-to-be rejected man; he empathized with the pain of loving Catherine. Although Dillon never really knew where he stood in her affections, she'd always been honest with him that she didn't love Boldwood, and never intended to do anything with him.

"Do you want me to speak with him again?" he asked, knowing that she'd tried to reject his advances, and that he himself had also previously tried unsuccessfully to reason with Boldwood.

"No, I need to do this, although I've run out of ideas of what to say—or do. Sometimes I think it would be easier for everyone if I gave in to his fantasy and pretended. He's neglecting his work and his responsibilities, but if I took on the role of his Domme in a non-sexual way, maybe I could command him to focus."

Dillon stepped forward and put his hand protectively on her arm.

"Catherine, I can see the sincerity in your thoughts—and your guilt at the initial card that you sent last Christmas—but for the past year, you haven't given him further reason to believe that this is the right thing for him. You've tried to tell him, and you've not flirted with him. You can't change yourself just to absolve yourself of that guilt. You were forced into Troy's web when he found ways to manipulate you—and yes, before you ask Liddy has since told me what he did to make you agree to marry him. What you need to see is that what Boldwood's doing is a manipulation of his own, and while it might not be an intentionally cruel manipulation, this is his fantasy—not yours. One of the things that I was told by a Mistress in London is that for BDSM to be right, it needs to be safe, sane and consensual. There's no consensual in something done from guilt, nor is it safe. You won't ever have the right bond to understand each other's limits. This definitely isn't sane for either of you—particularly in the long run. It would slowly destroy you to give up your identity. Boldwood is taking this too far—he needs to let you go if he truly wants you to be happy. If he really loved you, he would understand that."

Catherine's eyes began to well up with tears, "What will make me happy

Dillon? I don't know that I'm capable of love. Like you said, I work hard and I put that above everything. I let Troy nearly destroy me because of it. If I say no to Boldwood, he has more power. Unlike Troy, he actually can take this role away from me, and without my job, I have nothing."

"That isn't true. You have your friends, and you have me," he replied.

Catherine stared at him; she desperately wanted to have him at that moment. Dillon was a constant—and she needed him—but loving him was a weakness she couldn't risk for the sake of her work; her heart began to close in defiance.

"Dillon, if I chose you over Boldwood, the result would be worse. We would fall apart working together—if they kept us on that is—and Boldwood would fall apart, and then no one would be happy in the long-term. It's better, for all parties involved, if you and I never happen."

There was a heart-breaking truth to her words; she was his boss and they had a sexual dynamic that didn't fit into their working world. The two of them were stuck in a love-triangle which had the most senior figure in the company in the third point—a man who'd become so infatuated of late, that he'd never give Catherine up to Dillon without a fight—a fight that would result in Dillon becoming unemployed.

Dillon rarely cried, but on accepting the reality of their situation, he quickly excused himself from Catherine's office before she could see the tears now forming in his own eyes; strong men didn't cry.

Chapter Thirty-Nine

The elevator opened on the thirty-third floor. Catherine breathed deeply, drawing on every bit of strength she had, to face Boldwood; earlier that day she'd emailed him—a short request to see him that evening at 6:00 p.m. in his office. There didn't need to be further context; she knew him well enough to know that he'd read far more into the email—the time, the place, only them.

She'd contemplated meeting him at his home, but she'd never been to his apartment before and had no idea what might await if she did. Meeting at a public place was out of the question—this was a discussion for only them to hear. Finally, she'd settled on his office; she'd be able to leave him alone at the end of the conversation, and spare him the need to walk out of her office and risk running into people; it also meant that she wouldn't need to dismiss him verbally from the room.

It was the Friday before Thanksgiving week, and the floor was fairly deserted—her choice of date and time was deliberate—few people were about and there would be a weekend to gain distance from Boldwood. It would also give him time to change the arrangements for his party, the night before Thanksgiving, that he was hosting for DeChartine senior staff at his home—with Emilia in attendance. The invitation had been the final incentive for her to set him straight; coming only a day after the humbler delivery, Boldwood had attached a note to her invitation asking her to agree to be the joint party host.

Catherine knocked at his closed door, thankful that his PA had left for the weekend.

"I am ready for you Mistress," he said, reiterating the role he wanted to play; there was no 'come in' invitation.

How does he even know it's me?

Catherine hoped that he'd had the sense to check that his employees had all gone home before saying things like that through a closed door; increasingly she'd been worried that Boldwood was losing all sense of priority, risking discovery of his obsession and fetishes.

What does I'm ready mean?

She was tempted to run—not wanting to know what was on the other side of the door; the only thing stopping her was an overwhelming sense of responsibility. She'd sent the original card that started all this and she only seemed to encounter men who took drastic measures when rejected or abandoned; her father's suicide, Dillon's dungeon adventures, and now Troy's suicide were a reminder of that. Catherine knew she needed to do the right thing—whatever the personal cost.

Opening the door her worst fears came true; Boldwood was knelt on the floor beside his desk,—completely naked, except for a metal chastity cage clamped tightly around his cock with a padlock snapped to the top. Catherine didn't know where to look, choosing instead to keep her eyes looking upwards rather than down. Boldwood's naked body wasn't the turn-off— he kept himself in remarkably shape for someone in his fifties—but she wasn't at all aroused by the vision of him in that position; nor by the device he'd chosen to wear as his own personal restraint.

She recalled their conversation much earlier in the year when he'd mentioned the cage, and she hoped for his sake that he hadn't been wearing it all that time since. Thinking back to their Bahamas vacation, she remembered he never joined them swimming—he proclaimed not to like the water; now she suspected that was a cover excuse.

She couldn't deny that she'd thought about the concept of chastity cages after he'd mentioned it—turning to the internet for an understanding on what they involved. The image of a younger man wearing one had provided the most interest for her; his pubic hair on show was strikingly similar to that of Dillon's own hair colour, and her mind had wandered to putting him in the place of the chastity-bound internet man.

She snapped back to the reality of now—where Dillon wasn't the issue— she needed to focus on the man in the room with her. She closed and then locked the door—there were cleaners due around soon and this wasn't a scene to walk into.

"Bill . . .,"

"Yes Mistress," replied Boldwood, with the excitement of a child on Christmas Eve.

"You need to stand up and get dressed—now. I will count to three," she commanded, knowing that he'd never refuse to obey; she wasn't about to have a serious conversation with a naked man knelt on a floor—particularly not with that device as the glaring elephant in the room.

Boldwood looked disappointed, as though his appearance was the cause of her displeasure; Catherine felt guilty rejecting him in such circumstances—a male's ego was fragile, especially when so openly exposed.

"Yes Mistress, as you request," he answered sadly.

He stood and went into his private bathroom, returning a few minutes later dressed in a suit.

He started to kneel back down, but Catherine stopped him, "Sit in the chair please."

He obeyed.

"Bill, we're going to talk. However, I need you to talk to me properly; we aren't in a scene right now. We are two adults, and we are going to discuss the way forward for how this might work," she explained.

He nodded. Catherine had been hoping to see him adopt a more normal manner, but he didn't seem capable of getting out of the headspace he was in.

"If I consider your proposition—," Catherine started, then stopped when she saw him light up and move to the edge of his seat, ready to drop back to his knees. "Bill, what did I say about how this discussion was going to be? We are *not* in a scene. We are discussing terms as two adults. I need you to stay focused, and I want you to stay in your seat. Finally, I want you to consider this as though you were making a billion-dollar business deal. Can you do that?"

Yes Miss . . ., yes I can Catherine," he replied, faltering initially before composing himself.

"Good. What I was saying is that for me to consider your proposition seriously, we need to discuss the terms. My terms are that it would be strictly known to only us the nature of our arrangement and, for the moment, it would stay private about us being involved. By that I mean— no public appearances together, no dating, we would live separately, and no Thanksgiving announcement. My fiancé has only recently gone, and he hasn't been buried. It would be wrong for me to openly date you."

"I understand, but you will consider it? Next year you will allow me to be yours?" he begged.

"Hang on Bill, I haven't finished," she insisted; his eagerness was making her want to run and forget the whole, stupid idea.

"If, and I'm not promising, I do consent to this, I want you to stop with the gift deliveries. You will focus at work, and you will let me focus at work. Outside of work—when we're in private—we would work out how things would be between us, and by that I mean what you need and what I can give you. You do need to understand that I can't promise I would ever fall in love with you, nor could I agree to this being something sexual, or that I might change my mind in the future."

Catherine didn't want to give him false hopes; while she hadn't yet decided whether she'd definitely become his Domme in a non-sexual way, she was sure that she'd never want him to become her submissive for sexual pleasure. It wasn't his fetishes—nor his appearance—that made her sure; it was the complete lack of chemistry with him—no spark, and definitely no fire; where Boldwood was concerned, her mind was blank of fantasies, her heart was heavy and her soul was devoid of light.

She pitied him and felt responsible for his welfare—but that was where her emotions ended; if he needed to be dependent on her to survive—then this was a burden she might have to take on to save him.

"You're considering it, and that means more to me than anything Mistress. You will give me an answer before the Thanksgiving party?" Boldwood didn't even attempt to conceal his happiness—nor his renewed use of the title he wanted to use when with her.

Catherine sighed; this was going to be a difficult future.

"I promise I will consider it," she said wearily.

Chapter Forty

Catherine had been reserved since her meeting with Boldwood, and when Dillon offered to travel with her to Boldwood's home—her apartment being on the way from his—her acceptance had been instant; Dillon sensed that Boldwood—and this event—was weighing heavily on her mind.

"Penny for your thoughts?" asked Dillon. It was quite the old English expression, and Catherine smiled on hearing him say it.

"My Gran used to say that to me all the time. I think I could have been rich if she'd actually given me the penny every time, as I was always a bit lost in thought when I lived with her," said Catherine laughing. Strangely she felt a contentment remembering the memory and sharing it with Dillon; him saying something that a beloved family member used to say, bonded them that bit more and she needed that tonight.

"I'm sorry, I didn't mean to bring up a family memory," Dillon apologized, unsure whether her laugh had been a false one to hide sadness.

"It was actually nice to hear someone say that again, and it helped take my mind off the present issues," she said, this time with an obviously sad smile.

"Ah yes. Should I get a penny out, or aren't you up for sharing?" Dillon could be quite witty when he wanted to be, and had often lightened the mood—or set it in a rather different, arousing direction.

"I think these thoughts are worth at least a pound you cheap-skate," she said, laughing again.

"Catherine, knowing you, and all that you do, I think we might well be out of English coin territory and into paper notes. Plus I've only got a few bucks on me, and definitely no pound notes!" He smiled back cautiously; slightly worried that she might take offence at his quick banter response that may have crossed over the line.

Her offence was thankfully taken in humour, and she playfully whacked his arm as they walked along the sidewalk, "Oi you. You're hardly one to talk. I think you'd bankrupt me if I had to pay out for all your thoughts, *Mr. Regular Hard-On.*"

Despite the impending doom of Boldwood's party, Catherine was cheerful as she walked with Dillon; he was her rock, and she would need him in the future if she was going to get through the arrangement with Boldwood.

She had briefly entertained the idea that maybe she could have something with Dillon secretly—a friends-with-benefits arrangement alongside her more public-facing partnership with Boldwood; he'd said she could bring a third-party to the equation. However, the idea was full of flaws, and would eventually lead to the downfall of all three; she'd never forgive herself if she manipulated the attraction she was aware that Dillon had for her into an affair; her friend deserved love and happiness—something her own fucked-up life could never give him.

He laughed at her hard-on comment, but said nothing in response; there was no way he could lie to her, by denying that she still featured in every fantasy he had. Although Dillon had never resorted to a chastity cage, he'd spent more than twelve months craving only her, and his own sexual releases had been confined to those with her—or at least thinking of her when he jerked off.

They reached the entrance to the apartment building that Boldwood lived in at the right time, stopping their banter from moving into confessional awkward conversations that would only end in an argument. The concierge checked off their names, and they headed for the elevator towards the penthouse floor. Boldwood had done well over the years, and in his pseudo role as son of the late husband of Emilia DeChartine, he'd been bequeathed a sum of money to purchase their former apartment—Emilia not wanting to stay there after her husband's death.

Boldwood's home was an impressive apartment; panelled walls, leather Chesterfields and open fires—the decor fitting for a bachelor gentleman. Catherine, however, couldn't see herself living here—it lacked feminine warmth, and she'd probably find it easier to live in a contemporary modern apartment than somewhere like this.

She leaned towards Dillon, ensuring that Boldwood hadn't yet seen her; she didn't want him to witness their closeness. "He wants me to live here," she whispered.

"Well, it's kind of like an old English house," Dillon replied, trying to keep the conversation light and optimistic.

"Not my kind of English house," she retorted.

"Which is?" he asked, remembering the interior of her New York apartment. "You only ever told me once that it would be something in the country, with an orchard."

"You remember that?" she said, secretly flattered that he recalled the things she told him about herself.

"Of course I do. I remember everything you say. Now stop changing the topic. What's your kind of English house then?" he teased, knowing that humour was helping to settle her nerves at facing Boldwood.

"Something Georgian maybe; we lived in an old rectory in Surrey when I was a child. I remember the bay windows, the high ceilings and cream walls. It was very light and sunny. There was an Aga that my mother—,"

Catherine's description of the perfect, happy home was cut short; Boldwood had spotted them both and was heading towards them with a smile—usually he smiled less than a pouty catwalk model, and seeing his grin unnerved her.

"You made it Miss Everdene. Nice to see you Dillon," said Boldwood with over-animated enthusiasm. Dillon sharply took in his breath and slightly shook his head—not to contradict the obviousness that they'd made it, but in reaction to the man's continued referral of Catherine as Miss Everdene. Others might have overlooked it as old school, but Dillon understood the undertone, and had noticed that Boldwood never did the same when addressing other females—even Emilia was greeted by her first name, despite his lowered gaze in her presence.

"Dillon, might I have a moment in private with Miss Everdene?" he asked.

Catherine looked at Dillon, imploring him not to leave her. He stayed where he was, although it didn't matter—Boldwood took her arm and escorted her towards his study. She followed begrudgingly, anxious not to cause a scene in front of the few employees that were already present.

Once inside the study, Boldwood retrieved a small box from the mantle. "Mistress, in recognition of Thanksgiving, and all that it means, I am thankful to you. I know that you will make me a very happy man," he said, coming towards her with the box.

Oh fuck, what's in the box. Please no ring . . .

"Bill . . .," she was lost for words, praying that this wasn't going to be a proposal that she was going to have to definitely refuse; she'd been spared a proper one by Troy—his method of announcing he wanted to marry her was a far more public one, and there was never a ring.

"I know you said you would consider, but in the spirit of Thanksgiving, could you put me out of my misery and say yes?" he pleaded, kneeling on both of his knees; a proposal normally involved one bended knee, but Boldwood had a tendency for the extreme.

No, I won't marry you . . .

She opened the box; inside was an expensive-looking sterling silver necklace, and attached to it was a one-carat diamond teardrop. It was a beautiful piece of jewellery, and Catherine would have been flattered by the gift, had it not been for the additional adornment on the chain. For there, by the diamond, was a key—not an ornamental sterling silver key to match the necklace, nor a decorative symbol of what he wanted—it was *the* key; the key to that padlock on his chastity cage.

"Please say yes Miss Everdene—please wear it," he begged.

Catherine swallowed hard.

I need a drink . . . I need Dillon . . .

She needed many things right now, but she didn't need this—she didn't want this.

Keep breathing. Think about your career . . . Think what he might end up doing if you say no . . .

She looked up from the jewellery and straightened her hunched shoulders before replying, "Bill, if I say yes, there are two conditions: One, I cannot wear the necklace tonight, but I will after Christmas; Two, the key is to be taken off the chain and you're to take it now, and go and release yourself out of that cage."

Boldwood shrank back; he'd worn the cage for so long that it had become his protection. It kept him from carnal desires; an erection was too painful to endure in the cage and, through wearing it, he'd trained himself to stop thinking about what he wanted to do sexually.

"But don't you want to control me?" he asked, confused with what she wanted, as well as conflicted with his emotions.

Boldwood's childhood had involved a messy divorce between his parents—locked in arguments as they struggled for control over one another—yet when he'd joined DeChartine he'd discovered a role model relationship. He'd seen the love between Emilia and her late husband—where the man's love had seemed to feed off of the power Emilia had had over him—and watching them had manifested into his desire to become a submissive. The more he'd read since on what made such a dynamic—the more he'd been drawn to BDSM and all that it encompassed.

"You know I don't want to control you sexually, but if you agree to take it off, then I will agree to be your Domme—I will be the woman that ensures you keep focused. If that means being by your side publicly, I will do that once an appropriate grieving time has passed. However, I will not keep you, or any part of you, locked up. I can't do that."

Boldwood reluctantly nodded, accepting her conditions for the moment; a part of him still hoping that, in time, he could bring her around to all the things that he needed—including letting him retreat to the safety, and protection, of his chastity cage.

"Good. Now go and take it off please, and then come back to your guests," she commanded; her domination started now.

Catherine left the study, hoping that he'd go somewhere more private to remove the cage. She headed towards the main room, anxious to find a drink and Dillon—preferably in that order.

The search for a drink was an easy one—glasses of champagne were laid out on a side table; she'd hoped for something stronger, but the event followed the acceptable proprieties and it was still before dinner. With drink in hand, she proceeded to look for Dillon, or even Emilia, for some diversion from wondering if Boldwood was doing as he was told.

Scanning the room, Catherine saw Dillon and smiled, but as he smiled back at her, her face fell; less than a second later, as recognition sunk in, her glass followed suit, slipping out of her hands—the crystal shattering into hundreds of pieces and scattering across the floor, with expensive vintage flowing around the shards.

Everyone stared at her, at first thinking it had merely been an accident, but then registering the look of absolute horror on her face. A puzzled Dillon—to begin with unsure as to what he'd done to provoke such a reaction—realized she was staring right through him; he turned to look behind him.

Troy Selgent was standing in the doorway.

Chapter Forty-One

No one knew how he got past the concierge; dead men's names aren't included on guest lists,—even in honour of their memory. Not that it mattered how he'd got into the penthouse—the questions everyone was thinking; *how is he alive? What's he doing here? Why come back now?* Yet no one asked them—their shock had rendered everyone mute.

"Catherine, I have come back for you," he said arrogantly—his statement somehow implying that he'd left her in some other way than death, and now he'd realized his mistake and was returning for her.

The party guests that had so far only been looking at Catherine—oblivious to Troy's presence—turned at his words and gasped as they saw the speaker; they were all employees of DeChartine, or the partners of employees, and therefore aware of who they were looking at. Troy's suicide had been a continuous source of gossip and conspiracy theories within the company, but none of them were in any doubt that the man in front of them was flesh and blood—only Catherine thought that she was looking at a ghost.

"You're dead," said Catherine—her words strong and sure; she believed them, or, at the very least, wanted to believe them.

"No Cat, as you can see, very much alive as I stand here," Troy replied, holding out his arms to either side of him, then dropping into a dramatic little bow; a theatrical movement to show off his whole body, and reminiscent of a magician who appears after an invisibility illusion.

"How about—you're dead to me. Add those two extra words at the end," she retorted, her quick mind not hesitating to come up with a suitable response to his performance; her shock was rapidly giving way to anger.

"Now, now, my feisty little Cat, that's no way to talk to your fiancé who's been missing for months. Show some compassion when in the company of our friends and esteemed colleagues."

"I've never been *your* Cat, you bastard. I'm Catherine. You aren't my fiancé, because we're not engaged, and we never should have been. You blackmailed me. Plus, I doubt you've been in hardship and lost on an island without communication," she said with her iciness back in full force; if anyone could close her heart, it was Troy.

"Well, lost on an island is kind of where I was actually. In fact, I was enjoying it immensely until you all turned up a few months back, but seeing you made me realise just how much I missed you," he replied, faking remorse to trick Catherine into believing he felt for her, or gain sympathy from the others in the room and tarnish her reputation.

Troy started to walk towards her and Dillon held out his arm to restrain him, resisting his urge to punch him.

"Ah yes, Brit Boy. Tell me, are you still pining silently in a corner for my Cat? Or have you actually made a move since I saw you gazing longingly at her in the Bahamas when she was prancing around in front of you in her bikini?"

Dillon's anger was boiling up, and he knew he wouldn't be able to hold back much longer from physically assaulting the asshole in front of him. Just as he rose his other arm reading to strike, Catherine came to his rescue.

"Dillon don't—he's not worth it," she pleaded.

Dillon dropped both his arms, but wished he hadn't done so when Troy advanced forward and roughly grabbed Catherine's arm, before pulling her across the room towards the hall.

"Come on Cat, we're leaving this dull party. We have plenty to catch up on."

Catherine was embarrassed; she wanted to leave the party and run from the shame, only she didn't want to go with him. Looking around at the faces in the room, she tried to find a friendly one, but Emilia looked stunned and Dillon wouldn't look up at her; he was battling internally between with his alpha-male protective urge to give Troy a thump, and his submissive desire to respect Catherine's wishes.

"Let go of her."

The loud, angry shout caused everyone to turn towards Boldwood in the hall; red with rage, he was standing in a rare, dominant pose.

Troy laughed in response to the verbal and physical threat, but didn't release his grip on Catherine's struggling arm. The faces in the room all turned back to face him, as though they were watching tennis—their stares going backwards and forwards between the opponents in this game, only the ball being used was words.

"Well, well, well, I was wondering when the old man suitor would turn up—this being your house and all. Although I have to admit, I didn't think it was quite your style to issue the orders," said Troy with his arrogance showing no signs of weakening, despite there being no allies in the room.

Boldwood fell silent in response to the personal jibe.

"Stop being a bastard and get out," Catherine yelled, still struggling to free her arm from his grip; she was physically quite strong, but she hadn't kept up her workouts of late, and Troy clearly had.

Troy wasn't about to leave, or stop his show. "Yes Cat, *you* I can see giving the orders—well at least to some men—you never were particularly successful at getting me to obey though were you? Quite the opposite in fact; I seem to recall I made you whimper with excitement when I tied you down," he said with a smirk.

"Troy, shut up," begged Catherine, blushing with embarrassment at her sexual activities being so openly discussed.

"Not going to happen sweetheart. Remember I'm not the obeying type, but Boldwood on the other hand . . .," replied Troy, turning to look at his rival. "Tell me, has he been crawling around you on his knees again since I left? Begging you to whip him until he cries like a baby dressed in only a nappy?"

"You need to leave Mr. Selgent," said Emilia, finally entering the battle arena. Attacking Boldwood was an attack on family, and she'd realized that Troy was aware of his perversions; Emilia had never invaded Boldwood's privacy, but she'd helped to cover up the dungeon scandal of years earlier and therefore knew about his fetish for female domination.

Emilia DeChartine was a force nobody dared defy normally, but Troy had it covered; he'd planned this evening meticulously, putting more thought into it than his falsified suicide.

It hadn't taken much effort to find a woman who could get him the information he required—an event to attend with the right guest list and location. In DeChartine, there was enough staff turnover at administration level to allow him to find a suitable conquest that wouldn't recognise him, and once he had her besotted, the rest was easy. He'd even been able to stay with her free of charge—and off the grid—while he continued to plan, and he figured he'd keep her on as a sub once he had Catherine back.

Tonight though, he hadn't brought her along as his accomplice—that task was given to a hired submissive, and now it was time to introduce her to his audience.

"Oh, I don't think so Emilia. You see I brought a friend along. Meet—," Troy struggled to remember her name, then, realizing it was irrelevant, he continued. "Oh well, meet my friend here, who has this great thing called a smartphone. She's been recording this whole charade. The press are going to love this, and if there's one thing I know, it's that a video, once on the internet, is a much harder thing for even the likes of DeChartine to cover up. Words can be fobbed off, but video is right there on the screen."

The room was silent, the threat of the impending scandal weighing heavily on everyone's minds. They were all financially dependent on DeChartine, and here was the owner and two of the CEOs, about to have secrets about their private lives' exposed.

"Thought the video would change things and quieten you all into compliance," said Troy triumphantly. "Now, where were we? Oh, that's right, Cat was going to answer me about whether she's left me for Boldwood. Has he given you the key to his chastity cage yet?"

Troy was over-animating—enjoying being the centre of attention.

Catherine stared in disbelief; she'd never told Troy anything about Boldwood, but she was sure that they would all now think she'd blabbed about his interests.

"Troy, please shut—,"

Catherine didn't have a chance to finish her plea—the unmistakeable sound of a gunshot rang out through the room. Troy slumped to the floor—the single bullet piercing his chest and blood quickly covering the front of his pristine white dress shirt. Catherine screamed, falling onto him—the action caused by her loss of balance when his grip on her arm was suddenly released, rather than a manic reaction to save him.

The game's spectators again turned their heads towards the other opponent; Boldwood stood motionless with the handgun still pointed in Troy's direction. His position in the hall had placed him directly by the front stand where he kept his weapon—close to the front door for protection.

He'd needed protection now; already feeling lost from removing his chastity cage, suddenly seeing Troy had brought out every insecurity and fear in him. He was losing Catherine, and insanely he thought it was his own fault for taking off the cage. Witnessing Troy's hands on her, his words about Catherine's sexual submission and then the man taunting him about his chastity cage, made him angry—she'd betrayed him and told Troy things about him.

Boldwood wasn't sure to whom he'd aimed the gun at—his rival Troy, or his beloved Catherine.

There were still bullets in the gun and as he watched Catherine sprawled crying over the body of Troy, he felt defeated. He couldn't fire again at her—she looked weak, and he empathized with her sudden submission. Full of despair, he turned the gun towards his own chest.

Dillon was quick; he hadn't seen the gun until it was too late for Troy, and although his lunge for Boldwood couldn't stop the second shot, he did deflect it—the bullet powering through Boldwood's shoulder, but missing his vital organs. The wounded man fell to the ground, with Dillon on top of him.

Several other women joined in Catherine's hysterical screaming, and a few ran from the room in fear of who was next. Rising a little, Dillon kicked out at the fallen gun, sending it skidding across the floor out of reach. While there was no one else in the room that posed a threat—Troy was clearly dead—he didn't want to take any risks with the safety of those remaining.

The shoulder wound was bleeding profusely—the bullet deeply embedded. Boldwood was crying out in pain, begging to be left alone to die, but Dillon held him down and put pressure on his wound. He heard someone call 911 and request both the police and a paramedic, quoting a shooting and two men shot.

In the chaos, Emilia DeChartine was the tower of strength; her quickness to take action would be their saviour. No one had yet left the apartment— those that had fled were cowering in the hall waiting for the elevator. She addressed them all—she was their ultimate boss and they were going to have to listen to her.

"You all have to come back inside and go into the dining room to have a drink. If anyone asks, you saw nothing and you were in the dining room when it happened. If you want to keep your jobs, you will do this."

Emilia understood motivated her senior executives—they were either career-minded, money-orientated or both. Scandal wasn't their thing, and they were aware of the price for defying her—they would never work again. The more ruthless among them smelled blood of a different kind—the potentially empty CEO seats of at least one, but maybe two, companies might result in their loyalty being rewarded with promotion.

Emilia returned to the crime scene, where now only Catherine, Dillon, the wounded Boldwood and the body of Troy remained. She picked up the gun and walked toward Troy. Emilia was a fan of crime television—it gave an old woman something intellectual to fill her days—and her quick mind was constructing the details on how to amend the scene to confuse those who arrived to investigate.

"Catherine, you need to pull yourself together because you have to do something for Bill," said Emilia standing over Catherine's curled up body.

She shook her head, continuing to cry hysterically, and didn't look up at the older, bossier woman.

"What the hell do you need her to do?" Dillon asked, wanting to be beside Catherine to comfort her, but he was unable to leave Boldwood; if the man died, that would be a far worse outcome for Catherine.

"Dillon, I need you to stay down and keep Bill alive, and I need Catherine to put the gun in Troy's hand, then hold it there to take a shot well above your heads," explained Emilia.

There was a hint that she was experienced in planning the details of a scene—as though she'd done it in the past—albeit for the enjoyment of her husband, rather than for illegal cover-ups.

"What the fuck?" shouted Dillon, puzzled and thinking Emilia either in shock or insane.

"Do you want Bill to go down for murder? He's not a criminal, but he needs help. You know how his mental state has been, but manslaughter due to insanity is a hard thing to prove. Manslaughter in self-defence is different, and all you need is reasonable doubt. He could get off charges that would otherwise send him to prison, and instead he could get the professional help he needs."

Dillon, still relatively calm despite the circumstances, was baffled as to her intentions—he didn't understand why there had to be another shot. "Boldwood's shot. Isn't that enough?"

"No. Troy has to have gunshot residue on him, and only shooting in the direction of Bill and then missing would help with that. We have to make him hold the gun. It mightn't work, but we only need doubt. Doubt, plus the DeChartine name, is what will be the difference between murder and Bill being able to plead."

"But a third shot. What about the witnesses?" asked Dillon, not believing that they could feasibly deceive the police.

"Everyone here is a long-term, senior member of DeChartine and, for as long as I'm alive, what happened here will never be revealed by any one of them for the sake of their jobs and livelihood. That buys us time," she replied. "But right now we don't have time, because 911 have been called already and the authorities will be here any minute."

She turned back to Catherine, "You have to be the one to hold his hand and make it look like you were wrestling with him to get control of the gun. It will be difficult, but you have to focus and do it."

Catherine shook her head uncontrollably—now that she had recoiled from Troy's body, she didn't want to touch him again, and she certainly didn't want to touch a gun.

"Emilia leave her alone, she can't do it, especially not in her state. Don't make her handle the gun. She might shoot someone," he pleaded.

He was less worried about her shooting him, or Boldwood, and more concerned that in her despair—after everything that had happened in her life—she might take her own life.

"She has to take responsibility and get us out of the mess she put us in," said Emilia forcefully, but her blame only served to make Catherine cry more hysterically.

The words hit home; now it was time for Dillon to step up and protect the woman he loved—something he'd been failing at so far.

"Emilia, come and tend to Boldwood. I'll do it. I have gun residue on me already. We can tell them that Troy shot first, hitting Boldwood. He took aim again, and I wrestled him, causing a shot above the fallen Boldwood. I managed to make the gun fall out of Troy's hand, and when it skidded across the floor, Boldwood reached to grab it from the floor and then he shot Troy to stop him coming after the gun because he wanted to protect Catherine who Troy had threatened. Troy's faked suicide note accused Catherine of things that he might want revenge for."

Emilia stared at him. "You realise that you will need to perjure yourself? Catherine has the fact that she was a distraught woman in her favour, and they would more likely believe that she wrestled with Troy."

"I have the residue on me, which adds evidence, and there are people that know that it's in my nature to protect people. I would be perjuring myself, but then again we're all going to be doing that anyway. Catherine can't do this and, more to the point, I don't want her too," he replied. Dillon was determined, for his own conscience, to do this for her; he'd never forgive himself if anything happened to her when she had a gun in her hand.

"Fair enough, it's a noble thing you're doing," said Emilia, taking over his position at Boldwood's side to hold her hand on the bleeding wound. She watched him take the gun and complete his mission—Catherine wincing at the shot.

"Dillon, you take over pressure again," said Emilia. "There are two more things I need to do."

Putting his hand briefly on Catherine's shoulder to acknowledge and calm her, he reluctantly left her side to return to assisting Boldwood.

Emilia left the room, and shortly afterwards he heard her telling the guests the version of events that he'd created. Even he had to admit that it all sounded plausible, and the motives substantiated considering all the history of each of the people involved. Emilia then focused on the second thing she needed to do, and she passed Dillon as she led Troy's guest into the study. He prayed that Emilia wouldn't hurt the girl, and he looked at Emilia with worry when she returned and saw her with the girl's phone. Once she'd deleted the video, she looked up at Dillon.

"Don't look so worried, money talks," said Emilia, giving him a small smile; she was amused that Dillon thought her scary enough to threaten the girl—head of a media empire she might be, but Mafia general she was not. "Troy's preference for Madame Rose's more vulnerable girls made it easy. I offered her money and a new life for her silence and it also went in our favour that she wasn't American and was probably here illegally."

Emilia had dealt with everything—just in time for the police to arrive. The only things she'd not covered up, were the things she didn't know about, but was about to discover. The true state of Boldwood's obsession was yet to become known to them all.

Chapter Forty-Two

Dillon didn't know what made Emilia interpret Boldwood's delirious whispers in the way that she did; the pair were crouched over him, and all he'd heard was, "My Mistress, I protected her and she's safe in our special place in my room."

Listening to it said repeatedly, Emilia had increasingly looked concerned. As soon as the paramedics took over, and stretchered Boldwood from the apartment, she turned to Dillon, "Come with me. There's something we need to attend to."

"Are we going to the hospital?" he asked, unsure if they had permission to leave the scene—he definitely didn't want to abandon Catherine.

"No, my assistant will accompany him," she said, beckoning him to follow as she hurried out of the room.

If Emilia was concerned about the police officer who was now accompanying them to wherever they were going, she didn't show it—almost as if she wanted the police to be there when they found whatever it was she was looking for. She knew her way around the apartment, and Dillon recalled that she'd lived here before Boldwood had.

They entered his bedroom—an excessively neat room, with similar interior decor to the rest of the apartment. Dillon's mind cast back to Catherine's thoughts on the décor when they'd first arrived that night.

Catherine would hate this room.

Emilia walked straight towards the closed door on the other side of the bed—a door Dillon suspected would be into a walk-in-closet, considering he could already see a bathroom through an open door. Turning the knob, she looked relieved to find it unlocked and she switched on the light to the right of the door, revealing the previously pitch-black room's secrets. Dillon's facial expression, usually hard to read, couldn't hide his shock.

The police officer let out his breath with an audible whistle—not unlike the sound a television detective might make when making a discovery of epic proportions.

"Holy Shit," he said as he regained his voice.

Even the previously calm Emilia was visibly shocked.

"This might be *Oh Shit*, but it is *anything* but holy," she said in response.

This room was clearly the *'special place'* that Boldwood had been ranting about his Mistress being safe in—for here she was; the walls were covered with images of Catherine—her head pasted onto the bodies of dominatrix pornography models, standing over Boldwood in all sorts of poses. The realistic detail of Boldwood's figure indicated that the photographic images were indeed of him, rather than his face glued onto the bodies of others.

The walk-in-closet contained shelves piled high with designer shoeboxes, wrapped with red ribbons and heralding tags labelled either *My Mistress*, *Miss Everdene*, or even *My Beloved Catherine Boldwood*. On the counter below them were a chastity cage and a key—the former showing grotesque condensation evidence of recent usage.

"I'd been expecting different," Emilia said in bewilderment.

I was expecting clothes in a walk-in-closet, what the fuck were you expecting?

Dillon's questioning look towards her prompted her to explain her comment, despite the presence of the young police officer.

"There was a media scare once and Bill was spotted coming out of a venue. After the scandal was hushed up, he set up a private dungeon in an anonymous apartment. I knew a little—having helped cover everything up—and wanted assurance it wouldn't happen again. I didn't want to deny him whatever lifestyle he chose for himself; I just needed to know he was doing it safely, and privately, for the sake of the company. When I heard his whispers, I thought maybe he'd relocated the dungeon here. Last week he asked me what I'd think if he asked Catherine to move in with him. I never pried about the nature of the arrangement, only asking him to be sure that she wanted to—especially as I'd noticed the closeness between Catherine and yourself. I never knew much about her involvement with Troy, but what I did know was that I'd never seen anything to indicate she had an interest in Bill. I never would've guessed that his delusions would reach this," she said sadly.

"You knew about the chastity cage?" Dillon asked.

"No, not until Troy said it just now. It doesn't surprise me though, as I was always worried that he'd taken his lifestyle to the extreme."

"Surely you see that Catherine isn't responsible for all of this, especially now you've said about the media scare," said Dillon angrily, now that he knew about Emilia's previous concerns regarding Boldwood, and her admission that she'd noticed Catherine's lack of interest in the man.

Emilia ignored him, and turned to face the young police officer who was listening to everything said while he carried on staring open-mouthed at the walls.

"I trust that you will treat this room with the duty of care that's required. If any pictures of this room are leaked to the press—or discussed outside the necessary channels of the law—you can be assured that the full weight of the DeChartine resources will come down on your police department, and more specifically, yourself."

Her dominant pose, and her tone of delivery, reduced the young man to a petrified wreck, so much so that Dillon thought he was about to wet his pants with the fear that Emilia might do something similar to him as to what was being depicted in the faked images that covered the walls around them.

"Yes, Ms DeChartine. I . . .," he stuttered, his body trembling. "I personally will make sure that nothing happens in this room."

"Thank you," said Emilia, before turning her attention back to Dillon. "We need to return to the main room."

⁀ᴇ⁀ᴏ⁀

Dillon was glad to be back in the same room as Catherine. A female officer was comforting her, but she was sitting silent and motionless in an armchair. As he headed towards her, a detective stopped him to ask for his statement. He steeled himself, trying to summon the courage he needed to say the words that would perjure himself.

Before he could start to explain the events, Emilia stepped in, addressing the room, "There will be no statements taken here. All those in attendance will attend the station when required in the presence of a lawyer. The people that were in the room at the time of this unfortunate incident were Catherine Everdene, Dillon Oak, Troy Selgent, Bill Boldwood and myself; Emilia DeChartine. The three of us that are living and here, will come to the station willingly with you now, although in my car, rather than in a squad car, and Bill Boldwood can be interviewed—with his lawyer present—when his doctors clear him after surgery."

It wasn't a request; her order had been given, and the police were briefed enough to know that if they went against Emilia, the pressure from the Mayor's office would be intense.

⁀ᴇ⁀ᴏ⁀

Dillon and Catherine accompanied Emilia in her chauffeur-driven car to the station. They'd left the crime scene investigators at the scene, and the other guests were given permission to leave. Dillon was nervous about their alibis—while they were waiting to leave the apartment, he'd noticed the chaos in the empty crime scene; shattered glasses and knocked over items were all evidence that indicated more people were in the drawing room when the shooting had happened. For all their sakes, he needed Emilia to be sure her employees would be convincing when providing a statement.

In the privacy of the car, he voiced his concerns, "The room shows too many signs that the other guests were in there when it happened."

Emilia remained quiet, as did Catherine.

"Emilia, I'm talking to you. I fired a gun and perjured myself—I'm the one most at risk now," Dillon said, urging her to listen.

"I'm listening," she snapped. "You will be fine, it won't go to court."

He laughed in disbelief, "Even DeChartine can't stop a court case where someone has been killed through manslaughter."

"We can, and more importantly, we have," said Emilia, continuing to stare out of the car window.

Catherine and Dillon looked at each other with surprise, unaware what might have already transpired.

"How have you?" Dillon asked with curiosity, suddenly worried that he'd been sacrificed in order to protect Boldwood.

"I don't understand," added Catherine, who was speaking for the first time since she'd yelled at Troy, much earlier that evening.

"A deal has been struck. Bill has pleaded guilty to self-defence manslaughter on the grounds of mental insanity. His severe manic-obsessive state had deluded him into believing he was acting to protect his partner. The lawyers have already spoken with NYPD senior officials, and the Mayor has agreed. The whole thing will be kept out of the media, there will be no trial, and Boldwood will remain in a secure psychiatric facility for the foreseeable future," she explained.

Catherine didn't say a word in response—it wasn't the time to stubbornly insist that she wasn't Boldwood's partner, particularly as she could tell Emilia was blaming her for everything that had occurred.

Dillon, however, wasn't going to let it go. "You can't do that. You can't speak for Boldwood when he's still in surgery, and what about Troy—he might have been a bastard, but there will be some who will want justice for him—like his family."

"Dillon, don't argue," said Emilia, her bossy reprimand stronger than a Catherine one, albeit without the sexuality in the threat. "It's done. Troy alienated his family a long time ago, and his fake suicide only made that worse. He left a few estranged relatives with all kinds of debts—including unpaid rent—and there were no insurance policies to cover it. The only retribution they might be interested in, is monetary."

"You did all of this in the last hour?" he said in disbelief, wondering at the morals of the company he worked for; it was the first time he'd found himself truly questioning if he wanted to stay.

"Yes. Although I'd already looked into the Troy situation when his suicide was reported, so I knew about the debts. I'm only surprised that he hadn't ensured that Catherine was legally responsible for them."

Dillon said no more, and the rest of the short journey was undertaken in silence. An hour later, after saying very little in their statements due to the plea development, Dillon and Catherine were alone—Emilia took a car back to her hotel.

"Do you want me to take you to Liddy's house?" Dillon asked, despite the early hour of the morning.

She shook her head. "They're away for Thanksgiving," she said, starting to cry again. "Can you take me home?"

Hailing a taxi, Dillon sat beside her, with his arm wrapped around her protectively. Neither talked about what had happened—the backseat of a taxi wasn't the place for a discussion that was so personal and confidential. Fifteen minutes later, Catherine held onto his arm for support as she climbed the icy steps to her door.

"Don't leave me—at least not for a bit," she pleaded, unable to look him in the eye.

"I'll come in for a little while," he replied.

Dillon was full of mixed emotion, for while he didn't want to leave her when she was so vulnerable, part of him wanted to be as far away from her right now as possible. He too was suffering—events and revelations of the long evening had taken their toll. It was 1:00 a.m., and in the past five hours, he'd bared witness to Catherine's former lover gunned down by another man who wanted to be at her side. To see a man who was so obsessed, that he not only had a room dedicated to her, but was also prepared to take his own life because of his perceived rejection by her, scared Dillon—he knew how Catherine had affected his own mind, even leading him to cover up a crime—would he be her third victim?

Pushing aside his fear and memories of nine months earlier in the snowstorm, once again he set to building a fire in the grate to warm up her freezing apartment.

"Thank you," she said appreciatively as she curled up on the couch under a blanket.

Dillon looked over at her from his position by the fire. She looked as pale as she'd done back in February, only this time her vulnerable state was attributable to the cold reality of her life to date, rather than an icy blizzard.

"Do you want a cup of tea?" he asked, remembering her old '*keep calm*' tea-towel joke.

"No, and I don't have anything stronger," she said, looking down at her hands as she fiddled with her nails.

"What about something to eat?" Dillon was acutely aware of his stomach rumbling—they'd never eaten the Thanksgiving party dinner.

Catherine looked up and shook her head. "What was in the room you were all referring to?" she asked, changing the topic.

"You didn't know about the room?" Dillon doubted that she would have known—she'd have run to him to help her sort out her mess if she had—but he wanted confirmation that Boldwood hadn't taken her there on their arrival; he needed to know that she was completely naïve to its contents, and wasn't just angling for sympathy.

"No. You know I'd never been to his apartment before tonight, and when we arrived, he took me to his study for a talk. He gave me a necklace and a key, and I told him to go and use the key to take off his chastity device, while I went back to the guests," she protested.

"Well he obeyed your request. The device was in the room—or rather walk-in-closet, as that's the room we all mean," said Dillon, as he tried to supress his musings about anything that she might have promised to do to him if he took it off.

"So his chastity device was what they were so interested in? How was that sole object enough to go with an insanity defence?"

Dillon studied her inquisitive expression and wished he could just say 'yes, that was it', but she was far too intelligent to be fooled; the internal debate about what to reveal to her—that had been raging in his mind since he first saw the room—flared up again; he couldn't lie to her now that she'd asked.

"No, there were other things in there. Shoeboxes with labels, some even labelled Catherine Boldwood. Had you agreed to marry him?"

He prayed she would say no, and that he'd be able to see she was genuine in her denial; he'd noticed how she screwed up her nose, and averted her eyes, when she was lying.

"Hell no, do you really think I would agree to go that far?" she replied angrily. Although the overall intention of Boldwood didn't come as a surprise to her, it hurt that Dillon thought she would be willing to marry a man she didn't love.

Dillon turned away, unable to look at her as he replied, "You did with Troy, and you didn't love him. You did that for your career, just as you were going to agree to an arrangement with Boldwood."

"I did, but as you know with Troy it was about the pictures. To be honest, I was hoping that if I agreed to Boldwood's terms initially, and without a public announcement for a while, he'd eventually see that I was a rubbish Domme beyond his initial impression of me as a bossy woman. Then he would've ended it."

Dillon took a deep breath, and Catherine immediately realized there was more he was keeping from her. "A chastity device and labelled shoes are still not enough for insanity in the eyes of the law. What aren't you telling me?"

Averting her gaze again, Dillon sighed and searched for the courage within him to say, "There was something else in the room."

Something else . . .

A chill ran through Catherine. "Please tell me," she said nervously.

"He had loads of graphic, hard-core BDSM porn pictures on the walls."

"Oh . . .," said Catherine. After composing herself for a moment, she added, "I guess I expected that he might look at porn, and with his tastes running to the more extreme it stands to reason."

Dillon contemplated leaving her in her naivety at Boldwood's fantasies, yet he knew that if she ever found out that he'd withheld the truth from her, all their trust would be broken; he had to be the one to tell her, and he had to do it now. If she understood how extreme Boldwood had become in his affections for her, there would be a chance she'd accept that his insanity plea was the right thing for him and she wouldn't blame herself for all the events that had transpired that night.

"Catherine," he said gently. "The pictures were edited to have your face on the women. Boldwood had then added real images of his body in various poses. There were at least a hundred different scene images of you and him."

She was mortified at what Dillon had told her. "Do people think it's really me in them?" Do you believe it's me?" she asked desperately; while her professional reputation meant everything to her, Dillon's impression of her was what she was most worried about right now.

"No, I don't, and no one else would either," he said reassuringly, flattered that she'd separated him out in the question, therefore showing that she cared what he thought. "Thankfully, Boldwood had no skill in the use of photo-editing software. He used the old-fashioned approach of cutting out a circle around a head and then sticking it onto a body. Your face was the same photo repeatedly, and he'd obviously printed it from an internet image of you at a party where you were staring without a smile. For the images of him, he'd posed into the positions of the original models, and then cut out his image to paste it on top, but the dimensions were all wrong and you could see the outline of the man underneath. It was like a child had done it, but I think even Madison could have done a better job."

He cringed after he mentioned Liddy's daughter, particularly as the toddler was representative of happier things in Catherine's life. "Not that she would of course," he added quickly.

"But people will still know his thoughts and will wonder about me," she said, starting to well up again, her inner strength wasn't enough to withstand this latest threat.

"Catherine stop beating yourself up, there's no evidence to suggest that you ever did anything with Boldwood. There was nothing in his apartment to imply you lived there—or visited often—and he had nothing of yours that you'd actually worn or used. Did you ever send him anything other than the anonymous card? Did you ever write to him other than work emails? Did you ever call him outside of work?"

"No, you know I didn't," she said Catherine, thinking that Dillon thought she'd led Boldwood on further than she'd admitted to him.

"Look, I don't know if my opinion counts in your worry about what the world is going to say, but, for what it's worth, I know that you did try to put him off. I confess that, before tonight, I wondered if you hadn't tried hard enough, but when I saw that room, I realized that Boldwood had issues that went back a very long way—long before your arrival in New York. Even the most inexperienced criminal psychologist would see that the only prompt you'd ever given was the card in the centre of his picture wall. Besides, it was unsigned and they'd have had to match your handwriting to link it back to you. If you sent things, I suspect they would have been stored in there too, as would real pictures of you together."

Dillon's words were worth something—not only those that he'd said to make her see sense, but the implication that he wasn't blaming her beyond the initial stupidity of the card, and her reluctance to hurt Boldwood through rejecting him.

"Your opinion does mean a great deal. You're my friend," she said, unable to bring herself to admit more than that.

"Yeah . . . right . . . friends indeed," he said with an element of sad sarcasm, looking into the fire to avoid her stare.

Catherine kicked out her foot, the tips of her toes nudging his shoulder. "You always have my back," she added.

Seeing her toes so close to him would have normally set Dillon's heart racing. Even in the circumstances, a deep desire within him wanted to take hold of her foot and kiss it lightly; gentle butterfly kisses that took all her pain away.

His mind travelled to his own safe haven of dreams—the both of them sitting by the fire, with him shyly glimpsing up at her in her chair as he seductively sucked each of her toes. His cock began to twitch as his mind wandered into the fantasy, until the sudden crack of a twig in the fire brought him back to sinister thoughts—the crack of gunfire, the warmth of flowing blood, and the hysterical screams of women in shock. He wanted his fantasies with Catherine to have a crackling fire, the warmth of blood flowing through their living, loving bodies and the scream of her succumbing to pleasure.

Pushing her foot away, he snapped, "I won't always be able to be there. You need to start thinking about what comes next."

She bolted upright, glaring at him, "You can't quit, especially not now."

Dillon was irritated—she was always thinking the worst, and always wanted to tell him what he could, and couldn't, do.

"I didn't say I was quitting, but haven't you even considered what's going to happen come Monday? Emilia never said anything about work—in fact, she barely said five words to you all evening."

Catherine slumped back into the back of the couch—she had considered it; apart from Dillon's opinion of her, the shame she'd brought onto DeChartine, was the foremost thought in her mind. In her year's tenure, while she might excelled professionally in the deals she'd brought in, she'd been responsible for scandal and media exposure through Troy, and now Boldwood. Dillon was the one who had stepped up to the plate, covering Boldwood in the past few months, and then being the one to pull the trigger that helped to cover up his crime and save him from prison—if Emilia wanted someone dependable running her companies, Dillon would be the obvious choice.

"Emilia won't fire me—she will be in cover-up mode," she said obstinately.

"Yes, she will cover it up," agreed Dillon, saying nothing in response to her beliefs about her future at DeChartine.

He suspected that the day where he was going to have to make a decision—once and for all—between his career and Catherine, wasn't far off. With that impending thought in his mind, he stood and put another blanket over her, "You need sleep, and so do I. Goodnight Catherine."

"Stay," she said, holding up the blanket and moving over on the couch. "Please?"

"I can't. You take care of yourself, and I will see you on Monday if you make it into the office. But please, if you can, take the time to rest and think about things. I know you're strong and will get through this, but call Liddy if you find you need support."

Dillon hoped that he was right about her getting through this latest traumatic loss; however, for the sake of his own sanity, he needed to spend the next few days without Catherine Everdene.

Chapter Forty-Three

The following few days were a time of quiet solitude for Catherine—with Liddy away, and Dillon not answering the few texts and emails she'd sent him to ask how he was, she was quite alone and lost in her thoughts.

This should have been a time of mourning for Troy, but she'd already attempted to do that when he'd faked his death. Now that she'd confirmed his motives for the suicide were for maximum revenge, any trace of feelings she'd briefly felt for him had long gone. Where Troy was concerned, the only thing she could think about was what might have happened if Boldwood hadn't killed him—what might Troy have said at the party, would she have gone home with him, and would she have resorted to killing him herself eventually?

That last question was the biggest one of all; hate was an emotion she'd never experienced, yet it was raging through her now. Troy had used anything he could to manipulate her—even the anniversary of her father's death, and then his replication of the suicide. He'd been the worst kind of dominating personality—a narcissist who was hell bent on stripping his victims of any self-respect that they had; all to feed his own power trip.

His opponent in his final moments was on the complete opposite end of the spectrum—a submissive determined to give power away, rather than take it. The more Catherine compared the two men, the more she realised they had one thing in common; they both wanted to change her into what they needed most, and in the process would have stripped her of her identity—rather than encouraged her to flourish and find her way in life outside of work.

The third man in her complex love life was Dillon, and while he posted a threat to her career, the difference was that he'd never used that to manipulate her, instead stepping back from his own wants, and always put hers first. He'd wanted her change, but only to overcome the weaknesses in her personality—he challenged her to be a better person for her own personal development.

Dillon was also the only one of the three men who she'd constantly desired; he was the one she always wanted to turn to when she needed help, or when she wanted to share good news; he was the only one she felt comfortable with sharing past memories. However, even with her realization, Catherine still couldn't allow herself to fall in love with him; she was convinced she could never be the woman that Dillon would want forever.

By Sunday, after four days of ruminating about her love life, Catherine was still unable to decide what was more important—her career or love. Instead, she counted down the hours until Monday morning, hopeful that work would set her mind straight. Her hopes, however, were dashed when the intercom buzzed—Emilia DeChartine was paying her a Sunday afternoon visit.

❧

Catherine couldn't control the tremble in her arm as she greeted the woman that she'd once considered her fairy godmother—all of her insecurities resurfaced as she recalled Emilia's look of blame.

'She needs to take responsibility . . .'

Her usual warmth and humour was missing as she accepted Catherine's offer to take a seat in the armchair by the fire.

"Can I get you a tea, coffee or something stronger?" Catherine asked, relieved she'd been out to purchase the something stronger.

Please choose the vodka, so that I can have one . . .

Emilia shook her head. "No thank you, I can't stay long as I'm attending a dinner, but I wanted to check in and see how you were."

"I'm as well as can be expected," she replied, using a very English turn-of-phrase that had become an ingrained learning at boarding school after her father's death. "How is Bill—the hospital won't tell me anything as I'm not family, and they said he couldn't have visitors."

"Bill is no longer at the hospital. I arranged a transfer to a private facility where he can be cared for medically, and psychiatrically. It was part of the deal arrangement," replied Emilia.

Catherine couldn't read anything into Emilia's opinion of her, or the situation, through her response or body language. "I was going to go and see him," she said nervously, hoping that would show Emilia that she wasn't a callous bitch devoid of sympathy for the poor man.

"For many reasons, that wouldn't have been a good idea," said Emilia; this time blame was definitely evident in her statement.

"I didn't mean to hurt him and I do care about what happens," Catherine blurted out, as though she was a child defending herself after a playground war; she wanted Emilia to see that underneath she really was a caring person.

"None of us can change what has happened, and blaming each other isn't going to help, but you do need to understand that the only way you can help Bill is to not see him anymore." Emilia softened a little as she tried to get Catherine to understand the difficult situation.

"So you do think it was my fault?" said Catherine, feeling a lump forming in her throat—Emilia was like a grandmother that she didn't want to let down.

Sensing Catherine's vulnerability, self-blame and honest regret, Emilia's sense of compassion surfaced.

"I did blame you to begin with, but the room was my first clue that things weren't as they first appeared. When I discussed it with our lawyer, the hospital had provided the initial finds of his psychiatric assessment. They suggested his obsessive tendencies were there long before your arrival. They also said that they seemed wholly one-sided—unrequited by you in any way. I did see the card, but Dillon set me straight that this was a one off joke, sent a long time ago, and that you'd made significant efforts to make Bill understand that. He also explained how you recently hadn't accepted any of the gifts Bill had sent, nor worn any previous gifts blatantly in front of Bill or other people. I have discreetly spoken to his PA, and she confirmed that you cancelled any private meetings and dates that Bill tried to arrange. I do accept that you were out of your depth, and Bill saw you as something that you were never going to be, despite you trying to tell him. I too have to take some of the blame, because I should have spoken to him a long time ago about his interests. I should have taken on the role of his non-sexual Domme that Dillon tells me you were considering doing."

"I'm not a Dominatrix. I never did any of those things in the pictures—not that I even saw them—and other than the foolish card, I never acted inappropriately at work," said Catherine, desperate for Emilia not to judge, or fire her.

Emilia gave her a small, knowing smile. "No, Catherine you aren't that kind of dominatrix. I expect you're capable of being many things if you wanted to, but you have too much of a heart to be the kind of Domme that Bill needed—he wanted the full slave experience."

"I don't even know what the full slave experience even means," she replied, hopeful that this meant Emilia wasn't going to hold the whole Boldwood saga against her at work. "You aren't judging me?"

"I'm the last person to judge, but unfortunately there are others that will. This is another one of the reasons why you can't see Bill. You need to distance yourself from him, as that fits the story we've spun that he obsessed over you from a distance. The Board will no doubt have to be involved in this, particularly now we need to appoint a CEO, and they will become more involved as time goes on for reasons that don't matter right now. We need to kill the story, and you showing anything more than professional compassion for Bill won't do that."

"I understand," replied Catherine, secretly relieved that she'd never have to face Boldwood again; she was scared that he'd either want her gratitude for killing Troy, or confirmation that on his discharge from hospital they'd be together. "I will issue a statement at work tomorrow, even though I know it will be a busy day." Catherine was keen to show her dedication to career, and to ensure Emilia that she was capable of handling things.

"Ah. That won't be necessary, as I came to tell you that you're on compassionate leave for two weeks," said Emilia. She was trying to be tactful and compassionate, but even Catherine could tell this wasn't just kindness; Emilia was placating her Board.

"But I want to get back to work," she whined, pleading like a toddler insistent on getting their own way.

"I'm sure you do, and I understand the need for distraction in the circumstances. However, the Board need to see a demonstration that you're human. Taking time off after what happened is hardly a weakness. No reasonable person that has had their fiancé come back from the dead, only to be shot by another man that same night, is going to be back at work four days later as though it didn't happen. Hollywood couldn't make this kind of drama up, and so even if you don't give a shit about Troy, you have to look like you do—at least for a while. Your image needs to say that while you aren't an emotional wreck, you aren't a heartless bitch either."

Emilia's words made sense—Catherine was terrible at finding a middle ground between the two personality extremes, and veered far too often towards the heartless bitch persona.

"What will the company do for two weeks?" she asked, already guessing the answer; the knowledge that they could cope without her was a punch in the stomach, and the suspicion that Dillon would be the one to step up into her role—and do a sterling job in the process—was a further blow.

"We will manage," said Emilia, unwilling to add fuel to the fire; she was aware of the dynamic between Dillon and Catherine that stretched far beyond competitive rivalry.

"What will I do?" asked Catherine, genuinely now wanting guidance; she had no idea what to do with herself for two weeks—the past four days had been harrowing, as well as boring.

Aware that Catherine had no family of her own, Emilia paused to think for a moment before replying, "Spend some time with your friends, or take two few weeks away on a holiday, or to a place where you can go to find yourself."

"Place to find myself? What kind—,"

A phone interrupted Catherine's question, and Emilia took the call; when she finished, she headed for the door.

"I'm sorry, but I need to go, the car is waiting. Take care and I will see you when you return to work."

Catherine nodded sadly. "Goodbye Emilia, thank you for everything," she said, and as soon as the door closed, she ran to her bed and cried herself to sleep.

Chapter Forty-Four

Dillon had tried everything to shake off all that had happened to him, not just in the past few days, but for the past fifteen months; the question constantly in his mind—*is Catherine worth it?*

By Monday morning, he'd racked up nearly ten hours in the gym over four days, knocked back a bottle of whisky in between, and let the equivalent of an Olympic-sized swimming pool flow down his bathroom drain as he stood motionless under the shower trying desperately to wash his cares away.

Nothing had worked; as the elevator headed towards the twenty-eighth floor, he still didn't know what he would feel when he faced Catherine. There was no doubt in his mind that she'd come into work, and when her texts and emails had finally stopped after the first few days, it had taken all of his courage not to contact her to see if she was okay.

He had found, however, a discrete mechanism to check on her safety. Using his knowledge of the company's information technology, he'd tracked her logins to the network; Catherine—never one to let work go, even in this situation—had logged in every few hours over the past few days to check her work emails, giving Dillon the reassurance that she hadn't done something stupid in desperation.

Entering the lobby, he was surprised to find Emilia waiting for him. His heart sank as he wondered if he'd been right with his foresight of Catherine's dismissal from her job, despite his call to Emilia on Friday to explain everything that she'd done to reject Boldwood's advances.

"Let's have a coffee in your office—your PA is already making it," said Emilia when she saw him; she seemed friendlier than when he'd last seen her at the police station, and then later when they'd spoken on the phone.

"Sure," he replied, ignoring the fact that he was holding a takeaway coffee that tasted far better than anything his PA could ever make with the coffee-room machine; it would be impolite to refuse Emilia by pointing out his coffee needs were already met.

Once seated, she didn't waste time in getting to the point of her visit.

"Bill won't be returning to DeChartine in the foreseeable future. This may, or may not, be a permanent arrangement publicly, but between us, it's doubtful he will ever return. My Bahamas home looks a promising long-term destination for him after the hospital discharges him. In addition, you should be aware that Catherine is taking two weeks compassionate leave."

Dillon was expecting the Boldwood announcement; however, Catherine taking leave rattled him. He could understand a dismissal, but she was the last person that he ever expected to take compassionate level for that long—especially to grieve someone she hated.

"I see. Are they both okay?" he asked.

Emilia told him the facts about Boldwood—the same synopsis she'd told Catherine. She ended her explanation by requesting that Dillon also keep his distance so that Boldwood could heal without any prompts from the past twelve months. He agreed, relieved that he wouldn't have to see Boldwood and listen to him ranting of his desire for his Mistress Catherine—since seeing the pictures, Dillon wanted to punch the guy just as much as he'd wanted to punch Troy. He was repulsed that Boldwood had positioned Catherine in such a sexual way, even though she'd never explicitly given him permission to do so.

"And Catherine?" he asked, trying to conceal the extent of his concern beyond that of enquiring about a colleague.

"I can tell that you find her taking personal leave out of character. Am I right?" There was no fooling Emilia; her curiosity level was similar to what she'd shown in the Bahamas.

"Yes, it's unlike Catherine to take time away from work. I think we both know that she wouldn't be mourning for Troy, and any guilt she might be feeling, she'd channel into a more determined focus at work. She learned that coping mechanism as a teenager when her parents died."

"She has never said anything about her parents before. Did they die together?" Emilia asked, interested to learn more about Catherine and what made her tick—it had been hard to find much background on her personal life, even when they recruited her.

"Her mother died of cancer when she was nine, and her father, who was a doctor, committed suicide three years later, blaming himself for his wife's death. Troy knew this and used the fact about her father's suicide to hurt her further," explained Dillon. He felt guilty at betraying Catherine by revealing her past, but he wanted to Emilia to understand how strong she really was, so that she could keep her job.

"I see, she's had a very hard life," Emilia said, pondering on what she'd heard. "You do know her well, and she is lucky to have you. However, I know my Board, and they would see that determination to carry on at work as though nothing had happened, as a serious character flaw. That is why I made her take the leave—despite her protests. For the moment, you will take over management of both companies, with some assistance."

A sense of pride and achievement filled Dillon as he realized he was about to be the Acting CEO of not one, but two multi-billion-dollar companies. The proud puffing of his chest only lasted a moment, deflating through his concern for Catherine—this would crush her.

"Thank you for the offer, but I can't take over DeChartine New Media. I will cover Boldwood's role though," said Dillon with genuine regret.

Emilia sighed and put down her coffee. "Dillon, while I admire your loyalty, you need to understand the consequences of your refusal. If you decide to be noble for Catherine's sake, I will have to find myself a temporary CEO for two weeks from within DeChartine. That person is not likely to be noble, nor will he be in love with Catherine—in fact, he will probably be someone who hates her for getting the job in the first place, especially a foreign outsider. He will want her job permanently, and therefore will openly find faults with her work to undermine her return. My Board, who have already seen scandal in her wake, will then have more doubts about her. So either you can stay as only the temporary CEO in Bill's position, and I find another person to backfill Catherine—therefore leaving her vulnerable—or you can take the olive branch that I am, for some unknown and highly romantic reason, offering you Brits. You cover both roles, with some support reporting to you, and you get to ensure that Catherine is protected—which is something I have a sneaky suspicion that you have a tendency to do."

There were no untruths in what Emilia had said, even if Dillon was mortified that she'd guessed how he felt about Catherine.

"What makes you think I'm in love with Catherine?" he asked, his cheeks flushing pink.

Emilia sighed again, and sunk back into her chair. "Men can be so stubbornly naïve sometimes. I know you love her because you wear your heart on your sleeve whenever you're with her. You can't take your eyes off her, and want to be close to her. When you're not with her, you can't help but defend or praise her—depending on the situation." She watched as Dillon squirmed in his own seat. "I do feel for you though, as Catherine is even more stubborn and blind where her heart is concerned. I might be an old woman, but a good optometrist, along with a happy marriage of over fifty years, allows my eyes to see love between two people."

"Catherine is a focused woman, and she doesn't love me," said Dillon, trying to bring around the conversation from romantic notions.

Emilia smiled. "Focused is one word for her. I wish I could tell you that she will thank you for taking over the company for the next few weeks, but we both know that she won't—well not initially anyway. One day she might realise you did it out of love—rather than ego—and that you'd have given up your own chance to take the lead had I not given you a valid reason to change your mind. As to how Catherine feels, that is something the pair of you needs to resolve. Right now though, I need to head off to resolve some things of my own, and you need to get on with running two of my companies."

Dillon stood to see her out of the office. "Thank you for everything you're doing for us both," he said, holding out his hand to shake.

"My pleasure," she replied, shaking his hand. "There's one other request though. You are to ensure that Catherine doesn't work the next two weeks—no emails, no calls, or home working of any kind. Is that clear?"

"Crystal clear, you have my word," he promised.

Chapter Forty-Five

Two weeks seemed like months, or even years, to Catherine. Neither a holiday, nor a retreat, had appealed, so instead she'd commandeered all of Liddy's spare time. In between cocktail drinking sessions with her friend, she'd shopped and worked out at the gym, beating the hell out of her personal trainer. Everything was avoidance therapy—designed to distract from the much bigger issues about whether she was actually happy in her career, and how she felt about Dillon.

On Day Two of her exile from the office, they'd cut off her remote access; the passwords changed to her laptop, phone and tablet. When she'd called Mary-Anne to resolve what she assumed was a network connection issue, she'd shortly afterwards received a curt email to her personal account from Dillon—a few words stating that, for her own sake, she needed to stay away from work completely.

ᶜℓⁿᵍ

Bastard . . .
Whack. "Great upper cut Catherine."
Taking over my job . . .
Whack. "That was a forceful hook. Five more seconds to go."
Cutting me off email . . .
Whack. "Steady on with the blows."
I was the one who gave him a fucking job when he got here . . .
Whack. "Whoa there, far too low an upper cut—no punching the groin please!" yelled her personal trainer.

The imaginary punches to her stomach had just kept on coming, and she retaliated by punching her trainer even harder in reality, until she'd nearly punched him in the balls.

ᶜℓⁿᵍ

On Day Five, Dillon's hard-line no-contact stance weakened—he couldn't stand the thought of her suffering from boredom or becoming depressed; while he didn't come to see her, or even call her, he did reach out another way—couriering a gift bound with a red ribbon to her home.

At first, she had a sense of Deja-vu and, thinking that Boldwood has escaped his facility, she refused to sign for it. Only when the courier asked if she could confirm she wanted it returned to Mr. Oak, did she hastily sign—excited that he'd secretly sent her work in a ribbon-tied parcel.

Tearing it open like a child at Christmas—expecting to find bid documents—she was surprised to find that the contents were nothing to do with work. Inside was a bundle of novels with a handwritten note to accompany them.

> 'The strongest female heroines that Brits ever introduced to the world—a gift for a strong woman to keep her mind occupied. Love from your nearly-Oxford-educated, history-buff-bookworm friend.'

Catherine looked at each novel in turn, their covers annotated with sticky-note explanations from Dillon.

The first novel was Charlotte Bronte's *Jane Eyre*; with the note;

> 'This orphan never gave up and always remained true to herself.'

Next in the pile was in Jane Austen's *Pride and Prejudice*, complete with a note saying;

> 'Elizabeth Bennett sure knew how to argue with her men, and she overcame the attentions of Mr. Collins.'

Catherine smiled a sad smile, before taking the next book out of the box—the first of J.K. Rowling's Harry Potter books, with a note;

> 'if all else fails, do a Hermione and turn the man into a toad. P.S. I've never read it, so who knows if she used magic to really do that, but my niece reckons she wants to be like Hermione, and I most definitely wouldn't put it past my niece to want to turn boys into toads.'

Catherine laughed—she could almost hear the way Dillon would say that line, jokingly shrugging when queried about whether the toad-changing thing was true.

The fourth book was another children's title, Frances Hodgson Burnett's *A Little Princess*, with a more mischievous as well as sombre note;

> 'her fantasy story-telling captivated her audiences, but even in her darkest hours of missing her father, and losing everything, she showed kindness and strength.'

Catherine felt a tear forming in the corner of her eye, and she put the book to one side as the first one she would read.

The final book was Elizabeth Gaskell's *North and South*, with a note;

> 'she stood firm and held her own in a man's world, and even after

she discovered the workings of her heart, she still found a way to manage the business with the man she loved.'

Dillon had chosen the literature titles exceptionally well, and she wished he were there at that moment so that she could thank him—she missed him more than she ever thought possible. For the first time that week, she didn't hate him for taking over the company—or for cutting off her control from it.

The books were a comfort, and their purpose was fulfilled; she spent the following week reading them and taking in all the lessons Dillon was covertly trying to teach her. For nothing more than the time that it had taken him to select them, and about twenty dollars at the bookstore, Dillon had sent her a method of therapy far deeper than any retreat could have provided.

By the time her forced leave had reached its end, Catherine felt absolutely no animosity towards Dillon, and she couldn't wait to see him again.

Dillon couldn't believe that he'd tried on four different suits that morning. Catherine was returning to work and he was nervous.

His indecision caused him to be late, and she was already waiting in his office when he finally arrived. Two-and-a-half weeks had been the longest he'd gone without seeing her since he'd arrived in New York, and she looked exceptionally well; her eyes shone bright, and her face had lost the puffiness of tears shed.

"Hello Dillon, you're late," she scolded with playful assertiveness.

"I am, but it's your fault," he replied, determined not to yield to her.

"I don't recall doing anything to make you late, so clearly not my fault," she retorted, winking at him as she did.

Unable to think of a suitable comeback, Dillon settled on changing the topic, "I'm pleased to see you back Boss."

"Thank you, and also thank you for the books." Catherine wanted to show her appreciation, remembering Emilia's words that people wanted to see she had a heart.

"Did they keep you out of mischief?"

Dillon kicked himself at his choice of words, but he found it difficult to be completely professional when Catherine was standing in front of him after he hadn't seen her for a while.

"They did; I enjoyed re-reading those that I'd read before, and reading the ones that were new to me. You selected some good titles—it was Oxford's loss that they turned you down."

Dillon blushed, and looked down at the floor. "I admit I may have looked up a few on the internet to assist with the comments. I've been a bit busy looking after things here."

It was time to get the subject back to business.

"You have, and I hear you've done well. Emilia said it was fine to return, so I'm back now."

"Yes, you can have your job back. I'm going to cover Boldwood in the interim," said Dillon nervously, waiting for her reaction to his move. When she said nothing, he continued, "I'll update you now on all the work here before I head upstairs."

Firing up the computer, he steered forward their catch-up meeting at lightning pace. Catherine was disappointed that it was all serious business talk, and that she wouldn't get to spend much time with him anymore once he moved to another floor. She was sitting so close to him that she could smell the alluring scent of his aftershave and she noticed the muscles in his arms under his shirt.

He smells like sex. Has he been pumping iron to distract himself?

Now it was Catherine's turn to be totally distracted from work—lost in her fantasies of Dillon turning away from the computer to first eye-fuck her, then hitch her up onto the desk and finally—after more than a year—sink that all-too-often hard cock of his into her.

After an hour of half-heartedly listening to the update, her fantasising came to an abrupt halt; rocked to the core with Dillon's bombshell.

"If there's anything you need further clarification on over the next week, I will be upstairs in Boldwood's old office finishing up things there for the handover. Then after that, you'll be flying solo when I return to London at Christmas."

Catherine focused; all thoughts of his strapping arms around her—and his cock deep inside her—disappeared.

"You're going home for Christmas?" she asked. In one of her moments by the fireplace, she'd thought about the upcoming holiday, fantasising about inviting Dillon away with her for it—especially as Liddy would be elsewhere for Christmas—but now that fantasy was nothing more than a pipedream.

Dillon fumbled with a piece of paper, not looking at her. "I'm leaving permanently," he said quietly.

Catherine pushed her chair back suddenly, standing to attention with her mouth open and her head shaking in disbelief. "No, you're not going. They can't get rid of you, I won't let them. I'll . . . I'll . . .," she was almost going to say she'd quit.

Dillon looked up, "They didn't fire me, I resigned from my post here, and I also turned down the role of CEO of Boldwood's company that they offered me."

"Why?"

The part of Catherine's brain that was so career-driven could not comprehend why someone as equally focused as she was, would want to turn down such a career opportunity. Tellingly, where once she would've been jealous that he'd been offered the more senior CEO job within DeChartine over her, she was nothing but proud of him.

Dillon paused before replying, "Can we go for a walk—maybe to the park?"

If Catherine wanted an answer to her question, she had no choice but to agree to the walk. Collecting their coats, the pair descended the elevators in silence; Dillon relieved that they were not alone in the elevator and therefore their conversation halted.

They continued in silence as they walked to Central Park, picking up coffees on the way. There was still a little snow on the ground from the weekend flurries, but the paths were clear. Selecting a bench for them to sit on, Dillon finally answered her question, surprised that she'd been patient enough to not press on it while they walked.

"I thought about taking the job," he said, turning to face her. "It's an opportunity of a lifetime, but I'd been questioning a lot of things in my life and one thing I definitely knew was that I didn't want to become Boldwood, and—,"

"You're nothing like him—the man wasn't in control of his senses," interrupted Catherine.

"Don't interrupt," he scolded, glaring at her.

Catherine rolled her eyes back at him, but said nothing, instead taking a sip of her warm coffee.

"That's not what I meant. I don't want to end up in my fifties still trying to work out how to balance my working and personal life. Also, I can't deny that there are some things that do turn me on, and you do have an effect on me. What happens if I start to channel that like Boldwood did, particularly if we can't be together."

Dillon had dreaded saying that aloud, but it was all he'd been thinking about; would he turn into Boldwood if his desire for Catherine went unrequited for so long? While he wasn't wearing a physical chastity device, effectively he'd created a pseudo one by not pursuing a relationship with anyone else since he'd met her.

"I thought you didn't blame me for Boldwood?" Catherine replied with anger and hurt in her voice.

"You've missed my point. You're making this about other people, when this is about me and what I'm afraid of. This is about me admitting what you do to me."

The pain of hearing him remind her of all the unfair things she did to him was excruciating. "I've said I'm sorry that I hurt you—I don't know what else to say. You know we won't work, and we've discussed there can't be an us. You leaving only confirms that you know that."

She took his reprimand, and his departure, to be proof that he didn't want her—that she was no good for him long-term.

Dillon's eyes focused on two ducks squabbling over some bread; it was a metaphoric scene to watch given their conversation.

"Yes that's one reason why I have to go, because there's a part of me that will always want us. I know that you're right about it not working in our current situation."

"Can't you accept that, find someone who makes you happy, and stay?" she pleaded; she couldn't lose Dillon when he was nearly all she had apart from her work—especially when she was already questioning whether her career was truly making her happy.

"Why do you want me to stay?" asked, Dillon managing to maintain eye contact; he was anxious to see into her eyes, and read her body language, as she responded.

She hesitated and turned away, unable to hold his gaze, "You know why."

"No I don't. Tell me," he asked, persistently trying to crack open her emotional armour.

"I need you. The companies need you. You won't get the opportunity back in England, and you deserve it. You want success." Catherine delivered her justifications like the bossy CEO that she was—devoid of emotion.

Dillon's body slumped back against the hard back of the bench, disappointed in her response, yet not expecting the outcome to have been anything different. He wanted to say more, and disclose the other reasons for his decision—the ones told to him in confidence, with the request not to impart to Catherine. They were the instigator for him to not only resign and return to England, but they were what had given him the courage to take steps towards a happier future.

Why can't she say she wants me, not just that she needs me for work.

Dillon's hand clenched nervously in his pocket—inside it, the Valentine's Day Tiffany box containing the snowflake necklace, with the addition of another item. The note now amended to read:

'A snowflake necklace for happy memories in the past, and a diamond ring for the happy memories to come in the future.'

"I'm getting cold. We should head back," said Catherine, interrupting his silent, internal search for a moment of insane courage that might change his life.

"You're right; I have a lot to do this week before I leave," said Dillon, letting go of his hold on the box as he gave his monotone reply in agreement; Catherine was never going to love him the way he wanted her to, and he need to move on with his future back home.

Chapter Forty-Six

Catherine tried to find as many reasons as she could to contact Dillon that week; but unless it was work-related and required a response, he avoided her. She was unsure when he was departing for England—he'd only said that this was his last week—so when Friday came around, she set off for the thirty-third floor with a gift for Dillon—not a farewell gift, but a Christmas present, as she wanted to hold on to the belief that he would return after the holiday.

It had taken her a bit of time to select the right present; something that would outshine the cufflinks from the previous year was hard to find. Her first ideas centred on his promotion to CEO, but she later dismissed the idea, considering his turn down of the job offer. The second idea was even more controversial—something symbolic of their sexual desires—so she abandoned that too. She wanted to find something sentimental, yet not romantic—something that would convey how important he was to her and remind him of their bond.

In the end, she found the right thing—an inexpensive, unexpected find; walking past a street vendor on her way home, she'd spotted a snow-globe. The ornament featured a couple in a snowy scene, centred on a snowman, and the girl was holding up a snowball ready to throw it. There couldn't have been a more perfect depiction of their previous Christmas—the kitsch novelty of the item only added to the sentimentality and fun aspect—rather than on over-romantic gestures; Catherine was sure that Dillon would like it.

Exiting the elevator, she smiled at the receptionist, expecting to walk straight through towards Dillon's office.

"Good morning Miss Everdene. Are you here to see the new CEO? We weren't expecting you."

Catherine continued to smile, strangely happy to hear Dillon referred to as a CEO. "I hadn't scheduled a meeting, but yes I'm here to see Mr. Oak," she replied.

The woman looked back at her; puzzled that Catherine wasn't aware of what everyone else in the company seemed to know. "Mr. Oak left DeChartine yesterday. I thought you were here to meet his replacement."

The shock announcement hit Catherine as the truck had hit Faye; out of nowhere and knocking the life out of her—only Catherine was still breathing, albeit for the brief moment that her heart had stopped when she'd heard the word 'left'.

"He's left?" she asked, hoping that the woman had it wrong.

"Yes, yesterday. He said a few goodbyes, and then headed for JFK for his flight to London. He did go downstairs to DeChartine yesterday afternoon; didn't he see you then?"

Catherine had been at a client meeting offsite all the previous afternoon elsewhere; it nearly killed her when she realized that Dillon had known she would be out; he'd deliberately chosen a time to visit her floor that allowed him to continue to avoid her—just as he'd been doing since they left the park.

Standing in the lobby, welded to the one spot, Catherine had an overwhelming urge to burst into tears, cry out his name and demand him to come back.

You cowardly bastard asshole—why didn't you even say goodbye?'

Retrieving her iPhone from her bag, she was going to text, or email, all of those words; he would have arrived in London by now, and would still be awake.

How dare he rob me of the chance to say goodbye. How dare he abandon me.

Before she had a chance to act rashly, Boldwood's former PA approached her; on her way to DeChartine New Media, she'd spotted the opportunity to save a trip.

"Miss Everdene, I have some Christmas cards for you and the team downstairs. Some are from Mr. Oak, and the rest are from the new CEO. Would you be able to take them? Two are addressed solely to you—one of which is marked *'Private'.*"

Catherine wasn't sure if she'd nodded in agreement—the woman handed her the bundle before she said anything in reply. Looking down she saw the unmistakeable handwriting of Dillon on the one marked 'Private'.

Privacy—that was what Catherine needed right now, although even her office was the wrong place. Making her excuses for the afternoon's commitments, she dropped off the other cards, grabbed her coat and headed home.

༅

The card cover was blank; Dillon had used a cream notecard rather than a Christmas image and the lack of sentiment was even more hurtful than if he'd chosen an off-the-shelf pack of cards with a jolly Santa on the front. Flipping to the centre, her hurt intensified.

'I couldn't stay, but I couldn't say goodbye either. Please take care,

and I hope you find your happiness in the success I know you will achieve. Dillon'

No kisses, no emotion; Catherine snapped the card shut—anger filling her to mask the hurt. His words weren't only cowardly; she read sarcasm in his comments about taking care and finding happiness in success—a cryptic criticism of her choices, and all the tragedy her mistakes had brought about.

Storming around her apartment, she tried to think what to write back to him in an email or text—something to hurt him, or show him that she didn't care. Drafting the note in her mind, she ruminated over all that had transpired between them.

Only after doing this, did she start to realise that the direction of her anger was now towards herself. It was true she'd read sarcasm and criticism in Dillon's words, but only because they were wrong; her perceived successes weren't bringing her happiness, and she wasn't taking care in her actions—for far too long she'd been acting without thought as to the potential consequences for others, or for herself.

Dillon had been a victim of her naivety—even more so than Troy or Boldwood; in never entertaining the idea of a relationship with him—despite turning to him whenever she needed support, or sexual release—she'd hurt him repeatedly by rejecting him.

Looking at the gift she'd brought for Dillon, she shelved the idea of a retaliatory email or text. While a well-written apology note, along with the gift, might have opened up the communication lines with Dillon, her stubborn need to push aside romantic notions prevailed. Putting the snow-globe into an international express envelope, she added a one line handwritten card;

'A reminder of me . . . and snowball punishments.'

On Monday morning, she deposited the *'Private and Confidential'* parcel in his former PA's in-tray with a note requesting for it to be forwarded to his contact address in London; she didn't even bother to enquire as to his address—nor take the time to post it herself.

Dillon was gone and Catherine was going to focus on her future career.

Chapter Forty-Seven

As expected, hundreds attended the funeral in late February; Emilia DeChartine was a prominent figure in New York and had been so for over fifty years. Noticeably absent though, were those that had been closest to her in the last year of her life—Catherine's attendance was the exception.

It was her fault—Boldwood would've been there if she hadn't caused him to be psychiatrically-committed, and Dillon too, if he wasn't avoiding her. While no one at DeChartine was privy to the reasons regarding Dillon's failure to return for the funeral—especially as he wasn't yet busy working back in London—Catherine felt the weight of stares of accusation from the other mourners at the absence of Boldwood.

The mainstream media had avoided coverage of the whole, sorry saga to date, and only online gossip sites had reported the truth—albeit as rumors. Emilia's foreboding presence had continued to ensure a media blackout, but now that she'd passed away, the journalistic vultures were sharpening their pencil knives.

John Bradbury had warned his wife what was likely to unfold in the papers once Emilia was laid to rest, and when Liddy protested at his suggestion that she should persuade Catherine to return to London, he recommended that, at the very least, she should take her away for a few days. He would keep his wife informed of developments via phone, and Liddy could steer her friend to make the best decisions about her future—depending on the media's spin on who was accountable, and who would take over the ultimate helm of DeChartine.

❦

Catherine looked in the mirror at the puffy reflection staring back at her. It had been an emotional day, and she'd been appreciative of the silent journey to the Hamptons—thankfully in relatively calm traffic due to the day of the week, and time of the year. When Liddy had suggested an escape for the two of them to the beach-house—a chance to get away from the media coverage and the ghosts of the city—she'd gladly accepted; the wild, stormy coast would clear her head.

While she was grateful that Liddy had taken time off work to come with her, the one person she wanted right now was Dillon.

So often, she'd contemplated contacting him; her mind unable to decide between a long-winded, heartfelt email, or a short 'how are you' text—a phone call was too confrontational and felt invasive. Now, locked safely behind the bathroom door and away from Liddy's prying eyes, she felt compelled to reach out to him anyway she could. An email seemed preferable, but she would keep it very short—a simple 'thinking of you' sentiment, free of any accusation or judgment at his absence from the funeral, as well as from her life.

Reaching for her phone in the pocket of the coat that she'd not removed since arriving—the heating hadn't yet warmed up the house—she opened the application that was reserved for private emails. She hadn't checked her inbox for a few days; the endless tide of 'in deepest sympathy' seemed contrived considering she wasn't a relative of the deceased.

There in her inbox, amongst a host of subject lines all along a similar vein, was one titled *'in what I know will be a dark moment for you'*; the sender was Dillon Oak.

Catherine was a mess of nerves, ecstasy and anticipation—a hollow feeling in her stomach, a quickening of her heart rate, a pain in her chest and a sharp intake of breath. He'd timed the email to perfection; because not only had she wanted to contact him, but he would've pressed send at precisely the time she'd have left the church service—her phone switched to silent, she'd missed the tone set against his name to alert her specifically to his messages. He'd been thinking of her, yet she was nervous as to what tone he'd use—the subject line open to interpretation as to whether it was formal sympathy, or genuine caring emotion. Steeling herself for the possible content, she opened the email.

> 'Catherine,
> The subject line sums up the purpose of my email; I know
> you well enough to know that you will greatly feel the loss
> of Emilia and her death will no doubt bring up feelings of
> guilt, abandonment and vulnerability. You've never spoken
> much of these things, but I've watched you enough to
> know that your tough exterior is so similar to mine; a shield
> to hide the pain and suppress emotion.
> So often, we've been at battle with each other, even when
> we don't want to be. At least that's the case for me, and I
> can't believe that it's not the case for you; deep down you're
> not the icy woman you portray yourself to be. I've glimpsed
> beyond your walls, but sadly I was never able to knock
> them down, however hard I tried.
> I wish I could take your pain away; to say that you're

blameless in events. Much of what I've said to you has been the truth, but I have spoken with candor not because I wanted to bring you down, but because I wanted you to be the person that I know you are—not the person that you pretend to be in order to show strength. True strength comes from being comfortable in who you are, and finding the life path to suit that.

I left because I was no longer comfortable with who I'd become, or where I was headed. That was never going to change with the status quo, and you wouldn't have given up your career path for me.

I loved you, but as I didn't know if you loved me—or whether you would ever let yourself love me—I knew that I needed to stop torturing myself. I was tired of feeling second best, and tired of fighting. I was willing to submit to you in private, but you never gave me the chance to do that—you only allowed me to be submissive to you in the working world, and that was the one place that I couldn't submit without feeling I wasn't being true to myself.

When I felt that I was somehow betraying you if I took Boldwood's old job, I realized I needed a fresh start where we were equals.

I truly believe that, in another place and situation, we would've been very happy together and fitted well. I did confide my feelings to Emilia before I left, but she told me that I needed to let you make that decision on your own; forcing you to make a choice between me, and your career, was an ultimatum that I would always lose if I gave it. Our final meeting in Central Park confirmed her opinion, and I couldn't face you after that, because I knew I'd blurt out that ultimatum, and that you would reject me.

I contemplated not sending this email, but, with Emilia's message at the funeral about having lived a life full of love, if ever there is a right time to tell you that you will forever be in my thoughts and my heart, then this is it. You always reached out to me when you felt the rest of the world had abandoned you, and I couldn't let you believe that I had too. However, I couldn't return to New York to support you, as I'm embarking on the next chapter of my life back home where I belong—who knows, maybe I will be the Oxford-educated history bookworm after all, rather than only a 'rejected-nearly'.

Maybe we will meet again someday. Be strong, in the way that I know you're capable of.

Dillon.'

Teardrops dripped on the screen of Catherine's phone, blurring and magnifying the words Dillon had typed. He'd told her that he loved her—the first time that he had—but it was in the past tense, and he hadn't signed off with any affection. With her tendency to think of the worst emerging, she chastised herself for concentrating on the negatives rather than the overall sincerity of his words and the gesture in his well-timed communication.

A knock on the bathroom door reminded her that she wasn't alone in the beach-house; Liddy had heard her sobs and was offering tea and a warmer, cozier spot by the lounge fire. Right now, both of those suggestions were welcome, and Catherine had the overwhelming need for a hug from her friend; Liddy obliged as soon as she opened the locked white door, holding out her arms to embrace her tightly.

"He emailed," said Catherine, trying to choke back the waterworks.

Liddy didn't need to ask whom the email was from—she'd long since suspected Catherine's attachment to Dillon had run deep, and he'd been regularly contacting John to ask how she was over the past two months since his departure. "Come to the lounge and we can talk," she said.

The lounge had a warmth from the fire, but the room hadn't yet lost its iciness from being vacant throughout the winter—the cold was a poignant reminder of death. Liddy handed Catherine a steaming mug of tea.

"Are you okay?" she asked; it was a stupid question, particularly as she could see the obvious moisture of tears and a runny nose on her friend's face, but it was an opening line she'd successfully used in previous conversations with Catherine to break down her impenetrable emotional walls.

Where once Catherine would have provided a biased synopsis of an email from a man, she wanted a completely independent opinion on the content; she handed Liddy the phone. Sipping her tea, she watched her read Dillon's email; an eternity passing before Liddy looked up from the screen.

"He's said some tough things in here. How do you feel about it all?" Liddy worded her question carefully, anxious to understand if Catherine felt attacked. While she didn't openly defend Dillon, Liddy didn't think he deserved criticism for his honesty and sincerity; through her marriage, she'd discovered that sometimes loving someone meant being the one person that had to be brave and say things that would hurt.

"He didn't say anything that I didn't already know about myself," answered Catherine quietly, staring into her mug. "I'd hoped nobody else would ever get to know me that well, for fear they would use that knowledge against me."

"Dillon would never do that to you. He's remained loyal to you no matter what happened," said Liddy, trying to convince Catherine that not everyone was out to get her; while there would be plenty of people that would be in the coming days, it was vital that she appreciated she had friends who loved her.

"He might of though. If he'd stayed, right at this moment he would be leading the company through this because he wasn't publicly linked to last year's scandals. I'd always kept him at a personal distance in the eyes of everyone, so they perceived him the innocent bystander, who became the hero to step in and save Boldwood. In pushing him away all the time, I'd unknowingly protected him from the potential fall-outs of my other messes. Even if he'd been loyal initially, now would be his shining hour. The Board would have given him control, because they see him as the knight in shining armor that will steer DeChartine into the future now Emilia is gone."

Liddy nodded sadly, remembering John's premonition to her about the pending media backlash; she couldn't lie to Catherine by denying that the Boldwood incident wouldn't resurface, and that she'd escape unscathed. If she'd stepped down, Dillon Oak would be the one they'd trust to take over; if he'd defended Catherine—or refused the Board's offer—his own career would be in jeopardy and without DeChartine, his sponsorship visa would be withdrawn. Even the romantic in Liddy understood that their relationship would struggle to survive so many trials and tribulations.

"His actions in leaving were for your benefit, as well as his," said Liddy, wanting her to appreciate Dillon's selfless act in not accepting the promotion.

"What gives you the idea it was for my benefit? He said he wants a new life," retorted Catherine.

Liddy sighed at Catherine's continued blindness towards Dillon's stoical, loyal love for her, as well as her tendency to focus on the negatives. "You've worked out what would have happened if he stayed, but did you consider that maybe he'd worked that out too? That he knew he'd have to decide between you and the job. He says in the email that he spoke to Emilia while you were on leave. What if she'd told him that she was dying, then asked him not to broadcast it? Dillon hinted to John before he left that he'd had a decent payout. We thought it was hush money about Boldwood, but maybe it was an advance on a bequest, or a hush to keep her health a secret. If people knew she was dying, DeChartine would have been prime for acquisition, and Emilia would never want to see her husband's legacy broken apart in her lifetime, especially as she hadn't borne her husband a child to inherit."

"I suppose," said Catherine, pondering all of Liddy's point of view.

As she continued to stare blankly into the flames of the fire, Liddy left her alone with her thoughts while she went into the kitchen area to find something to tempt her to eat—Catherine's already slender frame had easily lost more weight in the last week. Returning ten minutes later to the silent room, save for the reassuring crackle of the open fire, Liddy put down two mugs of hot soup and a plate of crusty bread. She was surprised to see Catherine pick up the mug and a slice of bread almost immediately; this was good progress.

"Why did he leave? Why do they always leave?" Catherine asked softly when she'd finished her soup.

"If you mean Dillon, you know the answer to that; you just don't want to admit it. He left because you pushed him away, and—,"

"That's not true. I—," interrupted Catherine, trying to defend herself, but Liddy cut her off.

"You know it's true. You told him your job came first, and you couldn't have a relationship if you worked together. He knew that the only way he'd ever win you, or alternatively get over you, was to leave. Sometimes only realizing how much you miss a person, rather than just need them for everyday work things, is the only way you can admit what's in your heart." Liddy took a bite of bread before continuing, "As to your second question, who always leaves? Do you mean men in general that leave women, or do you mean Troy, Bill, your father, Emilia? A whole heap of people have come and gone in your life, but that's just the way of the world—people come and they go for loads of reasons. It's up to you to work out what those reasons were, and whether you should let the person go, fight for them, or find them once you know they're meant to be in your life again."

"When did you switch from law to psychiatry self-help mumbo-jumbo preaching?" Catherine teased, trying to lighten the mood.

"I haven't, I'm just doing what an awesome best friend does," replied Liddy, rolling her eyes at her friend.

Catherine didn't answer back, she was tired and her head was full of so many things to think about. Putting down her now empty soup mug, she pulled a blanket over her, laid her head on the cushion and closed her eyes.

ce⁓ಎ

"A delivery from a law firm came for you. I didn't want to wake you, and they let me sign for it once I said I was your lawyer," said Liddy, handing Catherine a jumbo mug of extra-shot *'wake up it's the morning'* coffee.

Taking a seat at the breakfast bar, Catherine looked down at the heavy manila envelope with *'Miss Catherine Everdene. Private and Confidential Legal Papers Enclosed'* written on the front.

Dismissal from DeChartine, subpoena for a court-case about Troy, or worse?

Catherine turned her head away from the foreboding envelope to glance at the front pages of the newspapers on the counter.

"Are there any stories in the papers about Emilia or DeChartine, or even me?" she asked with nervous curiosity.

"The papers have all reported that Emilia's personal estate has been bequeathed to some distant relatives and close family friends, while the wider company fortunes have been given philanthropically to a heap of charities. That's all they say today, but John says the unofficial talk is that the DeChartine company is likely to be broken up, as apparently her shares are to be floated so the profits go to the charities, rather than them owning actual shares," explained Liddy.

She looked at the manila envelope that Catherine had so far ignored. "The envelope is from Emilia's personal lawyers, not DeChartine, in case you were wondering."

Catherine smiled; Liddy could read her fears better than she could. "Thanks for the coffee. Do you mind if I go and read this in my room?" She picked up the envelope and her mug.

"No problem. If you need me, I'll be here."

When she was alone in her room, curled back up under the warm blanket, Catherine finally opened the envelope. Inside was a handwritten letter from Emilia, and a second sealed brown envelope. Setting the latter to one side, she began to read the letter.

> *'Catherine,*
>
> *I'm not going to bore you with the 'by the time you read this' lines. I've died after a short illness. Quite apart from my age, my idiot doctor seemed to think it was time to start wrapping up loose ends. Far from being sad, I'm happy that I will finally be reunited with my husband—the one who remained devoted to me until the day he died and whom I never gave permission to leave me. I want him back, and now the time has come to own him again in the next life.*
>
> *You know little about me Catherine, but you remind me so much of myself when I was younger. I've told few people my secrets, but now is the right time to pass on my story.*
>
> *Many years ago, I came face-to-face with the man who wouldn't only become my husband, but also my lover, my friend and my submissive. Yes, you read that last bit right. He was a powerful*

man, yet somehow he was in awe of me, despite the fact that I wasn't the most attractive woman in the building—or the city— and definitely wasn't from his class and upbringing. However, from our first interaction when I met him at the office, I held my own and my words, self-assurance and feminine charm captured his mind. Everyone thought I should immediately throw myself at him, idolize him and try to get a ring on my finger before he bored of me, but I wasn't drawn to him by his more obvious charms of power and wealth. We seemed equal in so many things that mattered and we could talk for hours. Our secret to success was that I had him wrapped around my finger when we were alone.

I made it my mission to find out everything about him on a deeper level, and in doing so I discovered I was everything he needed me to be. Even in the sixties, wives should have been good and compliant, and never stronger than their husband was—the man was the breadwinner and the one in charge. I didn't want to change who I was to get a husband, and thankfully, I was fortunate enough to never have to submit.

The best advice I can give you from nearly fifty years of marriage is that you only marry someone if you love them for who they are—not want you hope to change them to be. People will always change, but they will change because the person they are with brings out their strengths and makes them want to overcome their weaknesses. People forced to change against their will, will eventually rebel and that's when you lose them.

The second bit of married advice is that it won't always be a rosy life. My husband and I had a daily battle of wills, but we found a fun way to get through the battles. I learned how to take his stresses away, and he learned how to let me. Behind closed doors, we were always in our own world. I don't need to tell you all the salacious details, and I know your mind has been extended to BDSM in many ways—some not so good, but it's a lifestyle that can offer many pleasurable delights in the right relationship. Each couple learns what turns the other on, and how to derive pleasure from each other. The more they trust and communicate with each other, the more bonded they become. My husband and I were two of the lucky ones; the perfect fit.

You've been on a hard journey since you joined my company, and I understand that before that you suffered great trauma in your earlier life. I've seen you flourish professionally, but I've seen you hurt personally, and I've also seen you hurt those closest to you, *even though I know that you never intended to. You're not a cruel woman, and I see in you the ability to show great love if you let yourself. The right man for you was under your nose all along, and I think in your heart you knew it. You were just too stubborn to admit it for fear of the consequences. Instead, you headed down diversionary paths that had far worse outcomes.*

Now, if you want to be as happy as I was for all those years of my marriage, you have to make a change, and no one can force you to do that—you have to want to do it. Dillon needs you to not only be the woman he was drawn to when he first met you, but also the hidden woman that he then fell in love with—the happier, fun and loving Catherine. He isn't like Troy, nor is he like Bill; he's like my husband—a man who wants to do everything he can to make you happy, protect you and serve you, while feeling valued, appreciated and accepted for the great man that he is. I have faith that you can give him that if you let yourself love him. It would be my greatest dying wish to know that the great story that my husband and I had is being continued in a new generation; I would almost feel that we lived on.

There's one final thing to say though; you should return to England.

Dillon wanted to go home, but he didn't want to leave you, yet it was unfair for him to continue to be second to you in the working world. He didn't want to take over from you, knowing that you would resent him for taking over your position if it came to it. It was breaking his heart to carry on with things the way that they were. When he sought my counsel a few months ago to ask for my thoughts on a relationship between you, he told me that his greatest fear would be a situation where he had to make a decision between you and a job offer. Once I knew this, I had to be honest with him about my illness and tell him what would happen on my death in the near future.

As much as I wish it weren't true, when I depart this world, so does the protection I afford you. The wolves will descend, my empire will break up, and you will not be the one the Board will choose to try to keep it whole; had he still been here, it would have been Dillon—because not only is he the man, they will also think that it should have been Bill, had it not been for you. Once Dillon understood what was coming his way, and that he would be unable to protect you from it, he made the only choice his conscience would allow—to leave rather than fail to protect you, or have to make a choice that would hurt you. Please understand that he hasn't abandoned you—he chose the only option that still provided an ounce of hope for you both to be together one day.

You need to get past your willfulness and stubborn ego. If you're to succeed in a happy life, find something new that you can do without competition. You're both extremely talented, but you need some time out to rediscover yourselves and to develop your partnership, without external pressures. Dillon wants to study again and pursue a different career path and, as I have helped him financially in advance of my death, he can now do that.

I also have taken care of Boldwood financially and he is safe abroad, where his desires are being taken care of.

Now finally, as a percentage of my wealth the amount I bequeath you is very small, but it will buy you something bigger than your apartment should you decide to stay in New York. If you choose to return to London, it's likely to allow you a nice life, and if the happy ending that I hope you will have with Dillon becomes a reality, the merged pot should give you both a nice home, and financially-comfortable life, for some time to come.

Once I would have wished you all the success in the world, but instead I want for my final words to you to be a wish for all the happiness and love that a life should have. You deserve it.
Emilia DeChartine

P.S. Actually, your fairy godmother wants her final words to be 'Remember Cinderella, she is proof that a good pair of heels can snag you a prince.' Dillon told me that he's been besotted with you ever since he first saw your heels as you descended down the stairs; he is your prince. Let him be the one to put on your glass slipper every morning of every day. Don't be one of those idiots and lose him forever. These words are pretty much a wish for you to have a happy ever after.'

Tears rolled down Catherine's cheeks as she finished reading the letter, smiling only at the ending; how had Emilia known that she'd nicknamed her the fairy godmother. She opened the sealed brown envelope and withdrew the lawyer's letter stating the amount of money bequeathed to her; seven figures, even when converted to pounds.

The final, dying words of Emilia, Dillon's sympathy email and the discussion the night before with Liddy, were all the incentive Catherine needed to type her resignation to the Board. It was finally time to go home, and for the first time in twenty-six years—since her mother's death—she knew where, or more importantly with whom, her home would be.

Chapter Forty-Eight

"How can I turn fucking left when all there is to the left of me is a field gate?" yelled Catherine, cursing at the hire car's GPS screen.

"In ten yards, please turn left," repeated the monotone GPS robot.

"In five yards, please hit the fucking big oak tree directly in front," she replied, switching the stupid thing off and looking around for some indication of where she was—surrounded by fields and woodland, there were no houses or other buildings in sight.

She'd clearly missed a turning somewhere in the last mile, because now she'd reached a dead end. She cursed again, her short temper getting the better of her; Catherine was nervous, and when her nerves took hold, she always channeled them into abrupt outbursts; today's first opponent—the anonymous female navigation robot.

It was four months since Dillon had left her in New York. After Emilia's funeral, she'd fulfilled her six weeks' notice, and returned to London two weeks ago, but in all that time, she had never found the right words to send to Dillon, and instead had chosen to stay silent.

A week before her return to England, she'd been included in a round-robin email update from him—he'd moved into a new home in Evershot, back in this native Dorset. The arrival of this first communication from him since the sympathy email did nothing to help overcome her nerves regarding contacting him, and she'd therefore failed to respond—even to wish him well.

On arriving back in England, it had taken her two weeks to build up the courage to hire a car and drive the three hours south-west of the capital. Then, it had taken another day of mulling around in a bed-and-breakfast on the Jurassic Coast—staring out at the sea remembering Memorial Day weekend in the Hamptons with Dillon—before she finally retrieved his address email and typed the postcode into the stupid GPS.

Now, if the GPS was telling the truth, she was supposedly within a half-mile of his home. Catherine tried to calm her nerves by enjoying the scenery; she wound down the window and a cool breeze filled the car with the scent of the hedgerows; she could hear the happy sound of birdsong and she watched the spring lambs frolicking in the fields. As her senses adapted to the natural world—rather than the internal car smell of leather and cleaning agent—she relaxed and a deep sense of homecoming settled over her—even though she'd never visited the area before.

After ten minutes of clearing her mind, she started up the engine again and performed an eight-point turn to get the car facing back along the road instead of the oak tree. Catherine drove slower this time—not just because of not wanting to miss the entrance to where Dillon lived—but also because she'd adapted to the pace of the country. It didn't take long for her to spot the slightly concealed drive, recalling that a tractor had pulled into the space earlier to let her pass in the narrow lane. Flicking the indicator to flash left—more out of habit than an actual need to notify any traffic—Catherine turned the car into the graveled drive.

Cherry trees in full blossom stretched in a line either side of the long driveway; with the window still down she could smell their faint perfume and the occasional pink petal, carried on the breeze, fell onto her lap—reminding her of sitting with Dillon in Central Park a year ago.

Will he want to see me again?

Her nerves started to fray once more; he wasn't expecting her.

The house came into view; a former rectory with bay windows covered in wisteria and climbing roses just coming into bud. As she neared the building, she could see the scarred render on the façade—the marks in the stonework where the climbing plants had gouged their paths, year after year. It was an appropriate metaphor for her relationship with Dillon—him the solid foundation and her the plant that clung to it; reminding her of the beauty, rather than the ugliness in their symbiotic relationship.

After parking the car by the house front entrance, as casually as possible (just in case he was watching), she got out of the car and headed for the door. The old-fashioned bell's ring penetrated through the heavy wooden door and she waited as patiently as she could for someone to open it.

Please let him be home.

It hadn't even occurred to her that he might be away and she might have had a wasted trip.

Well I have nowhere else to be anytime soon . . .

The heavy door opened and Catherine froze.

Who the hell are you? This is definitely the right house.

In all her fantasies of how this might pan out, it had never crossed her mind that a young woman would open the door. On sight of the woman's left hand, and the sparkling diamond ring on a telltale finger, Catherine's world began to crumble.

"Hello, can I help you?" said the woman in a heavy local accent.

"Hi, I'm a friend of Dillon . . .," somehow her words were coming out in response. "I'm Catherine Everdene, and I used to work with him and I was visiting the area. I received an email a while back from Dillon to say he'd moved here, so I thought I'd call in . . .,"

Stop talking or she will think you are a psycho ex.

". . . but if it's an inconvenient time."

"He's not in at the moment. Not sure where he is exactly—probably gone for a walk," said the woman, shrugging as though she didn't really care where he was.

Don't let her see you're anything more than just a former boss.

Catherine tried to keep her emotions in check; she sensed the woman had heard her name before, but there was no suggestion that she felt threatened.

Dillon must really love her. Maybe he has told her I was an icy bitch that he hated.

"You can come in and wait for him. I'll put the kettle on and you can have a cup of tea," she said politely.

"Thank you for the offer, but I probably should be going," Catherine replied reluctantly; although her morbid curiosity to find out about Dillon's new love kept her rooted to the spot on the porch.

"Oh, that's a shame. Dillon would be disappointed not to see you—you being a friend and all." The woman didn't seem to care whether she was going to stay or go, but there was a knowledgeable amusement in her comment on Catherine being a friend.

"I guess I could probably do with a cup of tea," she replied, stepping into the hall. "I didn't catch your name."

"Oh, sorry I don't even think I told you it," said the woman, laughing as she carried on along the hall. "I was too busy admiring your dress. I'm Jane." Her reply gave no further clue to her identity beyond what people called her.

She doesn't look anything like Dillon—I'm sure I heard him say his only sister was already married with kids.

Catherine was about to find the courage to ask, when they arrived in a huge, bright sunny kitchen and Jane set to putting a kettle on the Aga plate; her jealousy about Jane having Dillon momentarily took second place to her envy about having a dream kitchen like this one. She looked longingly at everything, from the empty shelves of the huge pantry located off the main space, to the cushioned banquette seat in the bay window.

The things I could bake in this kitchen, or just sit and read the papers over Sunday breakfast.

The kettle whistled on the Aga plate and she heard a dog bark in the distance.

My dog always used to bark when the kettle boiled.

The happy memory quickly faded into the sad realization that this wasn't her kitchen, boiling kettle or the barking of a dog she might befriend.

"Milk, sugar?" asked Jane, putting one mug onto the counter.

"Bit of the first, none of the second," replied Catherine.

She knew if Dillon turned up, and she saw him happy with Jane, it would break her heart far more than wishing them all the best from a distance would do.

"There you go," said Jane handing her the mug. Catherine tried not to stare at the ring on her finger; relieved when she headed over to the table and proceeded to pull things out of a half-unpacked box. "I've got loads to do, so would you mind if I got on with the unpacking? Feel free to take a seat, or walk about the house or go out into the garden."

Catherine was puzzled; aside from the fact that it was rude to ignore a guest in your home, she couldn't understand why Jane was willing to let a strange woman, that had come to see her fiancé, go wandering around her house—without even giving her the third degree.

Everything about Jane seemed wrong for Dillon; she clearly wasn't a dominant woman and had more traits in common with a submissive—Faye Robine came into her mind, and Catherine quickly buried that painful comparison.

Has Dillon moved on to a rebound the complete opposite of me?

The last time she'd seen him and in his February email, he seemed so determined to move his life on from her, and maybe that included a very vanilla—or at least more traditional—wife.

He always said he wanted normal.

As Catherine's mind raced through all the possibilities, none of them explained Jane's complete lack of interest in her, or willingness to let her roam around the house. She was glad though to escape the gorgeous kitchen that the woman was happily making house in, and leaving Jane to find homes for the multitude of new kitchen appliances that kept appearing out of the cardboard box, she took her mug of tea into the hall.

The drawing room was a sunny room, with another bay window looking out into the garden. The imposing fireplace had the ash remnants of a recent fire in the hearth, and she spotted a hardback novel on the armchair by the fireplace; blinking back a tear as she remembered her two evenings with Dillon by her smaller fire, she tried not to imagine what he might have done with Jane by this fire.

It should have been me doing wicked things to him in front of the flames— me arousing him until he was begging me for his release—me cuddling him in my arms as he dropped out of sub-space.

A lump in her throat was rising up, and she quickly headed into the next room—away from the fireside and her fantasies of activities on the rug in front of it.

Off the larger drawing room was what looked to be a study, shelves lining the walls and a full-length south-facing window at the end; the sun was streaming through the glass panes and through them, Catherine could see a blaze of pink and white blossom in the orchard; Dillon really had purchased the property of their combined dreams.

Turning her attention back to the interior, she perused the few books that were unpacked—the dozens of boxes still sealed suggested that Jane had left this room for Dillon to do; the range of authors and genres on show confirmed his interest in history and literature.

She dragged her hand along the polished wood of the antique desk in the center of the room, and absent-mindedly picked up a metal ruler laid on it.

Oh, the fun we could have had on this bit of furniture.

"In all the unpacked chaos of my new place, trust you to find that ruler. You've only been here ten minutes."

The ruler came down harder than she was expecting into her open palm; the shock of hearing Dillon's voice behind her causing her to slap the ruler into her other hand.

"Oh fuck, that hurts," she screamed, dropping the weapon and clenching her fist tight.

Dillon was by her side in a flash, grabbing hold of her injured hand. Her pulse quickened at his touch, and the pain in her palm disappeared as she remembered what the ecstasy of his embrace—after all these months—still gave her.

"Don't even think about hitting me with it then!" he said, trying to mask his laughter.

Catherine pulled back, keen to put some distance between them—not least, because she'd heard Jane's singing stop after her scream.

"I . . . um . . . was in the area," she explained, stuttering through her nerves.

"So Jane said. John Bradbury had mentioned you were returning to London, and I did wonder if you'd visit, although you never replied to my new address email," remarked Dillon, still grinning.

Bastard John, he never said he'd kept in contact with him.

"I had some time free, so I thought I'd come and see how you were settling in . . .," she replied, hesitating for a moment. "Jane seems nice."

"Yes she is—always bubbly—and makes me sort of smile with all her singing. She also does as she's told—without arguments."

Dillon was goading her and she knew it, but his justifiable vengeful comment about her argumentative, moody and willful behavior still hurt. She turned away to study more of the book titles on the shelf and, in doing so, her eye caught sight of the snow-globe she'd posted to him. Alongside it were two photographs, displayed in an expensive, solid-silver frame—the first one, Dillon and her in the Bradbury garden at Christmas with a snowball in her hand, and the second, the two of them dancing together in Madison's playroom. Catherine had never seen either of the pictures before—Liddy had obviously taken the photos and shared them only with him.

"Why are these up?" Catherine doubted that Jane wouldn't have something to say about pictures of another woman on display—even if she was apparently adverse to arguments.

"The snow-globe makes me smile and, to be honest, so do the photos. I enjoyed that day," he replied, picking up the object and shaking it in his hand to make it snow; he was standing far too close to her again. Catherine blushed with embarrassment and arousal.

Why does he have to make my heart race to the point where I think I will faint into his arms?

"Jane really does submit! I'd break your balls if you put pictures of another woman up," Catherine snorted, thinking Dillon's fiancée even weaker than she'd first guessed.

"It was her idea actually—something about personalizing the space in here as my own man-cave," said Dillon, grinning again and puffing out his chest to appear more masculine and dominating.

"So Neanderthal—I've been dragged into your cave," she replied, rolling her eyes at him.

Dillon laughed. "Somehow I've always pictured *you* as the one to be dragging *me* by the hair back to your cave—or at least onto the floor," he joked, winking as he said it.

She quickly averted her gaze back to the books again, not wanting to succumb to her urges to flirt with an engaged man—even if she did love him and want him for herself; everything about Dillon right now—his relaxed, joking personality—showed he was happy.

Close to the photographs, she saw another treasure—the unmistakable aqua-blue box of the jeweler, Tiffany. It had to be *the* box; the one that had once housed Jane's sparkler until Dillon placed it on her finger. Catherine's stomach churned.

"I nearly forgot. Congratulations," she said, trying to fake happiness.

"Thanks, do you like the house then? I'm sorry if it reminds you too much of your parent's home, but I fell in love with it when I saw it online, and it was near the village I have always wanted to live in. I did look first for a village called Everdene, but no one seemed to have wanted to name a place after you—so Evershot it is."

Catherine's eyebrows furrowed in confusion, ignoring his jibe about the village name. "The house is gorgeous, you're really lucky to have found it, but I meant congratulations on your engagement."

"Engaged to who?" Dillon asked with a look of surprise.

There was a surreal Deja-vu to the conversation; a reversal of one they'd had almost a year ago to the day.

"Jane. I saw her ring when I came in, and—,"

Dillon burst out laughing, stopping her explanation. "You've been thinking that since you got here?"

Catherine glared at him, "Stop laughing. It's not funny."

He continued to laugh, even when she raised her hand as though to slap him.

"What's so funny then?" she asked.

I'm going to beat the shit out you if you don't stop laughing, you engaged, happy bastard.

"You," he replied, chuckling away still.

"I'm not funny," she said, picking up the lethal ruler again. "Now stop laughing, and tell me what's so funny, or I'll slap you with this and it bloody hurts." A wicked sparkle-smile began to form at the corners of her mouth—despite the Jane situation.

"Sorry *Boss*, my apologies. I was laughing at how you always miss things—or think the worst. Do you really think that John and Liddy would have been badgering you all week to get into your hire car and drive down here to talk to me if they knew I was engaged?" he said, screwing up his face as he contemplated his last comment. "Well actually Liddy probably would have, but John would've discouraged it."

Dillon was still smirking, aware though that he'd inadvertently revealed that he knew she was considering a visit any day; he could take the punishment if she did spot his admission.

"They said what!"

So much for confiding in my friends.

"Have to admit I was disappointed when you didn't show up last night. I had the fire going and everything, but then all that happened was me sitting up reading a novel until one in the morning, worried in case you were lost in the lanes in the dark. Liddy had sent an email yesterday to say you'd finally left London, bound for the greener pastures of Dorset. Where did you go?"

Catherine couldn't believe her friends were ganging up on her to this extent. "I stayed on the coast, but never mind that—who's Jane?"

"Well, apart from apparently my fiancée—which is something her own fiancé would have something to say about—she's my sister's best friend. Is that enough information for you, *Miss Bossy Boots*?" he replied, grinning as he enjoyed watching her squirm.

"No," she said, prodding him tauntingly with the ruler. "What's your sister's best friend doing here and playing house?"

"Are you going to put the ruler down?" Dillon reached towards the offending weapon.

"Hell no," she replied, dodging his grab by taking a step back. "Now get on with explaining."

"To help pay for her wedding, Jane has started up a cleaning, house-organization, interiors or whatever, sort of business that caters for useless-but-rich bachelors like me. To be honest, I think she and my sister started the business when I turned up back in the county, and it's highly likely that once my place is sorted, the business will wind up, and Jane will start a new one—probably a dating one, with me as its first, and probably only, male client. They'll probably charge extortionate fees to the single women of the county for a date with seven-figure Dillon—and that's pounds sterling, not inches, before you joke—recently returned from New York. I'm Dorset's most-eligible bachelor under forty I think—unless you count a few footballers in Poole. I wouldn't it past my sister and her friend to pimp me out."

Dillon took a step towards Catherine before continuing, "Now does that explain who Jane is, and what she's doing here? I'm really hoping it does, because you're welding that ruler in far too threatening a way."

He raised an eyebrow in amusement at her defensive stance.

"You know you could have just told me all that when I said she seemed nice," she scolded; the ruler stayed in her raised hand—a strike still an imminent possibility.

"What, and miss out on winding you up? I don't think so," he joked, laughing as he took a step back just in case.

"That's it," she said, advancing towards him. "You're going to get a slap. Bend down boy."

"Yeah right, you're going to have to catch me first," he teased.

Continuing to look over his shoulder at her, Dillon started to run from the study—straight into the petite figure of Jane, who was standing in the hall.

Catherine quickly hid the ruler behind her back, embarrassed to be caught by the stranger, who she'd now discovered was the best friend of

Dillon's younger sister—a woman that she hadn't yet met, but wanted to make a good first impression on. There was no way Jane wouldn't have heard her tell Dillon to bend over, and it inevitably would end up an amusing discussion with his sister.

Dillon helped Jane to her feet, apologizing profusely.

"I was coming to say that I was taking the afternoon off. I suddenly remembered I had a dress fitting," said Jane, looking over at Catherine and trying to hide a knowing smile. "It was nice to meet you Catherine." She turned and fled from the house.

Dillon turned back to face Catherine, "Nice one Boss. I think she saw the ruler." He winked and she hastily put the object down, her face becoming more serious.

"I saw the box on the shelf and I thought it was linked to Jane's ring," she admitted, unable to hide her sadness.

Stepping back into the study, Dillon picked up the culprit for the confusion from the shelf; the box looked smaller now that it was in his big hand, but the significance of it grew in size.

"No, sadly this little box has its own story. One that's far more complex than the story of Jane's ring. She went to school with her future husband and they've been happy together ever since," he explained.

Catherine's heart stopped.

Did Dillon buy me a ring because he'd been told I was on my way here?

"What did Liddy tell you?" she asked.

Dillon looked up from the box, guessing her assumption.

"Nothing, other than you were back in London and would visit." He looked back down at the box. "This goes way back. I'm not sure that telling you its story will do us any good," he said sadly.

The lump in her throat was back; she'd left it too late.

Would it have been different if I'd come to see him sooner—or even last night? Has my stupid hesitation cost me my chance with him?

"Dillon, tell me what's in the box," she demanded, hoping that her dominating tone might be the key to open the secrets inside that damn box. It worked; he handed her the gift.

"Before you open it though, there are two things I need to tell you. One thing in there I brought last February, and the first line of the message was written then. The second item, I added in December, along with the second line. I never found the courage to give you the box on either occasion, and I have gone over, and over, the consequences of that. I'd come into your office on Valentine's Day, but when I saw you so happy with the flowers from an admirer—at the time not known to me—I didn't want to ruin things for you. For a long time I blamed myself that everything that happened after was my fault, yet now I know that even if I had given you the box that day, you would have said thanks and still moved onto Troy. But, if you'd rejected my gift, I probably would have left for England soon after with a seriously wounded pride. Back then, you never would have followed me, and we'd never have gone through the things that made us closer. The time for this box, and us, wasn't then."

Dillon rubbed his hand along his chin and into his hair, steeling himself for the next part. "The second occasion I should have been stronger. We were in the park, and I told you I was leaving. I was never going to change my mind about that—I wanted to come home—but I did want you to come with me. You pushed me away before I could ask; saying only that you needed me. I needed you to want me in your life, not just that you needed me to sort your shit out. After that moment, I had to give you distance so that you could come to a decision of your own accord as to whether you missed me enough to want me. Only then would this box find out the ending to its story."

Catherine stared down at the box in her hand, too scared to open it. She had to lighten the mood.

"Have you finished, or do I need to gag you?"

He snorted a laugh; Catherine amused him—even when he was grappling with his emotions and was way out of his comfort zone.

"That won't be necessary. I'm done."

"Good," she said smiling. "Can I open it now?"

"You're the boss," he said, grinning.

Catherine gave him her sparkle-smile, and pulled the white ribbon to release the bow. With her hands trembling, she opened the box, and retrieved the jewelry case inside. Lifting the lid, she gazed open-mouthed at the ring—its size and sparkle outdoing Jane's bling. Surrounding it was a necklace chain adorned with a dainty silver snowflake. She read the message:

> 'A snowflake necklace for happy memories in the past, and a
> diamond ring for the happy memories to come in the future.'

The emotions stirred up inside her scared her; the idea of marrying Dillon—or anyone—terrified her.

Wow, for a guy, he really is a romantic, sentimental wordsmith.

"Dillon, I—,"

She didn't know how to respond; not wanting to say no, but unable to bring herself to say yes—or to tell him she loved him.

"No more 'we work together' excuses. I love you, and I'm pretty sure you love me too. Please don't keep pushing me away," he pleaded.

He could tell from her body language that she was leaning towards rejecting him, and he couldn't bear the thought of losing her—particularly not while standing in his new man-cave.

"I'm no good for you. You're always saving me, or protecting me, and I keep stuffing up. What happens when I really fuck up again? You've just admitted you blamed yourself for everything that happened after you didn't give me the necklace, and I'd never forgive myself if I caused you to end up like my father—depressed beyond anything imaginable because you couldn't save, or protect me. And what if we had kids and that happened," said Catherine, determined that no man—particularly one she loved—would go through that pain, and no child should endure what she had.

In her outburst, they'd finally reached the true issue that was holding her back from letting someone get close. Dillon pulled her tightly into his arms, and she reluctantly buried her head into his pounding chest, inhaling the smell of his nervous perspiration.

"I do love you, and you do drive me crazy because of that love. However, while I'd be distraught if anything happened to you, I would never take my life, however much I was hurting," he promised, stroking her hair as he tried to reassure her. "I'd rather have as much time together as life allows us, than go without you just because there are risks that might happen in some unknown future. As for kids, which I hope we'd have, I can sincerely promise you that I would never abandon them—no matter what. Besides, they'd remind me of all the things that I love the most about you. Although, I have to admit, I'm kind of hoping that they don't get your stubborn or bossy genes, because even though I secretly love that about you—one stubborn, bossy female is all I can take on."

Catherine muffled a laugh into his chest and then pinched his nipple with her fingernail.

"Stubborn genes hey—let's hope then, that any boys we have don't get your testosterone levels. I don't want to be the mother who is hauled into the school to see the headmistress every day because my son gets a hard-on every time a girl bosses him around—or slaps him for pulling her hair," she joked.

Dillon started to laugh in response, but the motion only made the pain in his still-pinched nipple worse. "Catherine, all this kid talk, does that mean it's a yes? You'll marry me?" he asked nervously.

She released his nipple, and pulled back from their embrace, to stare into his eyes with a blank expression.

"Catherine don't—," he started to plead, thinking she was shutting down again.

She put her hand over his mouth and said, "Stop talking."

"Yes Boss," he mumbled from behind her palm.

"On the floor boy," she instructed, pointing towards the ground.

Dillon's eyes showed his confusion.

"Now!" she added.

Dillon obeyed, dropping his knees onto the hard wooden floor.

"Good place for you at my feet," she teased, giving him the wicked spar-kle-smile immortalized into his brain since the day they'd met.

"Stay there," she commanded and then she left the room, leaving Dil-lon—and his erection—contained in his man-cave.

He heard the front door open and then close, then the distant blip of a car-door opener. His heart sank; she couldn't be that cruel to abandon him like that. A moment later, he heard the front door open again, and she returned with her handbag. His relief gave way to curiosity as she rummaged in the bag, standing in front of his kneeling, vulnerable body.

"I think the customary position for a proposal is one knee, not two," she stated, raising her eyebrow once again, to give him a dominant stare.

Dillon responded by adjusting himself onto one bended knee. This wasn't how he'd ever expected to propose—the scene was hardly dinner, twinkling stars, champagne and romance; this was unpacked boxes, threat-ening rulers, dominant stares and an all-too-obvious bulge in his trousers. Yet, it was the perfect proposal scene for them.

"Catherine Everdene will you be mine, and marry me?" Dillon got the words out as confidently as he could.

She gave him an even bigger wicked smile. "Dillon, you know that's not how it goes," she teased.

He hesitated, hoping to hell this wasn't one of one of her practical tricks and he was about to be crushed with her refusal. Then it dawned on him that she was reprimanding his choice of words—not his overall intention.

"Catherine Everdene, would you do me the honor of letting me become yours?" he said, gazing up at her expectantly—hoping that he'd now done it right.

"That's better," she replied, picking up the blue box and retrieving the diamond engagement ring. Slipping it onto her finger, she then held up her hand, showcasing her manicured finger that was now adorned with a sparkle that matched her eyes.

Dillon's quivering body, filled with joy and desire, wanted to stand and hug her, but Catherine wasn't done. She lowered her jeweled finger and ran her nail down his cheek.

"Your turn," she said.

Wondering what the hell she meant, Dillon watched her retrieve a leather collar from her bag. He shrank back onto his ankles, aroused yet apprehensive about the requirements of the collar—did she expect him to wear it all the time, as she'd no doubt wear her ring. His mind cast back to Boldwood and the chastity cage.

"Don't worry, it's only a fun symbol to wear sometimes when we're alone and playing. I want you to know that you're mine. I wasn't expecting your gift, but I did want us to be together in some way. I thought a collar was appropriate," she explained, as though reading his fears about not wanting to become like Boldwood.

Smiling up at her, for the first time in his life, Dillon felt an overwhelming happiness as she buckled the collar around his neck.

"Unless," she added. "A cock ring is more to your liking?"

Chapter Forty-Nine

Catherine took stock of what had just happened; here she was in a study—a room similar to her late father's place of refuge from family life—and she'd agreed to marry the man kneeling before her.

She didn't doubt that she loved him, and that they'd been through a lot together, but some things they still hadn't done.

Is this too soon, will he be crap in bed, will he tire of me? This is his house—could it be my home?

A million cold feet questions started to surface in her commitment-phobic brain, and she tried to fight the urge to take off the ring and run, knowing that it would be unfair to Dillon if she did.

Dillon wasn't naïve to Catherine's insecurities and he could read the fear in her face. Reaching for a remote control on the desk, he pressed a button, and from some hidden audio system the familiar opening sounds of her favorite piece of music filled the room; he'd remembered from her original story that that particular piece calmed—as well as aroused—her. His thoughtful tactic worked, erasing her mind of the fears that plagued them, knowing that she'd accepted a man who knew what she liked, and who would always have her best interests at heart.

Catherine ran her finger along the side of his face, ensuring that only her fingernail was gently touching him. As she saw the longing grow in his eyes and throughout his body, she ran the finger into his scalp, and then grasping a handful of his hair, she pulled back his head so that he was facing upwards to meet her gaze. She leaned down to kiss his lips, gently at first, but then more passionately as she let her desires take over. Her mouth, the part of her body that had so unsuccessfully communicated her feelings through words, was free to speak in a more effective way. As their tongues connected, she felt the true hunger that Dillon had for her—and her for him; it was a hunger that had started before they'd even met, and was unable to be satiated by anything either of them had done with anyone else—until now.

Time stopped while they remain locked together, tongues exploring each other's mouths. When they finally broke away for breath and Catherine released her grip on his hair, Dillon's body fell onto the wooden floor and his lips met the exposed parts of her foot showing through the gaps of her wedge sandals. He planted butterfly kisses gently on each foot in turn, and gradually moved higher over her ankles. Catherine lent back against the sturdy desk, not caring if the knobby metal rivets framing the top, dug into her firm, toned butt cheeks.

"Is this okay Boss?" he asked.

Why is he stopping, why is he talking, why is he asking if this is okay, why am I still Boss?

Catherine wanted him to take her, to lift her legs off the ground and wrap them around his waist, while he thrust his aroused cock deep into her. Yet she'd established the dynamic of her in charge and now he needed permission to continue; she had to give him the privileged access to worship her body.

"Yes my boy, that feels good," she cooed; he was her boy now, and would be forever when she married him.

Dillon took her 'yes' as an invitation to continue, and lifted her dress—planting more butterfly kisses on her thigh as he did. Her silk and lace panties were soaked with her arousal and, as he kissed her, any thought she'd had of him fucking her hard as she laid back on the desk, floated away as she relished the pleasure of the foreplay. The music increased its pace, and she contemplated re-enacting the scene from her story where she pleasured herself in front of him, but, for now anyway, she wanted the touch of his tongue on her—licking and sucking her more intimate places until she came.

"Higher boy," she commanded.

Her dominating nature had the desired effect—Dillon eagerly moving his mouth to the edge of her damp panties to place a few more gentle kisses, before a more forceful one on exactly the right spot, sending a short pre-orgasmic jolt throughout her body.

"Remove them," she instructed, and he obeyed without hesitation—his mouth returning to the same spot the second his hands had stripped the fabric covering it. Catherine breathed deeply as he ran his tongue over her clit. "Keep going and don't stop until I come."

There had never been a need to oversee Dillon at work, and she was grateful for his initiative as his tongue delved into her; now it was time to lie back and enjoy his oral skills, not issue micro-managing orders every few minutes. He'd always be willing to please her, learning what she liked best and thinking ahead to how he could make her life happier, and as she looked down at him kneeling at her feet, she could see his wholehearted enjoyment at the task he was undertaking. Seeing him there—with his head buried between her thighs—turned her on even more, and she felt an orgasm building inside her. Succumbing to her pleasure, her passionate cries drowned out the fading strands of the music.

As her orgasm subsided, she fell back onto the desk; they were still fully clothed, apart from Catherine being sans panties—the damp garment was dangling off the edge of the desk. Both of them looked at the hanging ornament, their daintiness not matching the masculine décor of the scholarly man-cave.

"Remember what I did with my knickers in the story I wrote you?" she asked, thinking back to what she'd written long ago about how she would gag him.

Dillon laughed. "Why are you laughing again?" she asked, playfully slapping his arm.

Continuing to grin, he looked at her with adoring eyes, "Because, coincidentally, I was imaging those knickers stuffed in my mouth and was wondering if I dared speak, whether I'd end up with the same fate right now."

"Tempting . . .," she replied, with a deliberate hesitation and raised eyebrow stare in order to raise his nerves. "It depends if you behave yourself."

Dillon was conscious that he still had an obvious erection, despite the loose fitting jeans he was wearing; her telling him to behave himself didn't seem to be an indication he was going to get his own release any time soon. His knees suffering on the hard floor, he dared to get up and take a more comfortable seat on the old Chesterfield by the window. Reclining back, he closed his eyes to bask in the sunlight—the spring sunshine, freed of the breeze by the glass, was warm on his face. As he started to doze, the transparent redness of his eyelids darkened as a shadow blocked the sun; not recalling seeing clouds overhead, he opened his eyes to see Catherine standing over him.

Without a word she straddled him, and kissed him once again as she unbuttoned his shirt. Dillon wanted to reciprocate by unzipping her dress but he was reluctant to take the initiative for fear of the consequences if he contradicted her command to behave himself; he decided to wait to gauge her intentions. She moved back on his lap, her thighs either side of his own, but now she had access to the top of his jeans; she wasted no time before unbuckling his belt and unzipping his fly. Raising up slightly, she tugged at the jeans to lower them, and he helped her remove them by lifting himself a little from the leather couch.

Only his boxer shorts remained on, and she traced her tormenting fingernail over the outline of his stiff cock; no one but Catherine had ever come close to delivering so many sensations throughout his body—or dominating his mind as completely—as she did.

She removed the boxer shorts with even more ease than the jeans, and the searing heat in his groin cooled as his genitals were exposed to open air.

"Nice cock," she said with a cheeky grin.

Dillon gave her an egotistical male pride smile that he instantly regretted when she glared at him.

"Stop grinning," she threatened, suddenly slapping his hard cock with her hand—the sharp sensation making his whole body tingle at the anticipation of slow, torturous pain and pleasure.

"Yes Boss," he replied, obediently wiping his grin.

He sat upright, and put his hands on her waist. Before she could issue him another command—not worried at all about the potential punishment that he might receive later—he lifted her forward and slid his cock into her. This time she didn't resist, instead adjusting her thighs to allow her to sink deeper onto him. Keeping his hands on her hips, he began to thrust, his butt rising off the leather with each push, and she dropped her body to meet his; the rhythm between them was equal, their kisses passionate and no one was in charge—they were two people in love, showing it in the most intimate way possible.

As all rules disappeared, their perfectness for each other was proved as they reached their climaxes together.

Chapter Fifty

'Love is a possible strength in actual weakness.
Marriage transforming a distraction into a support, the power of
which should be, and happily often is, in direct proportion to the
degree of imbecility it supplants.—Thomas Hardy'

Catherine re-read the literary quotation in the card that Dillon had given her when she'd kissed him goodbye the night before, then she peered out of the hotel's casement window; the late-August summer sky was clear—the perfect start to a happier future.

Two years earlier, when she'd met Dillon Oak in the office in Hammersmith, she never would have dreamed she'd one day marry him in a quaint parish church a few hundred miles away in Dorset—in a village with a similar name to her own. In that time they'd crossed oceans to escape one another, lived through tragedies that bonded them, and now were tying the knot to be together.

The morning passed in a whirlwind of people helping get her ready; some friends, but mostly hired professionals. Before Catherine knew it, the wedding car had passed the thatched cottages in the small street leading to the church, and she was standing at the entrance breathing in the scent of the pink roses covering the stone canopy at the church entrance.

She stared at herself in a full-length mirror, discreetly placed for last-minute bridal vanity. Not since before her parents had died—back when she was a happy child—had she envisioned herself in this way, dressed in a Stephanie Allin corseted wedding gown of white lace and satin with a bow at the waist; sky-high white satin and crystal Jimmy Choo heels adorning her feet.

"Ready?" Liddy's voice broke her from the dream; as her Maid of Honor, she was doing the final check to make sure Catherine wasn't going to bolt—they were already considerably, rather than fashionably, late.

Deciding that no one could take the place of her father, she'd opted to walk down the aisle alone behind her bridesmaids and flower girls—Liddy, Madison, Dillon's sister and his nieces. In her mind, she'd been independent for so long that there was no need for anyone to give her away to a man—rather she was taking ownership of one. The wedding was their way of showing the world that they loved each other, and was her concession to Dillon, knowing that he desired traditionalism alongside their more unusual arrangement.

As the bridal procession music commenced, Catherine remembered the first time she'd seen Dillon—locking onto his blue eyes as she crossed the office lobby. Back then, she'd been curious about him, but resentful that he was there to take her job—now she couldn't wait to lock eyes with him again as she walked up the aisle to stand beside him.

"Yes, I'm ready," she replied, giving Liddy a final, nervous smile.

᪥

As Dillon caught his first glimpse of Catherine walking towards him down the aisle, he recalled the moment he first saw her descending the stairs just a few years before. Then she was all black-suited, tailored perfection—with not a strand of hair out of place—but now her white lace dress, and loosely fastened curled hair was a contrast; a visual expression of how much she'd emotionally grown as a person. Back when he'd met her, his heart was beating with pure lust, now it beat louder from a different emotion; the sexual magnetism—although never having faded—had been superseded by his overwhelming love for her.

For years, his desire for her had driven him insane—their sexual dynamic a constant distraction from what really had been the whole truth; they were soul mates, compatible on every level—complimentary opposites, yet equals where equality mattered. Catherine had seduced his mind, and occasionally his body, but eventually they'd seduced each other's souls. Now—as he'd written to her inside the '*I love you*' card he'd given her the night before—it was time to turn his insanity, and continued lust, into something far more powerful; a strong partnership and marriage—just as Emilia had wished for them.

He continued to stare at her as she advanced closer to him, waiting for her eyes to meet his, and when they finally did, she stumbled slightly in her heels on the uneven stone aisle covered with carpet. He couldn't hide his quiet chuckle, and when she'd regained her composure, she gave him her wicked sparkle-smile and mouthed 'stop laughing'. He suspected she would punish him in some imaginative way when they were alone on their wedding night, but Dillon Oak didn't mind one little bit—Catherine Everdene owned every bit of him and that was exactly how he wanted it to be; he was finally hers—*forever*.

Epilogue

Deal with what haunts your present; face your fears and the demons of your past, and only then will you have the emotional maturity to accept what's in your heart. Never allow the ghosts of your past, risk you losing from your future the person who understands and loves you the most.

In the summarized words of Thomas Hardy, where happy circumstances permit the development of camaraderie between the sexes, the result is a compounded feeling that proves itself the only love as strong as death—a love that many waters cannot quench, nor the floods drown.

When you realize that the person you desire the most is not only your best friend, but is someone that will hold you when you wail with ecstasy, and cradle you when you cry with grief, you know that you have found a passionate love that can last—you know you have found the makings of your *Happy Ever After*.

Printed in Great Britain
by Amazon.co.uk, Ltd.,
Marston Gate.